Praise for *Bad*

'Leisa Rayven crashes onto the [scene] ... [fl]irting, and just daring us to put *Bad Romeo* [down. We] couldn't!'

Christina Lauren, *New York Times* bestselling
author of *Beautiful Bastard*

'An unputdownable debut! Filled with delicious tension that will make your palms sweat, toes curl, and heart race'

Alice Clayton, *New York Times*
bestselling author of *Wallbanger*

'The perfect combination of hot and hilarious, *Bad Romeo* is utterly dazzling. I loved it!'

Katy Evans, *New York Times*
bestselling author of *Real*

'I gobbled this book up in one sitting. The emotions between the characters were superb. The new hottest book couple!'

Jennifer Probst, *New York Times* bestselling
author of *The Marriage Bargain*

'*Bad Romeo* delivers perfect romance – emotional, edgy, and illicit. Every page is charged with off-the-charts chemistry. Don't miss this exciting debut'

M. Pierce, bestselling author of
the Night Owl trilogy

'I absolutely *loved* this book. This is a romance that you feel with all your heart and soul. Ethan and Cassie's chemistry was off the charts, and their connection so intense that it kept my heart racing the whole way through. The writing captured the emotional intensity of their epic love while balancing it out with hilarious scenes that had me laughing out loud, and other scenes that had me fanning myself from the hotness. It was the perfect balance! Absolutely freaking *adored* it. And I can't recommend it highly enough'

Aesta's Book Blog

'I loved reading this book. The heroine is infused with the perfect amount of believable hopefulness and charm. She is fully fleshed-out and possesses a sense of humour that is wry and witty . . . And the hero is perfectly drawn. The reader may want to throttle him for a sizable portion of the text, but they will equally want to make out with him. And that dichotomy is perfect for a New Adult hero. He is wonderful and believably bad for her in all the best ways'

Bibliopunkk

'A 100 per cent *must read*. There's drama, angst, humour, and sexy, sexy romance, and that ending . . . GAH! I wholeheartedly recommend *Bad Romeo* to those who enjoy contemporary romance with some angst but with the promise of humour and swoons to smooth the way'

We So Nerdy

'It's part second-chance romance, part friends to lovers, and part antagonistic romance, and the mixture is straight-up perfect. Especially when you add all the sexual tension. And my god, there was sexual tension!'

Kimberly Fay Reads

'There were times I was swooning and times I was fuming with these characters through their love-hate-love relationship, and as the plot was building, so was my heart rate. I swooned, I laughed, and I had those sweet chills up my spine from the intensity of two lovers approaching a second chance at making things right'

Romantic Reading Escapes

'WOW! This book! There isn't a single thing I didn't like about this amazing, fantastic read. An outstanding debut!'

Beauty and the Beastly Books

BROKEN JULIET

ALSO BY LEISA RAYVEN

Bad Romeo

Leisa Rayven

BROKEN JULIET

PAN BOOKS

First published 2015 by St Martin's Press, New York

First published in the UK 2015 by Pan Books
an imprint of Pan Macmillan
20 New Wharf Road, London N1 9RR
Associated companies throughout the world
www.panmacmillan.com

ISBN 978-1-4472-8299-0

3 5 7 9 8 6 4 2

A CIP catalogue record for this book is available from the British Library.

Printed and bound by CPI Group (UK) Ltd, Croydon, CR0 4YY

Visit www.panmacmillan.com to read more about all our books
and to buy them. You will also find features, author interviews and
news of any author events, and you can sign up for e-newsletters
so that you're always first to hear about our new releases.

This book is dedicated to my darling parents, who suspected I was being scammed when I told them I had a publishing deal. How d'you like me now, Bern & Val? Huh? (I'm kidding. I love you. Thank you for everything.)

When he shall die,
Take him and cut him out in little stars,
And he will make the face of heaven so fine
That all the world will be in love with night
And pay no worship to the garish sun.

—Juliet, describing Romeo,
William Shakespeare, *Romeo and Juliet*

ONE

BEAUTIFUL REPAIR

Present Day
New York City, New York
The Apartment of Cassandra Taylor

In Japan, they have something called *Kintsugi*—the art of repairing precious pottery with gold. The result is a piece that has obviously been broken, but is more beautiful for it.

It's a concept that has always fascinated me.

So often, people try to hide their scars. As if the slightest damage proves how weak they are. They equate scars with mistakes, and those mistakes with shame. Perfection forever marred.

Kintsugi does the opposite. It says, "There is beauty born from tragedy. Look at these precious fault lines of experience."

As I stand in my hallway, staring at the front door that reverberates with my former lover's knocks, it occurs to me that even though *Kintsugi* is a noble concept, it doesn't change the truth that once something is broken, it can never be anything else. Beautiful repair, no matter how elegant, doesn't make it whole again. It's still just a collection of pieces impersonating its former shape.

Judging from his soul-baring e-mail this morning, which included an epic declaration of love, I believe Ethan wants to repair me. Ironic, considering he was the one who broke me in the first place.

I know you think I left because I didn't love you, but you're wrong. I've always loved you, from the moment I first laid eyes on you.

I'd spent so long believing I got what I deserved when people left me that I didn't stop to think I got what I deserved when I met you. I couldn't comprehend that if I stopped being an enormous insecure jackass for five minutes, that maybe . . . just maybe . . . I could keep you.

I want to keep you, Cassie.

You need me as much as I need you. We're both hollow without the other, and it's taken me a long time to realize that.

There's the knocking again, this time louder. I know I have to answer it.

He's right. I am hollow without him. I always have been. But what do I have to offer other than a shell of the woman he fell in love with?

Don't be as stupid as I was and let the insecurities win. Let us win. Because I know you think loving me again is a crapshoot and that your odds are grim, but let me tell you something: I'm a sure thing. I couldn't stop loving you if I tried.

It's possible for him to love me and still leave me. He's proven that time and again.

Am I still terrified of you hurting me? Of course. Probably the same way you're terrified I'll hurt you.

But I'm brave enough to know it's absolutely worth the risk.

Let me help you be brave.

Brave is a word I haven't used to describe myself for a long time. My phone buzzes with a message.

<*Hey. I'm at your door. You in there?*>

Excitement and fear crawl up my spine, racing to see which one can paralyze my brain first.

When I'd finished reading his e-mail, I needed to see him. But now that he's here, I have no idea what to do.

As I walk down the hallway, I feel like I'm dreaming. Like the past three years have been a nightmare and I'm about to wake up. Everything feels slow. Important.

When I reach the door, I tighten my robe and exhale in an effort to calm my nerves. Then, with a shaky hand, I pull it open.

I make myself breathe as the door swings open to reveal Ethan, phone in hand. So handsome but tired. Nervous. Looking almost as nervous as I feel.

"Hey." He says it softly. Like he's afraid I'm going to chase him away.

"You're here."

"Yeah."

"How? I mean, I just texted you. Were you already here?"

"Uh . . . yeah. I've . . . well, I've been here for a while. After I e-mailed you, I couldn't sleep. Couldn't stop thinking about things. You." He looks down at the phone and shoves it in his pocket. "I wanted to be near you, just in case you . . ." He smiles and shakes his head. "I wanted to be here. Close."

His jacket is on the ground, crumpled next to a cardboard coffee cup.

"Ethan, how long have you been out here?"

"I told you, a whi—"

"How long, exactly?"

His small smile masks something deeper. Something desperate.

"A few hours, but in a way . . ." He looks at his feet and shakes his head again. "I kind of feel like I've been waiting out here for three years, just trying to find the courage to knock on the door. I guess that e-mail was my way of doing it."

When he glances up again, for the first time in a long while, I see fear in his eyes. "The real question is, are you going to let me in?"

I notice how I'm gripping the doorjamb with my right hand, while holding the door with my left. My whole body blocks the entrance. It's like everything I am is subconsciously standing in his way.

He leans forward slowly, being so careful. "You read my e-mail, right?"

Right away, the space between us feels very small.

"Yes."

He puts his hands in his pockets, expression wary. "And? Did it help?"

I don't know what to say. Does he expect some sort of declaration from me? Something to match his thousand 'I love yous'?

"Ethan, that e-mail was . . . amazing."

Apparently that's all he wants to hear, because his face lights up.

"You liked it?"

"I loved it." My throat tightens around the "L" word. "Did you really type out the . . . those phrases . . . individually?"

"Yes."

"How long did it take?"

"I didn't keep track of time. I just needed you to know. I still need for you to know."

I grip the door tighter.

I know we shouldn't be having this discussion in my hallway, but if I let Ethan in, he'll touch me, and then whatever fragile strength I have left will shatter.

"So . . . where do we go from here?" He moves forward. "I mean, I know what I want." So close, his feet almost touch mine. "I think I've made myself pretty clear. But what about you?"

I tense because of his proximity.

This man represents so many things to me. He was my first true friend. My first love. First lover. The master of more pleasure than I knew existed, and the architect of more heartache than I thought I could endure.

It seems almost impossible to translate all of those men into the one he wants to be. The one who just wants to be a single thing to me.

Mine.

"Cassie . . ." He touches my hand, then traces down my wrist and over my forearm. There's an explosion of goosebumps left in his wake. "What do you want?"

I want him. Can't want him. Need him. Hate needing him.

"I don't know," I whisper.

"I do," he says, leaning forward. "Invite me in. I promise, I'm here to stay this time."

TWO

DESPISED VULNERABILITY

Six Years Earlier
Westchester County, New York
The Grove

When I wake, I stretch, and it takes me a moment to realize why I'm sore. Then I remember.

I had sex. Incredibly passionate, muscle-trembling sexual intercourse. With Ethan.

I smile.

Ethan Holt took my virginity.

Oh, Lord, how he felt. All around me and inside.

Scenes from last night come flooding back and make the ache transform into tingles.

Surely I'll look different now. I feel different. Wonderful. Like a whole new world of experience has been opened up to me, and I can't wait to explore it.

With him.

As I sigh in contentment, I reach over to the other side of the bed, only to find it empty.

I open my eyes. "Ethan?"

I get up and check the rest of the apartment. Empty.

I go back and sit on my bed. The sheets are crumpled and still smell like him.

I check my phone. No messages. I look under the bed to make sure that a touching love note/apology hasn't slipped under there.

Nothing.

Great.

I'm pretty certain when a man leaves your bed in the middle of the night, it's not a good sign.

Later that morning, I jiggle my knees as I wait for our Advanced Acting class to begin.

Holt's late. He's never late.

I still can't believe he just left. I mean, if you sleep with a girl for the first time, you at least send her a text, right? If not an actual phone call to say, "Hey, thanks for letting me deflower you. It was rad."

I know that being open is a struggle for him, but doesn't he realize he's not the only one who needs reassurance?

Erika sweeps into the room, and I try to put Ethan from my mind.

"Ladies and gentlemen, welcome back. I trust you all had a refreshing Thanksgiving break." Everyone murmurs something vaguely positive, and she smiles. "Good, because for the next few weeks, I'm going to push you harder than ever before. This term we'll be working with masks, which is one of the most challenging and ancient art forms within the theater."

The door opens, and Erika frowns as Holt walks in and sits down. He looks tired.

"Thank you for joining us, Mr. Holt."

He nods. "Yeah, no problem."

"Can I get you anything? A watch, perhaps?"

He looks down at his hands. "Sorry I'm late."

She gives him a pointed look. "As I was saying, mask work is difficult and requires the actor to be completely honest and open. It's not an art form that forgives emotional blocks or insecurities. Be prepared for some brutal self-examination."

Holt glances at me and gives me a tight smile before he turns away.

Erika goes to her desk and collects a large box filled with masks. She spreads them out on the floor.

"These masks exhibit specific emotional traits. I'd like you all to take a few minutes and choose one that appeals to you."

Everyone goes over to the masks. As they talk and laugh among themselves, Ethan stands at the back, waiting for the crowd to subside. I go and stand beside him.

"Hey."

"Hey." He barely looks at me.

"You bailed on me this morning." He shoves his hands in his pockets, and the muscles tighten in his jaw. "Are you . . . upset with me? About what happened? I mean, I know you said we should wait, and I pushed you to do it anyway, but—"

"No." He shrugs. "I'm not upset with you. I was just . . . I had stuff to do and I didn't want to wake you. Everything's fine."

His words are reassuring, but they don't make me feel any better. "So, you . . . enjoyed it then? Me? What we did?"

He drops his head, and I see the hint of a smile as he leans down to whisper in my ear. "Cassie, only you would want to discuss sex in the middle of acting class. Can we please talk about this later, when we're not in a room full of people?"

"Oh, yeah. Absolutely. Later." I know he's right, but my ego deflates more every second. "When, later?"

He sighs and leans down again, so close his lips brush against my ear. "Yes, I enjoyed it. A lot. You were, without a doubt, the best I've ever had. But thinking about it right now isn't going to end well for me. So please, for the love of inconvenient boners everywhere, let it go."

His confession makes me beam. It doesn't excuse him leaving, but at least I know he had a good time.

Erika gestures to us. "Mr. Holt, Miss Taylor . . . less talking, more mask choosing, please. I'd like to get started."

By the time we step forward, there are only two masks left: one with a large nose and heavy, frowning brows, and one that looks like a child, all round eyes and soft cheeks.

"Aggression and vulnerability," Erika says as she leans against her desk. When I pick up the child and Holt goes for the other one, she clucks her tongue and swaps them around. "This is a far less obvious choice for you both, don't you think?"

Holt tenses, and for a second I think he's going to argue, but Erika stares him down until he turns and goes back to his seat.

Erika then calls people to the performance space in pairs. She gives prompts for improvised scenes that use only body language. It's difficult, and everyone struggles, but Erika pushes them to give more. She's scary today, and by the time she calls me and Ethan to the stage, my hands clammy.

"Miss Taylor, you're representing strength, but in a negative context. Bullish, domineering, uncompromising. Mr. Holt, you're the opposite. Sensitive, open, trusting. Begin when you're ready."

I slip on my mask. It's tight, which makes it difficult to breathe. My vision is limited to the small eyeholes, and I have to turn my head to see Ethan.

He glances at me for a few moments before putting on his own mask.

I take some time to center myself, then move toward him and make myself as imposing as possible. It's not easy when he towers over me. Still, I try to be aggressive and intimidating.

"*Feel* what you're doing, Miss Taylor. Inhabit the emotion of the mask." I grab Holt's shirt and silently order him to the floor. He shies away, feigning fear, but his movement is awkward.

"Mr. Holt, your mask represents submission and vulnerability. You have to embody those characteristics. Open yourself up."

Ethan tries to do what she's asked, but he throws out cliché gestures that make him seem more angry than vulnerable.

I can tell that Erika is disappointed in our efforts. A few minutes later, when she calls a stop to the exercise, Holt all but rips off his mask and stalks back to his chair.

Erika collects the masks and places them back in their box. "I know that today was difficult, but it should get easier. Your final assessment in this subject will account for fifty percent of your acting grade, so I expect you all to deliver your best work."

Ethan raises his hand.

"Mr. Holt?"

"Can we swap masks next time?"

"No. The mask you worked with today will remain yours for the rest of the semester. I think you'd better get used to exploring your vulnerable side, Mr. Holt."

The look on Ethan's face is so disdainful, it's almost funny.

THREE

MASK

The Grove's acting school is the most prestigious in the country, so it stands to reason that their standards are extremely high. Still, I don't think any of us were prepared for just how difficult some classes are proving to be. Especially masks.

Contrary to Erika's assurance that mask work would get easier, we all continue to struggle. But as bad as most of us are, Ethan is the worst. Erika has been pushing him harder than anyone else, and, of course, that means he's always in a crappy mood.

He's being distant, and even though I've made it very clear that I'd love to have more sex, it's been nearly a week since he's touched me anywhere interesting. He doesn't even hold my hand unless I initiate it. Good thing I always initiate it. If he won't let me have the rest of his body, I'm damn well going to have his hand.

"Erika fucking hates me," he says, as we head over to the Hub—a large, four-story building that houses the library, cafeteria, student lounge, and several large lecture theaters—to meet our friends for lunch.

"That's not true."

"Then why force me to work with that particular mask? Anger, sadness, aggression—I could nail any of those."

"Yeah, but she knows you have an issue with vulnerability, so she's pushing you to conquer it. Imagine how great it would be if you had a breakthrough. You'd probably top the class." *And become a more affectionate boyfriend.*

He shakes his head. "The likelihood of that happening is fucking nil. I can't do it, Cassie. In fact, I'm not even sure what *it* is."

I pull out my phone and google it. "Vulnerable. Adjective, meaning susceptible to being wounded or hurt; open to moral attack, criticism, temptation. Oh, wow! Next to the definition is a picture of you."

"Funny."

"Thanks. I try."

We're almost at the Hub when I spot a group of second years near the door. I recognize Olivia, Ethan's more-than-a-little-bitter ex, among them. She frowns when she notices Ethan holding my hand.

"I don't believe it," she says as we approach. "I thought all the stories about you having a girlfriend were bullshit, yet here you are with the same girl I saw you with at the beginning of the year. You're really putting the effort in to get her attached before you dump her, aren't you? I mean, what you did to me was bad, but this one? She's going to be cursing your name for years. Impressive."

Ethan tightens his hand around mine. "And today just keeps getting better." He tugs on my arm, and we head inside. I'm aware of Olivia staring after us.

"She really hates you, doesn't she?"

He nods. "Yeah, well, I gave her good reason to." He mutters that he needs food before disappearing into the crowded cafeteria.

I make my way to the far side of the room and find Jack, Lucas, Connor, Aiyah, Miranda, and Zoe at our usual table in the corner.

Jack looks around with a disgusted expression. "Damn, this place is depressing. Doesn't the student council have anything better to do than decorate the shit out of everything? It looks like Jingly the Glitter Fairy jizzed all over the damn place."

"It's nearly December," Aiyah says. "It's festive."

"Festive?" Jack gestures to the tsunami of tinsel and baubles surrounding us. "It borders on psychotic. Yesterday, they ripped down the Thanksgiving decorations like they'd personally insulted their mothers, and today, there's a metric shit-ton of Santa porn all over the damn place. No one needs this much fucking tinsel! If I show up to my rugby match this afternoon with goddamn glitter all over me, I'll make an official complaint to the dean. I will not be known as a human disco ball, no matter how fabulous that would look on me."

There are giggles before Lucas says, "So, what's everyone doing this weekend? Jack, did you finally convince that redheaded dance major to go out with you?"

Jack grins. "Hell yeah, I did. I'm taking her to that new Italian place in town. A little wine, a little pasta. And afterward, when I turn on the Avery charm, I predict I'll be face-deep in her ballet tights by bedtime."

Miranda glowers. "You realize that buying a woman a meal doesn't give you the right to bone her, right?"

Jack scoffs. "I'm aware. Plus, I actually like her. If sex was all I wanted I wouldn't go to all the trouble of taking her out, would I? I'd just invite her over to watch soft porn on Netflix in the hope that it would put her in the mood."

Connor nudges Lucas. "What about you, dude? Aren't you seeing that chick with the dreadlocks from visual arts?"

Lucas leans back and puts his hands over his heart. "Oh, sweet, sweet Mariah. I'm taking her away this weekend. Vineyard tour. Bed-and-breakfast. The whole nine."

Jack frowns. "Shit, that escalated quickly. Haven't you only been dating for two weeks?"

"What can I say, man? When it's right, it's right. She's amazing. I may suck at a lot of stuff, but taking care of my woman isn't one of them."

I feel a twinge as I hear them talk, because I'm reminded that even though Ethan and I have been officially going out for over a month, he still hasn't taken me on a real date. Usually we hang out at my place or his. Watch TV. Read. Study.

If I'm really lucky, we make out, but that's it.

Kind of depressing, really.

"What about you and Holt?" Connor says as he picks at his fries. "Any grand romantic plans this weekend?" His voice has an edge that says he already knows the answer.

I look over at Ethan in the cafeteria line. "Uh, I'm not sure. We haven't really discussed it yet."

"Uh-huh." Connor looks back down at his lunch, and I feel a stab of resentment that he brought it up.

Can everyone see how unromantic Ethan is?

I have a feeling that if I told everyone he bailed on me the morning after we had sex for the first time, no one would be surprised.

It's like our relationship is one of those stupid logic paradoxes.

When is a boyfriend not a boyfriend?

When it's Ethan Holt.

As everyone continues to chatter on about their romantic plans, I excuse myself and head to the bathroom. I guess I always knew Ethan wasn't the most demonstrative person in the world, but I figured once we came out of the relationship closet, it would change.

Apparently not.

When I come out of the stall, Olivia's there, bent over the sink and snorting something off the counter. When she sees me, she wipes her nose. "Hey."

I take a breath and slide past her to wash my hands. "Maybe you should do that where people can't see you."

"I usually do, but I figure you should see what's in store for you when Holt breaks your heart. It's not pretty."

I shake my head and wash my hands as quickly as possible. "I'm not into drugs."

"Not yet Give it time."

I dry my hands and try to ignore her snorting another line off the counter.

When I first met Olivia a few months ago, I couldn't help but notice how gorgeous she was. She made me feel inferior in every way. My hair was the most common shade of brown imaginable, while hers was a deep tawny color, thick and glossy. While I was curvy and well proportioned for my five-foot-five frame, she was about four inches taller and had the type of slender elegance I'd always envied.

I could imagine she would have looked fantastic standing next to Ethan, both of them equally stunning.

Sadly, the woman standing in front of me appears very different. Her hair is now greasy and dull, her skin uneven and sallow, and the slender elegance she used to possess has given way to sunken cheeks and too-prominent bones.

Whatever demons she's carrying around from her time with Ethan, they seem to be eating her alive.

As I turn to leave, I feel a pang of sympathy. "Take care of yourself, Olivia, okay?"

Before I can open the door, she touches my arm. "Look, I'm really not here to bust your ass. I just want to make sure you know what you're getting yourself into."

"I do, thanks."

"Do you? Because from where I'm sitting, the Ethan Holt who broke my heart looks an awful lot like the one you're dating."

"He's changed since then."

She leans back against the sink and crosses her arms. "Let me paint you a picture." I can already tell I'm not going to like this story. "He grudgingly agreed to let people know you were dating, but he doesn't act like a real boyfriend. No dates, very little public affection, and it's like pulling teeth to get him to talk about his feelings or mood swings. Sound familiar?"

I keep my face impassive, even though my adrenaline has kicked up a notch. "I don't know what to tell you. I like him. A lot. I'm willing to give him the benefit of the doubt."

Olivia shakes her head. "You don't get it, do you? You probably think it won't happen to you, because you're different or special, and maybe you're right. But that's not the problem. *You* may be different, but he's not, and he's the one who's going to destroy you. Tread carefully. That boy is an avalanche just waiting to happen."

"So this chick is, what, stalking you now?" my roommate, Ruby, asks as she struggles to open a can of tomato soup.

"Sort of, but I get the feeling she's kind of trying to look out for me."

"Yeah, well, bitch needs to step off. That's my job. Still, she's right. I can't believe he's never taken you on a real date. It seems like the man doesn't have a single romantic bone in his body." She dumps the soup into a saucepan.

"He's not that bad."

"Cassie, we did the 'How Romantic Is Your Guy?' quiz from *Cosmo*, and Holt's results were 'This Man Doesn't Know He's Your Boyfriend.' It's freaking ridiculous."

I check on the premade rolls I'd put in the oven a few minutes ago. They're still way too pale. "He's been hurt before. He just doesn't show his affection like normal guys, I guess."

"And how does he show his affection? Because from what I've seen, he doesn't kiss or hug you hello, he barely holds your hand, he slept with you once but won't do it again. There are no presents, no dates, and no epic love poems written while high on peyote."

I frown. "What was that last thing?"

"Never mind. Long story. My point is, the boy has zero romantic game, and you're the one who's suffering. I can't believe you're not more pissed about this."

"Well, I'm not happy about it, but what can I do?"

"Okay, here's my advice. You're being a doormat."

"That's not advice. It's a statement. And an insulting one at that."

"Dammit, Cassie, woman up!" She stirs the soup aggressively. "He's treating you like crap because he's got issues or whatever, but that's no excuse." She pours some milk into the saucepan. "Call him on his bullshit or else stencil *WELCOME* on your boobs and be done with it. It's your choice."

I know she's right, but I can't help feeling like one wrong move with Ethan could have disastrous results.

"Oh, crap." Ruby frowns at the saucepan, then picks up the soup can and reads the instructions.

"What?"

"I think I've fucked this up."

"How is that possible? It's soup. From a can."

"I put in too much milk. Apparently, I was supposed to measure it or some bullshit." She dips in her spoon and sips it.

"What's it taste like?"

She shrugs. "Tomato-flavored milk."

I sigh and lean against the counter. "Not the weirdest thing you've ever made."

"Nope."

"Serve it in mugs?"

"Okay. At least we have rolls."

"Oh, frack!" I open the oven door and smoke wafts out. When I pull out the baking sheet, the rolls are black. "Dammit."

"Who's the bad cook now? You were only in charge of reheating, for God's sake."

We stand there for a few moments and look at the pathetic remains of our horrible dinner. I don't know whether to laugh or cry. I have an urge to call Ethan to see if he'd come over and cook something for us, but I figure if he wanted to talk or spend time with me, he'd let me know.

"Wine?" I ask.

Ruby sighs. "Most definitely. I don't think I can fuck that up."

"Word."

Oh, God. Ow.

I wince as I open my eyes. Sunlight pierces my pounding brain like an ice pick.

I'm on the floor, surrounded by wine bottles and pizza boxes. Judging from the disgusting taste in my mouth, I not only drank way too much last night, I also smoked a crapload of cigarettes. My mouth feels like the floor of a cock-fighting ring.

As I stretch and rake my tongue across my teeth, I see Ruby lying on the couch, her arm thrown over her face.

I really hope she feels this bad when she wakes up. Even though I can't remember much about last night, I'm almost positive it's her fault.

My head throbs and my stomach churns, and when I put out an arm to steady myself, something on my hand catches my eye. My knuckles have the word "HOLT" written on them in black eyeliner.

What the . . . ?

My other hand has "SUCKS" scrawled across it.

I hear a groan and glance over at Ruby.

"I didn't do it," she says from behind her arm. "Well, okay, I did, but you told me to."

"You remember last night?"

"You don't?"

"Not really."

"Well, I ranted for a couple of hours about how much of a bastard Holt is, until you agreed with me. Then you did this to my face."

She lifts her arm to reveal the most horrendous makeup job I've ever seen. Her eyebrows are thickened, and her jawline has been drawn in, all sharp angles and bad shading.

"You tried to make me look like Holt, because you wanted to punch him in the face for being so closed off."

"Oh, God, Ruby, did I hit you?" It was hard to tell with all the makeup.

"No, but you did make a particularly yelly phone call to Holt at around two a.m."

"What?! What did I say?!"

She sits up, then grabs her head and groans. "You said a lot of stuff. I may have been doing drunken cheers in the background. By the end, I felt sorry for him. You really bitched him out. Then you hung up and passed out."

"Oh, God." I feel sick, and not from the alcohol. I scramble around the floor and uproot debris as I try to find my phone. "Why didn't you stop me?!"

"Honey, I was even drunker than you were. Plus, he totally deserved it. For a drunk chick, you were quite eloquent. Except for the part when you cried."

I stop what I'm doing and look up at her. "Please tell me you're joking."

"Nope. About ten minutes into it, you sobbed something about how he's your first boyfriend, your first lover, and you're supposed to feel giddy and in love, but all you feel is confused and lonely, because even when he's with you, he's not totally there."

"Oh, God."

"Then you said something like, 'Why don't you just let yourself love me? Don't you understand how good we could be?' And, well, by that point, I was crying, too, so . . ."

I rub my eyes. "Oh, Ruby, this is bad. Bad, bad, bad."

"Yeah, we need to never drink that much ever again."

I shove stuff off the coffee table, desperate to find my phone. At last, I find it under a pizza box. It's switched off and covered in grease.

When I turn it on, there are eight missed calls and two text messages.

"Crap, crap, crap . . ."

I read his first text message.

<Call me back. Now.>

I press the phone against my pounding head.

I don't want to look at the next message, but I know I have to. He sent it an hour after the first one.

<I fucking hate that I made you cry. Call me when you get this. I don't care how hungover you are. We need to talk.>

I stare at the screen for a long time as I reread his words.

"Cassie? Everything okay?"

"I don't know. He said 'we need to talk.'"

"Oh, shit."

"That's what I thought."

I dial his number. It goes to voice mail. *"Hey, this is Ethan. Leave a message. Or not. Whatever."*

I hang up.

"Dammit!"

"It's only seven," Ruby says, "and you did keep him awake with your drunken verbal abuse. Maybe let him sleep."

"I need to borrow your car."

"Uh . . . you don't think you're still too drunk to drive? I sure as hell am."

"I need to get over there, Ruby."

She rubs her eyes. "Fine. The keys are on my desk. But you might want to shower and get changed first. You have pepperoni stains on your boobs."

I look down, and I'm not at all surprised to see she's right. "Ruby, we are never drinking again."

"Amen."

Half an hour later, I knock on Holt's door while nausea and panic fight it out to see which can make me vomit first. When he doesn't answer right away, panic quickly takes the lead. I knock again.

After a few more seconds, I hear shuffling footsteps, then the door opens a crack to reveal Elissa's squinting face.

"Cassie?"

"Hey, Lissa."

"It's seven thirty in the morning."

"I know."

"On a Saturday."

"I'm sorry. Is your brother here?"

"No, or I'd freaking kill him. He bellowed something about going for a run about an hour ago. I hope he gets hit by a car. The hotheaded idiot banged around the apartment from like, three a.m. Swearing and slamming things around as he cleaned."

"He . . . cleaned?"

"Yep. He only cleans when he's beyond agitated. He started to vacuum around four. Did something happen between you two last night?"

"Uh, the thing is, I was drunk, and I . . . well, I think I verbally abused him."

"You *drunk-dialed* him?"

I screw up my face. "Apparently."

"Well, that explains a lot." She yawns. "Do you want to come in and wait?"

"Sure. If that's okay."

"It's fine." She pulls the door open, then shuffles back toward her room. "He shouldn't be long. Make yourself at home. I'm going back to bed. When he gets back, slap him over the head for me, would you?"

"Okay. Thanks. Sorry for waking you."

"No problem." She closes her door behind her, and I gaze around the living room. It's spotless.

Never before has a tidy room given me such a sense of foreboding.

My head aches, so I sit on the couch and flick through a magazine for a few minutes, until I realize I'm barely looking at it. I toss it back onto the coffee table and head into Holt's room. His bed has been made with military precision. Sitting open in the middle of it is . . . oh, God.

Is that his diary?

His neat writing covers both pages, and a pen lies along its spine.

Temptation, thy name is Holt's Journal.

The urge to read it is almost impossible to resist, but I know how it feels to have your privacy invaded, and even though I'd give my left arm to get a sneak peek inside his brain, the breach of trust wouldn't be worth it.

I close the book, careful not to look at what he's written, and place it and the pen on the nightstand. Then I crawl onto the bed and shove my face into his pillow.

Hmmm. Smells so good.

Please don't let him be angry with me. Let me be able to fix this.

Please.

Something brushes against my neck.

Lips. Warm breath.

I turn toward it, wanting more.

"Cassie?"

Shh. You'll scare away the lips.

"Hey . . . you awake?"

"No. Shhh. More lips. My boyfriend will be back soon."

The lips return. A different shape. Smiling?

They move up my neck, across my jaw. So soft but next to something rough. His chin. Cheek.

"Who do you think is kissing you?"

"Hmm. Orlando Bloom?"

Lips freeze, mid-kiss.

"Bloom? Seriously? Your boyfriend would kick that pasty Englishman's ass."

"Are you implying that you're my boyfriend?"

More kisses that linger on my neck, then press softly against my ear. "I'm not implying anything. I'm stating it as fact."

"Impossible. My boyfriend isn't this affectionate."

The lips stop. Breath exhales. Tension leaches from his body into mine.

I swallow, eyes still closed. "I'm sorry."

"For what?"

"What I just said. What I said last night. Please don't be angry. It was the wine's fault."

"No, it wasn't."

"Okay. You're right. I can't blame that entirely, but it helped."

He cups my cheek. "Cassie, it wasn't the wine, or you, or even Ruby, although I could hear her cheering you on. If it was anyone's fault, it was mine."

The excuse I'm about to say dies on my tongue. I open one eye. "Um . . . what?"

"You called me a fucking terrible boyfriend, and you were right."

Both eyes open. "Did I actually use those words?"

"Yes."

"Even the 'F' word?"

"Yes. Not gonna lie, it made me kinda hard."

I push up on my elbow and assess him. He must have just gotten out of the shower, because he's only wearing boxers. The sight of his naked chest distracts me. What's even more distracting is how he's not flinching away from my scrutiny.

I shake my head. "I'm sorry, but what exactly are you saying?"

He drops onto his back and closes his eyes. "Everything you said. All the criticism . . . You were right. I've been keeping you at a distance."

"Why?"

When he pauses, I stroke his arm to urge him on. After a few seconds, he opens his eyes and gazes at the ceiling. "Do you know what my first thought was when I walked in and found you in my bed?"

"What?"

"That you'd read my journal."

"But I didn't. I swear—"

He turns to me. "I know. When I stopped and thought about it, I realized you wouldn't do that. And yet, my first instinct was to think the worst of you, because that's how I cope with . . . things. People. I'm always prepared for the worst, so when it happens, I won't be surprised. Or disappointed. I figure, if I don't really try, I can't really fail, right? So that's what I've been doing."

"Ethan—" I put my hand on his shoulder, and he tenses.

He sits up. "I was angry with you last night, really fucking angry, not because what you said was wrong, but because it was all true. You brought up all the things I hate about myself. Shit from my past that has no right affecting you but does." He shakes his head. "I'm going to try harder. I know that sounds like bullshit, but it's all I can do, right?"

I don't know if he's trying to convince me or himself.

"Try to do what?"

"Be . . . better." He cups my face and kisses me. There's an edge of desperation in the grip of his fingers, the way his eyes are still closed when he pulls back. "I can do this. Be the boyfriend you deserve."

"I believe you."

As I say it, I know I'm lying, but I do believe he's going to try.

The next morning, I'm throwing the last of my books into my bag and shoving a piece of toast in my mouth when I hear a knock at my door.

I open it to see Ethan, smiling and holding out a cardboard cup.

"Dickachino?" I ask, concerned.

"No, just hot chocolate. Extra marshmallows." He smirks and gives me a quick kiss.

He's freshly shaven and wearing faded jeans and a blue sweater. For a moment, I can't process him like this. Here. Attentive. Smiling. Not dressed all in black like the grim reaper.

Does not compute.

His smile drops. "What the fuck is that look for? You're staring at me like I'm a serial killer. The cocoa isn't poisoned."

Okay, that's more familiar.

"It's just, you're not usually . . ." I'm distracted by how gorgeous and . . . unburdened he looks. "Uh, what are you doing here?"

He pushes past me and puts the cup on the table. "I'm being a better boyfriend, remember? Regular boyfriends walk their girlfriends to class, so here I am." He picks up my bag and slings it over his shoulder. "Fuck me, what do you have in here?"

"Books."

"Lead books?"

"I'm thinking regular boyfriends are nicer than you."

"I'm nice."

I snort. "Okay."

He wraps his arm around my waist and pulls me against him, then kisses me in a way that makes my body go from zero to hormonal overload in about two seconds.

He looks down at me in triumph. "You can't tell me that wasn't nice."

I nod. It's not a valid answer, but it's all I can manage.

"Ready to go?"

"Okay."

He grabs my hand and pulls the door closed behind us.

I think I like this new boyfriend.

FOUR

HOLD ON TO ME

Present Day
New York City, New York
The Apartment of Cassandra Taylor

"Let me in, Cassie. Please." He's so persuasive. Soothing and coaxing as he moves his fingers up my arm before grazing my neck, then gently cupping my face. "Just let go of the door."

He leans down, lips soft against my cheek. Then there's warm breath on my ear. I close my eyes as a tremor runs down my spine.

"I know that e-mail doesn't make up for everything I did—"

"No, it doesn't."

"—but I meant every word, and if you let me in, I'll prove it to you. Show you. *Love* you. Please . . ."

He brushes his lips against my ear, and it makes me tremble.

He wraps his fingers around mine and pulls them away from the door.

"You want to hold on to something?" he says. "Hold on to me." He brings my hands to his chest. When I curl my fingers into his muscles, he doesn't flinch.

"Ethan, I don't know if I can do this."

"I know. Let me help you."

"You never let me help you in the past."

"I should have. Don't make the same mistakes I did. Please. Let me show you how different I can be."

I close my eyes as he presses my hands against his chest and strokes my fingers.

Am I doing this? Considering trying again with him?

I stare at his chest. His shirt is a button-down. Blue. If I looked into his eyes right now, they'd mirror the color.

He squeezes my hands. "I know you're thinking that you've been shut down for so long, you don't know how to wake up. That all these messy feelings I bring out in you make you wish you'd never met me."

I sigh. "Pretty much."

He pauses for a few seconds, then says, "That's how I used to feel about you. When we started getting serious, everything I felt got too big. It didn't help that a paranoid voice inside kept whispering that you were going to destroy me. I'm sure in your head, there's a voice saying the same thing."

That's true. The difference is, I had nothing to do with creating his trust issues, yet he's the sole reason for all of mine.

"But you've told me you could do this twice before," I say. "Twice you broke my heart."

He strokes my hands again. "Cassie, look at me."

I struggle to lift my gaze to his. When I do, he doesn't let me look away.

"In the past, I *thought* I could be what you needed. But thinking and knowing are two different things. Now, I *know*. Let me prove I can love you the way you deserve."

I don't know what I deserve anymore. I used to think I deserved him, but he proved me wrong time and again.

If he were to fail this time, there'd be nothing left of me.

FIVE

PERFECT DISGUISE

Six Years Earlier
Westchester, New York
The Grove

For two weeks, Ethan is everything I'd ever hoped for. He's affection-ate and attentive, and we have standing dates on Friday and Saturday nights. He's even bought me flowers. Twice.

I can't believe the change.

Neither can anyone in our group of friends.

"What the fuck have you done to Holt?" Jack asks when Ethan leaves our table in the cafeteria to buy me a drink. "It's like that creepy-ass movie where everyone is taken over by aliens and become super-nice. He hasn't told me to fuck off in weeks. It's wrong and unnatural."

Connor shrugs. "Maybe the love of a good woman has changed him." He gives me a smile. "Personally, I'm glad he's stopped being such an asshole. It was starting to piss me off."

Zoe pulls out a compact and powders her nose. "Well, I call bullshit. No one as badass as Holt changes overnight, no matter how much he wants to. Did you see that look he gave Erika in mask class today? If his eyes were laser beams, she'd be dust. The real Holt is still in there, that's for sure."

I tune them out. I don't care what they say. Ethan has been amazing, and I'm going to enjoy it for as long as I can.

When he gets back to the table, he gives me a lingering kiss.

Everyone falls silent. Jack gets up and studies the back of Ethan's neck. "What the fuck are you doing?"

"Nothing," Jack says, and stands on his toes. "Just looking for the alien tentacle attached to your brain."

Ethan scowls and pushes him away. "Fuck off, Avery."

When everyone hoots and breaks into applause, Ethan looks at me with a confused expression.

I shake my head and pull him down next to me.

A few minutes later, Jack launches into one of his epic jokes. When I turn to look at Ethan, he's smiling, but there's something in his eyes. A weary sadness. Like being this version of himself is exhausting, but he refuses to give it up.

Part of me wants to ignore the wrongness and just believe him, but then I'd be pretending as much as he is.

No matter how much I want to deny the truth, it gets more obvious every day that he's a drowning man clinging to a sinking raft.

Whenever I try to talk to Ethan about what's going on with him, he either changes the subject, ignores me, or uses his sex appeal as a weapon to distract me from everything but my escalating need for sex.

That's what he's doing now.

He's between my legs, rocking and pressing his pelvis in a way he knows makes me crazy. I'm so desperate to have him inside me, I've resorted to begging.

"Ethan, please."

He kisses me again, then pulls me on top of him. His hands are on my ass, his lips on my neck.

"Not tonight."

"Why not?"

His mouth and tongue silence me. Wet, and warm, and so, so good.

I tug on his hair, and he makes that noise. My noise. The one that makes his chest vibrate.

"Ethan . . ." *Oh, don't stop. Yes, right there. Ohhhhhh, God.* He pulls down the cup of my bra and uses his mouth. Oh, sweet majestic Zeus. "Okay. Fine. I'll talk you into having sex later. For now, keep doing that."

"I have a better idea," he says as he unbuttons my jeans. "Let me put my mouth on another part of you."

My jeans are halfway down my legs before I register what he's said.

"Um . . . what now?"

He tugs my jeans off and throws them on the floor, then kneels between my legs and strokes my thighs. "Do you remember what third base is?"

"Uh . . . it's . . . well." I absolutely remember, and thinking about him going there makes me glow like a stoplight. "Are you sure you want to do that? I mean—"

He leans over and kisses me, deep and passionate. It leaves me so breathless, I can't talk. I think that was his plan.

He looks at my panties. "I've wanted to do this for a long time."

His eyes are dark. When he fingers the top of my panties, I suck in a ragged breath.

"Nervous?" he asks. I nod. "Don't be. You'll enjoy it."

He slowly removes my panties, then brings his mouth down . . . down . . . oh, mercy, all the way down. He keeps eye contact as he kisses my inner thigh. I can't stop the noises I'm making, no matter how embarrassing they are. When he kisses the other thigh, open-mouthed, I start to hyperventilate.

His eyes drift closed when he covers me with his mouth, and his accompanying moan vibrates all the way into my bones.

I have no idea what he's doing with his tongue, but it feels incredible. When I squirm in response, he grabs my hips and sucks harder. I've never felt anything like it. Then he adds his fingers, and I nearly pass out from the pleasure.

That night, Ethan teaches me about the explosive ecstasy of oral sex. Several times.

We don't end up talking about our issues. Or why he refuses to sleep with me.

Tomorrow, I tell myself as he leaves me in bed and lets himself out. *We'll talk tomorrow.*

Ruby turns bright red. "He still hasn't fucked you since he took your virginity?!"

"Shhh!"

Half the people in the cafeteria line have turned to look at us.

"Just rehearsing some lines," Ruby says. "Turn the fuck around, creepers."

We pay for our lunches and head out to the tables. "He does stuff to me all the time, but he always steers us away from . . . you know . . ."

"Penile penetration."

"Exactly."

"Jesus, Cass, what did you do the first time that made him so gun-shy?"

"Nothing! He told me I was the best he's ever had."

"Then why the hell isn't he hitting that every chance he gets? What's he waiting for? A presidential invite?"

I sigh and pick at my salad. "I don't know. He just seems to panic whenever we get close to . . ."

"He's such a dumbass."

"Ruby, come on. He's trying."

"To be a dumbass?"

"Stop."

I look over and see him crossing the quad. His hands are in his pockets, and his head is down. He looks nothing like the person I've come to know in the past few weeks.

He seems utterly defeated.

Weary.

Miserable.

A shiver runs up my spine.

He doesn't know I'm watching, and I realize what I'm looking at is the real him. My perfect boyfriend is nowhere in sight.

Out of the corner of my eye, I see Olivia watching him, too. She shakes her head and heads into the bathroom.

Outside, the rumbling clouds of an approaching storm sound a hell of a lot like an avalanche.

SIX

UNRAVELING

What do you do when you see someone you love unraveling? Do you try to stop it?

Of course.

I tell Ethan that he doesn't need to try so hard. That I care about him even if he doesn't bring me flowers or take me out on dates.

He still refuses to discuss it.

We go back to him not talking. Not touching.

Shutting down.

One night, we hear sirens outside and go out to discover an ambulance in the driveway of the apartment block down the street.

As we reach the small crowd gathered on the pavement, I see Ruby chatting with Liberty, one of the visual arts girls.

"What's up?" I pull my coat around me and glance over at the building.

Ruby's expression is serious. "Overdose. The paramedics revived her, but it was touch-and-go for a while."

"Oh my God. Who is it?"

She flicks a glance at Ethan. "Olivia Pyne. Second-year actor. That's the girl who was stalking you, right? Holt's ex?"

I turn to Ethan, who's gone as white as a sheet. "Yeah. That's her."

I'm about to say something when the lobby doors open and the paramedics wheel a gurney down the path to the sidewalk. Everyone cranes their necks to see. Even though Olivia's pale face is half hidden beneath an oxygen mask, it's clear she's in a bad way.

Ethan shoves people aside to get to the paramedics. "Is she going to be okay?"

The female paramedic gives him the once-over. "You her boyfriend?"

His expression hardens. "No."

"She's stable. That's all I can tell you."

"Was the overdose intentional?"

"That's not for us to say."

"What did she OD on?"

"I'm sorry, I can't comment further. We're taking her to White Plains Hospital where they'll do tests."

The paramedic shoulders past Ethan before she opens the ambulance door so she and her partner can load Olivia inside. I take Ethan's hand as the ambulance pulls away, its lights and siren blaring. He watches it with a stony expression until it disappears.

"Liberty said she'd been depressed," Ruby says. "Got hooked on drugs a while ago. Her roommate thought she'd gotten clean, but apparently not."

Without a word, Ethan pulls his hand out of mine and strides off.

When I catch up with him, his jaw looks so tight it could crack walnuts.

"Ethan—"

"I don't want to talk about it."

Yeah, well, I'm used to that by now.

I scramble to keep up with him. "You can't blame yourself for this. Seriously. She had a drug problem."

"Which she developed after I fucked her up."

"You don't know that."

"Yes, I do, because she sure as hell didn't have one while we were together."

"It's college. A lot of people do a lot of stupid stuff. At least they found her in time. She's going to be okay."

He stops and turns to me, his expression fiery. "You really wander through life looking through rose-colored glasses, don't you, Taylor? She's *not* going to be all right! Didn't you see her back there? She's barely alive! I know your life has been peaches and fucking cream, but not everyone is like you. Some of us live in the real world where shit happens that you can't take back, and no matter how much you wish things could change, they just fucking don't. Wake up!"

When he storms off, I tell myself he just needs time. That this will blow over, and we'll go back to normal. But I have no idea what normal is for us. I hate that we're becoming more and more undefined every day, and I'm powerless to stop it.

He doesn't call me that night, and when he shows up for his final mask assessment the next morning, he looks like he hasn't slept.

"Mr. Holt," Erika says, as he struggles through the first test. "How are you supposed to express the truth of this mask when there are so many barriers between it and the real you?"

I can see him really trying to get to the place of vulnerability that has eluded him for weeks, but he fails, again, and again, and again.

"Let go, Ethan! Strip away all the garbage you think is protecting you!"

He grunts in frustration and tears off his mask before throwing it across the room. "I can't fucking do it, all right?! Fail me!"

Erika looks around at the rest of the class. "You're all dismissed. I'll see you tomorrow. Mr. Holt, you stay."

There are cautious looks as everyone grabs their belongings. I loiter outside the door. Yesterday with Olivia, and now this? I have no idea how to help him. Or even if he *can* be helped.

I press my back into the hallway wall and eavesdrop.

"Mr. Holt, your behavior in this class has been unacceptable. Explain yourself."

"Okay, how's this? Masks are fucking stupid. I want to be an actor, not a two-bit mime. How the hell is this going to be relevant to me outside of this classroom?"

"An actor's job is to share himself with his audience. These masks challenge you to open up *fully. That's* how it's relevant."

"I've *tried* to share and be open and vulnerable! Every fucking lesson, I've tried. What more do you want?"

"I want you to just *be*. Stop trying to show me a sanitized version of yourself. Show me the guy underneath all of that crap."

"Don't you fucking get it yet? Under all my crap is just more crap. You think that somewhere in here is some magically well-adjusted individual, and all I have to do is find him? He doesn't exist! Believe me, I've looked! All I am is endless layers of shit. I thought that would be obvious by now." I hear him exhale. "So go ahead. Fail me. I don't fucking care anymore."

His voice cracks on the last word, and I so badly want to put my arms around him.

He struggles so hard with his self-esteem, but knowing what he's gone through, I understand why he finds being open so tough. He was a foster kid who wasn't adopted until he was three, and when he found out about the adoption at the age of sixteen, he didn't know who he was anymore. His rocky relationship with his dad didn't help. Charles turned parental disapproval into an artform.

If all that wasn't bad enough, in his senior year, Ethan discovered his high school sweetheart had been screwing his best friend for the better part of twelve months. I can't even imagine coping with all of that.

Clearly, judging from what's happening right now, neither can Ethan.

I chance a peek into the room. He's sitting in a chair, head in his hands, staring at the floor. Erika is opposite him. She leans forward as if trying to reach him with her words.

"Ethan, listen. I think we both know this isn't just about an acting exercise. You think you're the only one who's scared to let others see you for who you truly are? Everyone wears metaphorical masks during their lives. We all have different faces we show to our work colleagues, or friends, or family. Sometimes we wear so many masks, we forget who we are underneath it all, but you have to find the courage to drop all that bullshit and reveal your true self. That's all I want from you. It's all I've ever wanted from you."

He shakes his head. "What if my true self is . . . shit? Just defective and toxic and unlovable. Why would I ever let someone see that?"

"Because in the end, that's the only version of you that's real. It's the only one you can truly give to others. Everything else is just pretend."

"You're right," he says, his voice husky with emotion. He sounds hopeless. "I've been pretending. To so many people for too fucking long."

She puts a hand on his shoulder, but he flinches away.

"Ethan . . ."

"I'm not doing this anymore. I'll take the F. Can I go?"

"If there's nothing else you want to talk about—"

"There isn't."

I move away from the door just as he strides out. He doesn't stop when he sees me.

"Ethan?"

He ignores me.

"Hey, slow down. Where are you going?"

I grab his arm, and he spins around to face me. "Don't, Cassie.

Just fucking don't. You need more than I can give. I've always known it, and now you know it, too. Let's both stop trying to deny it."

"What are you—?"

"I tried. I really did. But I'm done. *We're* done."

He pulls his arm free and walks away, and I'm too stunned to do anything but watch him go.

SEVEN

STRONGER

Present Day
New York City, New York
The Apartment of Cassandra Taylor

I don't know if he's tired of talking or if he's just run out of words. He's talked a lot. About fear and how to conquer it. About learning from past mistakes. About how we're both better people together than we ever were apart.

He's saying everything I needed him to say years ago.

I've listened to it all but haven't said much in return.

I'd expect Ethan to be frustrated with me by now, but he's not. He's warm. Gently reassuring. More supportive than I've ever known him to be.

"I'm not looking for any guarantees here, Cassie," he says. "Just a chance. An opportunity to try."

Try to forget what happened in the past and just love him again?

That would be nice.

But trying isn't always enough.

I clear my throat and find my words. "Even if I agree to try, what makes you think I'm not going to act exactly like you did back then and ruin us?"

For the first time today, I see a hint of irritation. "Because you're better than I am. You always have been. Infinitely wiser and stronger."

If I weren't feeling so anxious, I'd laugh. "Ethan, the one thing I'm not is strong. If I were, I'd have gotten over you by now and moved on with my life. Not be standing here seriously considering giving you another chance."

"Bullshit. You're strong *because* you're here, facing your fears instead of running from them. If only I'd had your strength in the past, this story would have had a happy ending years ago."

I take a deep breath and let it out slowly. As much as I want to leave the past in the past, this conversation brings it all rushing back in stomach-churning detail. My chest tightens to the point of pain. I recognize the signs of a panic attack. I've had one or two before, all A.E.— After Ethan. Usually Tristan talks me down.

Today, I know it's my fight-or-flight instinct kicking in.

Ethan strokes my arms when he realizes what's happening. Of course he recognizes the symptoms.

His anxiety attacks were what destroyed us.

EIGHT

ONE NIGHT

Six Years Earlier
Westchester, New York
The Grove

The sun sets, and I don't move.

Ruby messages me to say she's bumped into an old flame and won't be home tonight, and I don't move.

I have a vague notion I'm in shock, but I don't know if I should be. I still don't know what happened.

Ethan.

Ethan happened, but . . .

Did he just break up with me?

No.

No.

If he'd broken up with me, I'd know, right? He was upset, sure, but he was angry with Erika, not me.

No. It wasn't even Erika's fault. He was angry with himself.

So why do I feel so . . . wrong?

I stand and stretch, but it doesn't help the ache in my bones. I need to do something. Help him.

I should tell him that whatever he's feeling, we'll work through it together. That's what couples do, right?

But are we still a couple?

I grab my backpack with shaky hands and dig around inside until I find my phone. A small voice warns me to stop. Says that if I talk to him, he'll clear up my confusion, and at this point, I'll take vague hope over grim knowledge.

But I can't not talk to him. I have to fix this.

I bring up his number and hesitate.

Please let him be blowing off steam. Let us get through this.

I pace the room as I wait for the call to connect. When it rings, I stop short.

I can hear Ethan's ringtone, AC/DC's "Back in Black," coming from outside my door.

I yank the door open, and there he is, phone in hand, shoulders slumped, leaning against the wall opposite my door.

"Ethan?"

"I don't know why I'm here."

I can barely hear him. His voice is rough, and his knuckles are scraped and bloody. His posture is so bunched and tense it sets me on edge.

"What happened to your hand?"

He talks as if he doesn't hear me. "Even when I'm trying to stay away, I can't. What the fuck is wrong with me?"

"Ethan? Your hand?"

When he looks at me, his eyes are red and swollen. "Punched a wall."

"Why?"

"Because I'm a pathetic fuck. You should know that by now."

I've never seen him so emotionally raw. My skin prickles. This isn't good.

"Hey, it's okay. Come inside." I take his hand to coax him through the door. "Let me clean that up for you."

He reluctantly follows me inside to the bathroom. I rinse his hand under warm water and cover the scrapes in antiseptic cream. He watches me carefully. His tension fills the small room.

I want to calm him, but I don't know how. When I try to touch his face, he moves back, just out of reach.

"Don't . . ." He strides into the living room and tugs at his hair. "I should've gone home. From the start I knew I'd be the worst thing to ever happen to you, but I was weak. You make me so fucking weak."

Panic crawls up into my throat as I watch him pace. He's unraveling. Pulling apart faster than I can put him back together.

I put a hand on his chest to stop him. He looks at it like it's a brand, burning into his skin. I drop my hand and try to keep my voice even. "Ethan, listen, whatever you're feeling right now, we can deal with it together. Please, just . . ." I take a breath and try to calm myself. "Tell me how to fix this." Then I have a horrible thought. "Can we fix it?"

He leans against the wall, brows furrowed, head back. "I don't know." His panic vibrates in the air, making all my hairs stand on end.

"How can I help you? Please—"

"Dammit, Cassie, I don't fucking *know*, all right? I don't know what the fuck I'm doing anymore. Since the moment I met you, I've been so turned around, I haven't known which way is up. All I know is that I want to be with you, but—"

I walk over to him and take his face in my hands. My desperation matches his. "No. No buts. You are with me. Look. You're right here."

"I shouldn't be." He squeezes his eyes shut.

"You should. You're with me, and I'm yours, and I . . . I love you."

He snaps open his eyes to stare at me, and I realize this is the first time I've told him that. It's strange that this is new information to him. I've felt it for a long time, but I guess I've been too proud, or too scared, or too stubborn to say it. But I have to tell him now because I'm losing him.

I watch for his reaction. Do I expect him to say it back? After all these months of compulsive passion, of course that's what I expect. But he doesn't say it. Instead, he drops his head like I've somehow opened Pandora's box and doomed us both. "Fuck. Cassie . . . don't . . ."

"It's true," I say, as the ache in my chest flares. "I love you, Ethan. You're . . . amazing. But I know you're scared. The last time you opened yourself up like this, your girlfriend cheated on you with your best friend. But you *know* I'd never do that. I love you. And I hope that under all your fear . . . you can find a way to . . . well, I hope that . . . you love me, too. Right?"

Please, Ethan. Tell me I'm right.

He shakes his head. "I can't . . ."

I hold my tears back. He needs me to be strong, and I need him to be okay. We can do this. "You can't . . . love me?"

I tense all my muscles so his answer can't hurt me.

"Cassie, it doesn't matter how I feel about you. I can't be what you need."

"You can. You are."

"How can you say that?" he says, frustration making his voice hard. "I keep proving you wrong, time and again. You deserve someone else."

"I don't *want* anyone else. But . . . if you do . . ."

He shakes his head. "You know that's bullshit."

"I don't understand. So, you want me, but don't love me?" My voice cracks, and I hate how pathetic I sound.

His expression melts from anxiety into pity. I hate that look. He sees how desperate I am for him to tell me I'm wrong.

"You think I don't love you?" he says as he steps away from the wall and draws up to his full height. "If I didn't, do you think I'd be in hell right now? You think I like feeling like this? Like pushing you away isn't ripping out parts of me? Fuck, Cassie, I know the right thing to do is to leave you alone. But when I think about doing that, it . . ." He grips his chest. "It fucking *hurts*. And I'm so *sick* of hurting. I thought you could make it better, but you only made it worse." Everything he's feeling is on his face. He can barely look me in the eye, and it makes mine sting with tears. "You want me to say it? Yes, I love you. But you have no idea how many times I've wished I didn't."

He curls his hands into fists, and he looks frayed at the edges, like he's going to split apart any second if he doesn't touch me. I feel the same way.

"Loving you," he says, "is the stupidest, most selfish thing I've ever done, but I can't stop. God knows, I've tried."

Before I have time to answer, he's moving. Within three strides, he has his arms around me, crushing me against him as he claims my mouth. The initial shock of it is quickly replaced by a white-hot fever. It melts my muscles and settles in my bones.

He groans and kisses me again, and again, becoming more passionate with each passing second. I can barely keep up.

He's never kissed me like this before. Never. It's like he's speaking directly to my body. Asking permission, and apologizing, and wishing for things that can never be. He pushes me back against the wall, and even though the kiss is full of the same hungry lust that's always lived between our mouths, it's also something else.

It whispers under my skin and heats the air in my lungs. I feel it tingling in all my nerve endings as he presses his weight against me and moans into my lips.

"Tell me how to stop loving you, Cassie. Please. I have no fucking clue."

He kisses me deeper. Longer. More intensely. It's seduction and yearning. Raw and unashamed.

It's everything.

Our mouths and hands become frantic. He says he wants to keep us apart, but our bodies have other ideas.

His movements are rough, impatient with need. When he tugs at my shirt, I lift my arms to let him pull it off. My jeans are next, and I have to lean against the wall as he yanks them down. When he kisses his way back up, my legs liquefy.

Heat is coursing from him into me and back again. Everywhere he touches me burns. All the places he's yet to touch ache. His mouth is everywhere, like he's trying to consume me. I know how he feels. I'm just as hungry for him.

I fumble with the buttons on his shirt, desperate to get to the skin beneath. I get most of them undone, but the last one won't give way. I grunt as I rip the fabric and push the shirt off his shoulders. When both of my hands finally land on his chest and press against the thrumming pulse beneath, I sigh.

This is more than lust. It's even more than love. It's imperative. Mindless, bloody-minded need. I can't kiss him deep enough, or hold him close enough.

"God, Ethan . . ."

He's not gentle, and that's okay with me. I'm not used to him like this. So raw and uncontrolled. Nothing is being held back. Nothing. And it's so thrilling to get so much of him, emotion catches in my throat.

He tugs at my bra and pulls the straps down so he can get to my breasts. All I am is breath as he kisses and nibbles, and when he pushes one hand into my panties, I'm one long, unending inhale.

I grip him so hard, it's like I'm trying to get inside his skin. As I unbuckle his belt and pull it free, he's still teasing me with his fingers and mouth, keeping me pinned to the wall to stop me from flying away. I yank his jeans open, and it's only when I slide my hand into his boxers that he falters in his intensity. All of sudden, he's still, and his whole body shudders as I palm the weight of him and squeeze.

Oh, how he feels. How he looks as I touch him. Muscles flex with grateful shudders and restrained urgency.

He puts a hand against the wall, head low, breath fast. He looks like he's in pain, but I know better. I stop long enough to work his jeans and underwear over his hips, and then I maneuver him back against the wall so I can kiss a line down his chest. When I reach his abs, he starts cursing. When I take him in my mouth, he's not even forming words anymore, just long, raspy vowel sounds.

If I had the power, I'd have him always feel like this. Loved and worshipped. I'd melt away his doubts and insecurities with soft suction. Brush away his fears with reverent touches and low, appreciative moans.

Before long, he's gripping my hair and pulling me away. Then he's kissing me with renewed passion. He pauses to unlace his boots and pull off his socks. I take the opportunity to kiss his back, his shoulder, his bicep. He comes back to my mouth, and I pull off his jeans and underwear. He's barely kicked them away before he's sliding down my panties.

I'm not quite sure how we get on the floor, but we do. I push him down so I can taste every inch of warm, sweet-smelling skin. Every tense muscle and delicious groove. As I'm working on his chest, I'm vaguely aware of him pulling his wallet from his jeans and rolling on a condom.

When he's done, he pushes me onto my back and settles between my legs. I don't think I'll ever get used to the intensity of him like this. Naked and glorious. He towers over me with eyes that are somehow black but also full of fire. He studies my face as he braces on one arm, his broad shoulders tense, and then I feel him, pressing forward.

Oh.

The sweet, ecstatic pressure.

I look at him in awe. This feeling. This slow, intense filling. So different from the first time we did this. There's still some discomfort as my inexperienced flesh gets used to being stretched, but there's none of the previous resistance. No pain. Just the incredible miracle of one body joining with another.

Within a few gentle thrusts, he's inside, and oh, God, I'm not big enough for the inferno of feelings he ignites in me.

His mouth is open. Eyes heavy and blinking.

How can he possibly think we can't work when we're like this? This is bigger than fear. More important than doubt.

He starts to move, slowly at first, his jaw clenched in determination. Then, his need takes over and he gains momentum. Every thrust brings him deeper. I clutch at his shoulders, and watch as his face morphs through different layers of pleasure. He's magnificent.

He tangles his hands in my hair. Kisses my chest. Suckles on my neck. Through it all, he's moving, long slides that make me quake and gasp. Heat crawls up my neck as pleasure spins inside me. When he increases his pace, I know I'm making embarrassing sounds, but I can't stop. He's too much.

When I can't stand his beauty any longer, I look at the ceiling. It swims and sways. I give up and close my eyes. Lift my hips to meet him. Grip his lower back and urge him on.

In the end, I just submit to panting. Adrenaline courses through me as I walk a tightrope of sensation, and when he reaches between us and presses his fingers in tight circles, I'm gone. Falling and flying at the same time, and giving plaintive voice to the long, heavy pulses that overtake me.

I'm still spinning when he lets out a long moan. He bucks and presses in as far as he can, then he slows, and eventually stops. By then, we're not even two people anymore; just one orgasmic, panting mass, clinging to each other with trembling limbs.

Incredible.

What more could two people want from each other?

I let out a deep sigh.

Ethan's body is heavy against mine, his face pressed into my neck. I run my fingers through his hair and try to get enough oxygen.

"I love you, Ethan Holt," I say, soft and breathy. "No matter how tough things get, just remember that, okay?"

He tenses for a second, and just when I think my heart is going to bottom out from him not saying it back, he exhales. "I . . . I love you, too."

For the rest of the night, we don't talk. We make love, time and again. In the shower, in the kitchen, on the sofa, and, finally, in my bed.

When exhaustion finally takes us, I curl into his side and rest my head over his heart.

Whatever internal dilemma he's going through, we'll find a way to make it right, because that's what couples who love each other do.

I go to sleep with Ethan's heartbeat in my ear and his arm around me.

The next morning, light bleeds through my eyelids, and I'm dimly aware of birds singing in the trees outside. I smile as I register the warm body beside me.

The first time we slept together, he left before I woke. This time, he stayed.

I breathe in his scent and run my hand over his chest and stomach. He's warm, and it seems so decadent to feel the length of his naked body pressed against mine. This amount of Ethan should be illegal. He feels too good.

Just being beside him arouses me, and I contemplate which sexual positions we could try this morning. There are so many new things I want him to teach me.

As I snuggle into his chest and sigh in contentment, I realize his heartbeat is fast. Too fast.

I open my eyes to find he's awake. Staring, stony-faced at the ceiling. A rush of heat crawls across my skin. "Hey."

He blinks and turns to me. "Hey."

His posture is stiff. Alarmingly so. The arm that held me close last night now lies straight out from his body, barely touching me at all.

I sit up. "What's wrong?"

He blinks a few times, jaw tense. "I have to go."

Before I can protest, he swings his legs over the side of the bed, grabs his underwear, and pulls it on.

"What? Ethan . . . ?"

"I need to go home and pack before heading back to New York for the holidays," he says, not looking at me. "Plus, I have to go see Erika about what extra credit I need to do over the Christmas break to make up for flunking this term's acting class. Merry fucking Christmas to me."

He pulls on his jeans and buckles his belt before going in search of his shirt.

"Well, I could come with you. Back to your place, I mean. After you pack, we could get breakfast. My flight home isn't until this afternoon . . ."

"No." He disappears into the hallway and sickening knots form in my stomach. I sit up and pull the sheet to my chest as he reappears, buttoning up his shirt.

"You don't want me to come with you?"

He sits on the bed and grabs his boots and socks, not even sparing me a glance as he pulls them on and laces the boots. His movements are tense. He looks angry, and I don't know why. Doesn't he remember last night?

"Ethan . . . talk to me."

He finishes tying his shoes and stares at the floor. His jaw tightens as he takes a deep breath.

"Cassie . . ." He sighs. "I can't . . . we can't do this. I thought that maybe . . ." He squeezes his eyes shut. "We just can't."

"No," I say, my panic rising. "Don't start with that crap again. We can. We did last night. Do you even remember how amazing it was? How incredible we are together?"

His breathing speeds up as he turns to look at me. "Last night was a mistake."

I freeze. His words hang in the air like a toxic cloud. Something inside me cracks and ruptures.

He's not saying this. He can't be.

He was there. He felt it. How could he not? It wasn't just sex. We *made love*. Many times.

"A . . . a mistake?"

For a moment, I see pain flicker across his face, then it's gone.

"Last night was . . ." He shakes his head. "Yesterday, I flunked acting because I couldn't open up. But that shouldn't have come as a surprise to you, because you've been asking me to open up for freaking months, and I failed at that, too." He looks over his shoulder but doesn't meet my eyes. "I'm not capable of being a proper boyfriend. We both know it. Last night doesn't change anything."

My cheeks burn with anger. "How can you say that? You proved how you feel about me all night long. We said we loved each other, for God's sake! It changes everything!"

He turns to me, his eyes filled with tears. "Yeah, well, sometimes, love doesn't magically fix things. I shouldn't have allowed things to go as far as they did. We're never going to work, and I can't go on pretending that we are. You shouldn't, either."

I've felt this coming, but I still can't believe he's doing it. "This is ridiculous! You think we can't work, so that's it? Game over?!"

He pushes off the bed and spins around to face me. "Yes! Because I know I'm too fucking screwed up to be in a relationship right now. *Any* relationship. I will *hurt you*, Cassie! I've done it to others, and I'll do it to you. Have you forgotten there's a girl lying in a fucking hospital bed right now, thanks to me? Because I sure as hell haven't! And every time I picture Olivia half dead on that gurney, all I can think is, that could be *you*. It *will* be unless I get the hell out of this relationship."

"Ethan, no."

"*Yes*, Cassie. I'm no good for you. I never have been. I'm demanding and moody and jealous as all hell, and as much as I *hate* being like that, it's who I am. Don't you think I've tried to be different? The past few weeks it's *all I've done*. I've fought all of my natural reactions to be the boyfriend you deserve, but it was all fake. Don't even pretend you haven't noticed, because I know you have."

"Of course I've noticed, but I didn't know what to do, because you never *talk* to me!"

He throws up his hands. "That's because what I'm feeling is usually petty and fucking illogical! I see you dancing with Avery, and I can't stop wondering how long it's going to be before you fuck him. You're ten minutes late, and I think you've finally decided I'm not good enough for you, and you've left me."

"That's crazy."

"I know! That's the problem! Yet I can't help thinking it. I don't trust you, even though you've done *nothing* to make me doubt you." He exhales. When he speaks again, his voice is softer. "I've done a lot of things in my life I regret. Treated people badly. Taken out my issues on others. I feel myself doing it to you, and I can't fucking stand it. You don't deserve someone like me, and I sure as hell don't deserve someone like you. Just accept it and get on with your life. That's what I'm going to try to do."

My blood is hot, simmering beneath my skin.

I grip the sheet so hard it hurts. "Are you even listening to what you're saying?"

"Cassie—"

I slap the bed in frustration, hating the hot tears that slide down my cheeks. "I love you, you *ass*! How on earth is breaking my heart *protecting* me?!"

He stares at me with a pained expression for a few seconds, and I hold my breath, hoping he's going to take me in his arms and comfort me. But he doesn't, and the knife piercing my ribs twists a little more.

Instead, he shoves his hands in his pockets and stares at the floor, and every angle of him screams of self-loathing and unshed tears.

"Cassie," he says, "if I don't do this now, I know that in three months' time, I'll have ruined both of us, and you'll hate me forever. Or worse. At least if I end it now . . . maybe there's a chance we could still be . . . friends."

"Friends?" My breath hitches, and I hate it. *"Friends?"* Fat, ugly tears fall, and I hate them more. He's actually doing this. Despite everything we mean to each other, everything we've shared . . . he's doing it.

"Am I just supposed to forget how I feel about you?" I say, quiet and bitter. "Or how you feel about me? We both know we'll never be *friends*, Ethan. Ever."

Incredulity heats my face as we stare at each other. My chest is tight, and my throat is sore. Still, I can't stop myself from leaning forward and touching his arm. "Please . . . don't do this."

I know I'm begging, but I don't care. He loves me. There's nothing he can do or say that will make it untrue.

"It's already done." He steps away from me, and his breathing is uneven as he stares at the floor. "I have to go."

He turns his back and crosses the room, and something ruptures inside me. All my seams pull apart, flooding me with gut-churning pain. I hug myself, and try to hold it together.

"I love you," I whisper, barely able to get the words out.

He freezes with his back to me, shoulders tense. Silence smothers the room, screaming like thunder in my ears. My heart curls in on itself when I realize . . . I *know* . . . he's not going to say it back.

His hands tighten and release, but still, his feet are pointed squarely toward the door.

I have so much to say, but I know it doesn't matter. He's decided to ruin us, and I can't do a thing about it.

He turns his head. "Good-bye, Cassie." His voice is quiet, but he might as well have yelled. "I'll see you in the new year."

He strides out of my bedroom and down the hallway, and I swear I hear him groan as he opens the front door.

There's a long pause—long enough for me to think he's changed his mind, but then the front door slams behind him, and any chance I had of holding myself together shatters into a million pieces.

The first sob is so painful, I think I've injured myself. The second is no better. Then, all I am is pain, and tears, and wrongness, and when I press my face into my pillow, all I can smell is the man responsible for it.

NINE

FLOODGATES

He tries to soothe me as my breathing becomes harsh, but the echo of heartache fills all my empty places.

"Hey," he says, and brushes hair away from my face.

"Cassie . . . it's okay . . ."

"You hurt me. Broke me."

"I wish I could take it back, but I can't."

"Is this how you used to feel? Angry? Out of control? I hate it."

He cradles my face. "I know. And it's my fault. I'm sorry." He strokes my back. I shove him away. He pauses for a second, then steps forward to put his arms around me once more, patiently riding out my frustration. I shove him again, and my face is hot with too many emotions to identify. I want to lash out.

To punish him.

He knows. It's easy to recognize his former self in what I've become.

"Do it," he says. "Hit me if you want. Slap me. Yell. Do it, Cassie. You need to."

I'm choking on emotion. I try to swallow, but it refuses to be suppressed any longer. I groan as the floodgates open, and hot tears spill down my cheeks as I slap at his chest.

"Yes. Let it out. Do it."

I slap him once . . . twice . . . three, four times, and then I'm swearing and sobbing, and he stands there and takes it, all the while whispering that he loves me.

"I'm sorry I hurt you, Cassie. I'm so sorry. I'm not going to hurt you anymore, I promise."

My sobs get deeper as I grasp at him, purging the rage, all the pain he caused, all the time he wasted. Letting out years of venom until I have nothing left. No fuel for my fire. No bitter voice telling me he's not worth it.

At last, all I have left is exhaustion. Then his arms are around me, and he supports me as my legs buckle.

He just stands there and holds me, murmuring that everything's going to be all right. That *we'll* be all right.

I'm too tired to fight anymore. Too lonely.

Too much in love with him.

When the wetness on my cheeks begins to dry, I hug him back and let myself believe him, just a bit.

Just enough.

I don't know how long we stand there, but neither one of us seems eager to move. It's like we don't want the moment to end.

After a while, he loosens his grip. I guess he realizes I'm not going to run.

He kisses the top of my head, then my forehead, then my temple. He cups my face and kisses my cheek, and every touch makes me shiver. The soft brush of his lips tingles down my limbs and collects in my stomach, lighting up places that have been dark for too long.

Everything else fades into the background when he touches me. His heart pounds fast against my breasts as he holds me close and kisses my neck.

"Cassie . . ."

The way he says my name is like a groan of frustration and a sigh of relief. A promise. An apology. A prayer.

He rubs his thumbs over my cheeks as he leans down and pauses for long seconds before finally kissing me on the mouth. He presses his lips to mine but doesn't move. I inhale as my pulse doubles, pounding blood filling tense muscles. Making me want so much more than I'm ready for.

He pulls back and leans his forehead on mine, eyes closed. "One more chance is all I need to prove how different we can be, Cassie. Please. I know second chances are hard to come by and here I am asking for a third, but . . . fuck, I need you. And despite everything, you need me, too. Just say yes. Please."

I clench my jaw against habitual panic. "After my outburst, are you sure you still want this mess of insecurity dressed up like a woman?"

He lifts my chin and searches my eyes. "Cassie, I can safely say I've never wanted anything as much as I want you. Even if you tell me no, that's not going to change."

I sigh. Trust him to say exactly the right thing to melt me. "Well, okay then, I guess we'll give this thing one more try."

His answering smile is so dazzling, it's blinding.

"But," I say, "I'm not going to lie and say it will be easy. I'll need some time, so we need to go slow, okay?"

He exhales. "Okay. No problem."

Then he kisses me in a way that's in a different universe to slow.

I pull back, breathless. "Ethan . . ."

"Slow. Yeah, I know. Right after I do this." He takes my face and kisses me, unashamedly desperate.

In a blur of mouths and desperate I-need-you noises, he walks me backward, guiding me through the doorway I was blocking a little while ago. Then the door is closing, and my back is against it, and his body is warm and hard as he presses into me.

"Ethan . . ."

I can't catch my breath. He's everywhere, pressing and tasting. Reclaiming what's always been his.

"God, Cassie . . . Thank you for this. For you. Thank you."

He stops kissing and wraps around me, and I bury myself in him, my face in his neck.

We just stand there for a while. Breathing each other in.

Being.

Still not fixed, but far less broken.

TEN

THIS TOO SHALL PASS

Six Years Earlier
Somewhere Over Middle America

For my whole life I've heard people throw around the term "heartache," but I never truly understood what it meant until now. I mean, how is it possible that an emotion, something that has no mass or form except what we give it, is able to wrap around our hearts like a python and squeeze until every valve and chamber aches? Until the blood itself, which has no feeling at all, pulls barbed wire through our arteries with every broken beat? It shouldn't be possible.

And yet, as I look out the window of the plane taking me home for Christmas, that's exactly how I feel.

Everything's wrong. I'm alone, and all the parts of me that shouldn't hurt, do. The parts that thought love could conquer anything feel stupid. The parts that were firing with pleasure less than twenty-four hours ago feel tainted and cold.

I'm so angry, I want to rage and smash things, but the pain . . . the illogical heartache . . . keeps me curled in my window seat, fighting tears and trying to ignore the sick rolling in my stomach.

I hate what he did. I hate the reasons he did it.

The word resonates hot in my chest.

Hate.

Such a strong emotion. So easy to call upon. Loud enough to shout down all the pain.

It's easy to hate him, so I do.

It distracts me from how much I love him.

When we land, I exit the plane in a fog of cultivated numbness.

"Sweetheart." Mom hugs me before pulling back to give me her usual once-over. "That's what you wore to travel? They'll never upgrade you if you wear jeans, honey."

I sigh and turn to Dad. He wraps his arms around me and squeezes, and when he whispers, "I've missed you, kiddo," everything breaks loose.

Mom *awww*s and *shhhh*s as I sob into Dad's shirt. She thinks this display is because I've missed them. She gets teary and says she's missed me, too. Dad shuffles nervously as he pats my back. He never was good at dealing with emotion.

By the time we collect my luggage and get to the car, I'm beyond drained. The trip back to Aberdeen passes in a hazy blur.

When we get home, I go straight to my room and get ready for bed. As I brush my teeth, Christmas carols echo up the stairs, along with my mother's out-of-tune voice.

She loves Christmas.

Usually I do, too, but not this year.

It's only when I crawl into my childhood bed that I find relief in deep, desolate unconsciousness.

The next morning, I zombie-walk downstairs.

"Merry Christmas, sweetheart!"

I get hugs and a large box. The hugs make me feel claustrophobic. The box contains a leather-bound copy of the complete works of Shakespeare. It's beautiful, but I have an immediate urge to tear out *Romeo and Juliet* and throw it in the fire. That play will forever remind me of my first lead role. And the first time Ethan kissed me. It was backstage on the second day of rehearsals. He told me he wasn't capable of being my Romeo. That if he tried to play the romantic lead, he'd choke and take me down with him. I should have listened.

I put the book down and thank my parents. My smile feels sickeningly fake, but they don't seem to notice.

I give Mom perfume. Dad gets a detective novel. They both hug me, happy with their daughter even if they're not speaking to each other.

When I've had my fill of Tofurky and nutloaf, I claim I have a headache and go upstairs. My room is small, yet the space around me screams its emptiness. Like I'm too shriveled to fill it.

I unpack the rest of my bag, and when I find a small package at the bottom, the room gets a lot smaller.

I don't know why I brought it with me. Maybe because I didn't know what else to do. I peel off the too-bright paper and stare at the leather cover for a long time. I was going to give it to Ethan yesterday, but I got sidetracked by him breaking up with me. I was so excited when I bought it. My first gift for my first boyfriend. I was worried he'd think it was lame.

Turns out, his Christmas gift was the last thing I should have been concerned about.

I flick open the empty journal and run my fingers along the lines that should be filled with his thoughts.

Maybe I'll keep it for myself. Make it the place I pour out all toxic emotions.

I pick up a pen and try to write. Nothing happens.

I close my eyes, but all I get is a cavalcade of Holt. Kissing me. Holding my hand.

I wrap my arms around myself to stop the pain.

God, I miss him.

Being away from him is one thing. Being emotionally severed from him is another. Both together are unbearable.

My last thread of self-control snaps. I grab my phone.

He said he wanted to be friends, right? I draft five texts before settling on one that sounds casual enough to be friendly.

<Hey. Guessing your Christmas lunch was better than mine. Nothing says "Christmas" like fake turkey and nutloaf, right? Hope you're doing well.>

As soon as I hit send, I want to take it back.

I spend the next hour in purgatory, waiting for him to reply.

The hour after that I spend making up excuses as to why he hasn't.

The hour after that I feel more stupid than I ever have in my entire life. So ridiculous, and pathetic, and viciously dumb. I cry hot tears, and my chest nearly cracks with the effort to stay silent so my parents don't hear.

I throw my phone on the floor and try to sleep.

A tiny masochistic part of me keeps waking during the night to check if he's texted.

When morning breaks, he still hasn't.

"Cassie?"

Go away, Mom.

"Sweetheart, come on."

"I'm sleeping."

"It's two o'clock in the afternoon. You need to eat something."

"I'm not hungry."

The bed dips. A hand touches my head and strokes hair that hasn't been washed in the five days I've been home.

"Honey, I wish you'd tell me what happened. Maybe I can help."

You can't.

"Does this have something to do with that boy you were seeing? Ethan?"

I don't answer, but Mom knows. Only love gone wrong could make a woman behave like this. I've seen her after she and Dad have fought. Heartsick looks the same on everyone.

"Sweetheart," she says as she strokes my back. "Surely no boy is worth this. If he didn't want you, then he's obviously defective."

She's right. He is.

That was one of the things that attracted me to him in the first place.

"He didn't . . . hurt you, did he? Physically, I mean."

I shake my head and block out images of how I gasped when he pushed inside me.

"So this is all just emotional?"

Just emotional? There's no such thing. Emotions are nothing without a corresponding physical response. Adrenaline-fueled joy, heart-thumping fear, gut-churning loss.

Sure, Mom. It's *just* emotional.

I nod, because I know it'll make her feel better.

"Do you want to talk about it?"

I shake my head again, really needing this conversation to be over.

She sighs and squeezes my shoulder.

I wait until she closes the door before I turn my face to the wall and go back to sleep.

"He's a fucking idiot." I can almost see the look of disdain on Ruby's face through the phone.

"I don't want to talk about him."

"Yeah, well, I do. He hasn't called you at all? Not even on Christmas Day?"

"No. I texted him."

"What? Why?"

"I don't know. I missed him, I guess."

"Did he text back?"

"No."

"Cock."

"I don't know what I expected," I say, and lie back on my bed. "We broke up."

"No, *he* broke you up. There was no 'we' in that scenario. And don't make excuses for him. He doesn't deserve them."

I really wish she were here.

Mom and Dad don't understand, but Ruby does.

"What are you going to do when you see him at school on Monday?"

"I have no idea. Drop out?"

"Cassie, don't even joke about that. Don't you dare let that douche nozzle ruin your college experience. Just block him out. Do your work and kick ass. Don't give him power over you, and you'll be fine."

I sigh. It's not like I want him to have power over me, but I can't stop thinking about him.

"So, I'm coming back on the ninth," I say.

"I'll be back from my parents' by then. I'll pick you up from the airport."

"Thanks, Ruby."

I'm just about to hang up when she says, "Cassie?"

"Yeah?"

"You're going to be okay." Her voice is soft and sympathetic. "I know it probably doesn't feel like it now, but you will be."

I nod. "Yeah, I know."

I hang up and rub my eyes. The truth is, I know no such thing.

I pretend to read even though I've been staring at the same page for over an hour. My headphones block out the sound of Mom and Dad bickering downstairs. I have Simon & Garfunkel's "I Am a Rock" on repeat. I kind of hate the song, but the lyrics speak to me.

They talk about a rock not feeling pain and an island never crying. Sound good to me.

I'm sick of the pain, and if I never cry again, it will be too soon.

I just want to be over Ethan. Now. I don't want to be wondering how his holidays were. If he fought with his dad. How drunk he got.

If he thought about me.

I don't want any of it.

I want to be mine again and not his.

The way forward is to purge and cleanse. Push every positive thought about him out of my system. It's the only way I'm going to survive seeing him again. I refuse to pine for Ethan Holt for the next two years. No freaking way.

I close my eyes and try to focus. I picture him as I listen to the song, over and over again, and I let the lyrics harden my paper-thin layers.

I'm going to become a rock.

Ruby drops me off at our place before heading to the store for supplies.

I look around my apartment. Everything's the same yet seems totally different. That's the door that opened to him, as he stood there wide-eyed with panic. That's the wall I pressed him against as I told him I loved him. The same place where he said he wished he didn't love me. Right over there is where he undressed me and kissed me until I was breathless. On the floor was where we . . .

I shake my head to clear it.

When I step into my room, my stomach coils.

My bed.

It's stripped back to the bare mattress.

The morning he broke up with me, I'd ripped the sheets off and taken them to the laundry room. Then I'd turned the machine to "hot" and doused everything in far too much detergent.

I remake the bed with fresh sheets. I breathe deeply as I tuck and smooth, and palm over the areas where we made love like I can wipe them clean of memories.

When I'm done, it's perfect. Pristine.

I look at it for long minutes as phantom lips suckle my neck. Ghost hands trail across my thighs.

Screw this.

I shower. Wash my hair. Finish with water so cold it shocks me into distraction.

When Ruby gets home, we fall into a pattern of easy familiarity. We reheat frozen dinners, drink wine, watch TV, laugh.

We don't talk about him.

When eleven p.m. rolls around, we yawn and say good-night.

Ruby goes into her room.

I sleep on the couch.

The classroom is noisy, filled with chatter about who did what during the break. I've missed my friends, and I can't deny their hugs are welcome.

Aiyah and Miranda are holding hands. Like Ethan and I, they got together last year. Unlike Ethan and I, their love survived the holiday. Jack is telling jokes, and I smile as Connor and Lucas crack up. Heck, I've even missed Zoe and Phoebe and their shrill conversations.

They all seem happy to see me, too.

None of them know about the breakup. How could they?

I guess they'll figure it out soon enough, but I'm not going to be the one to tell them.

The second Ethan enters, I know it. A bone-deep vibration shudders up my spine and sets every hair on edge.

People say his name. Ask how he is. He answers, his voice low and quiet.

I don't want to look at him, but my body turns of its own accord, and there he is, towering over most of the people around him, even as his shoulders sag.

Excitement tries to fire in my veins, but I suppress it.

Unwanted fantasies about kissing him crawl through my brain. It all seems so unlikely now that I almost laugh out loud.

He glances over at me, and that's when all the air goes out of the room. His mouth sets into a hard line, and he looks away several times before returning. It's like he wants to look anywhere but at me, but is incapable.

I know how he feels.

This is what I've been preparing for.

I breathe steadily and make myself over. Smooth down the rumbling waves of emotion. Make myself a rock.

I stare at him without apology and let him see my indifference. Dare him to challenge it.

For a moment, he frowns, like he expected something else. Hurt, maybe. Or longing.

If he expected to find me a blubbering, emotional mess, he must be sorely disappointed.

His expression is one of indescribable sadness, before his familiar barriers slide into place and it's almost as if nothing happened between us.

We're two perfect characterizations, flawless in our denial.

No one can tell how bitterly unleashed I am on the inside. Not even him.

Especially not him.

A line from *As You Like It* comes to me: *All the world's a stage, and all the men and women merely players.* Standing here, staring at Ethan, that concept has never been more true. The Grove is now our stage, and these are our new roles.

Separate.

Loveless.

Unaffected.

I take a deep breath.

Curtain up.

ELEVEN

OPEN BOOK

Present Day
New York City, New York
The Apartment of Cassandra Taylor

My head is on his chest, my arm draped over his waist. I'm gripping his shirt like it can keep me here in this place. Where everything that happened between us hovers on the edge of my consciousness like white noise. Not forgotten but dimmer.

After our hallway confrontation, he brought me in here. Laid me down. Reassured me we'll be all right.

Now he has his arms around me and is stroking my arm.

I can't quite believe he's in my bed, the scene of so many angst-driven fantasies about him. We're both fully clothed and completely silent, yet this is the most intimate I've been with a man since . . . well, since him.

He takes my hand and places it on his chest, then presses it down against the pulse of blood and silent promises. I can feel him willing me to trust him.

I want to, but it's like my heart's too small for him now. When he left, it collapsed like a balloon, empty and deflated, and over time it atrophied into that shape. And now he wants me to make room for him again, but I don't know how.

"Ethan?"

"Hmmm?"

"When did you know you were capable of . . . changing?" He strokes my hand for a few seconds, but doesn't answer. "I mean, you tried to change when you were with me, right? To become more open?"

"Yes. Jesus. I tried so hard. And failed spectacularly."

"So, how did you go from the guy who left me twice to the guy you are now?"

He looks down at me. "I did mention I've been in therapy for three years, right? And I'm not talking just one session a week. In my darker days it was two . . . three sessions a week. My therapist had the patience of a saint."

"Yeah, but you could have gotten therapy when we were together, couldn't you?"

"Technically, yes. But the thought of it scared the crap out of me, and we both know that back then, I was ruled by fear."

"Then how did you decide you weren't scared anymore?"

He takes a deep breath and lets it out. "I was hoping I wouldn't have to tell you this story, but I guess you deserve to know."

"What story?" I break out in goose bumps, certain I'm not going to like what I hear.

He grabs my hand and pushes it under his shirt. On the left side of his rib cage, my fingers graze a clump of scar tissue. I'd noticed it when we ran our love scenes, but I was always too distracted by his kisses to find out more.

I lift his shirt and lean over to get a better look. "What is that?"

He strokes my forearm as I continue to graze the rough skin. "That's where a tube was shoved into my lung to drain out the blood that was drowning me."

I look up at him and frown.

"And there's this . . ." He takes my hand and lifts it to his head. At the back, there's another patch of raised skin. "That was where my head smashed into a tree. Fourteen stitches."

Bile rises in my throat. "Ethan, what the hell . . . ?"

He takes my hand and plays with my fingers. "After I left you in senior year, I hit my low point in France. The show was a hit, and I was getting great reviews, but I couldn't stop thinking about you. I felt so goddamn guilty about failing you. Again. I already told you I was drinking a lot. Getting into fights."

I nod.

"Well, after our season, we had a week off before we moved on to Italy. The rest of the cast was going to do a tour of the wineries, but I couldn't cope with being a miserable bastard around them, so I hired a motorbike and just . . . left. Traveled aimlessly around southern France, thinking I had the world monopoly on self-loathing. Driving drunk, driving too fast, taking crazy risks. I was a fucking mess. I don't think I had a death wish, but deep down . . ." He looks at me. "I guess I wanted to hurt myself more than I'd hurt you."

"Ethan . . ."

He shakes his head. "Pathetic, right? Well, one night, after hitting a French pub, I decided to make a play for the Italian border. It had been raining. Too much alcohol, too much speed, zero self-esteem. I took a curve too fast and slammed into the guardrail. My bike went cartwheeling across the road as I flew over the rail and crashed down a steep embankment. Pretty sure I hit every damn tree on the way down. By the time I'd reached the bottom, my helmet was cracked, my leather jacket was shredded, and it felt like someone had shoved a dagger into my ribs."

"Oh, God . . ."

"I lay there for a while, just trying to breathe. When I moved, I was hit with so much pain, I almost passed out. I managed to pull off my helmet, but that was it. There was pain in my shoulder, my wrist, my chest. I could feel blood running down my leg."

"What did you do?"

He shrugs. "I tried to figure out if I was dying. And when I seriously thought I was, I took a moment to try and figure out if that was a bad thing."

"Ethan . . ."

I take his hand and he lets out a shaky breath. "It's weird, you know, facing your own mortality. People talk about their life flashing in front of their eyes, but I didn't get that. All I got were flashes of you. They were so vivid, it was like I could reach out and touch you. I wondered how you'd react if I died. Would you mourn me? Or would you be happy I'd never hurt you again?"

As I listen, anxiety begins to coil in my chest. Thinking about him dying makes my throat close up.

He strokes my face. "Hey, it's okay."

"How could you think I wouldn't mourn you?"

"I was in a dark place. I wasn't thinking straight."

"God, Ethan, if you'd died . . ." I can't finish the thought, let alone the sentence. Even at the height of my enmity, I couldn't imagine living in a world without Ethan. The mere concept was distressing beyond words. "Okay, tell me what happened next before I freak out about the death thing."

He wraps his arm around me and pulls me in to his side. "I don't know how long I was lying at the bottom of that hill. Most of the night, at least. I slipped in and out of consciousness, and as time passed, I realized no one was going to find me down there. Unless I did something, I was going to die. I had to get back to the road."

"But your injuries . . ."

"Yeah, I found out later that I had a dislocated shoulder, a fractured wrist, three broken ribs, and a punctured lung, as well as a concussion and multiple lacerations."

"Oh my God! How did you even move?"

"Willpower. Stubborness. The thing is, I knew that climbing up that hill was going to be the most painful thing I'd ever done, but it was necessary. I had to survive, because if I didn't, I could never get you to forgive me, and that was not fucking acceptable."

He touches my face, soft and reverent. "So, I climbed. Every step made me scream in agony, but I kept moving, one foot in front of the other. By the time I reached the top, I was sure I'd died and gone to hell. The pain was blinding. I managed to crawl over the guardrail before collapsing on the road."

"How did you get out of there?"

"A delivery driver found me a couple of hours later and called an ambulance. When I woke up, I was in a French hospital, tubes everywhere, dosed up on morphine. Elissa and the company manager were there. They told me I'd been out for a couple of days. Elissa was fucking furious. She'd been lecturing me for months about my drinking and self-destructive habits. When she was done yelling, she started sobbing. I'd never seen my sister cry like that before."

"Of course she was upset. She could have lost you. We all could have."

"But the ironic thing is, the way I was living . . . it was like I was already dead. It took the accident to bring me back to life. While I was recovering in the hospital, I had a lot of time to think. It occurred to me that, for most of my adult life, I'd had this thing for self-sabotage. When I broke up with you the second time, it was me slamming into the barrier of my goddamn issues. I knew if I didn't do something to fix them and find a way to get you back, my life was pointless. So, yeah. I decided to live. As soon as I got out of the hospital, I tracked down a therapist who specialized in abandonment issues and climbed the fucking painful hill of recovery. Three years later, here I am. Scarred, but grateful."

I want to be grateful, too, but I'm too busy being fixated on a mental image of him lying in a hospital bed, crumpled and broken.

"Why didn't you tell me? You could have asked Elissa to contact me."

He shakes his head. "I couldn't. I mean, I'd almost killed myself because I was pining for you. How fucking lame is that? Plus, I vowed the next time you laid eyes on me, I'd be the man you deserved, not some scared little boy."

I look up at him. "And now, here you are."

He brushes his thumb over my lips. "Here I am."

He leans down and kisses me, warm and open and soft. When he stops, I'm boneless.

"You were always my incentive to get better, both physically and mentally. You were my reward."

He wraps around me before burying his face in my neck. "Thank you."

I take in a shaky breath and try to keep it together. He tightens his arms around me, and I almost can't breathe.

"You know," I say, and wheeze for effect, "there's a difference between snuggling and holding someone captive."

"Yeah, well, I've waited a long time for this, so I'm going to enjoy it." Nevertheless, he loosens his grip.

We stay like that for long time, intertwined and breathing each other's air. Seeing who'll pull away first. My bladder makes sure it's me.

When I come out of the bathroom, he's sitting on the edge of the bed.

I stop in front of him, and he takes my hands. "I want you to come to my place for dinner tonight. I'll cook. I have something I want to show you."

I smile and shake my head. "Ethan . . . I think we really need to take things slowly for a while. Besides, I'm pretty sure what you want to show me, I've seen before."

"Not that," he says as he lifts up onto one elbow. "Although if you play your cards right, I could be persuaded to show you that, too. In fact, cards aren't necessary. A simple eyebrow raise would do it."

I roll my eyes.

He pushes my hair away from my face. "Hey, I'm kidding. I promise, my pants will stay on. Please, I really want you to come." I make a face. "Over! Jesus. Come *over*, and let me make you come. *Make you dinner!* Shit!" He shakes his head. "Sorry. My brain is distracted. When I look at you from this angle I can see right down your robe."

I slap his arm and pull my robe around me. He tries not to laugh.

I push him, and he falls back onto the bed. Part of me hates how right he looks on it.

He grabs my hand and pulls me down, then rolls on top of me. He's so happy and comfortable, I barely recognize him.

"I really can't be blamed for ogling," he says, as his hands frame my face. "It's all your fault for being so goddamn beautiful. Do you even understand how attracted I am to you?"

When he leans down to kiss me, I put my hand on his chest to stop him. He immediately rolls off like he's expecting it.

He sighs and stares at me, unashamedly lustful. "So, yeah. I'm going through this phase right now where I don't seem to know the meaning of the word 'slow.' I promise that from now on, I'm going to try harder not to hit on you every five minutes."

I laugh and shake my head. "I feel like I should apologize."

"For what? Not jumping into bed with me the moment you've decided you don't hate me anymore? How dare you? I'm fucking appalled."

I dig my fingers into his ribs. He squirms and makes a very unmanly noise.

"Hey! You know tickling is now against the Geneva Convention. Quit it before I call NATO. I don't want my girlfriend to be an international war criminal."

I flinch. He notices, and his smile falls.

"Fuck. Cassie . . . I didn't mean to—"

I laugh, but it's forced. "It's fine."

A few years ago, I couldn't convince him to call me his girlfriend without coercion and testicular clamps, and now he's throwing around the term like he's Mr. Commitment?

"It slipped out, okay? I mean, what I feel for you is a few hundred light-years away from just being my girlfriend, but I'm trying really hard not to freak you out here so I've been keeping my epic feelings on the down-low."

"Well, except for that whole thing where you typed 'I LOVE YOU' over a thousand times, right?"

"Yeah. Except for that."

"Ethan—"

He runs his fingers through his hair as his frustration peeks through. "I know it's too soon, but I'm not going to lie to you and say I don't want it, because I do. I want to be your boyfriend. No, wait . . . boyfriend sounds so fucking lame. I'm nearly twenty-seven years old. I'm not a boy anymore. I want to be your man. Your lover. Your . . . damn it, I don't know. Your Ethan. Whatever the fuck you want to call me, that's what I want to be. My end game is to simply know that I'm yours and you're mine, and that neither one of us is scared or ashamed of that. I want to take you out and put my arm around you and know that every other man in the room is jealous as hell that I'm the one who gets to take you home and paint your skin with my mouth."

I don't know what to say. Getting used to this new version of him is going to take time. He's so sure of himself.

He leans forward and brushes a stray piece of hair away from my face. "Now, do you have any other questions about how I feel? Or would you like me to describe exactly which parts of your body I'm going to paint with my mouth?"

A crawling heat spreads across my shoulders and creeps up my neck. He's not allowed to be this sexy when I'm trying to take things slow. He's really, truly not.

"Ah . . . no," I say as I fixate on his mouth. "That was an excellent explanation. I'm good."

He nods. "Good. Because really, that second part was kind of a trick question. When I get my mouth on you, there won't be any parts untasted. I want all of you." He takes a long, slow appraisal of my body. "Every . . . delicious . . . inch." He continues to stare, and I feel myself leaning forward. He clenches his jaw as I get closer, and just when I think he's going to try to kiss me again, he shakes his head and stands.

"Okay, I seriously have to get out of here, because if I stay, I'm going to make you uncomfortable with all my filthy, relentless lust." He exhales and rakes his fingers through his hair. "So, tonight. Dinner at my place? I'll cook whatever you want."

"Sure. What time do you want me?"

He takes a deep breath. "I want you all the time."

I shake my head and smile.

"Sorry, but you did ask. If you don't want innuendo, rephrase the question."

"Fine. What time would you like me to arrive tonight?"

"Six thirty. I want to discuss something with you before dinner."

"About?"

"You'll see." I'm immediately cautious. He gives me a half smile. "Don't panic. I think it's going to be a good thing. Trust me."

I'm trying. I'm really, really trying.

"Do you want me to bring anything?"

He stares for a few seconds. "Just you. That's all I need."

Time is a fickle whore. Whenever you want it to pass slowly, it speeds up, and whenever you're full of nervous impatience, it crawls like a sloth on sedatives.

The entire contents of my closet lie on my bed. Everything has been tried on at least twice. My hair is sleek and straight. Makeup light but careful.

I remind myself that this is not a date. It's dinner.

Just dinner.

Then why am I wearing underwear that cost more than the national debt of some small African countries?

I shouldn't be going to this much trouble. I shouldn't be this nervous. And I really shouldn't get so flustered when I imagine the look on his face when he sees this sex kitten underwear.

Shit. *If* he sees this underwear. *If*, not *when*.

I sit on the bed and drop my head in my hands.

Maybe I should cancel. I'm not ready for this.

I take some deep breaths and look at the clock. Tristan, my Zen-master roommate and life coach, will be home soon. He'll know what to do. What I should wear.

My phone buzzes with a message from him.

<*Hot yoga student asked me out for a drink. Home later, if at all. There's a new bottle of Shiraz in the kitchen. Use it wisely.*>

I text him back.

<*Fuck you, Tris. I hope he has a tiny dick.*>

He replies with a smiley face and what looks like a giant schlong emoticon.

Where the hell did he even get that?

Damn him.

To be fair, he doesn't know I'm going to Ethan's place for dinner. If he did, he'd probably cover me in barbed wire, strap a chastity belt on me, and then insist on coming with me to protect my vagina chakra, if there is such a thing.

I sigh and take off my pretty underwear and replace it with my most boring white cotton thong and bra. Then I put on comfortable jeans and a plain T-shirt, pull my hair back into a ponytail, and take my makeup back to just mascara and lip gloss.

Done.

No pressure.

Just dinner.

And him.

Nothing more.

I've barely knocked when the door opens, and he's there.

Oh God, he is so there.

Freshly shaven, navy shirt, dark jeans, no shoes.

I think I gape. I can't be sure.

He's staring at me, too, dragging his gaze slowly over my body before settling on my face.

"Hi." He looks nervous. For some reason, that makes me feel a little better.

"Hi."

He doesn't move.

"You look . . . I just . . ." He blinks. "You're so fucking beautiful."

How does he not understand that statements like that make me want to murder my resolution to take it slow with him and bury it where no one will find it?

"Uh . . . thanks. You look good, too." Really good.

He ignores my compliment as he continues to stare.

"Uh . . . Ethan?"

He shakes his head and remembers his manners. "Shit, sorry. Come in."

"Thanks."

He steps back and lets me enter. A rush of goose bumps crawls over my skin as I pass. The hallway smells like him, and I automatically take a deep breath.

I haven't seen his New York place yet, so I drink in every detail.

His apartment is compact but stylish. More grown-up than his Westchester digs. More refined.

"Elissa decorated," he says.

I nod. "It's nice. It's just you here?"

"Yeah. Ever since I got back from Europe. Elissa is living in the East Village like the bohemian she is. I miss having her around, but it was time, you know? Can't live with my baby sister forever."

"Uh-huh."

We lapse into silence as I wander around and check out his knick-knacks and photos. I run my fingers along the spines of his book collection as I try to get to know him again.

I can feel him watching me. Waiting for my approval. It's kind of strange.

I stop when I spy a familiar title. "Kristin Linklater—*Freeing the Natural Voice.*"

I turn to him, and he laughs. "Every time someone mentioned the title of this book in class, Jack Avery would fart." He laughs harder.

"Is that why you keep it on your shelf?"

He shrugs. "What can I say? Avery was a dick, but the boy was funny. Plus, Linklater really knew what she was talking about."

I shake my head. "You have all our old textbooks here."

"They've been useful over the years. They were also . . . reminders . . . of our time at drama school."

"I burned all of mine."

I say it before I register how he'll feel about it. Judging by his expression, it doesn't make him happy. I hadn't meant that to be a reflection on him, but I guess it is. I purged those books just like I purged everything that reminded me of him.

He drops his head. "I'm sorry."

"Don't be. Everything I needed from those books I learned by heart."

He nods.

He knows.

"Would you like something to drink?"

"God, yes."

"I have a red you're going to love."

He disappears into the kitchen and I continue to explore, looking for something. I don't know what. Something about me, maybe. About us. Something real and familiar.

On the wall opposite the windows, I see them. At first I'm not sure what I'm looking at, but then I realize what they are—masks. Two of them. From a distance, they seem like the standard comedy and tragedy faces so many actors have in their homes, but a second look causes me to catch my breath. Not comedy and tragedy. Strength and vulnerability. The same masks we used at drama school. The ones we both had trouble with.

"I convinced Erika to give them to me." I turn to find him a few feet away, a glass of wine in each hand. "I bought her a whole new set in Italy."

He passes me a glass, and I take a sip. "Why did you want them? I mean, you failed that class. Erika kicked your ass for weeks."

"Yeah, but only because she expected more from me. It took me a long time to expect more from myself. To see that being vulnerable takes a shitload more strength than being closed off and sullen." He takes a step closer, and I take another mouthful of wine while trying not to look at him. "Every time I look at those masks, it reminds me. Every time I look at you, it reminds me, too, but you weren't around for a long time, so the masks were a good placeholder."

I keep my eyes on the masks, but I can feel him staring at me. As I tip the glass back, I realize my wine is almost gone. I need to slow down, or I'm going to get drunk and do things I may regret.

I feel warm fingers on my wrist, and he's right behind me, warm breath on my neck as he says, "I want you to have something."

He takes my hand and guides me over to a large bookcase with doors. His palm is sweaty, and I wonder what has him so anxious.

He puts our glasses on the side table, and when he takes my hands, I swear I feel him tremble.

"Cassie, for so long I kept you guessing as to what I was thinking and feeling. I never want you to have to guess again. So from now on, anything you want to know, I'll tell you. Anything."

He pulls open the doors and gestures to the rows of books inside. "You want to know my motivations for all the shit I put you through in drama school? It's all there. Every fucked-up thought process and bad decision. Every time I broke both our hearts in an effort to avoid pain. Read them if you want. Burn them. Whatever works for you."

I look closely at the spines of the books. Dates. Years. Rows and rows of journals, starting from when he was in high school. Some years have a single volume, others have several. The year we met has five. No surprise there.

I pick up the last one from that year and open it to a random page.

November 18th

Tonight, she went down on me for the first time. And . . . Jesus Christ . . . I'm still shaking. I can't get the image of her out of my head. So eager to please me. So trusting.

So beautiful.

I can't handle it.

One day soon, she's going to realize I'm no good for her and leave. Destroy me.

Every single brain cell is telling me to get out while I can. To run so far and fast she'll never find me. Forget that someone as fucking perfect as she is even exists.

But some part of me believes I can do this. That I'm capable of ripping open my chest and just handing over my heart like it's not going to kill me.

That part is obviously deranged.

I look up, shocked by the depth of emotion in his writing. He's watching me. Gauging my reaction. He doesn't flinch from my incredulity.

"I take responsibility for everything I did," he says, "because even though I can't change it, I do regret it. I thought seeing these may . . . I don't know. Help in some way."

I'm not so sure.

I go back to the journal.

December 4th

2:48 a.m.—She won't fucking answer. She calls to abuse me in the middle of the night, and then WON'T PICK UP HER FUCKING PHONE?!

3:36 a.m.—I can't stop thinking about her crying. She sounded so lost. And I did that to her. Me.

What a stellar fucking human being I am.

As much as I'm terrified she's going to ruin me, I'm afraid I'm going to do far worse to her.

So now I'm faced with the decision—man up and be the boyfriend she deserves, or get the fuck out while there's still a chance we'll both survive.

Yeah. Easy choice. It's like asking someone if they'd rather die by drowning or electrocution.

Whichever way it happens, you're still dead.

11:18 a.m.—She just left. I can still smell her. Fuck, I love her smell. I want to bathe in it.

She was asleep when I got home from my run. So perfect in my bed.

I had a major freakout for the three seconds I believed she'd read this journal, but I quickly realized if she had, she wouldn't still be here, let alone sleeping. She would have finally seen the level of fuckery she's burdened with and run for the hills. And I wouldn't have blamed her.

But no, she's proven yet again that she's not like the others. Made me realize she deserves so much more credit than I give her.

I want to be a better man. A better boyfriend.

Don't fuck this up, Holt. Seriously. If you do, I'll never forgive you. She'll never forgive you.

Reading his thoughts gives me a strange sense of déjà vu.

I turn the page and read the last entry in the journal. As soon as I see the date, my stomach lurches.

December 23rd

I did it. Cut the cord.

I feel sick.

I feel more broken without her than I ever did when we were together.

I thought this was the right thing to do . . . for me . . . for her. But now . . .

I can barely swallow, my throat's so tight.

What the fuck have I done?

Why do I feel so wrong?

Fuck.

And yet, part of me knows I had to do it.

If we'd stayed together, I would have systemically broken her. I'd have tried not to and hated every moment of it, but I would have. She'd have spent all her time defending her actions, reassuring me, putting out fires she had no hand in starting.

I couldn't bear doing that to her.

I tell myself I want her to move on and be happy, but petty fucking creep that I am, I really don't. I want her to pine for me and not let another man touch her until I can figure out how to be better. I want to be magically cured of all the shit that runs through my brain on a daily basis and be the man she deserves.

But most of all, I just want to be with her. Especially after last night.

Jesus fucking Christ. Last night.

I didn't mean for it to happen, but when she stood in front of me, thinking I didn't love her, I couldn't stop myself. My brain was screaming that it was a bad idea, but my body wouldn't listen. I thought maybe it was a good thing. That it would . . . I don't know . . . fix me. Help me be with her, somehow.

But it didn't.

If anything, it made things worse, because now, I'll always know what I'm missing. The first time we made love, I was so obsessed with being gentle, I couldn't let myself go. I didn't have that problem last night.

I wanted to consume her. Brand my name on every part of her body.

By the time we were done, I think I had succeeded.

The trouble is, she also branded me.

I cried in her arms. I don't fucking cry. I don't even know why I did. It just happened.

But then my brain kicked in. My stupid, paranoid brain.

Lying in bed with her as she slept, I felt like one of those animals whose leg is caught in a trap, knowing if I wanted to survive, I'd have to gnaw off a part of myself and leave it behind.

That's how I feel now. Like I've carved out a huge chunk of my heart and left it with her.

It hurts. Fuck, it hurts like hell. But I know it was the right thing to do.

She doesn't see it like that.

I hope one day she will.

I almost laugh, but there's too much simmering anger to allow it.

When I look up, he's right in front of me. I don't think I've ever seen him look so serious.

"I'm not him anymore, Cassie. Never will be again. You have to know that."

I nod. Every day, I understand that more.

From the moment I met you, it was all about you. I just tried to deny it."

"And now?"

He gives me a hopeful smile. "Now I know I was a deluded asshole."

I nod. "You were."

"I know."

"I mean, really."

"I'm not arguing with you."

We stare at each other, and the push and pull of how we are now makes me disoriented.

"So, what do we do now?" he asks and glances at the book in my hand.

I pick up my wineglass and drain it. "I guess we have dinner. Then . . . I don't know. See what happens."

Dinner is delicious. Conversation is full but tense. I drink too much wine. It helps me relax.

The thing is, relaxed is dangerous around him. Makes me think I'm ready for things. Builds a different kind of tension. One that has nothing to do with our past and everything to do with the here and now of us. The Cassie and Ethan who lapse into silence every few minutes because our brains are too distracted by each other to speak.

Instead, we stare. Avoid touching. Stare some more.

Gentle music plays as he leads me to the couch. The lights are dim, but he sees everything. Studies every movement. Watches me exhale and makes me tingle with need.

He squeezes his eyes shut and drops his head back. We both struggle to stay at opposite ends of the couch.

"I should go," I say, more out of self-preservation than anything.

He sighs. "That is both the best and worst idea in the world."

"It's really sad that I know exactly what you mean by that, isn't it?"

"No. It's just another reason for you to get out of here while you still can. My noble intentions to take it slow with you only go so far when you look at me like that."

"Like what?"

"Like you want to make every sexual fantasy I've had about you for the past three years a very dirty reality."

"How dirty are we talking?"

"So dirty we'd have to do it in the shower."

"Wow." He's good at shower sex. I remember.

"Are you sure you don't want to stay?"

"No."

He exhales. "Fuck. I'm calling a car for you before I lose all self-control."

We both stand, and I stare blatantly when he adjusts himself.

"Can I borrow some of these?" I ask, and gesture to the journals.

"Take as many as you want. From now on, I'm an open book. Even Past Me has no secrets."

While he pulls out his phone and dials for a car, I pick up a selection of journals. I purposely avoid the ones from our senior year. I can't even look at them without breaking into a sweat. It's a safe bet I'm going to need a lot more to drink before I tackle them.

He walks me to the door, and with every step, the desire to leave him lessens. He leans forward and grabs the handle as his chest presses against my shoulder. For long seconds, he stays there, not opening the door. Just pressing against me and breathing.

"Cassie, I'm going to ask you some questions now, and I really need you to answer 'no' to them. Do you understand?"

"Yes."

He inhales, and I feel the tip of his nose graze the side of my neck. I close my eyes and shiver as I press back into him.

"Will you stay with me tonight? In my bed?"

He can't—How can he . . . ?

"Ethan—"

"All you need to say is 'No.' That's it."

I squeeze my eyes shut. "No."

"Will you let me peel off your clothes and put my mouth on you? All over you? Taste all the parts I've been dreaming of since we've been apart?"

Jesus.

Breathe.

"No."

"Do you want me?"

"No."

Lies.

"Do you love me?"

"No."

All of it.

"Will you stop me if I pin you against the wall and kiss you like my life depends on it? Which it kind of does."

My heart kicks into overdrive. We both stop breathing.

Finally, a truth.

"No."

In a second he's pressed me back against the wall. Our mouths are open and desperate. Then his hands are on my ass as he lifts me. I wrap my legs around his grinding hips and gasp as I drop the books and my bag so I can anchor my hands in his hair. I open myself up to one tiny corner of my need for him and let that part grip his shoulders and biceps as he works himself against me.

"Fuck. Cassie . . ."

There's too much of him, all straining, all hard. The deep parts of me ache for him the most. Not just my body. It's more than that. Some parts spark. Others melt. A flux of chemistry and catastrophe, the same compulsive need that keeps bringing us back together.

A car horn blares. He freezes and pants against my neck while his muscles slowly uncoil beneath my hands.

"You probably should have said 'Yes' to that last one," he says, lips against my throat.

When he lowers me to my feet, I can barely stand. "Probably."

He picks up the journals and my bag and opens the door, then escorts me downstairs to the waiting taxi.

When I'm inside, he leans in and kisses me gently on the lips. "Thank you for coming."

I smile. "I didn't quite—"

"To dinner." He smiles and kisses me again.

"Oh, that. Thanks for having me."

"Uh, I didn't quite—"

"We could do this all night."

"Is that an offer? Because I could send the taxi driver away and take you back upstairs."

I smile. "Good night, Ethan."

He kisses me one more time, lingering this time. I almost forget why I have to leave.

"'Night. I'll call you tomorrow."

He closes the door, and the taxi pulls away.

When I get into my apartment and collapse on the bed, I can still feel all the places he touched me. I turn off the light and strip as I let my hands wander, needing to finish what he started, or I won't be able to sleep.

I don't mean to close my eyes and picture him, but I do. Of all the many characters and faces I've seen over the years, the expression that's clearest in my memory is the one when he's touching me. How his mouth drops open in wonder as he brings me pleasure.

It's that face that lingers behind my eyelids. I pretend my hands are his, and when I cry out in my dark room, I have to stop myself from saying his name.

I'm on the verge of dozing off when my phone buzzes with a message.

<Are you touching yourself right now & thinking about me?>

I laugh. He always did know me too well.

<No.>
<Me neither. Definitely not doing it for the 2nd time.>
<TMI>
<Really? I can give you more details if u like.>
<Going now.>
<Going or coming? Put your phone on vibrate & I'll text the hell outta you.>

My laughter sounds way too loud in my silent room, and I realize it's the first time that's happened in a very long time.

<Good night, Ethan.>
<G'night, Cassie.>

I'm about to put my phone down when another text arrives.

<Really want to tell you I love you, but I'm not going to. How hard am I rocking this 'taking it slow' thing, huh? (Please don't take out a restraining order.)>

He signs it with a smiley face, and I snort with laughter. After waiting to make sure we're really done this time, I snuggle down into my bed. His journals sit on my nightstand, gray in the half-light.

I know they're probably going to bring up more questions than answers, but I think that inside their pages, I might find some sort of closure. If we're even going to have a chance of being together, I know I have to find a way to forgive him.

The problem is, I've had more practice hating him than loving him.

TWELVE

HOPEFUL INDIFFERENCE

Six Years Earlier
Westchester County, New York
The Grove

Two weeks.

Two weeks without talking to him. Two weeks in which every glance has been furtive and fleeting. I can't say his effect on me is lessening, but I'm certainly getting better at ignoring it.

It's only when I'm forced to look at him that my control wavers. When he stands in front of the class to perform, the cell-deep magnetism that draws me to him kicks into overdrive and tries to unstitch my resolve.

It's in those long, surreal moments, when all I can think of is how much I still want him, that the cast iron around my heart threatens to bend.

But then I dial up my bitterness, and just like that, anger is my insulation. It allows the rush of lust to drain away like murky bathwater.

His performances are consistently good, but I roll my eyes when he continues to hold back, keeping those last few fragile pieces of himself safely hidden away, stifled from either shining or shattering.

When he finishes, I clap with everyone else, but I'm applauding his self-delusion more than his performance.

Bravo for faking it yet again, Ethan.

You're a perfect counterfeit copy of someone I thought I loved.

We're singing, loudly. Twirling and dancing after having smoked some of Lucas's home-grown pot. Class doesn't start for another half hour, and I'm glad because it's been so long since I laughed, I don't want it to end.

I don't know how I know the words to "Can't Take My Eyes Off of You," but I do. We all do.

We're obnoxious and off-key, but some of the weight I've carried in my chest since the breakup is finally lifting. Miranda twirls me toward Jack. He picks me up and passes me to Lucas. Aiyah hugs us both and strokes my hair. Lucas yells a heads-up to Connor, then throws me into his arms. Connor laughs as he overbalances, and then we're on the floor. Everyone's laughing. Connor has his arms around me, and as I laugh with him, his smile drops slowly, like paint dripping off a canvas.

He stares at me, and before I know it, I'm not laughing anymore, either. His face is too close. His expression is asking for too much as he sings to me about being too good to be true.

For long seconds, I think he's going to kiss me, but instead he flops onto his back and pulls me close against his chest. People dance and sing around us, like we're the centerpiece in some bizarre pagan ritual, and even though it feels wrong to be in such an intimate position, I stay there, testing out my reaction. He's warm and smells nice, and I like the way he gently strokes my arm.

But I don't want him.

When Ethan dumped me, I filled all the holes he left with concrete. It protects me against feeling too much. Then again, that's all there is. No room for anything or anyone else.

I close my eyes. All I get are images of Ethan.

I feel claustrophobic.

"Hey, you okay?" Connor's worried. So am I.

His voice is wrong. His face is wrong. I want to be in other arms. Have a different heartbeat pounding under my hand.

I stand and stagger toward the water fountain.

I drink forever, and then just let the water flow over my lips and tongue. I feel desiccated.

"Cassie?" Connor's there, so caring and nice. So different from Ethan. "You okay?"

I nod and try to smile. "Yeah, fine. Just a bit dizzy, I guess."

No, that description's too simple. I have full-blown emotional vertigo. I'm completely turned around. Upside down and inside out.

I hate how freaking wrong I feel without *him*.

I let Connor put his arm around me and escort me to class. I let Ethan see as he hugs me when we arrive. I allow myself to smile when Ethan's face transforms into a storm cloud of the darkest dimensions.

Good. Let him be pulled inside out, too.

At least now my wrongness has company.

"Miss Taylor?"

Erika is watching me with concern on her face. I've been standing near her desk, staring for minutes at the group assignments listed on the board, unable to process what she's done.

She knows about Ethan and me. How could she not when everyone is still buzzing about it like flies on a rotting carcass? It's been more than two months, and yet there's no way she could be completely oblivious to the thrill of expectation that still ripples through the air every time we step into a room together. It's as if everyone's praying that we'll fight. Or fuck. Or both.

Is my facade so flawless that she believes there's any chance in hell I can perform with him again?

I glance at Holt. He's staring at the whiteboard with a similar shell-shocked expression.

"Miss Taylor?" Erika says, louder. "Is there a problem?"

Most people have packed up and left, but the few who remain go silent, as if frightened that if they move, they'll scare off the drama that's about to happen.

"Erika . . . I just—" How can I say this without everyone . . . him . . . realizing how weak I am? "The groups for scene work. I'm not sure I can be in that group."

Jack and Aiyah are lingering near the door. Lucas is pretending to fiddle with his shoelace. Phoebe and Zoe are keeping one eye on their phones as they slyly watch us. Erika politely tells them all to get out.

Then she turns to Ethan.

"Mr. Holt? Perhaps you should join us. I have a feeling this might have something to do with you."

Ethan tenses his jaw and unfurls himself from his chair. As he slings his backpack onto his shoulder and walks over, goose bumps prickle my skin.

"Now," Erika says when he's standing as far from me as he can without making me look like a plague carrier, "why exactly can't you work in the group to which you've been assigned, Miss Taylor?"

She knows, yet she wants me to say it. In front of him. Sometimes, I think she enjoys watching us squirm.

"I just don't think me and . . ." I can't say his name. If I say it, both he and Erika will see how not over him I am. "I don't think having both of us in a group would be very fair to other members. There would be . . . tension."

Erika looks between us. I don't look at Holt, but I sense his frown.

"Mr. Holt? Do you agree?"

"Yes. There would definitely be tension."

"So, you both expect me to give you preferential treatment because working together would be uncomfortable?"

Neither of us answers. That's exactly what we expect, but saying so would make us seem like selfish assholes.

Erika sighs. "I want to make it clear that during your careers, you'll have to work with many people you don't like. People you'd rather avoid. But you can't run away every time things become difficult. Plus, you're asking me to give you special treatment simply because you're no longer dating. If I do this for you, I'll be setting a precedent that will quickly become a major pain in my ass."

I know what she's saying is true, but I still want her to do it.

Ethan and I say nothing. Our silent pleading speaks volumes.

Erika sighs again. "Because of the mix of characters I've assigned within each group, the only person I could swap Mr. Holt with would be Mr. Bain." Ethan tenses. "Would that be acceptable to both of you?"

Ethan asks, "What kind of scenes are we doing?"

Erika's onto him. "Does it matter? Either you want to stay in Miss Taylor's group or swap with Connor. What will it be?"

I say, "Swap," at exactly the same time Ethan says, "Stay." Then, to make sure we truly embarrassed ourselves, we do it again, louder.

Ethan and I stare each other down. It's the first time we've really looked at each other in the past eight and a half weeks. My face and body flush with fierce heat.

It doesn't escape my attention that Ethan's ears have also gone bright pink.

"Fine. Whatever," he says, waving his hand. "Swap me with Connor. Do whatever she wants."

"Oh, no, by all means, keep Holt in my group. What he wants is far more important."

"I don't want this," he says as he steps closer, "but we both know it's for the best."

"Are we still talking about the acting groups? Because if not, I know no such thing."

Erika rolls her eyes and grabs her folder off the desk. "I don't have time for this. Give me your decision by the end of today, or the groups stand, unchanged."

Ethan and I are too busy fuming to even notice her leaving.

He's too close. My body's involuntary craving to touch him makes me even angrier.

"Just take the swap, Ethan. You know we can't work together."

"Yeah, and it's real convenient you get to work with Connor instead."

"What the hell are you talking about?"

"Like you have no clue. Tell me, how long did he wait to hit on you after he found out we'd broken up? Every time I see him, he's all over you."

"Connor's a friend. That's all. Unlike other people, he actually cares about me."

"Bullshit. He cares about the possibility of you riding his cock. You're just too naive to see it."

"Whatever he cares about is none of your business! You broke up with me, remember? Just because you don't want me doesn't mean other men don't."

His expression clouds over, and his voice drops to a harsh whisper. "My breaking up with you had nothing to do with how much I wanted you. You know that."

"You said that you loved me, then you dumped me. Even to a crazy person, that seems nuts."

I guess this is the part where we fight about our breakup. I'd predicted it would have happened sooner, but I'm ready to come out, guns a-blazing.

"Just admit you broke up with me to protect yourself, Ethan. End of story."

"That's bullshit, and you know it. If we'd stayed together, I would've hurt you—"

"News flash! You hurt me anyway!"

"I would have hurt you more!"

"So you broke up in the hopes that we could have a chance at being friends, and yet this is the first time we've said two words to each other in over two months."

He lets out a bitter laugh. "We can't handle being friends."

"There you go again, making assumptions about what I can and can't handle."

"Oh, really? You think you could deal with us getting close again? Fine. Let's workshop that."

His expression turns predatory, and he takes a step closer. I step back.

"Do you seriously believe we could pretend we don't want more?" He advances. I retreat. "Just imagine it. 'Hey, Cassie. Wanna have lunch?'" He's struggling to keep his expression casual. "How about we study together? Let's run lines."

My back hits the wall. He's so close, we're almost touching.

"Aw, you're feeling bad? Let's hug. That's what friends do, right?"

His body heat is scorching. My skin is crawling with electricity.

He puts one hand on the wall beside my head and leans down. His voice is quiet and dark. "Once we get our arms around each other, we won't want to let go. It will be an avalanche of 'kiss me,' 'touch me,' 'put your hand down my pants.' 'Take off your clothes, so I can be inside you.'"

"Stop." I can't breathe.

"That's the problem. We wouldn't stop. We'd keep going and all of a sudden we'd be neck-deep in a relationship in which my issues would fucking strangle us all over again. Would that be less torturous than what we're going through now? Because I don't know about you, but I'd rather have none of you than little pieces that just keep me wanting more."

I take a breath and look him in the eye. "So then why the fuss about swapping with Connor?"

His expression softens, and he steps back. "Because the only thing that would kill me more than touching you right now would be watching someone else do it."

"You gave up your right to decide that. This time the decision's mine, and since I can't have you, I choose Connor."

I don't realize how I've worded it until it's out of my mouth, and by then, it's too late.

He looks like I've punched him. "Of course you do. Fine. I'll go and tell Erika."

He grabs his bag and heads to the door. When he reaches it, he turns back to me.

"Just out of interest, if I have to do a love scene with Zoe in my new group, would you care?"

Now it's my turn to feel like I've been punched, but I don't let him see.

"Ethan, I've just spent the past eight weeks teaching myself not to care every single time I see you. I'm getting pretty good at it by now."

He nods and gives me a bitter smile. "Good for you."

The campus gym.

I've been at this school for over eight months, and this is the first time I've stepped inside. It's big. Just like everything else at this school.

The main floor is filled with cardio equipment and weight machines, and on the second level, there's a free-weights area and various specialized rooms for things like yoga, Pilates, and boxing. There's even a racquetball court.

It seems Eva Bonetti, whose name is plastered over the door, was a generous patron of the arts.

Ruby said I should try out the boxing room. *Relieve some stress*, she'd said. *Stop being a mopey bitch*, she'd said. *Pretend the punching bag is Holt's stupidly handsome face*, she'd said.

I figure it can't hurt. So here I am, brand-new boxing gloves in hand, resolve firmly in place. Determined to purge some of the emotional pressure that's been building inside me for the past few months.

It's Friday night, so the place is practically empty. Of course, most college students have more exciting things to do on the weekend than punch out their frustrations. I'm not one of them.

As I approach the boxing room, I hear grunts coming from inside.

Dammit. I hadn't considered someone else would be using it.

I reach the door and peer in through the glass panel.

My breath catches.

It's him.

Broad shoulders in a wifebeater, his arms pumping as he pummels the bag. Jabs and uppercuts blend into thumping roundhouses. His riotous hair drips with sweat.

Every time he hits the bag, he grunts, his face intense and angry. Time and again the gloves thump and smack. I can nearly feel the force of it through the door.

A cold shiver runs up my spine.

He looks desperate. Like he's fighting for his life. Hitting and hitting and hitting, and seemingly getting no satisfaction from it. It should make me happy to see him suffering so much, but it doesn't. It makes my throat tighten with emotions I don't want to feel.

He continues punishing the bag, arms flying, body pivoting to give him more power. Then he kicks it, knees it. Uses so much force, I feel the vibration through the floor. He gets faster and faster, and his noises become more frustrated, until at last he stops and grips the bag as he gasps for breath. His face morphs into an expression of total defeat.

"Fuck it," he groans as he presses his forehead into the Everlast logo. "Fuck, fuck, fuck, fuck, fuck."

I'm desperate to know what's going through his mind. I long to tell him he's making it too hard. That it could be so easy and right between us if he'd just give in.

But I know he wouldn't believe me.

It's too late for that anyway. The damage has been done.

At this point, we're beyond repair.

When he rips off his gloves and throws them at the wall, I sling my gym bag over my shoulder and walk away. Every part of me complains. Begs me to go back.

I don't.

Each step away from him is like dragging my feet though quicksand.

By the time I reach the stairs, the grunting has started again.

"He misses you, you know."

I didn't think anyone knew about my secret reading corner at the far edge of the drama block, but I should have realized Elissa is part bloodhound.

I close my book, not sure what to say. She helps by flopping down next to me and filling the silence. "I know you think he's an asshole or whatever, but . . . I've never seen my brother so ruined over anyone before. He's like a ghost of who he was when he was with you."

Bitter laughter bubbles out of me. "Maybe he shouldn't have dumped me, then."

She picks at the grass next to her. "He thinks he's protecting you."

"Well, he's wrong."

"What if he's not?" She holds her hand up to shield her eyes from the sun's glare. "What if he'd stayed and all his issues forced you to be the one who walked away? Would that have been less or more painful?"

I shrug. "I guess we'll never know, will we?"

"Guess not."

She's quiet for a moment, then says, "He's not a bad person, Cassie. He's just . . . damaged. Scared."

I blink and pick at the grass, trying to calm the heat that's rising up my neck. "I know. And now, thanks to him, I know what that's like."

She doesn't reply to that. I don't expect her to. It's a conversation killer, and we both know it.

She stands. "Do you at least miss him?"

More than I've missed anything or anyone in my short and unremarkable life.

"I'm trying really hard not to."

"How's that working out for you?"

"Miserably."

"I'm sorry."

"Elissa, you have nothing to apologize for. Your brother, on the other hand . . ."

She nods. "Do you think you'll ever forgive him?"

I sigh. "I don't know. I honestly don't."

It's the truth. I'd like to think I could get past all of this, but I don't know if I'm strong enough.

"I hope you do," she says. "You two are meant to be together. I can feel it in my bones."

The thing that frustrates me more than anything is that I know she's right.

I just don't see how it's possible.

It's performance day.

We've been rehearsing our excerpts for four weeks. Holt and I have hardly spoken the entire time.

Avoidance has become an art form, for both of us.

My group is performing scenes from *A Streetcar Named Desire*. Connor's playing Stanley. I'm Blanche.

I know now why Erika initially wanted Holt to play Stanley. He's perfect for the role—moody, intense, full of turmoil and passion, unsure of himself and aggressive because of it. Connor's doing a good job, but Ethan would have been spectacular.

Blanche is a challenge for me. She's an aging Southern belle. Distraught over the suicide of her husband. Haunted by having walked in on him having sex with a man. Embarrassed by her sister's violent oaf of a husband, and fighting her primal attraction to him.

As we prepare to go on, I sneak a peek into the auditorium. All of our classmates are there, as well as the second-year actors. I see Holt, tight jawed and restless in his seat, trying to look interested in something Lucas is saying.

Just as Erika announces our scenes, Holt stands and strides out of the theater.

Even though I'm a little hurt, I'm also relieved.

Now I can pour everything into my performance without being self-conscious about him watching me with Connor.

It also makes me not feel so bad about hiding in the bathroom when he did his love scenes with Zoe earlier. I couldn't watch them together. I just couldn't. Just thinking about it made my head pound with rage.

Yep, this not caring about each other thing is going well.

Ruby points to a third-year drama student with shaggy hair.

"Kiss him."

"No."

She gestures to a guy I've never seen before but who bears a striking resemblance to a young Matt Damon. "What about him?"

"*No.*"

"Here, have some more tequila."

"It's not going to make me want to kiss random boys."

"Yes, it is. Trust me."

I sigh and slump against the couch. "Ruby, I don't want to kiss anyone."

"Yes, you do, but you want it to be that douche who dumped you freaking months ago, which is why I'm staging this intervention."

"Okay, taking me to a party and getting me drunk enough to mack on strangers is not an intervention."

"It is in my book."

"Also, I do not want to kiss Holt."

She rolls her eyes. "Sure you don't. That's why, in the five months since you broke up, you haven't even looked at another guy."

"That's not true. I've looked."

"Yeah, you just haven't touched." She throws up her hands. "Cassie, don't you understand that the best way to get over one guy is to get under another?"

"I just don't feel like getting into anything, okay?"

"I'm not saying you have to pick out china patterns or anything. Just have some fun. Kiss. Grope. Fuck. It doesn't have to be with the love of your life. You're nineteen, for God's sake. You can't just swear off all men because Holt broke your heart. Men are like vibrators. Just because they're dicks, it doesn't mean you can't use them to have a good time."

She hands me another shot of tequila and I down it, mainly because I can't be bothered to argue with her.

I'm starting to feel blurry. Like the room is filled with Jell-O and everyone's moving slowly.

Ruby's still talking, but I've tuned her out. I don't want to be here. Also, I know she's right.

I am afraid of getting hurt again.

Part of me wants to take Ruby's advice and hook up with someone, purely to feel wanted again. To remind myself that I'm attractive and desired, and not as hollow as I feel. But I know I'll always feel the twinge of what Ethan did to me. It will always hold me back.

I get up. "I'm going home, Ruby. I'm sorry. You stay. Have a good time."

She stands and hugs me. "Well, me having a good time is a given. I just wish I could help you get over Mr. Dickface."

I laugh. "I am getting over him. I swear. I haven't fantasized about punching him or fucking him for weeks now."

She pulls back and looks at me in shock. "Seriously?"

"Yep."

She strokes my cheek. "Awwww, I'm so pwoud of you."

I smack her hand away and hug her again. She really does give the world's best hugs.

I call for a cab and head toward the door. Just before I get there, I see a familiar shape silhouetted in the hallway, tall and lanky, chaotic hair. I slow down and lean against the wall for support as I contemplate squeezing past him.

To my relief, when he turns around I see that it isn't Holt. It's a guy I've never seen before. Dark hair. Dark eyes. Kind of gorgeous. He gives me a smile and moves back against the wall to let me pass.

"Please tell me you're not leaving," he says, obviously a little drunk. "It would be a total crime if the most beautiful girl at this party went home before I got a chance to talk to her."

I shrug. "Sorry. I have some very important sitting around to do. Can't waste my whole night partying."

He holds out his hand. "I'm Nick, by the way. Third-year visual arts."

I put my hand in his, and when we shake, I'm surprised to find it gives me a small thrill.

"Cassie. First-year actor."

"Very nice to meet you, Cassie."

"Likewise, Nick."

He doesn't let go of my hand, and I don't remove it. There's something about the way he's looking at me that makes me feel less empty. I know we're both a little drunk, but it's nice to know someone finds me desirable.

"KISS HIM!" Ruby yells down the hallway.

I pull my hand free and cover my face.

Nick looks at Ruby, clearly bemused. "Uh . . . is that a friend of yours?"

"Not anymore."

He laughs. "Does she often scream at you to kiss people you've just met?"

"Yeah. More often than I'd like."

He steps closer. "Well, she seems nice. I'd hate for her to be disappointed."

Before I register what's happening, he leans down and presses his lips against my cheek. My skin tingles in a not-unpleasant kind of way, and I instinctively grab his shirt. He pulls back and smiles.

"I hope that was okay."

"Yeah," I say, a little dizzy. "That was okay."

I wait for the guilt to hit me, but when it does, it's far less potent than I expect.

Maybe I am getting over Holt after all.

Or maybe it's just the tequila.

Whatever the reason, when my cab pulls up and blares its horn, I say good-night to Nick feeling a lot more confident about my romantic future than before I arrived.

Being sort of attracted to someone means I'm on my way to being completely indifferent to Ethan, right?

I'm in the costume cage down in the basement level of the drama block. It's cramped and dusty, and innumerable costumes from hundreds of productions have been squeezed onto row after row of floor-to-ceiling racks. Students are allowed to borrow them by permission of the facilities coordinator, but finding exactly what you want is always tough. I've been looking for something for my monologue from *Twelfth Night* for almost an hour, and the stale air is making me feel light-headed.

When all the hairs on the back of my neck stand on end, I know I'm not alone. Sure enough, I turn around to find Ethan watching me.

"I didn't know you were in here," he says, seeming annoyed.

My heart rate speeds up. "Yeah, well, I am."

Stop it. You're indifferent, remember? He has no effect on you anymore.

He exhales and shoves his hands in his pockets. "Are you nearly done?"

His tone irritates me. "I have no idea. Why?"

"I need a costume. I guess I'll wait 'til you're gone."

I sigh and turn to the rack. "Just find your damn costume, Ethan. I have more important things to do than avoid you right now."

I flick through costumes, studiously ignoring him.

He says, "Fine. Whatever," and disappears from my aisle. I hear him a few yards away, scraping hangers just as aggressively as I am.

After another twenty minutes of searching, I find a dress I think will suit Viola, and I head into the small curtained-off dressing area to try it on. When I pull the curtain back, Ethan's there, shirtless, bent over the button-fly of what look like leather breeches.

He looks at me and grits his teeth as he pulls at his crotch. "I can't get these fucking things done up. It's like trying to thread a goddamn needle with a banana."

I'd laugh if I wasn't so devastated by seeing him half naked and practically touching himself.

"Ah, fuck it," he says as he abandons his efforts so he can slip on the matching jacket. The style is part biker, part Elizabethan doublet. The effect is all sexy.

He steps out of the dressing room and gestures for me to go in. "Go for it. I can wrestle with this stupid fucking costume out here."

I step inside and pull the curtain across. I'd be lying if I said I didn't peek through to watch his chest flex as he struggled to button the jacket.

You're totally and completely indifferent, goddammit!

"What monologue are you doing, anyway?" I say as I drag my attention away from him and pull off my T-shirt and bra.

He grunts in frustration. "Hamlet. I swear to God, these buttons don't fit through these holes. Do I need an engineering degree to get into this goddamn costume?"

I take a moment to register that we're having a relatively normal conversation. It's strange but also kind of cool. Maybe we really will be able to become friends one day.

I pull the dress over my head and try to reach the zipper. "Hamlet's a bit of an obvious choice for you, isn't it? Moody. Troubled. Self-destructive."

"Yeah, well, I'm not really in the headspace right now to play light and fluffy."

"Are you ever?"

He pauses. "What's your point?"

I twist my arms up behind me and tug, but the zipper isn't cooperating. "Fracking crap."

"Let me guess, you can't get your costume zipped up."

The curtain pulls back and he's standing there—jacket open, bare chest, pants half buttoned. His eyes widen when he registers how low cut my dress is.

"Uh . . . you want me to . . . ?" He gestures with his finger, obviously trying to drag his focus up to my face. He's successful for about half a second before he drops back to my cleavage. "Uh . . . help with the . . . uh . . ."

"Zipper?"

"Yeah. That. I'll help you if you help me."

I turn around and feel him step behind me. He tugs the zipper up to the middle of my back, then warm fingertips brush across my neck as he sweeps my hair over my shoulder. I think I hear him swallow. The zipper protests as he pulls it all the way up, but he gets it done. The bodice is so tight, I can barely breathe. Taking shallow breaths, I turn and press my hands against my waist.

"Jeez, how did women wear these things every day? I feel like my internal organs are going to merge together in a giant blancmange of gross."

There's silence.

When I look up, Ethan is staring. The lust in his expression makes a shiver run through me.

"Uh-huh."

He steps closer, and now it's not the dress that's making it hard to breathe. I stare at his neck because I really can't look at his face. I study the pattern of his scruff and how it gives way to smooth skin. Even now, after all these months, I remember so clearly how that skin tastes. How he used to moan when I nibbled it.

"Cassie?"

"Hmmm?"

"The buttons? Your fingers might be more dexterous than mine."

"Oh. Right."

I take the edges of the jacket and pull them together. His chest is too broad, so it's not easy, and he's right, the buttons do seem too large for the holes. I struggle with the thick fabric but have success with the bottom few buttons before running into problems.

"Have you put on weight?"

"A bit. I've been working out."

"Boxing?"

He pauses. "Yes. How did you know that?"

I shrug. "Lucky guess."

I pull again but the button's not cooperating.

"I can't get it."

"Leave it then," he says, his voice tight. "It's fine."

Once more the button pops out. "Dammit!"

"Taylor . . ." He closes his hand over both of mine. "For God's sake, just fucking . . . stop."

I freeze. Time slows down.

He's touching me.

The effect is instantaneous and debilitating. My heart skips into overdrive when he lets out a ragged breath. I stare at his hand covering mine. So alien. So familiar. Wrong and right twisting around each other and into my stomach.

I watch in sick fascination as he rubs his thumb across my knuckles in slow motion. I want to step away, but I'm frozen. I can't look up at him, afraid of what I'll do. Or what he'll do. Even through the thick leather of the jacket I can feel his heart pounding, faster than mine. His chest is rising and falling rapidly, and I know that whatever happens in the next few seconds could very well undo the past eight months of cultivated aloofness.

"Cassie . . ." he groans.

He presses my hands more firmly against his chest, and my resolve fails. I want to pull the jacket open and press my mouth to his skin. Taste the warmth there before moving up to his neck. He seems to want it, too, because he grips my hands and pushes them beneath the fabric. When my palms press into his bare chest, he inhales so sharply, it's like he's in pain.

I close my eyes and seek the strength to stop. I have to. I can't be like this again. Desperate and needy. The obstacles keeping us apart haven't changed. Especially not him.

I open my eyes to meet his gaze. It's searing. Dark and intense and way too compelling.

Resolve, where are you when I need you?

This isn't him wanting me back. It's just him wanting me. And me wanting him. Pounding hearts and hormones screaming at us.

I move my hands over his chest and feel the fast pulse beneath it, looking for an excuse to let this happen. To allow me to have his body without needing anything more. To relieve the aching sexual frustration that's haunted me since the day we broke up.

But there's no excuse. No alternate reality in which this would make things anything but immeasurably worse.

I curl my fingers into his muscles before I snap back to reality. Finding strength I didn't know I had, I pull away, embarrassed and irritated. I hate that I'm practically boneless with desire. That one fleeting touch from him can *still* affect me so completely.

I stare at him and try to find my voice.

He stares back, apparently just as shocked.

"What the hell was that?" Adrenaline is storming through my veins, making me hot and shaky.

He blinks and shakes his head. Angry. With himself or me?

"I have no idea." His jaw flexes, and he drops his head. "That was fucking stupid. I . . . I shouldn't have—"

"No, you shouldn't."

He snaps his head up to look at me. Definitely angry with me this time. "I didn't see you stepping back too quickly. You were breathing just as hard as I was."

"That doesn't mean you can . . . that we should—" I rake my fingers through my hair. "Goddammit, Ethan, we're supposed to be past this by now! I shouldn't feel this way when—"

"When what?"

"When you're near me! When you touch me. You can't just . . . do that to me."

"Believe me, I know the feeling."

I throw my hands up. "I didn't do anything!"

"You don't need to. Just fucking existing is enough to completely ruin me."

The sadness in his tone makes me pause, but it doesn't make me any less angry.

"Whatever," I say as I try to unzip my dress. "Forget it."

He pulls off his jacket and says, "What the fuck do you think I've been trying to do all year?"

The bodice of the dress seems to tighten like a python, squeezing me to the point of asphyxiation. "Get this damn thing undone."

I turn so he can unzip me, and when he does, I stalk into the dressing room. I rip off the dress and pull my bra and shirt back on. Then I gather up my stuff and throw back the curtain. He's standing there watching me, like he's about to apologize or something.

I pause. We stare at each other. No apology is forthcoming.

Of course not.

Freaking typical.

"Oh, hey, guys."

We both turn to see Jack Avery, holding an armful of costumes. "Oh, wow, did I interrupt something? Need some privacy? Or condoms?"

I make a disgusted noise and push past him. "Shut up, Jack."

As I walk down toward the exit, I hear Avery say, "Dude, are you still pretending she doesn't have you totally and completely whipped? How fucking deluded are you?"

As I reach the door, Holt says, "For once I agree with Cassie, Avery. Shut the fuck up."

Hours later, when I get home, I'm still tingling from the memory of my hands on his chest. They crave to feel him again. Want more of him beneath them.

I groan and collapse onto my bed, frustrated beyond belief.

Indifference? Yeah, right.

I have no freaking idea what that word means.

My only consolation is that neither does Ethan.

THIRTEEN

AVOIDANCE

Present Day
New York City, New York
The Apartment of Cassandra Taylor

I snuggle into the warmth beside me.

Hmmm. Boy. Soft skin. Smells good.

Ethan?

An arm wraps around me and I snuggle further, reliving the memory of lips and tongue. It wakes me up from the inside, making me greedy for more.

I put my hand on his stomach. Feel the taut muscles there. So many muscles.

Wait. Too many muscles.

I trail down to his belly button.

"Sweetheart, if you go much lower we're going to have to re-examine my sexuality, and I don't think either of us is ready for that right now."

I open my eyes. My roommate, Tristan, is lying next to me with one of Ethan's journals open in his hand.

"You know, I always thought your stories about this guy were embellished out of hurt or bitterness, but reading this? It's a wonder he could walk upright and talk at the same time. There's some serious self-flagellation going on in here. Did he actually have his own whip? Or was it all just in his mind?"

I grab for the book, but he tightens his arm around me and holds it out of my reach.

"Nuh uh uh. I've been hearing about his antics for three years. I think I've earned a little peek inside his crazy. Of course, the important question is, where did you get these journals? Please tell me you didn't steal them like a crazy stalker-lady."

I rub my eyes. It's too early for one of Tris's interrogations. "He gave them to me."

"Really?"

"Yep."

"At rehearsal?"

"No."

"Then where?"

"At his apartment."

He pauses. "Uh-huh. So you went over there, picked these up, and left, right? No romantic contact? No reminiscing about how obsessed you are with his cock?"

"Tristan . . ."

He pulls back so he can glare at me. "No, don't you *Tristan* me. You swore you were going to take things slow with this guy, and I get home this morning to find your sex-kitten underwear on the floor, loverboy's journals on your nightstand, and scruff rash all over your face. Seems to me you're determined to screw this up before you've even given it a chance."

"Nothing happened."

"Do I actually need to check if your pants are on fire, Miss Liar? Because it looks like your face has been exfoliated with a sandblaster."

"Okay, nothing *much*. We kissed."

"*Just* kissed?"

"And . . . humped against a wall."

He exhales. "That's not nothing."

"It's not sex."

"It's also not slow."

I know he's right, but admitting it is beyond me. "What do you want me to say, Tris? That it was stupid? It was. Do I know what the hell I'm doing with him? Absolutely not. Did I have highly pornographic dreams about him last night? Hell yes. Honest enough for you?"

I slump against his chest as he tightens his arm around me and rests his head against mine.

"Sweet girl, I'm not trying to be a dick here. I just don't want this to go south again. I know he probably turns you inside out, but if you go too fast, too soon, then you're going to do exactly the same thing he did—freak out and bail. I'm pretty sure neither of you wants that, right?"

"No. But whenever I'm with him, all I can see is him, and that terrifies me. And when we're apart, I think that maybe we're better that way, and that also terrifies me."

He rubs my arm. "Fear is natural in this situation, but the key is to not let it call the shots. Scared people either shut down and avoid the thing they fear, or get angry at it and lash out. The bad news for you and Ethan is that you've tried both of those options and neither has been successful. The ultimate tragedy is that ever since you met, you've been completely nutso in love with each other and wasted too much time being stubborn asses about denying it."

I close my eyes, not liking how this conversation is tightening my chest. Tris sighs.

"If it's any consolation," he says quietly, "the one thing these journals prove is that he always loved you."

I laugh. "Even when he was breaking my heart?"

"Yep. Even then. I mean, listen to this one from six years ago: '*New Year's Eve. I can barely function with so many thoughts of her running through my head. I feel like a crazy man. I keep thinking, "What if she could have fixed me?" If anyone could have, it would have been her. I'm dreading next year. It's going to be a fucked-up charade of pretending I don't want her. I'm exhausted just thinking about it. I could barely hold myself back when she texted me on Christmas day, and that was just a freaking message on my phone. How the hell am I going to resist her when she's right in front of me? All sad eyes and trembling mouth and broken heart.*

Part of me kind of hopes when I see her again, she'll break down and beg me to be with her. If she did that, there'd be no way I could deny her. Please let her beg me. No, wait, don't. Fuck. I hate this. I want to peel off my skin. Happy fucking New Year.'"

Hearing about his past turmoil isn't helping my own, but somehow, knowing he was as miserable as I was is strangely satisfying.

Tristan turns the page. "And here are his New Year's resolutions: *'Stop thinking about Cassie. Stop dreaming about Cassie. Stop fantasizing about Cassie when I masturbate. Be kinder to my mom and sister. Try not to imagine smashing my father in the face every time he says something annoying. Run more. Drink less. Be a better person. For Cassie.'"*

He puts the book down and looks at me. "You have to admit, despite his issues, the boy was totally crazy about you."

"It doesn't excuse what he did."

"I don't think he wants you to excuse him. I think he wants you to understand that he was confused."

"And stupid."

"Well, yeah, obviously stupid. I mean, you turn me on and I'm a bona-fide cock lover. I have no idea why that hot-blooded straight boy thought he could be anything but totally obsessed with you."

He keeps flicking through the pages. I lie there and listen to his steady heartbeat as I try to sort through my feelings about Ethan.

"Tris?"

"Hmm?"

"Do you think it's possible that soul mates who love each other aren't actually supposed to be together?"

He pauses, and then puts the book down. "I think a better question would be, do *you* think it's possible?"

I don't answer him, because if I admit that it's crossed my mind, the small spark of hope inside me will sputter and die.

FOURTEEN

PASSION

Five Years Earlier
Westchester County, New York
The Diary of Cassandra Taylor

Dear Diary,

Humans are strange creatures. We lie every day, in a thousand different ways. The most common lie is, 'I have read the terms and conditions.' The second most common lie is, 'I'm fine.'

Some people believe that actors are just professional liars, paid to manufacture personalities that aren't our own. We create characters from our imaginations, interpret someone else's words, dress in someone else's clothes, become a different person for hours, days, months. We're good at fooling people. We're less adept at fooling ourselves.

The best actors keep all the parts of themselves in little boxes and bring them out in an unending parade of various combinations.

I used to be pretty good at doing that, onstage and in life, but ever since Ethan and I broke up, my compartments have been confused. In the filing cabinet where I keep my feelings for him, the drawer labeled 'lover' is now firmly locked. So is 'boyfriend.' The 'friend' drawer rattles and tries to squeeze open, but it's so squashed beneath 'hurt' and 'resentment,' it's practically buried.

I don't talk about him anymore. Not to Ruby. Not to Mom. Not even to Elissa, who I confided in the longest because she always sought me out. Talking about him maintained tiny cracks in my resolve, and always made me bristle and want.

It's better now.

I've locked my passion away. Put it in a strongbox and covered it in concrete.

Ethan and I go to class, do our work, avoid each other when possible, and snark at each other when we can't. We have no patience for these platonic versions of ourselves. Even now, more than a year after our breakup, our hearts and bodies fight against the distance and suppression, but we've gotten good at ignoring them.

We're second-years now, and so far, we haven't been cast in anything together. I think Erika has given up trying to mediate.

And so Ethan and I orbit each other. Get on with things. Learn the art of pretending. Hone our craft to lie to others as skillfully as we lie to ourselves.

And every morning, the first thing that goes through my brain when I see him is, "I'm fine."

Erika leans on her desk.

"This term's acting assignment focuses on passion. Romantic, sexual, suppressed, violent, artistic. I'll be assigning each of you excerpts designed to confront and challenge you. Some of the material will make you uncomfortable. Turn those feelings into something you can use. A lot of the plays are controversial and contain issues of a sensitive nature. I expect you to handle it with maturity. Mr. Avery, please note, I'm looking at you."

Jack gives his best "Who, me?" expression, and everyone laughs.

"You'll have four weeks to rehearse and will present your pieces the week before Presidents' Day weekend. Questions?"

Jack puts up his hand.

"Mr. Avery?"

"Please say you've given me something from *Equus*. I've always had a thing for horses."

People laugh.

"As a matter of fact, no. You'll be performing with Aiyah in a little piece called *Soft Targets*. It's quite controversial, sexually."

Jack rubs his hands together. "Ooh, tell me more."

Erika suppress her grin. "It's about men who enjoy having their female lovers sodomize them with monster strap-ons."

Jack's face drops. "What?"

Erika hands out the group lists as Jack turns to Lucas and says in a whiny voice, "She's joking, right? That was a joke?"

I take the list and skim it to find my name.

The Killing of Sister George

Cassie—Sister George. Chain-smoking alcoholic lesbian. Ex-soap opera actor. Psychologically sadistic.

Miranda—George's lover, Childie. Passive. Simple.

The character description makes me nervous. I like to think I can rise to a challenge, but this character is so far out of my wheelhouse, I have doubts I can pull it off.

I look through the list of the other plays. They all have an element of the shocking or taboo. It turns out Erika wasn't joking about Jack's excerpt. He'll be playing a married businessman who pays a Dominatrix to regularly spank, degrade, and sodomize him. When I look over at Jack, he's a little green. Aiyah, on the other hand, is grinning with sadistic glee. She often tells Avery how much she wants to smack him. Now she's going to get her chance.

Miranda, Troy, and Angela are doing something called *Picture Windows*, in which people fall in love with inanimate objects. Lucas and

Zoe are doing *Unwrap Me*, a play examining a married couple who enjoys cross-dressing, and Holt has been cast with Connor in . . .

I almost laugh out loud. It's bad enough that Erika cast two guys who hate each other in the same play, but to make matters worse, *Enemy Inside* is a touching love story about a gay soldier coming to terms with his homosexuality.

Oh, my.

Connor is playing the closeted gay soldier. Ethan is the experienced and caring love interest who convinces him that loving another man isn't a sin.

My, oh, my.

I find the concept vaguely arousing. In reality, I think the likelihood of Ethan pulling off a character who's loving and patient is a major stretch. Also, he regularly glares at Connor like he wants to pummel him. Trying to convince an audience he's attracted to him? Erika couldn't have come up with a more difficult challenge.

I glance over at him. He's frowning down at the piece of paper like he can make it say something different if he just concentrates hard enough.

A sharp laugh bubbles out of me. He looks up and scowls, so I suck the insides of my cheeks to stop myself.

Oh, this term is going to be fun.

Erika rubs her forehead and sighs. "Miss Taylor, you have to stop laughing. We're wasting time."

"I'm sorry," I say as I fail to stifle my giggles. "I know it's not funny. I just—"

I'm lying on the floor and Miranda is straddling me, and every time I laugh, she bounces up and down, which makes me laugh more.

"Miss Taylor!"

The giggles abate, and I take a deep breath to try and calm myself. "I'm sorry. I'm ready."

Miranda sighs. She's used to kissing girls. I'm really, really not.

"Right. Let's try it again. Remember, this is one of the truly intimate moments in the play. It's when we see a brief glimpse of George's vulnerable side. How she genuinely cares for Childie despite how she treats her. We need to feel the sexual tension between you. Are you clear?"

"Yes. Clear."

It doesn't make this any easier. Doing a love scene with Ethan was difficult enough. Doing one with another girl is totally out of the realm of my experience. Still, that's what this whole term is supposed to teach us. That passion is passion, no matter who it involves.

My passion is kind of rusty. Maybe that's why I'm having so much trouble.

"Okay. Stand and go to first positions. Take a moment to center yourselves."

I stand opposite Miranda and close my eyes. Breathe. Remind myself to treat this just like any other character. I project myself into George's mind, so I can discover her motivations. She's experienced with women. With Childie. She loves her even though she torments her.

We start the scene. I'm agitated, but Childie calms me. Strokes my face. For once, she makes the first move. She kisses me gently then pulls back, hesitant as to how I'll react. I'm shocked by how forward she is, and although my first instinct is to punish her, she's looking at me with such hope, I can't bring myself to do it.

I kiss her back, passionately. She's so beautiful. As innocent as I am corrupt.

We fall to our knees and continue to kiss. Then, in an act of unparalleled boldness, she pushes me onto my back, straddles me, and grinds against me as she buries her fingers in my hair. I pull open her shirt and palm her breasts before flipping her onto her back and becoming the aggressor again. She wraps her legs around me as I kiss her neck.

We say the last few lines as we pant into each other's skin.

The scene ends, and Miranda and I stand and await Erika's notes.

"Well, ladies, that was—"

"Fucking *amazing*!" Jack leaps to his feet and applauds wildly. "Best play *ever*!"

"Mr. Avery!"

"No, seriously, Erika. Can these girls do that scene for the rest of the year? Because . . . yeah. It's seriously . . . stimulating. Stirring stuff."

"Dude," Lucas whispers, "You might wanna sit down. It's kind of obvious how much you enjoyed it."

Avery immediately covers his crotch and sits. Everyone laughs.

"Shut up, bitches. There are hot chicks making out in front of me. What do you expect? Every straight guy in this room is currently sporting wood. Hey, Holt. Let's see the size of your tent."

Ethan rolls his eyes and flips him the bird, but I notice his legs are crossed in such a way that his crotch is hidden from view.

He looks at me for a moment before dropping his gaze and shifting in his seat.

The passion I've just dredged up for the scene is now snaking out toward him.

I shove the emotion down. It's like trying to shove a pillow into a shoe box.

Stupid passion.

This is why we're not friends anymore.

A huge roar of "Asshole!" comes from the next room, and Connor and I exchange a look. Our friends are playing some asinine card game, and as usual on these Wednesday night get-togethers at Jack's house, Connor and I are in charge of snacks. I may not be able to cook, but I can open a bag of chips with the best of them, and Connor is the King of Frozen Pizza.

We make a good team.

I watch as he unwraps a couple of frozen pies with the finesse of a magician.

I find myself staring at his hands. He has lovely hands. Actually, most of him is lovely. Sandy brown hair. Brown eyes. Handsome face. Nice body.

Best of all, he's one of the sweetest, most caring men I've ever known.

It's a pity that doesn't seem to be enough for me.

"Do I have a booger?"

"Huh?"

Connor smiles, and suddenly the whole room seems brighter. "You were staring. I thought I might be sporting nose poop."

I shake my head. "Nope. Just admiring the pretty."

He shrugs. "Okay. I can live with that. But if you think those bags of chips are going to open themselves, you're sorely mistaken. Get to work, lady."

He passes me a bowl, and as I dump in the Doritos, he raises an eyebrow. "You making your famous salsa to go with that?"

I nod. "You know me well enough to not doubt my awesomeness by now." I pull out a jar of salsa and open it. "Voilà! Cost me a hot buck and a half to get it just perfect."

He smiles as he sprinkles extra cheese on the pizzas. "You're so talented."

"I know, right? You, too."

He holds up the bag of cheese. "Yep, if I don't make it as an actor, Pizza Hut managers all over the country will be lining up to hire me."

"You make it sound like that's your fallback plan. May I remind you that even if you do make it, you might still have to take a job as a pizza artist? Theater paychecks can be crappy."

He laughs. "Yeah, but becoming stars in any capacity means we have to first pass this term's acting class, and it seems like Erika's making that as hard as possible with these passion scenes."

He puts the pizzas in the oven and sets the timer while I grab two beers from the fridge and pass one over. "Well, I'd better start looking for my second job now, because I can barely get through my scene without giggling like I'm high."

"Oh, please." He uncaps his beer and takes a drink. "You have nothing to worry about. Your scene with Miranda was amazing yesterday."

"Are you saying that because you're a guy who gets off on two women kissing? Or are you basing it on our actual performance?"

He rolls his eyes. "Cassie, give me a break. I'm not Jack. I am capable of watching two women make out like demons without objectifying them."

I raise an eyebrow.

He turns away as he mumbles, "No matter how fucking hot it was."

At the mention of his name, Jack walks into the kitchen.

"Are we talking about Miranda and Cassie again? Cool, because I've been meaning to ask you a question, Cassie. Is Miranda a better kisser than Holt? Softer lips? Smoother skin? I'm sure the answer is yes, but I'd like to hear it in your own words. Be specific." He goes to the fridge, grabs a beer, and opens it before looking at me expectantly.

"Forget it, Jack. Miranda and I don't kiss and tell." Plus, I've perfected the art of blocking out what it was like to kiss Ethan. I'd like to say that time dulls the memories of his mouth, but it really doesn't. "Besides, Connor will soon be able to give you a play-by-play of Holt's kissing technique. Aren't you guys up to rehearse tomorrow?"

"Unfortunately," Connor says, and takes a long pull of his beer.

Jack rubs his hands together. "I think Erika was going for maximum crowd entertainment when she cast you two together. I'm taking bets that it's going to be the most awkward kiss in the history of lips. Cassie, you want in on the action? You could clean up."

"No way. I have faith that Connor's going to make it work."

Jack laughs loudly before heading back into the living room.

Connor takes another slug of his beer. "Thanks for the vote of confidence, but we both know Holt and I are going to suck. Ethan's never made a love scene work with anyone but you, and if he can't pull it off with the girls in our class, he has no chance with a guy. Let alone a guy he very clearly hates."

"I don't think he hates you."

He gives me a look. "Every time I'm within five feet of you, he glares like he wants to beat the shit out of me."

"Yeah, but that's only because he doesn't know you've done twelve years of karate so you can defend yourself against your asshole brothers."

"Even if he did know, it wouldn't matter. He's still hung up on you, and I pity the guy who dates you next, because Holt will probably murder him."

I lean against the counter and sigh. I doubt what Connor says is true. It seems as though Holt's becoming more indifferent to me every day.

Connor chuckles and I look up to see him staring at me. "What?"

"Nothing."

"Don't 'nothing' me, what is it?"

He shrugs. "I was just thinking that I should flat-out kiss you one day in front of Ethan just to see if his head would explode with rage. I suspect it would."

I smile and shake my head. "Yeah, let's not do that."

He puts his beer down and places his hands either side of me on the counter. He's not as tall as Ethan, but I still have to look up to see his face.

"You're right. Even with my karate training, I'd run the risk of him landing a lucky punch. A better idea would be for you to kiss me. He'd never hit a girl. Especially not you."

He stares at me in a way that says, *I'm joking, but not really. Kiss me.*

I'm spared the humiliation of turning him down when Jack comes back in to retrieve more beer.

"If you two are going to make out in here, just know there is no fucking on the kitchen counter. I don't want my meat going anywhere near where your meat has been, if you know what I mean."

Connor grabs the chips and salsa, and mutters, "I'll take these in to the guys," before exiting to the living room.

I feel myself blush, and hate it.

Jack shakes his head as he takes the caps off four more beers. "Goddamn, Taylor. You're not content to have Holt completely tied in knots? You have to bewitch poor old Connor, too? The boy has it bad."

I scrunch up the empty Doritos bag and throw it into the trash. "I'm not bewitching anyone, Jack. Connor sees me as a friend. That's all."

He lets out a short laugh. "Okay. Sure, he does. And I watch porn for the plotlines."

I know he has a point, but thinking about it makes me tense. Since the breakup, Connor's become one of my closest friends, and I love him like I love Ruby. But every now and then, he stares at me in a way that reminds me he wants more.

Ethan, on the other hand, stares at me less often these days.

I'm ashamed to say I miss it.

"Okay, stop there."

Ethan drops his head and steps away from Connor. They've been working on this part of the scene for the past forty-five minutes, and it's not getting any better. Both of them are faking the emotion.

They're both frustrated, and so is Erika.

"This is a lesson for everyone here," she says as she stands and walks onto the stage. "There will be times when you have to perform scenes with people who hold no attraction for you, but you still need to find a way to make it work. If you share a natural chemistry, that's great, but if not, you need to train yourself to manufacture it."

"Easier said than done," Holt mutters.

Erika ignores him. "This sort of scene is particularly difficult for men, because there's a heterosexual indoctrination that implies being gay means you're not a real man, and let me tell you, that's absolutely not the case. This story is about homosexual men who put their lives on the line for their country. And it's written by a man who lived it."

She turns to Holt and Connor. "So, you two need to get past whatever macho bullshit is holding you back from being intimate with each other, and understand that sometimes, you can't choose which body your soul mate resides in. Love is love. Passion is passion. And people who are lucky enough to feel it should grab it with both hands. *That's* what this play is about."

Holt slumps onto one leg and rubs the back of his neck. He seems completely at a loss as to how to make it work. Connor's much the same.

Erika calls them over. "Might I suggest you both take a moment to close your eyes and recall a person with whom you've shared a strong emotional or sexual connection? Picture that person in your mind. Let the way they made you feel invade your body, stir your emotions, boil your blood." Both men close their eyes and breathe. Their postures relax a little. "Do you feel that?"

They nod.

"Stay in that moment. Let the sense memory of that connection infuse you."

I feel a hand on my shoulder, and turn to see Jack leaning forward. He whispers, "How weird would it be if they were both thinking about you? Like, seriously?"

He smiles and sits back, and I try to squash the rush of flutters in my stomach.

Yeah, that'd be too weird.

Erika preps the boys for a few more minutes, then gets them to start the scene again.

Ethan closes his eyes and breathes, and when he opens them, his whole demeanor has changed. His expression softens. His voice lowers. As he speaks, he slowly moves closer to Connor.

"You want me, Ty. You can deny it all you like. Doesn't make it not true." He's calm. Self-assured.

Connor counters his calm with barely suppressed panic. "I do deny it."

"I can see it in your eyes."

As Ethan closes in, Connor crosses downstage to put distance between them. "We're not just mindless animals. We control our actions. Our actions don't control us."

Holt isn't deterred. He maintains his slow pursuit. "You can tell yourself that, but it doesn't change the fact that you watch me."

Even now, Connor watches him. Mesmerized. "I don't."

"Everything about me turns you on. It scares the hell out of you, and so you yell, and rage, and push me away, but it doesn't change anything. You could live a hundred lifetimes and never find what you have with me."

They're really inhabiting the scene. Becoming their characters. Ethan has transformed. He's incandescent. It's good. So good, a whole mess of emotions I can't grasp or stop wells up. My heart kicks into overdrive, and there's a roaring sound in my ears.

"Rage all you want," Ethan says. "Curse my name. Pretend all of this passion is coming from a place of hate, but I know better. Your passion for me is strangling you. Telling you that you're someone different than who you thought you were. Urging you to be bigger and braver than the tiny box you've shoved yourself into for all these years."

Then he touches Connor. Lovingly. Reverently. Connor is vibrating with indecision. Terrified by their obvious connection.

The way Ethan is, the words he's saying . . . it's too much. Something primal stirs inside me, low and snarling. It wants what it sees. *That* Ethan. The strong and brave one. The one staring at Connor and speaking words that resonate through all of my layers.

"It's not working, is it?" he says as he strokes Connor's face. "You're miserable. Unfulfilled. Hollow and aching for the one thing that's going to make all the whispers of longing shut up, once and for all. Me."

"No—" He touches Connor's lips, and Connor closes his eyes and sighs.

"Yes. And the sad thing is, you know the more you deny it, the more miserable you'll become, and still you're desperate to continue pretending."

"Mark—"

Then Ethan steps in and cups Connor's face before he leans down so their lips are almost touching.

I can't breathe. Jealousy fires in my belly, blasting outward until there's a firestorm under my skin.

"Ty, what we feel for each other isn't the enemy. Why do you insist on continuing to fight it?"

"I know how to fight. I've been doing it my whole life."

"Isn't it time you found some peace?"

"I—"

Ethan leans down. "I'm going to kiss you now. If you don't want me to, say stop."

"This isn't who I am." Connor squeezes his eyes shut.

"No excuses. Just one word."

"You're asking too much."

"You're expecting too little. Say it."

"I . . . can't."

"Good."

They seem to go into slow motion as they move closer while gripping each other. Then Ethan kisses Connor. They both inhale, and I want to look away but can't. Ethan's jaw tenses as he kisses Connor again, and my lungs are burning from lack of oxygen.

I clench my hands painfully around the armrests. I can't see this. I really, really can't.

I stand and stumble out into the aisle. People berate and shush me as I squeeze past, but I ignore them.

I all but run for the exit, and as I throw open the door, the class bursts into applause. I can still hear the cheering and whistling as I sprint toward the bathroom.

* * *

Music thumps straight into my bones as I throw back the shot and then slam the glass onto the table.

"Another!"

Usually at these weekend parties at Jack's place, I spend the night trying to avoid getting drunk. Tonight, it's my only mission.

Ruby holds the tequila bottle just out of reach. "Cassie—"

"Shut up, Ruby. You're forever trying to get me drunk and handsy, and the one night I want it, you tell me to ease up? Just pour me another damn shot."

She shakes her head but does it. "You're going to regret this tomorrow, you know that, right?"

I down the shot and breathe through the burn. "Don't care. Worth it. More."

She complies. "What happened with you today? Zoe said you stormed out of acting class. Something about Holt kissing a guy?"

She's taking too long, so I grab the bottle and drink from it. "Don't wanna talk 'bout it. More booze."

"No." She snatches the bottle and holds it out of my reach.

"Ruby!"

"I'm cutting you off until you tell me."

I wave at her. "Whatever. I'm gonna dance."

I stagger to the dance floor. The music is loud and bass-y, so I close my eyes and sway to the beat. People surround me. I don't know who they are. Don't care. Just wanna feel part of it. Of something.

The beat echoes through me. Of course it does. Noise is more reverberant inside big, hollow spaces.

One song merges into another. Arms wrap around me. Someone nuzzles my neck.

"Hey, beautiful."

I open my eyes. It's Nick. We've been flirty. Gone out a few times. Shared a couple of mediocre kisses and some light groping.

It never goes any further. My choice, not his.

Why does he keep coming back? Doesn't he get it by now?

Still, he smells good and keeps me upright, so I sway with him.

He kisses my neck. I shiver, but not in a good way. When I turn around, he cups my face and kisses me. I almost gag. Not because of him, but because the room is spinning.

I pull back and close my eyes. Doesn't really help.

"Cassie?"

"I'm fine."

"Really? Because it looks like you're going to be sick."

"M'okay."

"Want me to take you home?"

"No. You go, have fun. I'mma go t'the bathroom."

"Do you need help?"

"Nope. M'fine."

I push through the crowd and head toward the hallway but stop short when I see Ethan there, his expression like thunder.

He's been coming to more and more parties recently. Of course he'd be here tonight. The one night I really didn't want to see him.

All of my control systems are confused. Malfunctioning. Having him here isn't helping.

I push past him and stumble to the bathroom. Inside, I just make it to the toilet before most of the tequila makes its way back up.

Ten minutes later I emerge from the bathroom, still drunk, but more in control. Ethan has disappeared. Despite not really wanting to be alone, I don't feel good, so I find Ruby and tell her I'm leaving.

"Want me to drive you?"

"Nah. I'm gonna walk."

"Really? It's cold out there."

"I want some fresh air. Clear my head."

"You sure?" Ruby asks. "It'll take you nearly an hour."

"I don't really have anywhere else to be." Or anyone to be with.

"Okay, but keep your phone in your hand and call me when you get home."

"K. See you later?"

"Probably not. See that big guy in the corner? He doesn't know it yet, but he's going to be taking me home tonight."

"Haven't you slept with him before?"

"Yep. But he's definitely worth a repeat performance. Hung like a horse and knows how to ride."

I laugh and grab my purse. "In that case, I'll see you tomorrow."

"Probably."

I'm nearly at the front door when a hand closes around my wrist.

"Hey, you're not leaving?" Nick puts his arms around me, and I can smell the alcohol on his breath. "Why is it that you always seem to be running away from me, Cassie Taylor?"

I sigh, too tired to pretend. "Not running. Just going home."

"Let me drive you. I could . . . come in. Tuck you into bed." His tone suggests he has a little more on his mind than just tucking, although it rhymes with it.

"Not tonight, Nick." Or ever. Despite his physical hotness, I'm completely disinterested. "I'm wiped. Seriously."

He sighs and leans his forehead against mine. "Okay, fine. But at least kiss me good-night."

"Probably not the best idea. I vomited a little while ago."

"Your breath smells minty."

"Well, yeah, I rinsed with mouthwash, but still—"

"Good enough for me."

He kisses me, and even though I'm not really into it, I try to kiss him back. I don't really understand why he doesn't arouse me. He's nice enough. Handsome. Decent kisser. Good sense of humor. But no matter how hard I try to feel it, there's just nothing there.

When I'm with Nick, it always feels like there's a tiny Ethan sitting on my shoulder whispering, "*It doesn't matter how similar we look. He's not me. He'll never compare to me. Give up now and accept that for the rest of your romantic life, no one is even going to come close to making you feel what I could.*" The sad thing is, I know that tiny shoulder-sitting Satan-Holt is right. And it depresses the hell out of me.

I should just tell Nick we're not going to work out, so he can move on with someone else. He deserves passion. Mine's currently unavailable.

Before I can say anything, he shoves his tongue in my mouth and presses me back into the wall. I pull back, but he grabs my face and kisses me again.

"Come on, Cassie," he says as he grinds against my hip. "We've been dancing around each other for months. Let me make you feel good."

"Nick, stop—"

He pushes my hand between us and leans into it. "Just touch me. Please. Dammit, I've been hard for you since the first time we met."

"Nick—"

A hand closes over Nick's shoulder and pulls him back.

"She said stop, asshole. Are you fucking deaf?"

Ethan's there, scowling and angry. He steps in front of me and stares down a confused Nick.

"Who the hell are you?"

"Someone who can tell from across the room that she's not interested. Have some fucking respect."

"Ethan, I'm fine."

Nick laughs. "So a guy's not allowed to kiss his girlfriend around you?"

Ethan and I react in absolute unison. "What?!"

Ethan spins around to face me. "You're his *girlfriend*?"

"Nick, I'm not your girlfriend."

"Cassie, come on. We're dating."

"Not really," I say. "I mean, we've been out on a few dates, but that's it."

"Well, I think our relationship is a bit more meaningful than that."

Holt glowers. "You're in a relationship with this tool?"

"No."

Nick throws up his hands. "Cassie, what the hell is going on here? Who is this guy?"

"He's . . . my ex." The words still feel wrong.

"Really? He's not acting very *ex*." Nick squares off with Ethan. They're about the same height and build. In a fight, you'd expect them to be evenly matched, but to me, there's absolutely no competition.

And that's the problem.

Ethan leans in. "Nick, is it?" He makes his name sound like it was something he scraped off the bottom of his shoe. "You were pawing Cassie like a creeper. Learn to take no for a fucking answer."

Nick draws up to his full height. "Do you go around stalking all your ex-girlfriends, or just this one?"

"You were groping her in the goddamn open. What the hell is your problem, man?"

"What's *your* problem? Can't handle that she's moved on with someone else?"

I sigh. All I wanted to do tonight was get drunk and forget about my stupid emotions. Now I'm stuck in the middle of some sort of macho pissing match.

I push between the two men still glaring at each other. "I'm leaving, but by all means, you two keep arguing. It looks like you're enjoying yourselves."

Nick grabs my hand. "Wait, Cassie. Please. I'll drive you home."

Ethan bristles. "The hell you will."

"No, Nick," I say, and turn to face him. "You're drunk, and I'm walking. Also, I don't think we should see each other anymore. You did paw me like a creeper, and I'm not cool with that."

Nick frowns but doesn't let go of my hand. "Can't we go somewhere to talk about this?"

"No. Now let me go, or I'll let Ethan hurt you, and you really don't want that. He's good at inflicting pain."

I don't miss the expression that passes over Ethan's face.

When Nick drops my hand, I walk to a pile of coats near the front door and dig until I find mine. Then I pull it on and walk out.

As I close the door behind me, the chill hits my cheeks. When I exhale, a cloud of steam pours from my mouth.

I really just want to go to bed and forget about today. Maybe tomorrow will be better.

I've barely gotten to the sidewalk before I hear footsteps behind me.

"Cassie, wait."

I keep walking. After all this time, why does Ethan choose tonight to break our unspoken rule to stay away from each other?

"Hey. Stop."

He grabs my arm, and I shove my hands in my pockets as he walks around and stands in front of me.

"It's fucking freezing out here," he says. "Let me drive you home."

"I'm fine."

"You're shivering."

"So are you."

"Yeah, but I'm about to get into my nice, warm car, and you're about to freeze your ass off. Come on, I can have you home in twenty minutes. Don't be stubborn."

"Hah! *You're* calling *me* stubborn?"

"Well, I would have said '*fucking* stubborn,' but I'm trying to fucking cut down on my fucking cursing."

"Funny. Why do you keep swooping in and trying to save me tonight? I don't need you."

His mouth twitches. "Oh, I realize that. Over the past year, you've made it abundantly clear."

"Then why are you even bothering?"

He pulls his jacket around him and looks at the ground. "I don't know. I just figure it's about time we start being civil to each other. You looked upset tonight, and more than a little drunk. If you stay out here, you could freeze to death. Or worse, run into a drunk asshole like Nick. I'm leaving anyway. Why not let me drive you home?"

I can think of about a thousand reasons, but he's right. I am freezing my ass off. Still, the thought of spending time with Ethan sends an unwanted thrill of anticipation through me. I inhale the chilly air to dampen the fire.

"Whatever. Take me home."

He breaks into the most genuine smile I've seen on him in a long time.

The fire inside me grows.

Bad idea. Such a bad idea.

His car is like an airtight chamber of Ethan-essence. I'm sober enough to know how much it's affecting me and drunk enough to not really care. I lean my head back.

Inhale.

Shudder.

Exhale.

Resist watching him drive.

"You okay?" he asks.

"Fine."

"You look . . . hot."

I turn to him.

He blinks and looks away. "Temperature-wise, not . . ." He shakes his head. "Never mind."

He grips the steering wheel harder. I close my eyes so I can avoid staring at his hands. Or thighs. Or jaw. Or lips.

Dumb tequila. Lowering my defenses. Making me horny.

We drive in silence. It's uncomfortable. And arousing. We haven't been this close to each other in ages. In a strangely masochistic way, it satisfies something in me that's been severely lacking.

When we pull up in front of my apartment building, I almost don't want to leave. There's an energy firing between us. One that we've both suppressed for a long time. I've spent so much time training myself to be numb, I was getting worried that was all I'd ever be. It's a relief to feel this lusty simmer; like someone who fears they'll never walk again getting an unexpected tingling in their toes.

I'm about to reluctantly get out of the car when Holt turns off the engine.

I glance over at him. He's still gripping the steering wheel and staring straight ahead. Tense always did look sexy on him.

He turns in my direction without actually looking at me. "So, you've been dating that Nick guy?"

"Sort of."

"I didn't know."

"Why would you? We don't talk."

He leans back in his seat, and stares at the clock on the dash. "Did you sleep with him?"

It takes a moment for me to register what he just asked, but when I do, my hands curl into fists.

"Who I'm sleeping with is none of your business."

"I know that, but—"

"Is that what was happening tonight? Cock-blocking him?"

He turns to me. "Do you seriously believe I'm that petty? I was trying to *protect* you, or were you okay with him shoving your hand down his pants and ignoring your pleas to stop?"

I fiddle with the button on my coat, knowing very well he was looking out for me. I just prefer to make him the bad guy. It means whatever is currently happening between us is easier to ignore.

He sighs and cracks his knuckles. "Forget it. You don't have to tell me anything. What you do is your business. It was stupid of me to ask."

He doesn't say "sorry" but his tone is apologetic enough to persuade me to tell him the truth.

"I didn't sleep with him."

He loosens up just a bit, and the look of relief on his face is nearly laughable. "Good. He seemed like a prick. Better to be celibate than sleep with someone not worthy."

"I didn't say I was celibate."

He blinks. "What?"

"You asked if I was sleeping with him. I'm not. But I'm not celibate."

His brows furrow. "So, what? You're sleeping with someone else?"

"Well, you could hardly call what we do sleeping." I shouldn't torture him with the details, but I really want to.

Silence hangs in the air between us for a few seconds.

"Who?"

"His name's Buzz. He screws my brains out several times a week. Sometimes multiple times a day."

Even in the dim glow of the streetlight, I see him go pale. He grips the steering wheel a little tighter. "Is he a student?"

"No."

"How long have you been . . . seeing him?"

"About eight months."

The muscles in his jaw go crazy. "What the hell, Cassie? You were fucking this Buzz asshole while you were going out with Date-Rape Nick?"

"Well, sure. I mean, Nick was okay, but Buzz and I are just about the sex." I try not to laugh.

He leans his head against the steering wheel. "Jesus Christ."

"Don't you want to know how we met?"

"No."

"Ruby introduced us. At a sex shop."

"Please stop talking."

"She knew just by looking at him that he'd be able to make me come."

He groans. "Fuck . . . Cassie. Please . . ."

"For a while I thought you were the only one who could get me off."

". . . stop . . ."

"But once I figured out he had multiple speed settings, he made me see stars, and I've been devoted to him ever since."

"Too much fucking information. Literally." Then he stops, and turns to me. "Wait . . . multiple speed settings?"

I have to smile. "Yep."

He stares. "So Buzz is your . . . uh . . ."

"Vibrator. His full name is Sir Buzzalot. Best orgasms money can buy."

He closes his eyes. "Yeah, you'd think that would make it better than fucking another guy, but it really doesn't. You've been making yourself come . . . with a vibrator. I can't even . . . God—"

I'd be lying if I said I wasn't enjoying his discomfort.

"Since we're being all chatty and whatnot . . . what about you?"

He rubs his eyes. "I don't own a vibrator."

"You know what I mean. Are you sleeping with anyone?"

"No."

"Dating anyone?"

He makes a noise that's almost a laugh but not quite. "No."

"Why not?"

"Because if I were capable of dating someone, why the fuck would I have broken up with you?"

The silence solidifies between us. It feels like we have so much left to say after not speaking for so long, but neither of us knows where to start.

At last, he comes up with something appropriate. "Do you have any alcohol in your apartment?"

"Yeah. Tequila. Or wine."

"Can I come in? I need a drink. Plus, I don't really feel like going home. If I have to spend another night in my apartment alone, I'll—"

He shakes his head. "If you don't want me to, it's fine."

I think of all the days he sits by himself to eat lunch. The way he separates himself in most social situations. Even when he started coming to parties again, he'd keep to himself. Was he just there to escape his solitude?

Throughout this whole thing between us, at least I've had people to support me. Ruby, Mom, my classmates. Hell, even his sister.

Who's been there for him?

My pride is mad at me for feeling sorry for him, but I can't help it.

"I could use something else to drink, too. If you want to come in, you can. I suppose."

He nods and tries to hide his half smile. "Fine, I will, but please, stop begging. It's embarrassing."

"What can I say? I don't like drinking alone."

He turns to me, eyes almost black in the shadows of the car. "Me neither."

The air between us becomes stifling. Crazy thick.

He lets out a breath before saying, "One drink, then I'll be on my way."

Flutters tickle my stomach and then move lower. "Okay."

I'm laughing so hard, I can barely breathe. Ethan's in the same boat. He's wheezing like a cartoon character. I don't even know what we're laughing about. This is surreal. After more than a year of bitterness and snark, how the hell did we get here?

I topple to the side and collide with his shoulder. He leans back against the couch, and I'm so busy marveling over how stunning he is when he's happy, my head slides down his arm and lands in his lap. We keep laughing. My head bounces off his stomach. It makes me laugh more. I sound deranged.

He spills some of his drink and licks the liquid off his thumb and forearm before it can drip onto the carpet. I'm transfixed by the motion of his tongue. I want to find out if it tastes like tequila.

He drops his head back and says, "I think we're drunk."

"I think you're right."

Gradually, our laughter dies down, and I flip onto my back and let my head nestle on top of his thigh. It feels strange to be with him like this. Like these are versions of ourselves from an alternate universe in which things are totally different, and we're both happy. Touching him with such ease after all this time feels more like déjà vu than something I've done before.

I close my eyes and let myself enjoy it. I know this is a stolen moment, but it's exactly what I need right now.

I feel fingers on my forehead as he strokes my hair away from my face, and I open my eyes to see him staring down at me. All laughter has left his face. There's an intensity in his expression that makes goose bumps flare across my skin. He threads his fingers through my hair, and everything seems to slow down. Like the air is charged with extra gravity.

I inhale with effort.

Within three seconds his fingertips have aroused me more than Nick could in three months.

The box in which I've locked my passion explodes open.

Ethan licks his lips. "I'm starting to think this was probably a bad idea. Being alone with you."

I'm mesmerized by the movement of his mouth when he talks. "Yeah. Probably."

"It's easier when there are other people around. They distract me, you know? When it's just us . . . it's—"

"Harder."

His expression softens. Fingers trail down my cheek.

"You're so fucking beautiful," he whispers, like he's afraid I'll hear. "Every day I think that but can never tell you."

His touch is feather-light, but each stroke sinks into my bones. Sets them ablaze. "Why tell me now?"

"Because I'm too drunk to stop myself. And because neither of us is likely to remember this tomorrow."

His chest rises and falls in fast, shallow breaths. Eyes are hooded. Deep and needy.

Lonely.

Sad.

"I miss you, Cassie."

My heart races. I've wanted to hear that so many times, but now that he's said it, I have no idea how to respond.

He's still stroking my face. Studying me. Trying to keep himself together.

Seeing him like this instantly pulls me apart.

I look away.

He sighs. "On a scale of one to wanting-to-kick-me-in-the-balls, how much do you hate me for dumping you? Be honest."

I pick at the outer seam of his jeans. "Some days, I hate you lots. Most days, to be honest."

"And other days?"

I run my fingernail down the stitching while ignoring how his thigh is tensing beneath my head.

"Some days, I . . ." He grazes his fingernails down the back of my neck and then up across my scalp. It makes a quake of shudders roll through me. "Sometimes I don't feel like kicking you in the balls at all."

"What about right now?"

I turn to face him as I fight the burn that's rising up my chest and neck, and the hungry ache that's pounding down low. "Right now, I have no idea how I feel."

He stares at me for a long time, then nods and takes a mouthful of booze. He frowns at his glass.

I sit up and wait for him to say something. He doesn't.

His knuckles go white as he grips his drink.

"What are you thinking?"

He shakes his head. "I'm thinking I really want to kiss you, but I can't." He gives a short laugh. "While I'm admitting stuff, I'll tell you that's what I'm thinking pretty much every day. It's fucking pathetic how often I fantasize about it. I thought I'd be over you by now. But I'm not."

His words floor me. So honest and unexpected. So similar to things I stop myself from thinking.

I can't respond. For once, he's braver than I am.

He drinks again and looks as if he's waiting for a response. He's going to be sorely disappointed.

At last he gives up. "So, care to tell me why you walked out of acting class today?"

The question takes me by surprise. "Not really."

"I thought we were pretty good by the end."

"You were. You were amazing."

"So, why did you walk out? You looked pissed."

I stop and think about it. The answer isn't easy to put my finger on, but when I do, it's so obvious.

"For so long, I've tried convincing myself that we broke up because you were incapable of being truly intimate. Of letting your guard down. Then today . . . in that scene with Connor, you did it. You were everything I knew you could be and more. Passionate. Brave. Loving. Patient. So open and strong. And I was so . . . jealous. And angry. I couldn't cope. It made me even angrier that you could be like that with a *guy* you *hate*, and yet you couldn't do it with me."

"Cassie, I was acting."

"No. You were living it. You think I can't tell? I've watched you hold yourself back in every acting class since our breakup. Today was different. You made a breakthrough. A huge one."

He downs the rest of his drink, pulls his legs up, and crosses them in front of him. Then he levels me with the most honest look he's ever given me.

"You want to know why that scene worked so well today? I was . . ." He shakes his head. "Jesus, if I wasn't drunk, there'd be no way I'd be telling you this." He takes a breath. "It worked because I imagined I was you, talking to me."

It takes me a moment to comprehend what he's said, and even then, I think I have it wrong. "What?"

He tugs on his hair. "I thought about all of those times you talked me through stuff. Tried to help me be strong. It seemed appropriate considering the text I had. If you think I was amazing today, it's because I was pretending I was you."

He shakes his head and fingers the hem of his jeans. "The funny thing is, I never thought I'd have the balls to be like that. Open to being hurt and not giving a shit. But when I did it today . . ." He slowly lifts his head and looks me in the eye. "I could see how different things would be for me if I was. How much better they'd be."

He doesn't say, "with you," but I swear to God, I hear it in my mind.

"I want to be like that," he says softly. "The strong one. I'm fucking ashamed of how weak I am. About so many things."

I'm stunned into silence. My heart pounds, and my breath comes too fast. He's staring at me. Waiting for a reaction. He's so close, but I want him closer.

Seconds pass. Time stretches around us.

He leans forward. Our legs are touching. Two layers of denim do nothing to insulate me from the effect of his body next to mine. Faces are close. It would be so easy to move forward. Brush against his lips. See if he still tastes as sweet as I remember.

"Cassie . . ." The dark edge in his voice isn't helping my restraint. It's like he's drowning and begging me to save him.

I take a deep breath and dig for strength. "I'm thinking that one of us should probably leave this room before we do something stupid."

He leans forward a fraction more and inhales. Then he closes his eyes for a second and says, "Yeah. I think you're probably right."

With a grunt of frustration, he pulls back, stands, and walks unsteadily to the table. Then he puts his glass next to the bottle of tequila. When I stand and follow suit, I have to lean on the back of a chair to keep my balance. Gripping it also helps stop me from launching myself at the gorgeous man beside me.

Ethan stares for a moment before sighing and running his hand through his hair. "I can't drive. Is it cool for me to sleep on the couch?"

No. Get out before I mount you.

"Sure."

I go to the linen closet and grab extra blankets and pillows before I dump them on the couch. He thanks me.

"No problem."

We stand there for a moment, at a loss as to what to do. We both know this is a bad idea. What we're feeling? The nearly irresistible pull toward each other? That's the reason we've been avoiding each other since the breakup. Sure, we're now experts in ignoring our desire, but constantly living like that is exhausting.

Soul destroying.

Although tonight has danced on a tightrope between spine-tingling excitement and disaster, the potential for it to go to hell is still very much there. It's in every lingering glance, every touch, every ache and tug of body and heart.

My fear is telling me to run before it's too late, but part of me is getting off on it. The adrenaline he brings out in me makes me feel more alive than I've felt in months. The danger of him is part of it. This is why people jump out of planes and swim with sharks. To feel this muscle-trembling rush.

Judging by how he's staring at me, he feels the same way.

"I should go to bed," I say in barely a whisper.

He nods but doesn't look away. "Yeah. It's late."

"Yeah. So . . . sleep well."

"You too."

I only take three steps before warm fingers close around my hand.

"Cassie . . ."

He tugs on it. There's hardly any pressure, but I move like he's pulling me with a steel cable. I step into him, and when he wraps his arms around me, I press my cheek against his chest.

His breath comes out ragged and shuddery as he buries his head in my neck and sinks into me like honey on warm toast.

So warm, he melts me.

Our hearts thunder against each other, and right now, there's only one thought inhabiting my head.

Ethan.

Bastard Ethan. Beautiful Ethan.

My Ethan.

Forever mine, regardless of whether we're together.

"Do you think we're ready to be friends yet?" he whispers.

"No." What I'm feeling for him is in a different universe from friendship.

"Me, neither."

"One day?"

"Stranger things have happened."

"Really?"

He laughs. "No. It's highly fucking unlikely."

"We could pretend," I say, not wanting to let go.

He brushes his nose against my ear. "What do you think we've been doing all this time?"

I nod.

He strokes my back. Breathes against my neck. "I've thought about holding you a lot recently. I thought it would somehow feel different than it used to, but it doesn't. You feel exactly the same."

"I'm not."

I can feel the weight of his guilt when he says, "I know."

I bring my hands down onto his chest. "You feel different. Hard."

"Yeah, ignore it. I've been like that since you and Miranda made out in acting class on Monday."

I laugh. "I was referring to your new boxing muscles."

He pauses. "Oh. Of course you were. Forget I mentioned the arousing lesbianism."

"You liked that?"

"No, I *like* pie. *That* was like a religious experience. It was one instance in which I was in complete agreement with Avery. You two should totally make out more often."

He lets me go, and when I step back, I immediately want to hug him again.

"Don't go to bed," he says and takes my hand. "Stay for one more drink. Please. I'm too buzzed to sleep. I promise to keep my hands to myself and sit on the other end of the couch."

I grab the bottle and our glasses from the table. "I guess one more would be okay. We're already drunk. What's the worst that could happen?"

Even before I open my eyes, I can feel them aching. They throb slowly behind my lids. My stomach rolls and I press it against the warmth I'm holding, searching for relief.

The warmth moans.

I stop breathing.

Warm.

Large.

Acres of man-skin.

Most definitely naked.

I open my eyes to see Ethan, unconscious and unguarded, both arms wrapped around me, legs tangled between mine, parts of his body already awake and attentive even as he slumbers.

No.

God, no.

We didn't.

We're not that stupid.

It was tequila, not a full-frontal lobotomy.

I would never . . .

And he *definitely* would never . . .

Ethan moans again and rubs his erection against me.

"Hmmmm. Cassie."

No, no, no, no.

I try not to launch into a full-blown panic attack.

I must still be dreaming.

I close my eyes and breathe. It doesn't help.

The room smells like him. And me. And sex.

Lots and lots of sex.

Images of last night come back to me.

Darkness and light. Long blinks and gentle touches. Fingers. Palms. Barely there. Tentative and surreal.

Hair between my fingers. Hot breath on my neck. Then his mouth.

Oh, Mary. His sweet, talented mouth. Silk lips. So soft at first, then ravenous. Cleansing all the bitter words from my tongue. Exorcising every sliver of restraint until all that's left of either of us is primal, and desperate, and writhing.

His thigh presses between my legs and I grind . . . and grind . . . and grind. All of him, hard and swollen.

Floating. High on alcohol and sensation. More skin revealed. Clothes pulled. Half-naked stumbling.

Panting breaths against my ear, begging me to tell him to stop. Pleading for strength. Praying to be inside me.

The weight of him, heavy and electric. Stirring all my synapses. Transforming everything he touches into insatiable flesh. Mouth and fingers, all

over me. Making me dizzy. Crazy. A frenzy of wrongness and "God, yes"
and please, please, please.

And then he's inside me.

I can barely comprehend the pleasure.

I speak to God. Say his name over and over again. Sigh and pant and
very nearly cry.

He's gentle. Holding still and swearing. Also speaking to God. Telling
Him how good I feel.

He prays through my skin. Bites my shoulder. Kisses it better. Groans
like he's riding an angel all the way into the pits of hell.

I can't get enough.

God, please, Ethan, move.

Thrust.

Let me feel the perfect deepness of you. Sliding home and rolling
through me.

There are strong arms and low moans, and how can he feel this amaz-
ing after all of this time? He fits perfectly to my body. Plays its rhythms.
Hits every beat until everything is wire-tight and singing.

The couch, the floor, the hallway, the wall, the bed. Time and again he
fills and refills me. Guides me through every type of ecstasy there is. Shows
me all of its gasping forms. Just when I think we're done, he touches me
again and the fire roars back to life.

In the end, we collapse, exhausted. I fall asleep, smiling. Refusing to think
about what morning will bring.

I open my eyes and stare down at Ethan.

Already, my chest is tightening.

What we did . . . what we shared last night doesn't fix anything. Not
one of his issues.

If anything, it complicates things even more.

We tried to suppress our passion, but in the end, she ended up making
us her bitch. She waited until we were vulnerable. Stalked us on ninja

feet. Pried us open with longing and loneliness. Stripped away our anger and common sense and doused us in lust.

Then she lit a match and danced as we burned.

Even now, everywhere he touches me blazes to life. I should climb out of bed and wash every trace of him away. Try to forget how incredible he felt.

But I can't move. Can't bear to drag myself away.

Then he opens his eyes and looks at me. Panic fires in his expression. He looks down at himself, naked and hard, then takes in the catastrophe of clothing littering the floor and bed, and frowns when he sees the slew of condom wrappers strewn across the nightstand. He stares for a long time before comprehension and disbelief dawn behind his bloodshot eyes.

"Fuck, Cassie."

"Yeah, well, seems like you've been there, done that. Now what?"

FIFTEEN

JUST SEX

Sex.

It's a primal, ancient instinct stamped into every corner of our DNA. We must screw to survive.

But sex is greedy. Addictive.

It's an infinite, aching appetite that reduces us to base impulses capable of clouding all reason and logic.

It's instinctual.

Simple.

Except when it's not.

After the initial shock of waking up in bed together wears off, Ethan and I talk. Agree that it was a mistake. That we couldn't and shouldn't do it again.

Ever.

Then we screw two more times and fall asleep in each other's arms.

Yep.

Simple, this is not.

"So . . ."

"Yeah. So . . ."

We've made it as far as the front door. After several failed attempts, he's wearing clothes, and I'm wearing a robe. His hair is ridiculous. Mine is even more so. I look like Hagrid if he'd been electrocuted in a wind tunnel. Ethan's looking at me as if he'd like to do very bad things to Hagrid.

The urge to touch him again is swelling like the tide under a full moon. It's vaguely ridiculous.

"I'd better go."

"Yeah."

He doesn't move. Neither do I. We know we have to. We can't do it again. I hurt everywhere. He's given me scruff rash on every inch of exposed skin, as well as some that isn't so exposed.

"Okay."

"Okay."

Fifteen minutes ago we were fitting together in the very definition of rightness, gripping each other through countless layers of pleasure. But now? Here comes the awkward. The separation.

Walls and masks and tectonic plates of emotion slide back into safe formations. Stand us on our feet. Tilt us away from each other once more.

Whisper to us that it was just sex.

Just sex.

He opens the door, then pauses. "So . . . is it going to be weird between us now?"

"You mean more weird? No."

He nods. "No. Exactly. I mean, it was just breakup sex, right? Everyone does it."

"Right." *Just sex.* "We might have waited a little longer than most, but it's totally normal."

"It's out of our systems now, so, we can . . . you know . . . move on."

"Yeah. Absolutely. Move on."

He inhales and stares at the exposed flesh my robe reveals.

He talks to my boobs. "See you Monday?" At last he makes it up to my face.

I want to tell him to stop it. The longing that's peeking out. It's too much. This was *just sex*.

"Yep. See you then."

He hesitates, and for a moment I think he's going to kiss me, but instead he hugs me and buries his head in my neck. I'm not sure what he's thinking, but it feels like *thank you* and *I'm sorry* all wrapped up in one.

It makes me feel things. Buried and bound things.

I push him away. I don't want him to go, but I need him to.

He seems to understand. Shoves his hands in his pockets and lets out a disbelieving sigh.

"You smell like me. Like me and . . . sex."

He fingers the tie of my robe. "I mean, you've always smelled like sex to me, but today . . . you smell like the very definition of incredible, earth-moving, seeing-the-face-of-God sex."

This man. Forever stealing my breath.

We have a moment of *maybe once more* before we both realize there's no way. Our bodies are done.

I push him out the door. "Get out while you can. Thanks for all the sex."

All the *just sex*.

"Yeah. Okay. Bye."

"Bye."

After I close the door, I collapse against it, breathless and aching. I expect the regret and bitterness to swallow me, but strangely, it doesn't. Instead, I'm smiling.

I did it. I fucked Ethan Holt and survived. Thrived, even. And now, I'm too filled with satisfaction to regret what we did.

Later, I feel bad when I take a shower and change my sheets, but it's only because I can't smell him on me anymore.

It's at that moment a dull ticking starts up inside me. It pulses in my blood and keeps time with my heart. When I think of Ethan, it speeds up.

A countdown clock. A slow detonator.

Cataloguing the seconds until he makes me explode again.

When Ruby arrives home mid-afternoon, she flops down next to me on the couch.

"Hey."

She also has Hagrid hair and a satisfied smile. Seems good sex looks the same on everyone.

My hair's washed. I've untangled the sex knots.

No one would ever know that just five hours ago, Holt had it wrapped around his hands as he took me from behind.

"Hey," I say and push the image away. "Have a good night?"

She stretches. "Oh, yeah. God, there is nothing . . . and I mean *nothing* to relieve tension like riding a hot piece of man-meat all night. It's like a full-body massage from the inside out. You really need to try it one of these days. I know you think Buzz is all you need right now, but, honey . . . there's only so much fake dick a girl can take before she needs to rumble with the real deal."

He tugs my head back and grips my hip to hold me in place as he thrusts, strong and deep. He hits unexpected places inside me. Kisses my shoulder as I swear and call out his name.

I eat a spoonful of yogurt and try to keep my face impassive. "Uh-huh."

She leans against me. "So, what did you get up to after the party? The usual? Book and bed?"

I nod. "Yep. You know me. Boring old Cassie."

I lower myself onto him, prideful as I watch his eyes roll back into his head. My body trembles with the effort of containing this power. This magnificent, confident version of myself. Sex-Goddess Cassie. I ride him slowly, drag him to the edge of climax so often he starts to beg. Punish him by weaponizing his pleasure. Reward him by letting him see mine. Time and again.

"Poor baby," Ruby says as she snuggles up to me. "You need sex."

I fan myself. My blood is pumping way too fast. Too close to the surface. Hot and demanding.

"Yeah, well. Maybe one day."

I don't know why I don't tell her. Maybe because she'd take it the wrong way and think Ethan and I are getting back together, when we're absolutely not. Or maybe because she'd confirm it was the worst thing I could have done.

Whatever her reaction, I don't want it right now. I just want to enjoy this feeling of relative bliss. Before Ethan drove me home last night, I was miserable and lonely, and today I feel . . . empowered. Like a sexual genius. I did things to Ethan I'd only ever dreamed about. I made him shudder. Groan and plead. I dominated him and let him dominate me in return. I was able to give him pleasure like no one else ever has. Then I made him admit it and brought him completely undone.

After being powerless for so long, I finally feel like I have some control.

And what's more, I managed to have him without drowning in unwanted emotion. I kept myself shielded and protected, even while he filled me in ways no other man ever will.

Sexual catharsis? Is there such a thing?

If so, that's what Ethan and I shared.

I just wonder how long it will be until we both need to be purged again.

Monday morning. I walk to class feeling a thousand feet tall. I still hurt, but it only serves to remind me of my power. I'm Aphrodite. A force of nature, ready to be worshipped.

I should be nervous about seeing Ethan, but I'm not. Whatever happens, I can deal with it. I'll smile if he shuts me down, because I'll know he won't be able to resist me for long. I own him. And he knows it.

I walk into class and immediately feel him staring at me. He looks angry.

Wait, not angry.

Hungry.

He glances away, but it's only a few seconds before he's back. Surprised. Awed.

The *tick-tock* inside me speeds up. Gives me a powerful thrill. I'd kind of expected him to retreat back into his emotionally distant shell, but for once, he's not being totally predictable.

I like it.

With only a trace of his trademark fear, he gives me a lusty half smile. I give one back. I feel like we're collaborators in a private joke. No one else has any idea what happened between us, but if he keeps looking at me like that, they're going to realize pretty damn quickly.

I walk past him and whisper, "Stop undressing me with your eyes."

He whispers back, "Would you rather I do it with my hands? Or teeth?"

Oh, this is interesting. He wants to play? Fine. For once, I'm confident I'll win.

"How's your penis?"

"You don't know by now? It's magnificent."

"So conceited. I meant, are you sore?"

"Oh. Yeah. There's definite . . . chafing. He's exhausted, to be honest. I doubt I'll ever be hard again."

I give him a slow smile. "That sounds like a challenge."

"It's really not."

I accidentally/on purpose drop my book and bend over in front of him to pick it up.

Then I glance behind me to see him wincing and adjusting himself. My work here is done.

The rest of the class chatters and moves around us, oblivious. We barely register on their radar anymore. We're old news.

If only they knew.

I sit down, and when I turn back to Ethan, he's crossed his legs and is staring at his shoes, his face still painted with discomfort. And arousal.

It looks good on him.

"I thought we agreed it was a mistake," he says, not looking at me.

"We did."

"Then why do I get the impression you'd like to do it again? Right now."

I whisper, "Even if I do, it doesn't mean I'm going to. I'm not that stupid."

"Oh."

"You look disappointed."

"Nope. Just . . . you know . . . relieved."

I lean closer so my mouth is right next to his ear. I know what I'm doing. If this were chess, I'd be demolishing his queen right about now. "Relieved I won't be taking you in my mouth again? Riding you? Scraping my nails down your back as I come?"

In the past, I never really understood why girls play games and use their gender and sex appeal to get what they want.

I understand it now.

Sometimes sex is the only thing that will bring a man to his knees. And sometimes, it does a girl good to know that after losing so much, she can occasionally win.

After seeing how affected Holt is by my words, I sit back, triumphant.

He closes his eyes. Then he adjusts himself again. "Yep. Definitely relieved none of that is going to happen again. So very . . . happy . . . about that."

"Good."

Checkmate.

It doesn't escape my attention that he's hard for nearly the entire lecture.

SIXTEEN

LITTLE ACHE

Present Day
New York City, New York
The Apartment of Cassandra Taylor

I sit up and clutch my chest as sweat and the too-real remnants of his dream-hands prickle my skin. My heart is pounding. It makes all the wrong places ache for him.

It's the memory of him that really sets my nerve endings into overdrive. The phantom brush of his fingers. The ghostly weight of his hips pressing against my thighs. The soft noises as he rocked and filled and exploded me.

Is it any wonder I have trouble taking things slow with him when he affects me like this?

After a quick shower to cool myself down, I pull out another of his journals. I'm tired and my eyes are gritty, but I can't seem to stop reading. Getting inside his head is like a drug.

I spoke to him on the phone last night. It's easier to deal with him when we're not face-to-face. When we're together, he has this way of staring at me that almost has me convinced he can melt my clothing with the power of his mind. It drives me crazy. At least on the phone, I have some insulation. Plus, if his voice gets to be too much, I can always hump my pillow, and he's none the wiser.

Not that I'd do that.

Much.

We didn't talk for long. He wanted to check how I was and apologized for molesting me at dinner on Saturday night. I told him it wasn't entirely his fault. He promised to try to keep his hands to himself. Certain parts of me booed.

He asked about the journals. I told him I'd almost reached the end of our first year at The Grove, then we both went quiet as if caught up in our own thoughts of that time.

This morning I found all of his journals from our second and third years waiting on my doorstep, along with a bottle of Valium. I think it was his idea of a joke. If I hadn't felt so nauseated, I might have laughed.

As it is, I'm wading through entries that make me simultaneously weepy and horny. I may have thrown something at a wall about an hour ago. Tristan has understandably been avoiding me.

So far, entries from our second year have been few and far between. Curt. Almost boring. I'd expected long prose passages about how much he missed me while we were apart, but I got the opposite. Like he'd shut down.

Then, I see the entry for the day after the night that changed everything.

February 11th

Last night. Jesus.

How do I even describe it?

Stupid? Yeah.

Beyond amazing? Hell, yeah.

The best night of my life? Absolutely.

I'd like to say I have no idea how it happened, but that's not true. I was drunk, but not that drunk. I knew when I sat next to her what I was doing. I knew when I touched her face. When I leaned in to taste those fucking amazing lips I'd been staring at all night.

When she started kissing me back? That's when I knew I couldn't stop. No amount of logic or fear could have stopped me then. The tequila was a good excuse, but the truth is, I wanted it. More than anything in my entire life.

Lucky for me, she wanted it, too.

I can't put into words how it felt to finally touch her again. I've fantasized about it too many times to count, and then it happened, and I got lost in sensation after not feeling anything for way too long. Nothing has ever felt as right as being inside her. The moment I sank into her . . . fuck. It felt like my chest was going to explode. Too much emotion. Too much love.

Too much everything.

I tried to tell myself it was just fucking, but I knew it wasn't. It never could be with her. As much as I like to think I'm getting desensitized to how she affects me, I know it's bullshit. I'm desensitized as long as she doesn't touch me. Or look at me. Otherwise, I want to launch myself across the room and tackle her. Kiss her until she can't stand up. Make love to her until she can't sit down.

Pretty sure I achieved both of those things on Friday night. And again this morning.

The bastard part of me hopes she's sore and that every time she winces, she remembers the feel of me deep inside her.

Fuck.

Now I'm hard again.

I can't masturbate. I seriously can't. Apart from how I'd probably scream in agony if I even looked at my cock right now, I just couldn't go back to fucking my hand when I've known the perfection of being inside her. There's no way.

I know we agreed it was stupid and that we shouldn't do it again, but I want to.

If I wasn't such a pussy, I'd ask her if we could try again, but I know that's not an option. I've screwed things up so badly with us, I don't think they'll ever be right, no matter how much I want them to be. Plus, despite how amazing our sex marathon was, it doesn't change how my brain works. It just gave it something more pleasurable to focus on than all the ways the universe can screw me.

Still, the distraction is addictive. If I have sex often enough with her, would it make me feel like I could make things work between us?

It's so tempting to find out.

So tempting.

February 13th

Yeah, I'm in trouble. I'm not sure what I thought would happen when I saw her today, but I didn't expect her to transform into someone who makes my dick even harder. She walked into class like she owned it and fixed me with a look that was so sexy, I don't think I'll ever be flaccid again. I mean, she's always been fiery, but today . . . I don't know. It's like Friday night awakened something inside her. Something powerful. As soon as she stepped into the room I couldn't take my eyes off her. She was thrumming with energy. Sexual confidence.

It was fucking mesmerizing.

I have no idea how to deal with it. It's like she's now this supernova—dazzling and deadly—and even though I know she'll make me blind, I can't look away.

She flirted with me, and even stranger, I flirted back. What the fuck is going on?

Can it be that one incredible night can make us work correctly? Overcome so many of our issues? It seems unlikely.

I think we're just both a little high from the experience, but I'm sure when that wears off, I'll realize she's too good for me, and she'll remember she hates me, and we'll go back to being dysfunctional and distant.

To be honest, I hope that's what happens, because this new Cassie? If I'm not careful, she's going to fucking ruin me. And God help me, I'd enjoy every second of it.

I caught her staring at me today, and I could tell she knew. It's like a game to her and, like it or not, I'm letting her win. Seeing her like that? All powerful and confident? It almost makes the massive ache in my balls worthwhile.

Actually, no. It really doesn't. I need to have sex with her again. Now.

For so long, I dictated how our relationship would go. Tried to control it and my feelings for her. Now, she's in the driver's seat, and even though I'm certain she's hurtling us headfirst into a massive fucking wall, I know that if she wants me again, I'll come running. Depending on how horny I am, that last statement may be literally true.

I laugh. He's pretty spot-on in his assessment.

Back then, teasing him was always one of my favorite ways to exert control. It wasn't something I was proud of, but it was addictive. The power. The temporary intimacy.

I put down the journal and ignore the tingling between my legs. That hungry little ache was the cause of so much trouble at that time. It convinced me I could have him physically without wanting more. Demanded him, time and time again. Shushed my heart when it complained we were getting too close.

It just *wanted*, and didn't care how many lines became blurred in the process.

I close my eyes and ignore it while I cuddle my pillow and resist the hypnotic whispers of my stupid, power-hungry libido.

SEVENTEEN

COLLISION COURSE

Five Years Earlier
Westchester, New York
The Grove

As winter melts into spring, the distant orbits in which Ethan and I circle each other change, and morph into something new. A spiraling ellipse of heat and sexual frustration that has definite overtones of catastrophe, but which neither of us seems inclined to avoid.

In fact, Ethan has been actively seeking me out.

In the past weeks, he's been around more. Instead of going off by himself, he's been loitering, occasionally joining in with banter and conversations, not only with me, but with the rest of our friends. When he started joining us for lunch, Avery gave him shit for deigning to chow down with the peasants. Holt told him to fuck off but cracked a smile while doing it.

He's even tolerating Connor. Well, except for when Connor touches me—then Ethan gets a look like he's trying to figure out how to murder him and stash his body where it'll never be found.

His jealousy is strangely reassuring, but I try not to think about it too much.

Every now and then, I stare at him and fantasize. Replay all the ways he lit me up on that incredible night.

At those times I think it's a tragedy it won't happen again.

When he catches me staring, I know he feels it, too. My countdown clock gets louder. It makes me restless and impatient.

Horny.

Oh, so very horny.

Would it matter if we did it again? We survived it once, didn't we? In the big scheme of things, it's just sex.

Right?

I jiggle my leg as I watch Holt and Avery argue across the table in the cafeteria. He's so freaking hot when he argues. I want to suck the acid right off his tongue.

"Fuck off, Avery. In 2006, *Crash* deserved to win Best Picture. No doubt."

"That's bullshit, man. *Brokeback Mountain* should have won. Are you kidding me? Two straight guys playing queer? You only had to hear Erika gushing over you and Connor to know how much people eat that shit up."

"Erika loved it because we were fucking flawless. It's not my fault you couldn't fake enjoying being sodomized. Maybe you need to practice that."

"Why don't you teach me, sweetheart? Connor said you're a sensitive lover. Best he's ever had."

"That's true. Even used the warming lube."

He's talking about sex. Why does he think this is acceptable? Even though he's joking, my imagination is exploding with scenarios. In all of them, lube is redundant.

"Care to comment, Taylor?"

"Uh . . . what?"

Avery grins at me. He's up to no good. "You've had firsthand experience, right? Is Holt a good lover? Or is it all a big act? Come on, be honest. He couldn't find your G-spot with both hands and sat-nav, am I right?"

"Shut up, Jack," Ethan says as his smile fades.

Avery laughs and slaps the table. "Aw, come on! You guys have been broken up for a million years. Surely we can talk about this stuff now without Holt's head exploding. Give us the deets. Did he rock your world?"

Three months ago, this question would have made me apoplectic. Now, I'm kind of tempted to answer it, simply to see Ethan's reaction.

When I don't answer, Jack gives up on me. "What about you, Holt? Give us something! On a scale of one to ten, where do you put Taylor on the hotness meter?"

Ethan laughs and glances at me as he shakes his head. Crawling pinkness slides up his neck and onto his cheeks.

"Rate her!" Avery says, goading him. He starts up a chant. "*Rate her! Rate her! Rate her!*" Lucas and Zoe join him. So do Miranda and Aiyah. Random passersby, who have no idea what the hell we're talking about, stop and clap.

"For fuck's sake." Ethan runs a hand through his hair. The chanting continues. "You're a prick, Avery. Okay, okay! Shut up, and I'll tell you!"

The clapping dies down and Ethan looks at me even as he talks to Jack.

"You really want to know where Taylor sits on the hotness scale?"

"Hell, yes!" Jack is almost vibrating with excitement.

Ethan's stare paints every inch of my skin with tiny shivers.

"On a scale of one to ten . . ."

"Yeah?"

Ethan licks his lips. I do the same. I think I stop breathing.

"She's about a thirty-five."

Everyone exhales, me included.

For once, Avery's speechless.

It doesn't last long.

"Jesus Ass-Slapping Christ. Seriously?"

"Seriously." Ethan hasn't stopped looking at me, and I don't think I could look away if I tried.

"Taylor? Care to comment?" Jack asks.

"Not really." I'm too busy swallowing excess saliva.

"Don't make me chant again. Just give Holt a number."

"Out of ten?"

"Yeah."

"For sex?"

"Yeah!"

Ethan raises one perfectly sexy eyebrow. I reward it with a smug smile. "Ten."

Avery's jaw hits the floor. "Are you shitting me? Why does he get a ten?"

"Because that's how many orgasms he gave me in one night." The words are out of my mouth before I have a chance to be embarrassed.

Avery laughs. "No, really."

"Really."

His face falls, and he looks between us and blinks. Everyone is very quiet. Zoe is staring at Ethan like he's the incarnation of a mythical sex god.

"Well, fuck me. And you guys broke up, *WHY*?!"

It's a good question. Sitting here knowing the myriad of things he seems to be thinking about doing to me, I have no good answer.

Before I even get to the party, I know he's there. Every part of me is tingling in anticipation. I've waxed, shaved, and exfoliated so thoroughly, I feel frictionless. Like a shark. Hungry and ready for a victim.

Only one victim will do.

It's going to be tonight. It has to be. I can't take not having him anymore.

I've dressed the part in a skintight black sheath I've borrowed from Ruby, along with heeled boots. It's a little more dressy than my usual jeans and T-shirt, but I need every advantage. If he's going to try to resist, this dress will convince him.

As soon as I walk through the door, he's staring at me. He's trying to hide his desperation, but it's written all over his face and in every tense muscle that flexes as he ogles me. I don't let him see how violently he affects me. Showing him all my cards isn't part of this game. I feign disinterest and graze his crotch with my butt as I pass him on the way to the kitchen.

Not playing fair but definitely playing to win.

He's drinking beer. I grab one, too. Then I brush past him again on the way out. He makes a sound of frustration, but he doesn't touch me.

He's just delaying the inevitable.

Back in the living room, Avery is setting up shots of tequila. Holt and I share a look. It speaks volumes. Without talking, we line up for our turn. I grab his hand, lick it, then cover it in salt. Lick it again to make it perfectly clean. Graze it with my teeth. His expression is pure sex as I sip and suck. He uses my clavicle. Sprinkles me. Sucks me clean. Makes me feel dirty in a good way.

We line up again.

This time we use other people, because we don't want our friends becoming suspicious. We watch each other, though.

The shots are an excuse, and we both know it. We want to lose control. We're both strung so tight, the only choice is to snap.

Still, if his brain has anything to do with it, he'll get out of here before he does something stupid with me. His brain is fooling itself. Already, I can see layers of protection sliding away as the booze works on him.

It's only a matter of time.

Three shots later, I can't hide that I'm staring, while I imagine the parts I want to touch. He makes my mouth dry. I nurse a bottle of beer and suck on it suggestively. The front of his pants swells. He's trying to carry on a conversation with Lucas and failing, big-time.

When someone cranks up the music, I dance. I close my eyes and sway to the beat. There are bodies all around me, but as soon as he's there, I feel it in my belly. It's a low, hungry burn that will only be soothed by him. I find him behind me without even opening my eyes. He sways against me, one arm around my waist. I wind my fingers through his hair and tug as his groan vibrates into my back. I wonder if people are gossiping about us yet. Even if they are, I'm beyond caring.

He drops his head to my shoulder, a supplicant in the making. I turn and whisper, "I can feel how hard you are." He tightens his arm around my waist as he pulls me back against his erection.

"You walk into this party looking like sex in woman form and expect me to be anything but hard? That's fucking laughable."

I grind into him. Make him exhale between his teeth. Then I move away and turn to look at him as I dance with others to try to disguise how oblivious I am to anyone but him. Another arm winds around my waist and pulls me back to a firm chest. Shorter than Ethan. Smells good.

Connor.

"What the hell did you do to Holt?" he whispers as he spins me around to face him. "He looks like he wants to murder you."

I turn to look at Ethan. Yeah, he looks murderous, but it isn't aimed at me.

"Oh, you know," I say as I take a step back. "He's uptight, as usual." More than usual. Way more.

"You need me to . . . you know . . . protect you, or whatever?"

I almost laugh. If anyone needs protection tonight, it's Ethan. I'm the predator. He's my well-endowed prey. "No, I'm good. Thanks for the offer, though." I hug him, short and perfunctory. By the time I turn around, I've forgotten he was even there.

Then I push through the crowd and head toward the bathroom. I brush past Ethan on the way and run my hand across the front of his pants. Squeeze. Keep going. Don't look back.

I get inside the bathroom seconds before he's there, pushing me backward and slamming the door behind us. He grabs me, equal parts angry and horny.

Before he has a chance to speak I push him against the wall and kiss him. At last I get to show him the full extent of my need. It only takes a second for him to kiss me back, then all bets are off. We're rough and demanding, and even as he mutters that we shouldn't, he knows very well we're going to. Within three seconds, I have his jeans unbuttoned, and he's in my hand. So hard and perfect.

I squeeze, then pump him gently. His head hits the wall. I kneel in front of him and look up. A single pleading moan signals his utter surrender.

"Fuck. Please, Cassie." My ego explodes. This is the man who said we couldn't be friends. Who swore we shouldn't be lovers. Who broke my heart by listening to his ridiculous paranoia. Now, he's begging me to put my mouth on him. Pleading with his eyes and soft fingers on my face. His noble intentions are forgotten in the face of the things he knows I can make him feel.

I smile up at him. Sex is power. Sex lets me have this part of him and believe it's enough.

He begs me again, and I give in. His legs almost give out. I smile even as I take him in farther. I'll never not marvel over the texture of him. The delicious weight. The tight noise he makes in the back of his throat every time I sweep my tongue over him.

Within a minute, I have him on the edge. I leave him there. Stand.

Step back. He takes a moment to realize before he opens his eyes and delves into his jeans pocket. Then he rips the condom packet open with his teeth and rolls it on in record time.

Within seconds, he has my panties down and off. No foreplay. None is needed. That's what we've been doing for weeks now. He pushes me against the wall and pulls my leg up to his hip, then kisses me hard. He's rough, and I welcome it. I know he hates how much control I have when we're like this. He wants to punish me. All he achieves is getting me more aroused.

Then he's there, and pushing, and inside, and oh . . . oh . . . God, I needed this. Him. We both freeze, mid-kiss. I open my eyes and pull back. He's looking at me, frowning and trying to stay detached. But how can he when we're joined so completely?

He moves, slowly, sinuously. Takes his time and revels in my response. Nothing seems quite so black and white anymore. I cling to him as he enfolds me. We kiss and moan while we pant in time with the rhythm of our bodies. It all feels good. So right. Like we were born to be part of each other this way.

I shake my head to clear it of thoughts beyond this moment. Try to ignore the yawning hole that's spewing unwanted feelings into my chest.

I shut down and concentrate on the feeling of him thrusting. Where we're joined, the physical pleasure screams almost loud enough to drown out everything else.

Almost.

Our pace becomes frantic. The rougher he is, the harder it is for me to stay quiet.

After being so strung out for so long, neither of us lasts very long. Certainly not long enough to fully purge all of our tension. My orgasm is blinding. His seems to go on forever. I kiss him as he groans through it and let some of his essence bleed through a tiny chink in my armor. I hide it away and pretend it's not the most precious thing I own.

When we've both recovered, he tries to stay inside of me, but I have to get out. I've had my fix, and that's all I need.

Just sex.

I don't need him.

I clean myself up and leave without saying a word.

Just take my waning power and go.

EIGHTEEN

POWERPLAY

Present Day
New York City, New York
Graumann Theater

It's our first day rehearsing on the main stage in the theater. As I step through the door, a thrill runs through me. Being in a theater is always a magical experience. There's just something about the energy of it. The peeling walls and thick wool curtains. Memorabilia from decades of productions. Scrawled messages on the bricks backstage, cataloging the history and traditions of combining art and imagination.

Our production intern, Cody, meets me and hands me a cup of coffee before he shows me to my dressing room. Like most dressing rooms, it's not glamorous, but it resonates with the vibrations of all the performers who've been there before. I take a minute to just sit in front of the mirrors and close my eyes to drink in the ambiance.

I haven't spoken to Ethan since Sunday night, although I've thought of little else. I spent all of Monday and Tuesday reading his journals and alternating between wanting to smash him in the face and wanting to fuck him thoroughly.

I couldn't bring myself to look at his journals from our senior year. Right now, I think it would do more harm than good.

I hear someone behind me. When I turn, I find him there, leaning against the door frame and staring with an intensity that makes me look away.

"Hey."

"Hi."

The weight of a million questions hangs in the air, but he doesn't say anything. He wants to know what I think about what I've read. I'd tell him, but I have no clue. He wants to know if it's making things better between us, if understanding equals absolution. It doesn't, but it's not by choice. If I were able to banish every ounce of mistrust in the blink of an eye, this whole situation would be resolved by now. I'd be healed, he'd be grateful, and we'd spend countless nights gasping our happiness into each other's skin.

That would be nice but I'm not there yet.

"You okay?" he says, still in the doorway.

I stand and go to look through my costumes. It doesn't take long. I only have three. Still, I graze my hands over all the seams, suddenly nervous. Some of it has to do with him and some with the realization that in three days, we'll be performing in front of a preview audience. Either way, I'm terrified of disappointing someone.

"I guess," I say. "Feel a little bit like I'm going to vomit."

"Me, too."

"You're hiding it better than I am."

"I think I'm just more used to it by now. Want to snuggle?"

His question catches me off guard. My hand freezes on the sleeve of my dress.

"Uh . . ."

I feel him behind me before he runs his finger along my costume, just above my frozen hand. When he speaks, his breath is warm against my ear. "It used to help, remember? Both of us. Plus, I think I'll go insane if I don't touch you. Strictly platonic, of course."

I can't look up. Can't even touch his finger.

"Cassie?" He touches my hair and smoothes it back over my shoulder. "I'm not asking you for sex. Or even a kiss. I just want to hold you."

It's not just holding. It never was. It's intimate.

I'm saved from turning him down when Elissa appears at the door.

"Hey, you two. We're about to start the tech run. Can I get you on-stage in costume, please? Be prepared to be patient. Marco likes to take his runs nice and slow."

She disappears, and I step away from Ethan. He sighs and hands me my costume.

"This is what you're wearing for Act One?"

I nod.

"No wonder I fall in love with you."

He gives me a smile that's part affection, part patience.

For some reason, it makes me bristle and feel way too vulnerable.

He leaves, and I try to shake off the negativity. I don't need it today. I need to be focused and cool.

In control.

"Now, unbutton his shirt. Good. And put your head where it would be if you were kissing his chest. Okay, great. And hold that."

Ethan tightens and releases his hold on my hips as I keep my lips millimeters away from his chest. Marco's muttering instructions to the lighting designer, complaining that the spotlight's too shallow and the sidelights are too far forward. He wants the sex scene to be shadowy and moody, but apparently the only thing in the theater that's moody right now is him.

This tech rehearsal is moving at a snail's pace. I've never worked with a director who's so hung up on lighting and positioning. It's like he's doing stop-motion animation.

I focus on the smattering of hair on Ethan's chest and try to block out how much his scent is affecting me. It's not easy. Right now, I'm wound tighter than a Swiss watch, and he's trying so hard to respect my personal space, I want to punch him.

"Cassie?"

"Hmmm."

"I'm going to ask you something, and I want you to promise you'll answer honestly."

I'm immediately wary and look up at him.

"Cassie! Put your head back down. Lance is focusing the specials. Don't move!"

Holt groans. "Fuck this fucking tech rehearsal."

I stare at his chest again.

"Move your head closer!"

I dip my head. My lips accidentally graze skin. Ethan swears.

"What's your question?" I ask.

"Did you happen to have a psychotic break recently and decide to slowly murder me? Because I swear to fucking God, having your mouth hovering over my chest without actually kissing it is a cruel and frustrating version of hell I'd rather not be a part of."

He's so whiny when he says it, I laugh.

"Fuck," he says and exhales. "And now you blow air across my nipple? If I'm not dead already, then please, kill me now."

"Okay, Ethan, take off her shirt."

He sighs. "And the torment keeps coming."

He unbuttons my shirt and pushes it open. Then he closes his eyes and whispers, "Please, God, let Marco tell me to freeze with my hands on her boobs. Please."

"That's not in the blocking for this part."

He glares down at me. "Quiet, woman. I'm conversing with a higher being. Don't distract him with unhelpful logic."

He's slowly raising his hands to my chest when Marco calls out, "Okay, Ethan, pick her up."

"Goddammit."

He wraps his arms around me and lifts me, and I lock my ankles behind his back. It feels weird doing this in disjointed sections. Also, without the kissing. He migrates his hands down to cup my ass cheeks. I raise an eyebrow.

"Just getting leverage," he says, deadpan. "It has nothing to do with me wanting to grope your ass."

"And yet, you are groping my ass."

"Well, semi-groping. Please note my hands are over, not under, your skirt."

Please note, my body wants him to be under the skirt, fingering the elastic of my panties. Distracting me from all the conflicting emotions I'm too much of a coward to deal with.

The lights change again and Marco yells, "For the love of God, Lance! They look like a giant two-headed Quasimodo! Can I please get some blasted definition in the cross lighting? This is ridiculous!"

Lighting assistants rush around sidestage as Holt lowers me until I'm settled fully onto his crotch. Once again, I give him the eyebrow.

"What?" His innocent act has gotten better over the years, but it doesn't fool me. "It's easier to hold you like this."

"That's because I'm resting on your erection."

"I know. It's like a shelf."

I shake my head. "You have zero shame, you know that?"

"That's not true. I have a great deal of shame. I've just given it the day off. I've been working it hard recently, and now it's all exhausted and needs to recuperate."

"Unlike your penis."

"He rarely needs to recuperate. Not around you, anyway."

He sounds relaxed, but the way he's breathing and the subtle movement of his hips tell me otherwise. Seeing him like this, barely restrained, makes me want to torture him even more. Marco helps with my mission.

"Okay, Ethan, move her to the bed. Cassie, I want him between your legs."

"Oh, for fuck's sake."

Ethan lowers me onto the bed, then crawls between my legs. I pull off his shirt and wrap my arms around his neck as he settles against my crotch. He groans and drops his head onto my shoulder.

"This is fucking ridiculous. Why can't it be like a movie set where they get stand-ins to do this stuff?"

"More blue!" Marco says. "And bring up the pinks from behind!"

I try to hold myself still. If I didn't hate tech rehearsals before, this experience is enough to make me despise them. With every minute that passes, I feel more out of control. My instincts are telling me to take back my power. Fuck him. Let body-quaking sex dull all of my other thought processes.

Simplify things in the most complicated way possible.

"You okay?" he says as he leans on his elbows. "I'm not crushing you?"

"You're fine."

"Thanks. I've been working out. I was wondering when you'd notice. You're fine, too."

"Are you trying to be infuriating today?"

"Nope. Just comes naturally. Are you trying to drive me insane by moving like that?"

"Like what?"

He looks between us. I realize I'm rocking my pelvis against him. Just a little. Just enough to take the edge off the ache.

He lets out a low groan.

"Cassie . . ." He closes his eyes and puts more weight against me.

The added pressure is nice, but it stops my movements. "Have some pity, woman. You're killing me."

The lights brighten a little.

"Okay, Ethan," Marco says, "some thrusting please."

Ethan lets out a short laugh. "Thrusting. Of course. Just what I need right now."

He fake thrusts while keeping his erection away from me.

Evil thoughts fill my brain as I stroke the back of his neck and bring one hand down to his chest to graze his nipple.

His rhythm falters. "Stop it."

"Why?" I trail a finger down his abs, and his face turns red.

"You know why." His voice has dropped an octave. It's full of breath and dripping with want.

"Tell me."

"Cassie . . . please . . . not now."

I'm Aphrodite again. He can't hide how much he wants me, and it's intoxicating.

"Don't you want me to touch you? Don't you want me to be your girlfriend again? Break that three-year-long dry spell?"

I brush against the line of him through his pants. He hisses and swears. I smile and keep going.

"This isn't fucking funny. We're working."

I press my palm fully against him. His whole body tenses.

Ahhhh, there it is. The rush of power. My dominion over him is written all over his face. The way his eyelids flutter and close.

"Fuck . . ."

I keep stroking him, and he looks like he's being electrocuted. He grunts and drops his pelvis down, which traps my hand between us. I squeeze him, because it's all I can do. Apparently it's enough. He stiffens and clamps his eyes shut, then clenches his jaw to stifle a moan. After long seconds of tension, he relaxes and glares at me.

I try to play innocent, but I'm not as good as he is. After what I just did, that much is obvious.

He grabs my hand from between us and plants it at the side of my head. He's pissed. Really pissed.

"That was out of line," he whispers. "What the fuck did I do to deserve that?"

I look down, too embarrassed to answer. What the hell am I doing?

"You don't need to do this," he says, and it's clear he's trying to hide how angry he really is. "Whatever game this is, just fucking stop. You don't need it. You own me. You always have. I thought reading my journals would have proven that to you."

"Okay, everyone," Elissa says over the PA system. "That's a thirty-minute break while we reset for the next scene, thank you."

Ethan climbs off me and grabs his shirt. Then he stalks offstage without a backward glance.

My face burns as regret and guilt slither through my veins. I throw my arm over my eyes, as if I can hide from myself.

He's trying so hard to show me he's changed, and I'm determined to drag him back into our old patterns. Why? Because they're familiar? Because I feel safe in them? What the hell good is that going to do anyone, especially me?

"Cassie?"

I open my eyes to see Elissa standing over me.

"You okay?"

I have the urge to giggle hysterically. The one thing I'm absolutely not is okay. "Sure, Elissa. Great."

She nods, but the hard press of her mouth tells me she's not buying it. "Uh-huh. So, Ethan looks ragey. What did you do?"

I sit up and run my hands through my hair. Ethan's shame might be on vacation, but mine is very much present. "Oh, you know. The usual. Unleashed my inner bitch on him."

She nods again. Her disapproval engulfs me like a noxious cloud.

"As your stage manager, I have to remind you that maintaining professional conduct with all members of this company is required. As Ethan's sister, I want you to know that he's dragged himself to hell and back to become a better person for you, and if you know he has zero chance of making it work, tell him now and let him get on with his life."

"By hell and back, do you mean the accident?"

She frowns. "He told you about that?"

"Grudgingly."

"Then you know what he's been through."

I nod. "I do. And I want things to work with us, but I can't change overnight."

"I know that. Neither could he, but he wanted to. Do you?"

Marco walks across the stage, clearly agitated. "Elissa! I need you. I have every intention of hunting Lance down and flaying his skin from his bones. I need you to stop me."

"Coming."

She leaves, and it's just me, sitting on a fake bed in a fake house, trying to figure out how to make all the fake parts of me line up to form a real person.

I knock on the dressing room door.

There's no response. When I enter, Ethan mutters, "I didn't say to come in."

"Yeah, well, you didn't say 'fuck off,' either, so I figured I'd take a chance."

I close the door and lean against it. He's sitting on the couch opposite the mirrors, head back, arm thrown over his eyes. He's changed into his own jeans, which is understandable, considering what just happened.

"What do you want, Cassie?"

"To talk."

"No, I mean, what do you want from me? Tell me what I'm doing wrong. Because I'm really trying here, but it feels like all I'm doing is finding new ways to lose you."

He doesn't move. Doesn't look at me. I press my back into the door. It reminds me a backbone is there for a reason and not just to hang my bones on.

"I'm sorry."

I whisper it. Ashamed. Afraid after all this time, I'm not good enough for him. That he's now a better person than I ever was.

"You don't need to apologize," he says as he rubs his eyes. "I just had a grand romantic fantasy of how things would be when we got intimate again. Strangely enough, blowing my load fully clothed during a tech run wasn't part of the plan."

He still doesn't move. I go sit next to him and pull his arm away from his face. He's flushed. I don't know if it's from embarrassment or anger. Maybe both.

"Yeah, I kind of missed that memo. Sorry for orgasming you against your will."

He laughs. "It's ironic, considering the amount of times I've practically begged you to touch me like that. I'd almost forgotten how quickly you can make me come when you put your mind to it. It's mortifying."

He's still not looking at me. Instead, he looks at his hands as he fiddles with the hem of my skirt and occasionally brushes my thigh.

"I didn't know if I still affected you like that," I say. "I thought . . . maybe . . . you'd outgrown it."

Now he looks at me, incredulous. He opens and closes his mouth and blinks. Then he frowns at the floor, the wall, the mirrors, before he makes a disbelieving noise and looks back at me.

"You've met me, right? I'm Ethan. Late-night drunk-dialer. Compulsive ass-groper. Shameless boob-ogler. Forever-erect-in-your-presence serial masturbator. How the hell could I possibly outgrow that? If anything, it's gotten worse over the years. Did you not just witness me coming from you fondling my cock for less than three minutes?"

His complete bewilderment makes me laugh.

He shakes his head. "Crazy fucking statement. Not attracted to you? Jesus." He pauses. "So mystery solved. Was it gratifying to see me completely lose my shit in record time?"

"A little."

He nods. "At least you're being honest."

Honest. Right. He used to tell me I'd be horrified if I knew the stuff that went through his head every day. Now the reverse is true. Still, I know nothing's going to improve between us if I keep things from him.

I take a deep breath and say, "Elissa said I need to figure out if I can make this work, and if I can't, I need to let you get on with your life."

He turns to me, his expression intense and on edge.

"I love my sister, but she really needs to stop giving you sucky advice."

"She's trying to protect you."

"I don't need protecting."

"Don't you? Have you considered that maybe you're placing all your hope in something that's doomed to fail?"

That makes him pause. He studies me. "No. Have you?"

I want to laugh. "Ethan, that's *all* I've thought about for the last three years. I mean, I know the accident inspired you to better yourself and try to get me back or whatever, but until we started this show, I didn't know that. As far as I was concerned, we were over. We'd been over for a long time. I had my future all planned out, and as painful as it was to admit, you weren't going to be a part of it. Now, I have to entertain the possibility that you've changed and will stick around? I mean, come on. It's difficult to process. Did you ever think that your epic plan to get us back together should have included consulting me?"

"I tried to tell you in the e-mails."

"But you didn't. You told me you were getting help and that you wanted to be part of my life again, but you spoke about being friends, nothing more. You didn't even tell me you loved me, remember?"

He rubs his eyes. "I thought I had it all figured out, but . . . fuck, Cassie, I'm sorry. I'm kind of new to this whole winning-back-the-love-of-my-life thing."

He says it so easily. Like it's not one of the most momentous things he's ever uttered.

Love of my life.

It's such an cliché, but that's exactly what we are to each other. Even if we both walk away now and end up in other relationships, we'll forever be that. Some people never find it. Yet, here it is right in front of me, and I have no idea how to keep it.

"Cassie, remember how pissed you used to get when I was thinking important stuff but wouldn't tell you?"

"Yeah."

"Well, I can tell you're doing that right now. Care to share?"

I sigh. "I'm thinking that . . . I really want to change, but I don't know how, and part of me thinks it might be too late, anyway."

"That's not true."

"What if it is? Denying how badly this could end up doesn't mean it's not going to happen. I think you believe that if you ignore that I'm broken, it will somehow make it not true. But it is."

"Cassie—"

I stand and pace. He wants to know what I'm thinking? All of a sudden, I want to give it to him.

"And I sometimes think the only reason you want me back is because sexually, we're spectacular. But what if we get back together, and months from now we realize that apart from great sex, we really have nothing in common? Then we'll have gone through all of this for nothing."

"That's bullshit, and you know it."

"Is it? Maybe we're just one of those volatile couples who are supposed to fuck like animals for a few months, then go their separate ways. We've never really had the chance to get each other out of our systems. But what if we did? What if we finally realized all the crap that fueled our problems also fueled our passion, and without it we're dead in the water?"

He stares at me. "You don't honestly believe that."

"Maybe I do. I don't even know anymore."

He shakes his head and smiles.

Smiles.

Why doesn't he look terrified? I just spewed all of my crazy at him, and he seems completely calm.

What the fuck did that therapist do to him? Did she have all of his fear and panic surgically removed?

"Cassie, come here."

He's still so calm, he's like freaking Buddha. If Tristan were here, he'd have a Zen boner.

"Please," he says, as I stew in my agitation. "I need to show you something."

I go and stand in front of him. He takes my hands and strokes them gently, then pulls me forward until I'm straddling him.

Now I'm agitated and aroused. Not sure what this is going to prove.

"I thought we were keeping this platonic," I say as he grips my hips.

"We are."

I grind onto his growing erection. "Uh-huh. That guy is making a liar out of you."

He wraps his arms around me and pulls me against his chest. The contact is almost too much. A vicious ache immediately grows, reinforcing my point about our sexual chemistry driving the disaster train of our relationship. I want to soothe the burn, but he tightens his arms and just hugs me. Breathes into my throat and wraps me in reassurance as he urges me to relax more with every exhale.

"Just breathe," he whispers. "Ignore everything else."

I close my eyes and try to do as he says.

Within a few minutes my lust has ebbed to a vague simmer, but in its place is something else. An effervescence in my blood.

He strokes my back, and I melt into him. He leans back, and I follow. After a while the rest of the world ceases to exist.

Our universe is the hush of air between his lips and my throat. The brush of his fingers on my neck.

"Do you feel this?" he whispers. "This is what makes us keep coming back, despite everything we've gone through. This is why I had to change, and why, despite how much I hurt you, you can't walk away. The way we sink into each other. The way I can't tell my heartbeat from yours. We have this perfect rhythm, whenever we're together, and *that's* the essence of us. It's not just about sex. It's about this."

He pushes me back, so I can see his face. "Cassie, I want to be with you. Always. If that involves us being naked and making love in a hundred different ways, every day for the rest of our lives, that's fantastic. If it involves us sitting and talking, wearing barbed wire and cast-iron body suits, that's fantastic, too. I just want you. Now. A week from now. A year. A decade. Whenever you're ready. What I want is never going to change. It's you. Just you. Naked or clothed, doesn't matter to me."

I take in a ragged breath. What he's saying . . .

He strokes my arms. Keeps me grounded in this moment.

"That's why I haven't had sex for three years," he says as he runs his hands up my shoulders and caresses the back of my neck. "There were plenty of girls who reminded me of you. Similar hair, or eyes, or smile. If I'd squinted, I could have easily pretended they were you. But I didn't want a lookalike. I haven't been able to have sex without emotion since you, and considering you own all of my emotions, who the fuck was I going to have sex with? From the moment I met you, it was only ever going to be you."

I lean my forehead against his. "But—"

"No buts. If our relationship was based only on sex, do you think we'd have gone through all the shit we have? Sex is easy. It's an itch that needs to be scratched, and as much as I love having sex with you, what I want from you isn't easy. It's messy and complicated, and it's filled with so much fucking passion, I don't have a clue how to cope with it all. But I find a way, because I love you. And love is hard, but it's worth it. *You're* worth it. And I hope one day you'll realize I'm worth it, too."

I'm too choked up to speak.

I know he's worth it. I've always known that. I knew it before he did, I just need to stop doubting we can make this work.

"Ethan? Your therapist . . . would she maybe take me on?"

He frowns. "I don't know. Is that something you want to try?"

I nod. "I need to change. But I can't do it by myself. I need help. I don't want to be . . . like this . . . anymore."

He pulls me into a hug, and his breath is ragged against my throat as I stroke his hair. "I'm sorry."

"I know."

"We're going to get through this. Have no doubt."

I squeeze him tighter. "That's the plan."

NINETEEN

EMOTIONAL EVOLUTION

Four Years Earlier
Aberdeen, Washington

The thing about developing an addiction is that it happens so quietly, you don't know how much trouble you're in until it's too late. It tiptoes through the rooms of your mind and body, gently inserting hooks and strings into every cell, until you don't know where you end and it begins. And untangling that web is nearly impossible.

By the end of our second year at The Grove, my sexual encounters with Ethan have increased in frequency, but I tell myself I have it under control. Whenever we stray into areas that feel too intimate, I go cold turkey for a couple of days to remind myself he's a luxury, not a necessity.

It's not until I go home for the summer that it occurs to me I may be in trouble.

For the first few days, I'm fine. I sleep in. Spend time with my parents. Listen to music and pray for sunshine.

By the end of the first week, I'm antsy. Restless and horny. I think about him way too much. His face. His smell. What I wouldn't give for just one hit of his smell.

Halfway through the second week, I take a job at the local diner, partly as a distraction to stop me thinking about him, and partly to get me out of the house so I won't have to listen to my parents argue.

By the end of the third week, I'm in full-blown withdrawal. Irritable. Intolerant. Needing a fix of someone who's on the other side of the country and pissed at everything and everyone that's not him.

I guess he misses me, too, because on my way home from work at the beginning of the fourth week, I receive a text.

<Hey. Elissa just dragged me along to see Wicked *on Broadway. Ashamed to say I enjoyed it. Be right back, handing in my man card. Hope your summer is less lame.>*

And just like that, I'm high. Embarrassingly so. I do a little dance and skip up the stairs to the house.

Mom and Dad stop bickering long enough to welcome me home, and I head straight up to my room.

<Elissa dragged you, huh? Don't lie. Always suspected you're a closet music theater fan.>

A minute later, I receive a reply.

<Yes, you've discovered my dark secret. When I'm alone I put on the Funny Girl *soundtrack & do my best Babs impersonation. Forever ashamed.>*

I laugh before catching myself. *Dammit. Not good.*

I miss having sex with him, that's all. Not the way he brushes my hand when he passes in the hallway. Not the affectionate glances he gives me when he knows no one else is watching. Not the way he regularly drags me into stairwells, or bathrooms, or shadowy corners of the costume storeroom just so he can kiss me.

It's just the sex I miss.

I close my eyes and try to calm my racing pulse as I resist the urge to text him again.

Admitting you have a problem is the first step.

I admit nothing.

I don't miss him.

I don't.

"For crying out loud, Cassie, I'm going to start calling you Charcoal."

Exasperation is leaking into Ruby's tone, and even over the phone, I can imagine her eye roll.

"What? Why?"

"Because you're playing with so much fire, you're going to be incinerated."

We've been on the phone for more than an hour. She's told me all about a guy she met over the summer, and after she assailed me with far too many details of their sexual exploits, she started grilling me about Holt. To say she disapproves of our arrangement would be a massive understatement.

After Ethan and I started hooking up, I tried to keep it a secret from her, but everything went south a few weeks later when she came home unexpectedly to find us naked in the living room. I don't think I've ever seen Ruby so angry. She stood there and ripped into both of us. Didn't even let us get dressed, just stood there yelling while Holt and I did our best to cover ourselves with throw pillows.

After that, she didn't talk to me for two days. She was mad about me getting back with Ethan, of course, but I think she was even madder that I lied about it. Ever since then, I've vowed never to keep stuff from her, which kind of sucks, because when she asks me if I'm having feelings for him again, I have to tell her the truth.

"I don't know. Maybe."

She makes a disapproving sound.

"What am I supposed to do, Ruby? Cut off all contact?"

"I'm not saying that. I'm just saying to be careful. If you can't handle being straight up fuck-buddies, then maybe you should cool it for a while. I mean, he hasn't magically lost all his baggage, has he?"

"No, but he's the one who started texting me. I'm not making any moves here. I'm just reacting to his."

"That's going to be exactly zero consolation if he gets scared again and bails."

"I know. But he seems . . . different. Bolder. Happier. I don't know."

"Yeah, well, I suppose I can't complain too much. You have been a lot less mopey since you started banging him. Although, you owe me money for all the condoms you've stolen."

"I'll pay you back. Plus, I'm on the pill now."

"Really? So you two can bang bareback? Great. Can't wait to walk in on that."

"I've apologized for that a million times."

"Doesn't erase the mental images."

"We weren't even having sex."

"You were about to. By the way, did I ever congratulate you on Holt's cock? I meant to. Very nice. One of the nicest I've seen, in fact."

Despite my newfound sexual confidence, I still manage to blush. "Well, with the sheer volume of cocks you've seen, that's a huge compliment."

"It sure is. Huuuge."

We both laugh. I miss her so freaking much.

Unfortunately, I still miss Ethan more.

It's Friday night, and the diner is packed. I'm getting slammed from every side, and although I like to think I can handle it, I'm getting more frazzled by the minute.

"Order up!"

I swipe hair away from my forehead and hurry to collect the plates from the pass. Back and forth. Smile and drop.

"There you go. Enjoy."

The dinner rush seems to go on forever, and by the time I get a break at eight forty-five p.m., I'm exhausted and starving. I grab a burger and head out the back door to eat it. My phone buzzes with a message.

<Had a great idea today. Made up a T-shirt that said, "I got boned at The Museum of Natural History." Took it to Threadless & made a million dollars. Avery bought a dozen. Dropping out of drama school to become creepy bar-hopping douche who marries hotel heiress & becomes famous for his giant schlong in grainy sex tape. It was nice knowing you. Sincerely, Ethan (aka The T-shirt Baron).>

I laugh and shake my head as I text back.

<Hate to burst your bubble, Baron, but Chandler from Friends came up w/that quote years ago. Guess you'll have to stay in trenches w/the rest of us plebs. Sucks to be you.>
<Fuck. Ok, plan B. Get own reality show & get arrested for DUI. Then wait for movie offers. Gotta go. Booze to drink. Easy chicks to bang. (Just kidding. Only easy chick I'm banging is you. Well, not right now 'cause you're on other side of country, but . . . when you get back. Yes?)>

Goddammit.

How the hell do I reply to that?

<Maybe.>
<Don't tease me. It's cruel. Just say yes. Or, fuck, yes.>

And I'm back to laughing.

<Fuck, yes.>

<**(Pretend I've invented fist pump emoticon & insert here)** See you in 4 wks. I'll be the one w/the massive boner.> He signs it with a smiley face with the tag, *<That's my **Looking forward to getting laid emoticon**>*

I laugh again. All of a sudden I've forgotten about the sweat running down my spine, the ache in my feet, and the smear of grill grease on the front of my shirt. Thanks to him, I'm smiling like an idiot, and when I go back inside, one of the other waitresses asks if I just got lucky in the parking lot.

My parents are yelling again. Bickering like children over inconsequential crap. Nothing. Everything. I'd go out, but as usual this summer, it's raining. I put in my headphones and turn up my music.

I'm listening to Radiohead. Ethan always puts it on when I'm at his place. When I listen to it, I can almost pretend he's in the room with me as he wraps his arms around me and pulls me against his chest.

My phone rings, and when I see his name, my mouth goes completely dry.

God.

He's calling me.

He hasn't called before. He usually texts.

I shouldn't be this excited.

I let it ring. Don't want to seem too eager.

Two . . . three times it rings. I pick up on the fourth and feign nonchalance.

"Hello?"

"Hey."

"Uh . . . hey. Who is this?" *Good one, Cassie. Keep him on his toes.*

"It's Ethan. Your caller ID would have told you that. Or do you just have me under *World's Greatest Lay*?"

Hearing his voice does strange things to me. But I'd never let him know that, so I clear my throat and try to sound bored.

"Oh, hey."

"Hey."

This is awkward. People who aren't us do this.

"Why are you calling?"

"Uh . . . Well . . . I don't know, I was just . . ." The final word sounds like "jusht."

"Ethan, are you drunk?"

"Not totally."

"Drunk is like pregnant. You either are or you aren't."

"Then I'm not."

"Drunk or pregnant?"

"Both. Although, I don't know. I've missed my period. Pregnancy could be a possibility."

I smile without meaning to. "Is that right?"

"Yeah. What are the other symptoms of pregnancy? I'm worried now."

When I close my eyes, I can almost picture him lying on his bed, tugging at his dark, unruly hair. In my vision, he's shirtless, and the hand that isn't torturing his hair is grazing over the grooves between his abs.

I realize that in reality, at least one hand needs to be holding his phone, but the fantasy is hotter, so I roll with it.

"Cassie?"

"Hmmm?"

"I'm having a pregnancy scare here. You're supposed to be reassuring me." His words run together a little. It's kind of adorable.

"Okay, sorry. Well, I didn't really listen in freshman health class, but I think the first sign of pregnancy is fatigue. Are you tired?"

"Yes. Very."

"Irritable?"

"Fuck, yeah. Super irritable." I can almost hear him frown.

"Nothing new there."

"Shut up."

"Case in point."

"What else?" he asks.

"Sore breasts?"

"Hmmm. Hang on."

I hear rustling. "What are you doing?"

"Taking off my shirt, so I can check my breasts. Wait . . . mmm . . . yes. They are a little sore."

More fantasy images. This time of him running his hand over his naked chest.

It does nothing for my deteriorating composure. "Your . . . pecs are sore?"

"Yeah."

He clears his throat. "Maybe you should come home and kiss them better."

I freeze. Did he call for phone sex? We don't do that. Or at least, we haven't yet done that. I mean, he sometimes whispers stuff in class to make me blush, but he doesn't call me to flirt.

"Cassie? Are you okay?"

Maybe.

It's unclear.

My chest is tinged with pain.

"I shouldn't have called."

"Why did you?"

He pauses. "I was lying here, thinking about you, and . . . I just wanted to talk to you, I guess."

"Oh."

Ask him why. Ask him, and see if he has the balls to tell you.

Of course, I don't. What we have is working. We both get off, and no one gets hurt. It's completely free from "I called because I miss you," and "I miss you because I love you."

What we share is an emotional desert with an oasis of sex, and we're both happy with that.

"So . . ." he says, in an effort to push through the awkward, "what have you been doing?"

"Uh . . . I got a job."

"Yeah?"

"At the diner. It sucks, but I need the money. What about you?"

"I've been pulling some shifts at the construction company I worked at before I got into The Grove. Long hours, but the money's decent."

"Uh-huh."

We lapse into silence. I have the strongest urge to tell him I miss him, but I can't.

"Well, I'd better go."

He feels it, too. This is too personal. We can't just magically become talk-on-the-phone friends. Texting is different. We can pretend to be detached. Anything more, and we're heading back into areas that are murky and dangerous.

"Yeah, okay. Thanks for calling."

He laughs. "Yeah. No problem. Worked out well. I'll text next time."

"Okay. Sure. Bye."

" 'Night, Cassie."

I hang up and sigh. It's better this way.

Simpler.

Safer.

After the hideously awkward phone call, I expect not to hear from Ethan for a few days, but that doesn't happen. He goes from texting a couple of times a week to every day. Sometimes, several times a day. Little things. Things that make me smile. That make me miss him way too much. Not sex with him. Just him. I always reply. Our text conversations are getting stupidly long. It probably would be easier if we spoke, but as with everything in our relationship, we don't do easy.

As the end of the summer draws to a close, I'm counting down the days until I get back to Westchester. I miss everything about it: my apartment, college, my classmates, Ruby, even Ruby's atrocious cooking.

Everything.

Especially him.

Yet again, I'd gone to bed to the sounds of my parents arguing again, so the next morning when I stumble downstairs to find them sitting calmly together at the kitchen table, I know something's up.

"Cassie, honey. Sit down."

Dad's cradling a cup of coffee. Mom's eyes are red. There's a feeling of finality in the room that makes the air feel too thick. Nervousness prickles my spine and makes my throat tight.

"What's going on?"

Before they say it, I know.

"Honey, your dad and I have something to tell you. We . . . well, we're . . ."

Mom stops. Dad puts his hand over hers and stares down at the table.

"You're breaking up."

Mom puts her hand to her mouth and nods. I nod, too. Dad finally looks up at me.

"This has nothing to do with you, kiddo. Your mom and me . . . we're not good together. We love each other, but we can't live together anymore."

I nod and clench my jaw. I'm not going to cry. I look at the center of the table. Concentrate on it while they tell me how it's going to work.

Dad's going to stay in the house. Mom's going to move in with her sister. During the summer, I'll switch between them. They ask if I'm okay. I tell them I am.

Mom tries to make me eat breakfast. I take one bite of my toast and feel like I want to throw up. I excuse myself to go shower.

When the spray runs over my face, I pretend I'm not crying.

I sigh and berate myself for moping. It's stupid to feel like this. I'm twenty years old, for God's sake. Twenty-one in just over a month. I shouldn't feel devastated that my parents are separating, especially since I've known for years that they'd be better apart.

And yet, I am.

Thinking of coming home and not having them under the same roof makes me unreasonably sad. Imagining Mom moving out of the home where I was born and starting a new life without my dad makes me sad. Dad having to fend for himself for the first time since he was my age makes me sad.

As they drive me to the airport, I continue to act like I'm okay with it, but I'm really not. Maybe in a few months I will be, but not now.

I hug them good-bye and tell them I'll see them at Christmas, and then I wonder where we'll even be spending it this year. Will we all get together? Or will I have to shuttle between them?

The rest of my trip passes in a blur. I get on a plane. Doze. Get off. Sit glassy-eyed waiting for my connection. Get on another plane.

I feel displaced.

Lonely.

I spoke to Ruby last night. Explained what had happened. I tried to sound blasé, but she could hear something in my voice. She offered to cut her weekend short and pick me up from the airport, but I couldn't do that to her. She's happy with her new guy and deserves to savor the last few days of freedom before classes start. The last thing she needs is to have to console the latest victim of America's epidemic divorce rate.

When the plane lands, I wait until everyone else has passed before grabbing my backpack and making the long walk to the exit. The flight attendants are annoyingly perky as they bid me good-bye and tell me they hope I'll fly again with them soon. All around me in the airport, people are hugging and kissing, greeting loved ones. I pause to watch them, partly because they're blocking my way, but mostly because just observing them makes me feel like some of their happy might rub off on me.

At any rate, I'm not in any hurry to take a cab back to my empty apartment.

When the family in front of me finally moves, my breath catches as I see a familiar figure standing on the other side of the arrivals area. Tall. Unruly hair. Dark clothes. Pensive face. Tense and nervous, like he's unsure if I'll be mad about him being here.

I'm not. In fact, I'm so happy, I could cry.

He must recognize my sappy expression, because he pulls his hands out of his pockets and walks toward me.

He looks good. So very good.

He moves sinuously, but there's a repressed urgency in his gait. Like he's forcing himself to not run over and swing me around in front of all of these people.

There's so much I want to do to him. So much I want to say.

When he stops in front of me, he takes my backpack and places it on the ground. Then he wraps his arms around me and gently pulls me against him. I hug his neck, and when he says, "I'm sorry about your parents. That fucking sucks," I press my forehead into his shoulder to stop myself from crying.

The people around us slowly dissipate, and I just stand there and let him comfort me. As much as I've craved sympathy today, until this moment I didn't realize how much I needed it to be from him.

The rest of the world melts away as he holds me and strokes my hair, and when he whispers, "I've missed you," and I whisper it back, the glass-jawed delusion that we're just fuck-buddies goes down for the count.

By the time we get back to my apartment, it's late and I'm exhausted. Ethan opens the door and carries my suitcase to my bedroom. Then he turns around and hugs me. He's so warm and feels so good, I sag against him, almost drifting off. Only the thick layer of travel grime that covers me from head to toe prevents me from fully relaxing.

"I need to shower."

"Okay. You want me to make you something to eat?"

"We have no food."

"I could go out and get something."

He needs to stop with the sweetness. I'm in enough trouble here as it is.

"No, thanks." I push him to sit on my bed. "Just . . . stay. I won't be long."

I grab my robe and head into the bathroom. When the warm water hits my skin, it feels so good I moan. I lather everything twice, then get out and brush my teeth.

When I get back to the bedroom, he's exactly where I left him. He watches as I approach, and the way he stares tells me how much he wants me. The familiar rush of power is back, but it's accompanied by something else. A deeper need. Something I haven't let myself feel for a long time. It makes my skin prickle and my heart flutter, because I know this is one of those moments that is going to define something.

Me.

Us.

The thought makes me freeze in my tracks. We've been here before, and in the past, I was always the one who put myself out there. Pushed us to be more.

Not this time.

If he wants it, he's going to have to ask for it. If he doesn't, I have to walk away before my heart gets even more scarred.

I wait. He barely hesitates before standing and walking to me. He takes my hands and pulls me to him. Cups my face. Kisses me. Gently. So gently. Warm lips and soft tongue. Within seconds, an aching heat is twisting in my veins, but I don't let it take over. He needs to steer us this time. If I hang back, I can decide if I'm willing to go where he leads.

His kisses become hungrier, but still deliberate. It's like he knows any misstep will make me run, and he's determined not to let that happen. He leaves one hand on my face as he tugs at the belt on my robe and slowly unthreads it. Fingertips brush across my chest as he pushes it open. I feel too naked, but I stand there and fight the fear as he claims every inch of terrified, goose-pimpled skin in a way that's so much more than sexual.

He pushes the robe off my shoulders, and it slumps to floor. More of me exposed.

He takes his time. Mouth follows fingers. Lighting fires, then dousing them in kerosene. Branding himself all over me. I'm so dizzy with it, I have to grip his shoulders to stay upright. He takes the hint and picks me up before he lays me on the bed and continues what he's doing without missing a beat. He kisses across my chest, then down my stomach as his hands keep my breasts warm.

Hot breath sparks across everything it touches, and he moves lower. Pushes at my knees. Opens me up to him and moans as he puts his mouth on me. Muffled whispers tell me how much he's been fantasizing about this. I arch into him as he shows me what he's been dreaming about. All the ways he knows he can speak to my body.

Before long, I'm panting, trying to keep myself together even as he's determined to make me fall apart. I squeeze my eyes shut and gasp. I've been dreaming about this, too, but the reality is so much more powerful. I grip his hair. Clench and release. Faster and harder, in time with his rhythm.

This is different from how we usually are. I want to keep my eyes closed and pretend nothing has to change, but he doesn't let me. I'm arching so hard I'm nearly levitating, when he stops.

I try to grab him. To make him finish.

The bed dips as he stands.

I open my eyes as panic tightens my chest.

But he's just removing his shoes. He drops them heavily before tugging off his socks.

He clears his throat. I think it's nerves, but no. He wants my attention on his face, not on his feet. When I'm looking at him, he undresses slowly, first by pulling off his shirt. When it hits the floor, he pauses. Now he's nervous. He's never done this before. Become voluntarily bare.

I watch in awe.

He keeps looking at me, as if he's trying to prove himself.

He unbuttons his jeans and pushes them down, then shakes his head like he can't believe he's stripping for me. He's down to just his boxer-briefs. They hug every long inch.

I realize just how little I've looked at him during our sexual encounters. Watching him like this seems almost wrong. Like I shouldn't because he's not mine. Every feature is so familiar, but it's like a work of art I've admired from afar, knowing it will never hang on my wall.

And yet, this little display is telling me he wants me to own him.

He pushes down his underwear, and then, it's just him. Gloriously naked him. He's self-conscious, but he lets me stare. Does he see the way all my arteries dilate, sending crawling heat all over my body?

How totally ill-equipped I am to deal with how much I want him?

Every part of him.

The silence stretches around us. He's standing there naked, silently asking permission to be more, and I don't have the courage to answer him.

My heart rate escalates, and I lie back on the bed. Within seconds, he's there, warm and comforting. He kisses my face. Pulls my hand away from my eyes.

"It's late," he says. "You're tired. Tell me if you want me to go."

I don't want him to go.

"It's not that late," I say.

"Is it too late?"

I open my eyes. He's looking down at me, vulnerable and intense, and he's not asking about numbers on a clock.

My mind races as I try to figure out what to say.

I don't want to be this confused, but our relationship is like a Chinese rope puzzle, and every strand that pulls us closer together also pulls us apart. Will there ever be a time when we have the forward without the back?

He kisses me, and only his sharp inhale tells me he's anything but completely calm.

"Tell me it's not too late," he whispers into my lips, as if he can will me to say the words. "I need it to not be too late for us."

He kisses my neck, and I close my eyes as I try to think.

This is the moment. The one where I get to choose. From here, my future branches into two distinct timelines. In one, I pull him on top of me and let him show me the difference between fucking and making love. In the other, I push him away and resign myself to forever wondering, "what if?"

I'm not the gambling type. I've never understood how some people can get addicted to games in which the probability of losing is so high. They're not stupid people. They know the odds aren't in their favor, yet they risk more than they can possibly afford to lose.

Right now, I think I finally get it.

Losing isn't what drives them. It's the glimmer of that one spectacular win. The jackpot that's painted with bright lights and a giant check from The Bank of Happily Ever After. *That's* the rush that keeps them putting their hands in their pockets. The thrilling, heart-pounding moment the second before the ball drops, or the card turns, or the tumbler falls into place.

"Cassie?"

A thousand to one. Two thousand. Seventy thousand.

The first number is almost irrelevant. It's the *one* that makes people take the risk. That elusive, magical *one*.

"Please, look at me."

I do. I look and I see. The well-meaning heart of him. The damaged and skittish ego.

I kiss him, hard. He grunts in surprise before kissing me back.

I kiss and tug at him. Pull him on top of me. Try to step back over the "just fucking" line and see if I feel safer there. I grab at his hips and attempt to pull him to where I want him. He tries to resist, but I'm insistent, and I lift my hips and slide against him until he's breathing so hard, he sounds stricken.

"Fuck, Cassie, wait . . ."

He drops his head as I stroke him and wind his body so tight, he has no choice but to ease into me to relieve the burn.

The second he enters me, I realize I'm not remotely prepared for how good he feels. How my body sings as it swells around him.

Somewhere between the last time we fucked and our endless text conversations, I lost the ability to compartmentalize my feelings, and now 'just fucking' isn't even an option anymore. He lets out a long moan as his hips finally rest against mine. Then he stops and breathes shallowly for a few seconds.

Is it just as scary for him? Or does he feel that small thrill of possibility?

I try to move against him, but he holds me down.

"Stop. Wait."

He takes a deep breath and pulls back, then presses in again. Slow and determined. He's not fucking me. He wants me to feel it. The way his whole body is trying to tell me his intentions.

"Cassie, open your eyes."

I do. His face is more naked than his body's ever been. Every tender thrust shows in the way his mouth moves without making noise. He's not even trying to hide how he's feeling.

"I want to be with you. Please. Don't make me beg, because I'm desperate enough to do it, and I swear to God, it won't be pretty."

He moves faster. Lifts my leg to his hip. Slides deeper and watches my reaction. Holds my gaze. Silently begs me not to look away.

"Please say something."

His voice is tight. Low and rumbling. Punctuated by his movements. What he's doing. Physically. Emotionally. It's too much.

"Just say yes," he says, breathy and panting. "I'm so fucking tired of trying to live without you. Aren't you tired? Of pretending you don't want it all? I really think I can do it this time. Us. Please, I want to try."

His movements are becoming erratic, but he still doesn't look away. I dig my fingernails into his back, tug on his hair, grab his hip as I arch and crest.

"Cassie, please." He's barely hanging on. I'm the same. I can't say no to him. He might be the worst gamble I've ever made, but he also might be my *one*. *The* one. How can I not take a chance on that?

"Yes."

I hold on long enough to see the exquisite relief in his smile, then I can't keep my eyes open anymore, and I'm flying so high and fast, I babble against his shoulder. Repeat the word "yes," over and over again. Hold my breath as my whole world spasms in perfect unison with my orgasm.

I've never felt anything like it.

Even at our hottest and most desperate, it's never been this incredible. I'm still reeling when he buries his head into my neck and groans.

"Cassie—I . . . God . . . I love you. I love you."

I grip him as he shudders. I stroke his hair and hold him as I wait for us both to stop shaking.

So many emotions twist and rage in my veins, sparking and pounding in a rush that seems like it's never going to end.

When it finally ebbs away, he's still wrapped around me. Still inside. I don't let him go. I'm incapable.

For so long, I've tainted my vision against him. Closed my eyes to his beauty and my ears to his charm. But my heart . . .

I tried to harden it against the things I didn't want to feel, and yet, here I am, feeling them anyway.

For all its amazing strength, our hearts are made of eggshells, and sometimes all it takes is someone you'd almost given up on declaring their love for it to crack wide open.

TWENTY

NOW AND THEN

Present Day
New York City, New York
Graumann Theater

I splash warm water on my face to wash off the last of my stage makeup. After I pat myself dry, I look at the stranger in the mirror.

No extra-long lashes, fake-pinked cheeks, or Lolita-red lips. Just me. Pale, splotchy skin. Olive eyes too world-weary to sparkle. Brown hair too coated in hairspray to shine.

I don't dislike how I look. Everything is in proportion.

And yet, this girl staring back at me? Somewhere along the way, I think I lost track of how much I like her.

My new therapist is helping. In four sessions, we've covered a lot of ground.

We've talked about a wide range of topics: my childhood, my overly critical mother, my emotionally distant father, my need to please people, my parents' divorce, and, of course, Ethan.

Always Ethan.

She's made me describe how we met. Our first kiss. The moment I realized I was in love with him.

Making me remember all the ways he lit me up.

I know we have to talk about the bad times, too. I'm just hesitant to relive it.

There's a knock on the door.

"Come in."

I don't even have to turn around to know it's him.

He stands behind me, and his chest radiates warmth, even though he's not touching me. I watch him in the mirror as he studies me. The expression on his face makes me wonder what he's seeing that I don't.

"You were amazing tonight."

I shake my head. "No, you were. I just got infected by it."

"That's not how I recall it."

"That's because you know all the right things to say to make me feel good."

"Oh, really? I make you feel good?"

He steps closer but doesn't embrace me. He just presses, barely there. He's so much taller than I am, my head brushes his chin.

"All I want to do these days is make you feel good," he says, his voice low. "However you need me to do it."

I'm sure he doesn't mean that statement to be incredibly arousing, but it is. I can't help thinking that having him make love to me would make me feel pretty damn good, and God knows, I could use the tension relief. But in talking with Dr. Kate, I realize that would be a monumental step in the wrong direction. At least for now.

He knows it, too. He's been very careful to keep our offstage contact as platonic as possible. It's torture. Understanding why it's a good idea doesn't make it any less of a struggle.

Even now, I see him fighting to not touch me.

"You realize you're stunning, right?" he says to my reflection, and I lean back into him.

"I'm getting wrinkles."

He wraps his arms around me. "Bullshit."

"My skin's breaking out from the stage makeup." I wind my fingers between his as he rests his chin on my shoulder.

"Mine, too. So what?"

"I found a hair on my chin the other day. A long, dark hair poking out of a freckle. I'm officially turning into a witch. Run while you can."

He chuckles and presses his nose against my cheek. "I'm never running again. And please stop trying to convince me you're anything but absolutely gorgeous, because it ain't gonna happen. You're perfect. Always have been. Always will be. Just like this. Breakouts, wrinkles, witchy chin hairs, and all."

And just like that, he makes those imagined flaws disappear.

"You're biased," I say as I step away from him and brush on some powder.

He leans against the counter and watches. "Totally biased. Proud of it. Put on some lip gloss."

I turn to him. "What? You just told me you like me au naturale."

"I do. I also like watching that pouty thing you do when you put on lipstick. It's sexy as hell." He pulls out a chair and sits down. "Actually, put it on, then wipe it off. Then put it on again. Just keep repeating the process until I say stop. FYI, we could be here awhile."

I smile and pick up my lip gloss. Then I pull out the wand and hold it toward him.

"Is this what you want, big boy? This spongy, moist tip dragging across my lips? Does that turn you on?"

His whole body seizes as he digs his hands into his thighs. Then he closes his eyes and leans his elbows on his knees as he scrubs his face.

"You tease me with mental images you know I have zero defense against. Does 'three-year dry spell' mean nothing to you, woman? I'm working with a very short fuse here."

"I've seen your fuse. It's really not short."

He makes a noise and strides into my bathroom. "Wait here. This won't take long."

I laugh as he slams the door.

Approximately three minutes later, he's back. He sits on the couch as I finish packing up.

"So, how are you liking Dr. Kate?" he asks, taking our conversation back to being G-rated.

"She's great. Although, it's a bit weird calling her Dr. Kate. I kind of feel like she should have her own talk show, like Dr. Drew."

"Yeah, but unlike Dr. Drew, Kate is her last name."

I stop and turn to him. "I thought it was her first name."

"It is."

"But . . . that would mean her name is—"

"Kate Kate. Yep, she married some big property developer. William Kate."

"Huh. I guess it would be the same thing if I married Taylor Swift. She'd be Taylor Taylor."

His eyes glaze over. "Uh, so let's run with that idea. What would that wedding night be like?"

I slap his leg.

"No, seriously," he says and sits forward. "I really want to know. Start from where you kiss passionately and remove each other's clothing."

I laugh and continue packing up.

He watches me in silence for a few minutes, then says, "So, if you and I got married, would you take my name? Or would you expect me to be Ethan Taylor-Holt?"

And just like that, all the blood drains from my face.

He laughs. "Cassie, relax. I'm not asking you to marry me."

"Oh. Okay." My lungs start working again.

He gives me a half smile. "Yet."

I settle into the oversize leather chair as Dr. Kate crosses her legs. She looks like she belongs in an advertisement for sexy horn-rimmed glasses. All perfect blondness and designer shoes.

"Hi, Cassie. How are you?"

"I'm fine."

Dr. Kate gives me a look. I'm not supposed to resort to meaningless automated responses. I'm supposed to describe my feelings as honestly as possible. Identify and confront.

"Um . . . okay, I'm . . . nervous. Conflicted. A little nauseated."

"Uh-huh." My self-awareness is rewarded with a smile. "How's the show?"

"Good, I guess. Previews have been well received. The buzz around town is positive."

"Opening night is tonight, yes?"

"Yeah."

"What are your expectations?"

"I'll make myself sick with nerves. Then I'll do some focusing exercises and try to convince myself I can transform into someone else so completely, my rampant insecurities will be all but invisible."

She gives me a real smile this time. "Well, that sounds exhausting. How's Ethan?"

"Irritatingly patient. Understanding. Perfectly calm. About us, anyway. Nervous about the show, of course."

"It sounds like his patience frustrates you."

"It does. He makes it look so freaking easy."

"I'm sure it's not, but he's been working on it for a long time. This is only your fifth session. I think you're doing remarkably well."

"You do?"

"Yes. I'm impressed with how you're embracing this process."

"I want to get better."

"I know. And that's a fantastic platform upon which to build your recovery."

I smooth down my skirt for the tenth time. It doesn't ease my tension. Dr. Kate waits patiently. She knows I'll start when I'm ready.

"So," I say, "I dreamed about him again last night. How he used to be. I can see so many parallels to how he was back then to how I am now."

"How do you see yourself now?"

"Guarded. Desperate to protect myself."

"Was there a time when you felt you were successful in protecting yourself?"

"After our first breakup, yes. For a while."

She writes something in her book before looking at me again. "If you were to conjure a mental image of yourself from that time, what would it be?"

I think for a few seconds. "The first time he broke my heart, I tried to make myself into a fortress. A castle with high, impenetrable walls."

"And what was Ethan in this scenario?"

"He was this . . . irresistible force, and no matter how high I built my walls, he still managed to find a way in."

"So you fought to keep him out."

"Every single day."

"And when you embarked on a sexual relationship with him again, that became more difficult?"

"Yes." *A thousand times, yes.*

"In your analogy, you tried to be impenetrable. What changed?"

Everything.

"He asked me to open the door."

I wake up to tingling, down low and insistent. Then I register lips on my neck, hands on my breasts, hardness pressing into my butt, and I realize . . .

Ethan met me at the airport.

Ethan asked if we could try again.

Ethan told me he loved me.

Ethan told me he would stay the night, so he could make love to me in the morning.

Well, it's morning and . . . he didn't leave. Didn't get scared. And he seems intent on making good on his promise.

I'm encouraged, especially by the way he's holding me. It's like he's been wrapped around me all night and has been holding himself back from touching me like this.

He continues to kiss and suck. I reach behind me and wind my fingers through his hair. When he gently bites my shoulder, I make a mental note to always be woken up this way.

He makes a low, desperate sound as he continues to grind against me, and I want him so much, it's getting uncomfortable.

"Good morning," I say, my voice hoarse.

"Hmmm." His lips vibrate against me as he trails one hand down my stomach, then lower to press against where the tingling is the strongest. I arch into him, and with a minimum of repositioning, he slowly pushes into me.

I hold my breath. The sensation is too much. Then let out a long moan as he exhales against my shoulder.

When we're fully joined, he says, "Now it's a good morning."

He then proceeds to completely redefine how good a morning can be. Twice.

Dr. Kate writes in her notebook and asks, "So, you took him back?"

"Yes."

She studies the way I cross and recross my legs. "Was that a hard decision?"

I uncross again and sit with my hands on my knees. "Yes and no. I'd missed him so much, it was a relief to finally let myself have him."

"But . . . ?"

"But . . ." This is hard. I've spent so long hiding from these feelings, it feels way too raw to talk about them.

"Do you need a moment?"

"No, I'm okay." I take deep breath. "From the get-go, I was cautious. I was looking for the old him, but at first, he was nowhere to be found."

Thursday night. Friday. Friday night. Saturday.

He doesn't go home.

Apart from one trip to buy food, he doesn't get dressed. Barely leaves my side.

He cooks for me. Naked. His skill in the kitchen is almost as mind-blowing as his skill in the bedroom, and that's saying something.

On Saturday night, he takes me to a movie. Buys my ticket and everything. Holds my hand and acts like a real boyfriend.

It's kind of strange, but nice. I don't let myself enjoy it too much, in case it's just a passing fad. I mean, we've been here before and look how that turned out.

I really hope this time is different.

As soon as the lights go down, he leans over and kisses me. Within ten minutes, my hand is on his crotch, and his mouth is on my neck, and we leave just as things start exploding onscreen.

I resist fanning my face.

"It sounds like your prolonged emotional distance led to your reunion being quite . . . intense."

"You could say that." We couldn't get enough of each other. It was thrilling.

"And then?"

"And then . . ." I look down at my hands. "We had to stop being alone and start being around other people."

"And that was a problem?"

"It was the start of our problems, yes."

On Sunday night, we know our little cocoon can't last much longer. We have to shower soon and get ready to pick up Ruby from the airport.

She doesn't know we're back together. I can only imagine how thrilled she's going to be. Also, classes start back tomorrow, so Ethan has to sleep in his own bed tonight.

All the bits of reality we've been ignoring are starting to press their pointy edges into our delicate bubble.

I'm tense. It's quite an accomplishment given the number of orgasms I've experienced this weekend.

I press myself against him and I listen to his heartbeat.

"What are we going to do tomorrow?"

"What do you mean?"

"At school."

His heart rate stays reasonably steady. I'm surprised. I trace a pattern on his chest. He hovers his hand over mine, fingertips brushing my knuckles.

"Well, call me crazy, but I thought we might go to class. You know . . . learn stuff. Get good at acting. Perhaps even graduate."

"You know what I mean."

He rolls me under him and frames my face with his hands. He's heavy, but I like the weight. It's somehow reassuring. Like he's all here and not half somewhere else.

"Well, if you're asking if I think we should hide that we're together, then no. I want every guy at that school to know. Maybe then they'll stop sniffing around like a bunch of horny mongrels."

"No one sniffs around me," *I say as I stroke his back.*

He snorts. "Sure they don't."

"Who?"

He kisses my cheek. My jaw. My neck. "Everyone. Every prick-wielding cock jockey at that school wants a piece of you. Lucas, Avery, Boring Nick, that weird kid that looks like Matt Damon. They're always making comments they think I don't hear. And don't even get me started on fucking Connor—"

"Oh, I see."

He stops kissing me. "What?"

"This is about Connor."

He kisses back up from my neck to my face. "He's a douchebag."

"No, he's not. He's never made sexual comments about me."

"Exactly. That's the problem."

He leans on his elbow and brushes my hair away from my face. "I can cope with all those other dicks talking about how much they want to sleep with you, because that's all it is: talk. But Bain? That asshole doesn't just want to bang you. He wants more. He genuinely likes you."

He says it with so much disdain, I laugh. "That bastard! I can see why you hate him so much."

He smiles and shakes his head. "Oh, you can laugh, but every time you talk, he gets a sappy expression on his face that makes me want to punch him. He's crushing on you big-time, and I swear to God, he needs to stop."

He goes quiet, but I see the cogs of his brain turning. I trace his eyebrows, trying to get them to unfurrow.

"Ethan, I'm not interested in Connor. I'm interested in you."

It feels strange to reassure him. It used to come so easily to me, but now the words scrape like sandpaper in my throat. Still, it must work because his attention is now fully back on me.

He lifts an eyebrow. "How interested?"

He cups my breast. Gently rubs his thumb across the nipple.

I inhale, quick and shallow.

"Very."

It's getting hard to breathe. He does this so easily, it's scary.

He bends to kiss the swell in his hand. Soft lips. Open mouth. "Tell me again how much you missed me over the summer."

I try to form words. "I missed you a lot." Too much. Don't make me regret it.

The other breast isn't forgotten. He's just as gentle there. "On a scale of one to touching yourself and picturing my face?"

"It was up there." I grip his hair, needing more.

"How high?" He adds teeth. Just a little. Just enough.

I arch, and my voice is tight as I say, "It hovered around I-missed-you-so-much-I-renamed-Buzz-Ethan."

He comes back up to my face. "Good. Just the right amount, then."

I kiss him, and he pushes between my legs as he breathes hard against my lips.

"Do you see what you do to me?"

He kisses me, deep and slow, then moves down to where my neck meets my shoulder.

"I'm thinking if I use my tongue in exactly the right way, I can give you a hickey that reads, 'Cassie belongs to Ethan. Step the fuck off.'"

He starts sucking, and I squeal. "Ethan Robert Holt! Don't you dare give me a hickey!"

"Shhh. I need to concentrate to get this right."

"Ethan!"

He sighs and rolls off me, and I laugh when I see the massive tent that is now formed above his crotch.

"Oh, yeah, sure. Laugh at what you do to me, then negate all efforts to show other guys you're mine. That's fair."

I kiss him and reach under the covers to address his problem. He inhales as I wrap my fingers around him and pushes down the sheet so he can watch.

"We were broken up for over a year," I say. "If I'd wanted other guys, don't you think I would have had them?"

He pants in time with the rhythm of my hand.

"You dated Nick."

"Barely. You had nothing to be jealous of."

He presses his head into the pillow. "He kissed you at that party. I had everything to be jealous of."

"Yeah, well, you made up for it later that night, didn't you?"

"God, yes." I don't know if he's answering my question or reacting to my increasing pace. Doesn't matter. He closes his eyes, and the conversation's over.

For long minutes I watch his face as I bring him pleasure. How he could possibly be jealous of any other man, I'll never know. I get that he has issues about being adopted, as well as his track record with women, but how does he honestly not understand just how incredible he is?

When I was in high school, I remember a friend of mine confided that her boyfriend didn't think she was pretty. I couldn't understand that. When you love someone, they should appear beautiful to you, no matter what they look like.

As I watch Ethan's face, I realize he might be insecure about other guys because he doesn't love himself enough to see how truly spectacular he is.

As if to illustrate my point, he arches his back and lets out a long moan as he comes, and in that moment, he's the most beautiful, sexy, magnificent man on the planet.

To me, anyway.

Dr. Kate pauses, no doubt picking up on my building tension.

"Did you ever talk to Ethan about his self-esteem issues?"

I rub my eyes. "No. Not really." I should have, but I didn't.

"But you reassured him on occasion?"

"Yes. Probably not enough."

"For people with low self-esteem, it's hard to ever give enough reassurance. How much would Ethan have to give you now to make you believe you were special?"

I've lost track of how much reassurance he's given me since he's been back. "I see your point."

"So," says Dr. Kate as she leans back in her chair. "When you got back together, Ethan was happy to be open about your relationship?"

"Yes."

"How did you feel about that?"

Partly relieved, but mostly . . . "It made me nervous. I just wasn't confident this time would be any different."

"What about your friends? Were they supportive or did they try to steer you away?"

"I'm sure they all thought we were insane, but at the time, their judgment was a small price to pay."

The closer we get to the drama block, the more tense I become.

Everyone saw what we went through when Ethan and I broke up the first time. When they notice we're back together, I'm sure they're going to think we're the biggest idiots on the planet for trying again.

I wouldn't entirely disagree with them.

Ethan squeezes my hand. "You okay?"

"Yeah. Fine. You?"

"Great. Never better."

We're both lying, and we know it.

As we approach the building, I see most of our class congregating near the benches, chatting, laughing, and smoking. Zoe's the first to see us walking hand in hand. Her mouth drops open. She pats Phoebe, who turns to look. Within a few seconds, they're all staring at us.

"Hey, guys," I say as we stop in front of them. "Have a good summer?"

"I had an awesome summer," Jack says with his trademark smirk. "I got back together with the ex-girlfriend I dumped more than a year ago because I'm a miserable fuck who never stopped pining for her. Oh, wait, that was you, Holt, wasn't it?"

Everyone laughs, and the tension breaks, and for once I'm grateful for Avery's big mouth. Even Ethan smiles.

The only person not smiling is Connor.

He turns away a second too late to hide his incredulity.

"Connor was a friend of yours?"

"Yes."

She cocks her head to the side. "Why do I get the feeling there's more to Connor than you're telling me?"

I look down. Of all of my misguided attempts to forget about Ethan, I regret Connor the most.

"He was more. After Ethan, we were . . . lovers. For a time."

Dr. Kate makes an understanding noise. "Revenge lovers?"

I nod. I still can't think about how I treated him without being consumed by shame.

"You ended things, I take it?" Dr. Kate asks quietly.

"Yes. I know I hurt him, but it was for the best."

"But in drama school, you never . . . ?"

"No. We were just friends. I knew he always like me, but . . ."

"You weren't interested?"

"No."

"Was Connor resentful about that?"

I remember how supportive Connor had been after the breakup, and how that had changed after Ethan and I got back together. "I guess. He was never nasty about it, though. Just . . . protective."

"Ethan wouldn't have appreciated that, I'm sure."

"Not at all."

A hand presses into the small of my back.

"So you really took him back? After what he did to you?"

This is the first time Connor's spoken to me all day. I grab a sandwich and move forward in the cafeteria line.

"It's complicated, Connor."

"I bet."

He grabs a drink and falls into line beside me.

"Just promise me you'll be careful." He glances over at Ethan, who's sitting with the rest of our group. "The second he starts giving you warning signs, get out. Seeing you get hurt again would . . . well . . . that'd suck, okay?"

"Maybe it'll work out this time."

He gives a short laugh. "Yeah. Maybe."

Ethan looks over, and when he sees us together, his expression goes dark.

Connor sighs. "Why do I get the feeling you and I won't be allowed to be friends anymore?"

We pay for our stuff and head over to the table. As we approach, Ethan stands and puts his arms around me. Then he kisses me, long and deep, right in front of Connor. It couldn't be more obvious that he's staking his claim, unless he stapled a large "Property of Ethan Holt" *banner to my back like a cape.*

Connor rolls his eyes and sits next to Zoe. Ethan sits and pulls me onto his lap.

Everyone else seems oblivious, but all through lunch, the weight of the tension between the two men on either side of me sits squarely in the middle of my chest.

"So the conflict between Ethan and Connor escalated when you got back together?"

I sigh. "Yes. I mean, they never really liked each other, but at least they used to pretend."

"You said 'they all' thought you were insane earlier. Who else gave you a hard time?"

"My roommate, Ruby."

"She didn't like Ethan?"

"No. She saw what I went through the first time, and I guess my bitterness rubbed off on her. When we first got back together, she was sort of . . . intolerant."

"Ethan! Get out of the fucking bathroom! You take longer than a girl!"

Ruby bangs on the door and grunts in frustration. To say she's not pleased about me and Ethan getting back together would be an understatement.

"Why does your goddamn boyfriend take so fucking long in the shower?"

she asks as she drops down next to me on the sofa. "It's not like he needs to whack off anymore. You two are constantly fucking."

"He just likes long showers, I guess."

"Fucking prima donna."

"Ruby, be nice."

"I am being nice. Being nasty would be going into the kitchen and turning on the hot water."

Her face lights up with mischief.

"Ruby . . . no."

She laughs and runs into the kitchen. I hear the faucet running for about three seconds before there's a manly bellow from the bathroom.

"Fucking goddamn sonofabitch!"

I sigh.

It's like living with children.

Ethan appears in the doorway, dripping wet, towel draped around his waist, his expression like a storm cloud.

"Where is she?"

Ruby pokes her head out of the kitchen. "Who? Me?"

He glares at her. She smiles sweetly.

"Stop being a pain in my ass."

"Okay, as soon as you stop dating my best friend."

"Hardly the same thing."

"Wrong. You dating Cassie is a giant pain in my ass."

"Get used to it."

"For how long? Until you fuck up and dump her again? Are we talking weeks or months here?"

I glare at her.

Ethan clenches his jaw and stays silent. Then he stalks into the bedroom and slams the door.

Ruby deflates at the same time my anger flares.

"What the hell, Ruby?"

"I'm sorry, he just . . . I shouldn't have said that."

"Can't you give him a break?"

"I don't want him to hurt you again."

"Neither do I."

"And I know you think he's changed, or whatever, but it seems a bit too fucking convenient. I don't trust him. Do you?"

Hardest question in the world to answer. I want to say yes, but I swore to never lie to her again.

"I don't know."

She nods and comes over to hug me. "That's what I thought. Let me just say, if he does hurt you again, I'm going to knee his balls so far up into his body, they may never come down."

I squeeze her. "If he hurts me again, I'll totally let you."

"Good."

Thinking about Ruby makes me long for her. If it wasn't for her and Tristan, I would have become even more of a basket case than I already am.

"Is Ruby still in your life?" Dr. Kate asks.

"Not as much as I'd like." And I miss her every day. "Just before graduation, she got pregnant. Her boyfriend was an Australian businessman she met the summer before senior year. He asked her to marry him, and after graduation, they went to live in Sydney. Now they have three kids and are sickeningly happy."

"Does she know Ethan's back in your life?"

"Yeah. We talk online every few weeks."

"How does she feel about it?"

Whooboy.

"When I told her I'd agreed to do a show with him, she thought I was insane and bitched me out for a good half an hour. Then, when I told her he'd apologized and wanted me back, she threatened to jump on the first plane out of Oz to beat the crap out of him. When I told her how hard he's worked on his issues and how different he is, she went quiet for a long time."

"And now?"

I take a deep breath. "She's glad I'm getting therapy, and she's cautious about Ethan. *Very* cautious, but she wants me to be happy. She thinks I should make him jump through hoops before even considering taking him back."

"Does she believe he's different?"

I shake my head. "She's dubious."

"Why?"

"Because he convinced us he'd changed before."

He walks toward me, looking smug. Well, more smug than usual. Beside me, Zoe and Phoebe have gone mysteriously silent. I turn to see them watching him with their mouths open.

I can hardly blame them. Every time I see Ethan striding toward me, it's like the world goes into slow motion. I have no doubt he affects other women in the same way.

"Christ, he's hot," Zoe mutters under her breath.

It might make me a bad person, but seeing Zoe drool over the man who only has eyes for me makes me all kinds of happy.

"Morning, boyfriend," I say, a little too loudly.

When he reaches me, he murmurs, "Good morning, girlfriend," before cupping the back of my head and drawing me in for a kiss.

All thoughts of Zoe and Phoebe are immediately forgotten. Actually, all thoughts that don't revolve around how amazing his mouth is are also forgotten.

"Oh, for fuck's sake, you two," Avery says beside us. "I just had breakfast, and I don't need to see that. I think I liked it better when you were broken up and would just passive-aggressively eye-fuck each other all day. There was definitely less visible tongue. Get a freaking room."

"Good idea," Ethan says. He grabs my hand and pulls me down the

hallway toward the makeup room, then shuts the door and pulls some-
thing from his bag.

He holds it out and says, "Happy birthday."

I'm surprised he remembered. And pleased. I wanted him to remember
without reminding him. As petty as it sounds, he's passed some sort of boy-
friend test.

Having said that, I eye the thing in his hands dubiously. It looks like a
tornado of paper and tape got caught on something kind of rectangular.

He shrugs. "Yeah . . . so, I suck at wrapping. I've been trying to hide it
from you, but . . . there it is."

I smile and rip off the paper. Inside is Ethan's old, beaten copy of The
Outsiders.

"Oh, wow." Knowing how important this book is to him makes a lump
form in my throat. "Ethan . . ."

"Wait," he says and opens the front cover. "Look."

On the title page there's a message: "To Cassie, on your 21st birthday.
Ethan tells me you're a very special young lady. I hope your future is as
bright as the sun. Stay gold. Warmest regards, S. E. Hinton."

"Oh my God." I look up at Ethan. His amount of smugness is now off
the charts. "You got her to sign it for me?"

He nods. "E-mailed her over the summer. She was really nice and agreed
to sign. I mailed it to her a few days later, and she sent it back within the
week."

"Over the summer? But . . . we weren't even back together then."

He pauses, sheepish that he just gave himself away. "I know. But I
wanted to be. I couldn't stand the thought of getting through another year
without you."

"What if I'd said no?"

He shrugs. "I would have still given it to you. It's your twenty-first birth-
day. It's special." He kisses me gently, so open and relaxed. "You're special."

I stroke his face. "This is unbelievable."

He kisses me again. "So you like it?"

"Like it? This is . . ." I shake my head, trying not to tear up. *"This is the nicest thing anyone's ever done for me. I love it."* I want to say, *"I love you,"* but the words get stuck. Instead I kiss him and whisper, *"Thank you."*

Maybe I've been wrong about him being able to change. Perhaps this second chance is exactly what we need, and it took us being apart to make him realize what we have is more important than his fear.

Whatever the reason, I'm grateful. I feel myself falling for him even harder than before, and right now, I don't think I could stop myself even if I wanted to.

He hugs me, and I'm glad his T-shirt is black so the tears of happiness that bully their way onto my cheeks are camouflaged.

I look over at Dr. Kate, well aware that I'm blushing.

She gives me a small smile. "So, for a while, you were happy together?"

"Yes. Really happy. At least, I was. Looking back, I realize it was only a few months. Not long enough."

She writes in her notebook. "When did things start to change?"

My tension starts to rise. "I don't know the exact moment. It happened gradually."

"Did it have a specific trigger?"

"Connor."

I know I'm getting short with her, so I try to calm myself. I'm angry with Ethan, not her. "Every time Connor was around, Ethan would shut down and tense up."

Dr. Kate crosses her hands in her lap. "Cassie, tell me more about Connor."

I pause for a moment. "He was open. Sweet. Caring."

"Handsome?"

"Yes. Very."

Dr. Kate nods. "No wonder Ethan chose him to be the focus of his aggression and insecurities. The mammalian brain doesn't always work logically when it comes to a perceived threat. In Ethan's mind,

Connor had the potential to steal you away. His primitive instincts would have reacted to that."

"So that's why he turned into such a caveman every time Connor was around?"

"Sadly, yes."

I clasp my hands together and squeeze. "Unbelievable."

Dr. Kate pauses. "How's your anxiety?"

"Getting up there."

"So Ethan's jealousy upset you?"

I sigh. "At first I found it attractive that he was so possessive. But then . . ."

"It got worse?"

"Yes. When we got back together, he really did try to not let on just how bad it was."

"Did he succeed?"

"Up to a point."

"Which point?"

Sweat breaks out on my forehead. "Graduate showcase. Senior year."

Erika opens the large file on her desk and hands out stacks of papers.

"Ladies and gentlemen, as you know, the Senior Showcase is only a couple of months away, and these are your assigned scenes. If you haven't already submitted which monologues you'd like to perform, please do so ASAP. Remember, this showcase will be viewed by producers, agents, sponsors, and important industry professionals. Make it count."

I nibble at my thumbnail. The Senior Showcase scares the crap out of me. If you do well, you can fast-forward straight into a professional career. If you don't, you need to wade into the world of endless cattle calls and auditions. The pressure to be good is kind of ridiculous.

"Did you hear about what happened last year?" Miranda whispers. "Nearly half the class got offered contracts for shows all over the place."

"Like where?" I whisper back.

"*L.A., Toronto, London, Europe, San Francisco . . . even Broadway.*"

"*Seriously?*"

"*Yep. Shit's serious, man.*"

As if I wasn't nervous enough.

I'm just about to demolish my other thumbnail when Ethan grabs my hand and laces his fingers through mine. "Quit it. I like you with fingernails."

"*I'm freaking out.*"

"*I know. Stop. It's infectious.*"

"*Do you think we'll get a scene together?*"

"*We'd better. I'm never as good as when I'm onstage with you.*" *He squeezes my hand and smiles.*

God, I love him. Still haven't told him that, of course. Still waiting for the right moment. Every time I try, my heart pounds like I'm a frightened rabbit.

Doesn't mean I don't feel it, though.

Erika gives us our scene allocations and says, "Now, I've thought long and hard about these groups and pairings. I've tried to give you all scenes in which you're working to your strengths, but I also need you to show your range. Therefore, some of the scenes you'll have performed before, but some will be new. You'll all perform three scenes and two monologues. One of your monologues must be Shakespeare."

I look down the list. Ethan and I will be doing the balcony scene from Romeo and Juliet. *Thank God. Something I know I'm going to nail. Ethan and Connor will be performing their scene from* Enemy Inside. *No surprise there. They were excellent.*

It's interesting to see that Ethan is paired with Jack for Rosencrantz and Guildenstern Are Dead. *I've never really seen Ethan do comedy. I'm excited for him.*

My other two scenes are new: Jean Genet's The Maids, *with Zoe and Phoebe, and something called* Portrait, *with Connor.*

The scripts for all the excerpts are paper-clipped to the rehearsal schedule. I'm already familiar with The Maids, *so I flip through* Portrait *to see what it's about.*

I only get two pages in before stopping short.
Oh.
Oh, God. No.
Ethan is going to lose his shit.

Dr. Kate takes off her glasses. "I take it the play had some controversial content."

If I weren't so tense, I'd laugh. "You could say that. But I think if I'd been paired with anyone but Connor, Ethan wouldn't have cared so much."

"His reaction was extreme?"

A chill runs up my spine. "Actually, no. It wasn't the reaction I'd expected at all."

He's quiet. And still.

The thought of him ranting and raging was bad enough. This is so much worse.

"Please say something."

He blinks.

The energy in the room is beyond tense. I want to touch him, but I have no idea how he'll react.

"Ethan, it's no big deal."

He frowns and nods.

"I mean, Erika said she wouldn't make me do it, but it's what the script calls for, and I don't want the producers or directors to think I'm a prude. I mean, it's not like everyone is going to see them. My back is to the audience for most of it. The only person who can really see them is Connor."

He laughs, short and bitter. "Just Connor."

"I can wear pasties."

"What the fuck are pasties?"

"You know, sticker things that cover my nipples."

He laughs again. "Oh, well, that's okay then."

I drop my head. I almost want him to yell. That would be easier to deal with than this quiet, sarcastic fury.

"Ethan—"

"No, you're right, Cassie," he says and holds up his hands. "It's no big deal. My girlfriend is going to be topless in front of hundreds of people, but the only person who'll get a good look at her boobs is the one guy who's probably been beating off to images of her since the first day they met. No big deal. I have absolutely nothing to worry about."

"You don't. So he sees my boobs. So what? You're shirtless with him in your scene, too. Hell, he kisses your damn chest."

"You sound jealous."

"I am jealous. I hate seeing you do that sort of stuff with another person. Even Connor. But I know it doesn't mean anything."

"That's because Connor and I hate each other! Him ogling you is completely different. You don't hate him, and he sure as shit doesn't hate you."

I sit down next to him. I don't know what to say to make it better.

He sighs and rubs his face. "Can I at least see the script?"

I hand it to him and watch his face as he skims through it. I know there's stuff in it he won't like, but forewarned is forearmed, right?

He gets about halfway through when his frown reaches epic proportions.

He points to the stage directions. "Marla removes her shirt and bra. Christian sketches her, while glancing up with obvious lust. *'The more I stared, the more beautiful she became. The more I reminded myself that she was married, the less it mattered. She was more than my model. She was my muse.'* He walks over to her. She's unresponsive as he touches her body. *'The longer I painted her, the more realistic my fantasies became. Every stroke of my brush made my fingers tingle like they were caressing her.'* He runs his fingers up her side then cups her breasts."

Ethan shakes his head and takes a deep breath before continuing. "'Of course, the Marla in my mind wanted me just as much. She did things to me, too.' She stands. 'Wonderful things.' She unbuttons his shirt and caresses his chest. 'Things that real-Marla would never do.' She kneels in front of him. The lights dim as she unfastens his pants and begins to pleasure him orally. *'If only she'd do these wonderful fantasy things. Betray her husband. Let me love her. I could give her so much. A world of beauty, and pleasure, and magnificent art. Everything. Everything.'* Lights flash suddenly as he orgasms, then go to black."

He closes the script and drops his head. "Fuck me."

He's not angry anymore. Just . . . resigned.

I want so badly to reassure him, but I know that if the situation was reversed, there isn't much anyone could say to make me feel better. Instead I kiss his cheek, his brows, his forehead, then his lips. He pulls me into his lap and hugs me, and when our chests press together, I can feel the too-fast rhythm of fear in his heartbeat.

"Do you want me to tell Erika I can't do it?" I ask as I stroke his hair.

He squeezes me tighter and presses his forehead against my heart. "No. The script is amazing. It's a great role for you. Awesome role for Connor as well. That's why Erika chose it. I just . . . I hate thinking of him touching you. Jesus, watching you pretend to blow him is probably going to kill me."

He leans back and closes his eyes. When I touch his face, it's hot. I can see he's trying to defuse his emotions, but it's not something that's easily done.

"I wish Erika had cast you instead of Connor."

He opens his eyes and runs his fingertips over my lips. "Me, too."

That night, when we make love, he's different. Rougher. Like he's trying to fuck the thought of Connor and me out of his brain. Afterward, he doesn't talk. Just holds me.

The next morning, he seems calmer about it all, but I don't miss the haunted look in his eyes. He looks like someone who's foreseen a terrible tragedy and doesn't know how to stop it.

I take in a shaky breath.

"Cassie . . . ?"

Dr. Kate's voice is quiet.

"It's natural for you to get emotional about these memories. That's the purpose of these sessions. To expose the triggers for your anger and try to confront them. Letting the emotion out so we can deal with it is part of the process."

"I just don't see how he could have ruined us twice. Once I could have almost forgiven, but the second time? Why did he even bother trying again, if he knew he couldn't do it?"

She gives me a sympathetic nod. "Even the best motivations can be tarnished by hurtful outcomes. Have you ever heard the term 'unresolved abandonment'?"

I shake my head.

"It manifests in different people in different ways, but is usually self-destructive. For those who suffer from it, it's frustrating, because they recognize the patterns of fear, anger, and self-sabotage but feel powerless to change them. Sound familiar?"

I nod. "Yes." Not just regarding Ethan, either. I've been feeling that way for years.

"Some try to self-medicate with drugs, alcohol, sex, food, shopping, or gambling."

Ethan used to drink heavily. I lost myself in meaningless sex.

Dr. Kate sits forward a little. "People in these types of cycles think that if they change how they react outwardly, their inner processes might follow suit."

"Like wearing a mask," I say quietly.

"Yes. Exactly like wearing a mask."

I clench my jaw against rising emotion. "Ethan failed our mask assessment. He had to do extra credit to make up for it."

She pauses. "How successful was he in masking his emotions with you?"

"When I first started working with Connor, Ethan tried to be cool about it. In fact, I think I was more uptight than he was."

"Why do you think that was?"

"Because . . ." I pick at my fingernails and answer in a near whisper. "I didn't want to give him an excuse to break up with me again."

I don't look at Dr. Kate, but I can feel her staring at me.

"Cassie, your behavior is nothing to be ashamed of. You were scared of being hurt again. Clearly, Ethan wasn't the only one affected by abandonment. You're here because you're still being affected by it."

I nod. At the time, I had no idea why I was so emotionally bipolar. All I knew was that I was being pulled in so many different directions, I was afraid of moving at all.

I'm supposed to be confident as I take off my shirt, but I'm not. I'm even less confident as I remove my bra. I'm wearing skin-tone stickers over my nipples, but they don't make me feel any less naked. I'm supposed to look Connor in the eye, but I can't. It's Connor. My friend Connor. My friend who's now standing in front of me, staring at my chest and breathing too fast.

"Watch your posture, Cassie," Erika says. "You're a life model. You'd be used to being seen half naked."

I straighten my back. Connor says his lines, and then he touches me. Gentle hands. He runs his fingers up my sides, over my rib cage. He pauses before touching my breasts. I look up at him. He almost seems apologetic as he puts his hands on me and squeezes gently.

"Good, now Cassie, you transform into his fantasy: the Marla who wants him as much as he wants her."

I try. I really do. I feign confidence as I unbutton his shirt and push it off his shoulders. Then I put my hand on his chest and trace the planes of his muscles. He inhales and watches as his fingers flex at his sides, waiting for my curiosity to escalate into full-blown lust.

His chest is different from Ethan's. More hair. Slightly narrower. Still very nice. Just not him.

"Okay, stop."

I drop my arms and sigh. Connor steps back and rubs his eyes. I'm sucking like a Hoover, and he knows it. We all know it.

Erika drops her notebook and comes onto the stage. I pick up my shirt and cover myself.

"*Cassie, what's going through your mind when you touch him? Because I'm guessing it's not how much you want to sleep with him.*"

"*I'm sorry. I just can't seem to . . .*"

I glance at Connor. He's trying so hard to make this work, but I keep blocking him. At this rate, our scene is going to be the blandest obsessive love story ever told.

"*Mr. Bain, take a break. I'd like to work with Miss Taylor for a while.*"

"*Yeah, sure.*" *Connor gives me a sympathetic smile, then pulls on his shirt and heads to the exit.*

I tense up as Erika studies me and crosses her arms.

"*What's going on with you? I know you're capable of having chemistry with Connor. I've seen it, especially in the scenes from* Streetcar *last year. That's why I cast you together in this. Why are you holding back? Is it the nudity?*"

I shake my head.

"*Then what?*"

How can I tell her that if I fully commit to the scene, I'm worried how my boyfriend will react? It's the world's weakest excuse.

She frowns when I don't respond. She knows Ethan and me well enough by now to read between the lines.

"*Cassie, you can't let your offstage relationship affect your performance. They're two different lives. Mr. Holt is an actor. He should understand that.*"

"*He does, and he's being really supportive, but . . . it's going to be hard for him to watch, you know?*"

"*Then perhaps he shouldn't. For this showcase, you all need to be at your best. You should sideline anything that could hold you back or distract you.*"

"*I can't ban him from watching.*"

"*No, but you can suggest that it's not in his best interest. The last thing either of you needs right now is drama in your private lives. Keep it onstage. Am I clear?*"

I nod. "Yes."

"Good. Are you ready to rehearse now?"

"Yes."

I feel like I've been chastised by my mother.

"Take five and come back with a different attitude. We don't have much time to get this piece in shape, and I really believe it could be quite spectacular, as long as you both commit to it."

I put on my shirt and head outside for a cigarette. I don't smoke much these days, because Ethan doesn't like it. Just another way I'm modifying my behavior for my boyfriend.

When I go back in, I put all thoughts of Ethan out of my head and completely commit to the scene. Connor doesn't know what's hit him. I can see surprise in his expression when I become Marla. In her skin, I feel guilty for wanting a man other than my husband, but I need to explore the physical attraction to the enigmatic painter.

By the end, we're both flushed and breathing heavily, and I'm kneeling in front of him and pretending not to notice the bulge in his pants.

Erika seems pleased. "Much better. See you tomorrow."

She leaves Connor and me to get dressed. It's awkward between us. Connor's always been the one person I felt completely comfortable with, but this rehearsal has ruined that. He touched my boobs and got an erection. In my character's skin, I was aroused by him.

How do we not feel weird about that?

When we exit the theater, Ethan's waiting. Connor mumbles, "Good night," and walks off without looking either of us in the eye. I immediately bury my head in Ethan's chest and hug the hell out of him.

"Hey," he says as he strokes my hair. "You okay?"

"Yeah. Just tired."

"Rough day?"

"Yeah. Erika ripped me a new one."

"Why?"

"Because I was holding back."

He pauses. "With Connor?"

"Yeah."

"Uh-huh." He stops stroking. "Did you . . . not take your shirt off?"

"No, I did, but—"

His jaw muscles tighten against the side of my head. "But what? Did he touch you?"

"Yes." I can hear his heartbeat thundering in his chest. "But I kept thinking about you. How you'd react. Erika told me I needed to stop."

"So . . . what happened?"

I pull back so I can look up at him. Predictably, he's frowning. "I tried harder."

His frown deepens. "And?"

"And . . . uh . . ." I recall the breath-stealing tingles as Connor palmed my breasts. His bulge, right in my face as I pretended to fellate him. "I think by the end it was working okay."

He deflates, and the look on his face almost breaks my heart.

I stretch up to kiss him. I need to kiss him. Remind him he's the one I want. Remind myself it was my character getting turned on by another man during a scene, not me.

He kisses me back. Wraps his hands in my hair and moves my head to where he wants it. Lights me up more completely in three seconds than Connor did all night.

"Take me home," I say as my whole body flushes.

He does. And an hour later, when I'm sweaty and boneless beneath him, I tell him I love him for the first time since we got back together.

I say it because I mean it. Not because of the guilt.

Mostly.

Dr. Kate pours me a glass of water. I take it gratefully. At least it's something to do with my hands.

"Do you think you may have been overcompensating for what you were doing with Connor?" Dr. Kate asks.

"Probably." I sip more water. "But I didn't want Ethan to feel like there was some stupid love triangle going on, because there wasn't."

Dr. Kate gives me a few seconds, then asks, "Was there ever a time you wanted to justify Ethan's mistrust?"

I nearly choke on my reply, but these sessions are nothing without honesty.

"No, but . . ."

She waits for more.

"I often wondered how different everything would have been if I could have loved Connor. He was so uncomplicated. But I couldn't do it. Not even after I thought I'd never see Ethan again."

"So there wasn't even a hint of anything when you and Ethan were still together?"

I shake my head. "As much as I had to be attracted to Connor on-stage, I never wanted to continue things offstage."

"You told him that?"

"Connor and I never spoke about it, but I could tell he knew. As for Ethan, I told him over and over again that he had nothing to be concerned about."

I'd said it so much, the words began to feel like acid on my tongue.

"But he didn't believe you."

Bitterness bleeds through my skin like a rash.

"No."

Windscreen wipers thud from side to side as Ethan's number flashes on my screen.

"Hi." I'm exhausted but happy to talk to him. We haven't seen each other much this week, and I'm craving him. The Senior Showcase is in four days, and we've been rehearsing around the clock. We've only had to rehearse the Romeo and Juliet *scene a couple of times, because, clearly, we rock. Erika*

has been concentrating more on the new scenes, determined to get them perfect.

"Hey," he says, sounding just as tired as I am. "Where are you?"

"On my way home."

"Our rehearsal is almost done, too. I think Avery and I are finally getting the rhythm of this freaking Stoppard dialog. Not that we can hear much with this storm going on. This rain is crazy, huh?"

"Yeah. Hope your ark-building skills are decent, or we could be in trouble."

"We don't need an ark. I have some inflatable pool lounges. They have cup holders."

"Fancy."

"No expense spared to save my woman from the watery apocalypse."

"Nothing says 'I love you' more than quality recreational inflatables."

He makes a noise. "Now I have visions of that inflatable sheep Avery bought for his pool."

"We said we'd never discuss that."

"You're right. Can we talk about how much I fucking miss you?"

I smile. "Can you hold that thought? We're just pulling up outside my apartment. I need to make a mad dash for the door."

"We?"

"Yeah, um . . ." I take a deep breath. "Connor drove me home, so I wouldn't get drenched."

There's silence, then, "Uh-huh. You don't have your umbrella?"

His tone immediately sets me on edge. "Well, yeah, but it's a storm. Connor's car was parked behind the theater. Plus, it's ten o'clock at night."

Next to me, Connor shakes his head ever so slightly. It frustrates us both that Ethan gets like this every time we're together. He must know by now that his fear is unnecessary. Does he honestly believe I'll suddenly develop an overwhelming urge to fuck Connor, because we're alone in a car?

"Hang on," I say, and grab my bag. "I'll talk to you when I get inside." I push the hold button, and sigh. "Thanks, Connor. See you tomorrow."

"No problem. Have a good night." He gives me a look that says he knows the rest of this phone call isn't going to be pleasant. I exit the car as quickly as possible, then race through the downpour to my front door.

When I get inside, I strip off my jacket and take Ethan off hold.

"Hey."

"Hey." His voice is all kinds of pissed. I stifle a groan. I'm too tired to deal with this right now.

"Ethan, it was a five-minute car ride. What the hell do you have to be worried about?"

"I don't know, Cassie. You tell me."

"There's nothing to tell! Do you have so little faith in me that you think I'd even contemplate doing anything with Connor?"

"Well, you seem to be spending all of your time with him these days. Perhaps you're confused about who's your actual boyfriend and who's the annoying fuck trying to get into your pants."

"He's not trying to get into my pants! How many times do I have to tell you that?"

"Cassie, I've seen how he looks at you."

"Who cares how he looks at me? He's never, and I mean never, tried anything! He's been a perfect gentleman, despite how rude you are to him all the time."

"Oh, sure, a perfect gentleman who's spent the better part of six weeks groping your tits."

"Oh, for God's sake!" I rub my eyes. "I can't do this with you right now. I really can't. You're wearing me out. We have the most important performance of our lives in four days, and right now you're tying yourself in knots and taking me with you. You have to stop. Seriously."

He sighs and goes silent.

I hate fighting with him, especially over the phone. If he were here, I could touch him. Show I love him and only him. As it is, I can just picture him, tense-jawed as he jumps to all the wrong conclusions. Doubting himself enough to doubt me.

"Yeah. Okay. Well, I'd better go. Good night."

"Wait."

He pauses. "What?"

"Do you want to come over when your rehearsal is done?"

"Why?"

"Because . . . I miss you and want to see you."

"Cassie, you're exhausted. I'm exhausted."

"So? Just come over and sleep here. Please."

"I don't think so. You need to rest and you just admitted I'm wearing you out."

"Ethan . . ."

"I'll talk to you tomorrow."

The line goes dead, and I flop back onto the sofa.

Crap.

I pull off my wet shoes and socks, then send him a text.

<I'm sorry. I love you.>

Predictably, I don't get a reply.

Half an hour later, I'm getting out of the shower when there's a knock at the door. I put on my robe and answer it to see Ethan there, drenched.

"What are you doing? You're soaked!"

"You asked me to come over, remember? I've been knocking for five minutes." He looks past me into the apartment. "What the hell took you so long?"

"I was in the shower."

I can see suspicion all over his face, and I roll my eyes as I grab the front of his shirt and drag him inside.

"Stay," I say, and leave him dripping on the rug as I head off to grab some towels.

When I get back, I throw a towel over his head and roughly dry his hair.

"You're an idiot, you know that?"

"Why?"

I push him down onto the sofa and pull off his shoes and socks.

"Because you have absolutely no clue how much I love you." I unbutton his shirt and pull it off. "And you think stupid, impossible things, like I could want anyone but you."

"Cassie . . ."

"Shut up."

I pull him to his feet and gesture to the bedroom. "Go take a look."

He frowns. "What?"

"Go look to make sure Connor isn't in my bed. Check the closet, too. And Ruby's room. While you're at it, you might as well check my phone and computer. Make sure I'm not cyber- or text-fucking him."

He drops his head.

"Go on. Look."

He drags his fingers through his hair and pushes it off his forehead. "I don't need to look."

"Don't you?"

"No." He walks over and puts his arms around me. "You're right. I am an idiot."

He buries his head in my neck, and that's all it takes to defuse me. Then he presses his lips against my pulse, and I'm all wound up again.

Why doesn't he understand this is what I want? This crazy über-lust he can elicit with a single brush of his lips. Doesn't he get that no one will ever make me feel the way he does?

Dumb man.

He pulls open my robe, and gentle fingers trail apologies all over me.

"Tell me you love me again," he whispers.

I cup his face. "I love you. More than that, I'm completely in love with you. Stop being ridiculous, please." I kiss his chest and feel the rapid pounding beneath the muscle.

"I'll try. It's not easy. I've been this way for too long."

"You don't need to be."

"Please inform my brain of that. It won't listen to me."

"Take me to bed. That'll make your brain shut up."

He scoops me up and carries me to the bedroom. I kiss him and touch him in all the ways I know he likes, as I try to chase away his fears for a while.

When we finally join, I see him let go of the doubt. But I know from experience that this sexual exorcism won't last long though. We'll make love and fall asleep in each other's arms, and everything will be perfect, but in the morning the shadows will return.

I keep telling myself that if we can just make it to graduation, we'll be okay. Connor will go his way, and I'll go mine, and Ethan will have no reason to doubt anymore. But the logical part of me whispers that there'll always be a Connor. Someone who threatens him and makes him feel like he's going to lose me. And even though it will never, ever be true, I have no idea how to convince him otherwise.

After a few seconds, I realize I've gone silent.

I look up to find Dr. Kate staring at me.

"Are you okay?"

I don't answer.

"Just breathe, Cassie. Allow everything you're feeling to have its moment, then let it go. Every breath will lessen the anxiety. You don't need it anymore."

I take deep breaths. The more I do it, the easier it gets.

After a couple of minutes, I feel calm enough to open my eyes.

Dr. Kate gives me a warm smile. "Well done. How do you feel?"

"Drained."

"Good. That means you're purging. Each time you do it, your emotional burden will lessen, and that's our goal."

She looks at the clock. "We have a few minutes left. Is there anything else that's been weighing on your mind?"

I take another slow breath and let it out before saying, "I sometimes get this overwhelming sense of . . . guilt about Ethan, when things started going wrong."

"About what?"

I shake my head. "How I couldn't help him. I feel like a lot of this stuff is my fault, because I wasn't strong enough or clever enough or patient enough to help him change."

She puts down her notebook and takes off her glasses. "Cassie, let me assure you, it's not possible to change people. You can encourage and support them, but that's about it. The rest is up to them."

"But I feel like I should've done more."

She looks at me for a few seconds, then crosses her legs. "Do you like books?"

For a moment, I'm thrown by her sudden left turn. "Um . . . Yes."

"Well," she says as she laces her fingers together, "let's say people are books. Everyone who comes into our lives is given a glimpse of a few of our pages. If they like us, we show them more pages. If we like them, we want them to see the unedited parts. Some people may make notes in the margins. Leave their marks upon us and our story. But ultimately, the words that are printed—that represent us as a person—don't change without our permission."

She leans forward and gives me a smile.

"You had a huge impact on Ethan. No doubt, in the story of his life, you've left your mark everywhere. It's unfortunate that a lot of other people did as well. Ethan made a choice to delete their contributions and only keep the things that made him stronger. He reprinted himself, if you like. The only person who was capable of doing that was Ethan. Just like the only person who can rewrite your story and how it ends is you. Do you understand what I'm saying?"

I nod, because what she's saying makes perfect sense. And the realization that all the therapy in the world isn't going to help me unless I take the responsibility for helping myself is both terrifying and exhilarating.

She pats me on the arm. "Well, our time is up. I'll see you in a few days. In the meantime, try not to be too hard on yourself, and please wish Ethan all the best for me."

"I will. Thanks."

When I step out into the waiting room, Ethan's there. He closes the book he's reading and stands.

After the roller coaster of emotions I've just experienced, I'm amazed at how happy I am to see him.

The way he looks at me makes me warm all over.

"Good session?"

I smile and go to him. "Pretty good. Watcha reading?"

He holds it up for me to see.

"*The Art of Happiness*?"

"It's written by the Dalai Lama."

"So just a light read, then."

He shakes his head. "Not light, but definitely worth it."

"Yeah? What does it say?"

He steps forward, his expression serious. "In a nutshell, it says 'Make Cassie smile every day and tell her you love her even when she doesn't want to hear it.'"

"Really?"

"Yes."

Excess emotion wells up.

He doesn't help by wrapping his arms around me like he never wants to let go.

I don't want to let go, either.

The thing is, if people were books, Ethan would be a bestseller. A sexy, intelligent page-turner you'd find hard to put down, even after it reduced you to a sobbing mess.

TWENTY-ONE

OPENING NIGHT

Three Years Earlier
Westchester, New York
The Grove
Senior Showcase

We wrap around each other like we're all that's holding each other to the earth. Adrenaline pumps through me, and even though snuggling with Ethan helps channel my nerves, I can't get rid of them completely. Neither can he. This performance is too important.

A few nerves will do us good. Raise our energy. Keep us on point.

When the call comes to take our places, I pull back and look into his eyes. He strokes my face and looks back with love, but there are also flickers of something else.

Doubt?

Fear?

Both?

We head down to the stage, and the show begins. Our scene is first. *Romeo and Juliet.* Performing with him is so easy. We tap into our connection effortlessly. The scene is flawless, and after we take our bow, he leads me offstage and kisses me in triumph before running off to get changed.

The rest of the night passes in a blur. We do scenes and monologues, take our applause, and get changed into our next costumes. We see each other briefly backstage, but we're focused on what we're doing as we slip out of one character and step into another. Show our range. Impress the audience. It's not just people filling those seats tonight, it's representation and contracts, too. It's our futures.

Ethan and I rise to the challenge. Despite our nerves, we both perform incredibly well.

The last scene of the night is *Portrait* with me and Connor. I'm confident and in the moment. Connor and I are on fire. The energy onstage crackles with realism, and it's not until I take my bow that I see Ethan, stony-faced, in the wings. My smile drops. He hasn't witnessed this scene before. I'd made sure of that.

After our fight a few days ago, I'd begged him not to watch it tonight.

Obviously he's done listening to me.

I barely look at him as I exit the stage.

Present Day
New York City, New York
Graumann Theater
Opening Night

Every opening night is a mixture of excitement and fear, but this one . . . well, it's even worse. I have to do my eyeliner three times because my hand is shaking so much, and when the production intern, Cody, knocks on the door to find out if I need anything, I just about jump out of my skin.

"You okay, Miss Taylor?" he asks.

"Yeah, fine."

"You're ready early."

"Yeah, well, I have a lot of panicking to do. I need to allow enough time to fit it all in."

"You don't need to panic. You're amazing. The show's fantastic."

"Yes, but every Broadway reviewer worth their salt is here tonight. The asshole from the *New York Times* is out there, for God's sake, and he makes a habit out of not liking things just to piss people off."

"Well, that's just wrong."

"Tell me about it. He's already done a piece about how skeptical he is about this play. He doesn't like the script, and I'm pretty sure he doesn't like Ethan and me."

"Has he met you? Seen you perform?"

"No, Cody. He's a *reviewer*. He doesn't have to see something to know he doesn't like it."

I pull a brush through my hair. "How's Ethan doing?"

"Well, he vomited."

"How many times?"

"Three. Now he's lying down. Do you need me to get you anything?"

"Valium, a bottle of bourbon, and about ten pounds of self-confidence."

"I'm predicting that if I get you the bourbon, the self-confidence will take care of itself."

I turn to him. "Holt's been telling you stories about me being drunk again, hasn't he?"

"Just a few. I'm impressed."

"Let me just say this: that time in Martha's Vineyard? *Everyone* was half naked. Not just me."

"He did explain that. Okay. I'd better go raid a liquor store. Be back soon with your bourbon."

"Wait, you can't buy booze. You're, like, twelve."

"I'm twenty-two, Miss Taylor."

"Really? You're legal? Hmmm. I might have to rethink not sexually harassing you, then."

"Please don't. Mr. Holt is a large man. He'd crush me like a bug."

"He doesn't get jealous anymore." Cody gives me a look. "Okay, he does, but he's not an asshole about it."

"Did you tell him Mr. Bain sent you that massive bouquet of roses?"

"Are you insane? He'd tear the place apart."

"Really?"

"I don't think so. Still, maybe lose the card, okay?"

He takes the card and shoves it in his pocket. "It's gone."

"You're awesome, Cody. And pretty."

He laughs. "Have a great show, Miss Taylor."

"Thanks. See you when it's over."

When he's gone, I slip into my Act One costume and begin my focusing exercises.

I do three sets of tai-chi before giving up. My focus is screwed. I need . . .

There's a knock at the door. Perfect timing.

"Come in."

Ethan enters. He looks like crap. He's also in costume, but even through his makeup, I can see how green he is.

He walks over and collapses on my couch.

"You okay?"

"Yep."

"Really?"

"Nope. Did you hear the asshole from the *Times* is coming tonight?"

"Yeah, plus every other Broadway reviewer and blogger in New York."

He clutches his stomach. "Fuck. Also, my parents are here."

"They're going to love it. Mine are coming next week. I wanted to make sure I had some time to spend with them away from the craziness of opening night."

"They send you flowers?"

"Yes. One giant bunch each, because you know, divorced people can't possibly talk on the phone and organize a joint present."

"Of course not."

"Tristan sent me a gift-boxed vibrator with a card that read, '*If the reviewers don't like your show, give them this and tell them to go fuck themselves.*'"

He laughs, then groans. "That's the best thing I've heard all day. He coming tonight?"

"Yep. Bringing his new boyfriend."

"Oh, good. I'd really like to put a face to the inappropriate descriptions of his ass."

"Likewise."

He sits up and sighs. "I see Connor sent you roses."

My heart falters. "Uh . . . you did?"

"Yeah, he was dropping them off at the stage door when I arrived."

"Uh-huh. So . . . you talked to him?"

"Yeah. He wished us both luck."

"You seem very calm about it."

"I am." I give him a skeptical look, and he waves me off. "Connor was a blip on our radar. Despite my fantasizing about beating the shit out of him on the regular, he's a nice guy. The only thing he ever did wrong was take a liking to the girl of my dreams. Can't really blame him for that. You are fucking spectacular."

"So you're okay with him sending me flowers?"

"Yep. He can send you all the flowers he wants. At the end of the night, I'm the one taking you home."

"Well, you walk me home."

"Semantics. I take you back to your apartment, then we say good night at the door and share a marathon hug that ensures I'll be hard for hours afterward."

I laugh. "*Hours*? Really?" He glares, and I drop my smile. "I'm sorry. You must be frustrated."

"Nope. I'm fine. Because I know that one night, you're going to invite me in, and on that night, I'm going to make sweet love to you for hours on end, and Connor will be nowhere to be found. At least, I hope he won't. If he were, that would be creepy."

I laugh, and when I go over to him, he pulls on my hand until I'm straddling him. I balk for about three seconds before admitting to myself that I need this. I need him. Of all the things to be worried about tonight, he's not one of them.

He moves beneath me and makes a noise.

"Am I hurting you?" I ask.

"No. What you're doing is the opposite of hurting. God, you feel good."

I snuggle into his neck, and he wraps his arms around me. Within two minutes, our breathing is synchronized, and my nerves have calmed.

There's a brief knock on the door, and I murmur, "Come in."

I crack my eyes open to see Marco standing in the doorway, staring at us.

"What on earth are you two doing?"

In unison, Ethan and I say, "Focusing."

Marco blinks and shakes his head. "Erika certainly taught you some interesting techniques at that school. Still, whatever works. I was going to wish you both luck for tonight, but I don't really need to because I know you'll be magnificent."

Ethan says, "Thanks. We know," and tightens his arms around me. If I weren't so relaxed, I'd giggle.

"Well, all right then. Have a wonderful show, and I'll see you afterward."

"Bye, Marco."

When he closes the door, we both sigh.

"I pity those reviewers," Ethan says.

"Why?"

"Because by the time we're finished with them, they're going to run out of superlatives for how fucking awesome we are."

I smile against his neck. "So true."

Three Years Earlier
Westchester, New York
The Grove
Night of the Senior Showcase

The after-party is manic. Everyone is decompressing so hard, all sense of being civilized has flown out the window. The air heaves with primal energy. People throw back alcohol amid thick clouds of marijuana smoke, and I see things being done in public that should be kept private.

Ethan's on the other side of the room talking to Avery and Lucas but glancing at me intermittently. It's obvious he's angry about tonight. No problem. So am I.

"Trouble in paradise?" Ruby asks as she drapes her arm around my shoulders.

I roll my eyes. "Men. Why are they so stupid?"

"To make us look smart? I take it Holt didn't dig your little scene with Connor."

"Not at all."

"Well, to be fair, it was pretty steamy. And let's be honest, Connor is all kinds of easy on the eyes. If I were Holt, I'd be pretty pissed, too."

"Ruby—"

"Just saying."

I grab her beer and take a swig. "I'm just glad it's done. Maybe now he can get over it. I'm so tired of having to defend myself over nothing."

"I hear you. There's nothing more draining than having to constantly deflect suspicion. I had an ex-boyfriend who accused me of cheating every time he saw me so much as talk to another guy."

"Really? How did you deal with him?"

"I cut him some slack. After all, I was fucking several other dudes."

I hand her back her beer. "You're not helping."

"Oh, honey, lighten up. Go get your man, take him back to our place, and screw his brains out. In the morning he won't even remember why he was so pissed."

"You think?"

"Well, it *is* Holt. He has a talent for holding on to things. Maybe throw in a morning blow job for good measure."

I give her a hug. "I love you dearly, but you're useless at advice."

"Yeah, I know. See you tomorrow?"

"Yep. I'll be the one blowing my boyfriend."

"In your bedroom with the door shut, right?"

"If you're lucky."

I take a breath and walk over to Ethan. When I get there, Jack puts his arm around me, clearly inebriated.

"Ah, sweet Cassie Taylor. You were so good tonight. So good."

"Thanks, Jack. You too."

"I especially enjoyed getting a peek of side-boob during your scene with Connor. That was hot. Holt, your girlfriend has a spectacular rack. I hope you appreciate that."

Ethan shakes his head. "Yeah, and now everyone's seen it. I'm thrilled. Really."

Right. That's it.

I grab the front of his shirt and pull.

"Hey!"

"Where are you guys going?" Jack whines.

"I'm taking my boyfriend home to screw his brains out," I announce. "Maybe then he'll stop being such an idiot."

There's a chorus of catcalls as I drag Ethan out of the party, but I don't care.

I take his keys from him and push him toward the passenger door. I've barely had anything to drink but judging by the way he wobbles as he gets into the car, he's well over the limit.

As I pull away from the curb, he mumbles something about being careful with his car. I ignore it.

He turns on the stereo and AC/DC blares from the speakers.

I turn it off and slap his hand when he tries to turn it on again.

He slumps down into his seat and looks out the window.

"Did you mean what you just said?" he asks.

"Yes. I am indeed going to screw your brains out."

"No," he says, "I meant about me being an idiot."

"Yes. I can see how pissed you are over the scene with Connor, and it's dumb. We did what the play called for. You know that's how it works. I feel like you're blaming me."

"I'm not, it's just . . . I keep seeing him touching you. Do you have any idea how that makes me feel?"

"That's why I didn't want you to see it. Ethan, we can't keep doing this dance. You have to try to find a way to get past this."

He's quiet for a few seconds, then says, "I've been reading self-help books."

"What?"

"I have a whole stack of them. I've been meditating and trying to change how I react to stuff, but it's really fucking hard."

"Why didn't you tell me?"

"Like I want you to know how desperate I am."

"At least you're trying."

"Yeah, and failing," he says. "It's frustrating as hell, because I want to change so badly, then something like tonight happens, and I'm back to where I started."

I touch his face. His air of hopelessness is scaring me. "Please . . . keep trying, okay? Don't give up."

He nods, but I wonder if he's already too far gone.

We pull up in front of my apartment and head inside. When I close the door, he pushes me up against it and kisses me. There's a desperation in him that I want to extinguish, but I don't know how. It mirrors my own.

I don't think either one of us is a bad person. Why can't we just get to be happy together?

When we make love, it's rough. Almost angry. And when he falls asleep, I lie there and try to imagine being the one to leave this time. Could I do it? Get out before he destroys me?

It's a tempting thought.

Present Day
New York City, New York
Graumann Theater
Opening Night

The party's loud and flamboyant, just like most of the people attending. There's a cavalcade of *"Darling!"* and *"You were FABULOUS!"* and *"I loved it!"*, and through it all, I try to take the compliments and make small talk, when all I want to do is find Ethan and bury myself in his chest.

I spot him across the room, chatting with a throng of women all desperate to get his attention, but all the while, he keeps one eye on me. The way he looks at me keeps permanent color in my cheeks. Even across the room, he radiates sex. I pity the effect he's having on the poor women huddled around him.

"So what's the story with you and Ethan?" the reviewer from *Stage*

Diary asks. "I've heard you had a tumultuous love affair at drama school. Are you still together?"

Ethan takes a sip of champagne and nods at the woman talking to him.

I can't stop watching him. "No. Not together."

"Friends?"

He moves his gaze to me and stays there. "No. Not exactly friends."

"What then?"

Ethan frowns. Does he know I'm talking about him? "He's . . . Ethan."

"What does that mean?"

"I'm still figuring that out."

"Hmmm, intriguing."

"Yep. Definitely that."

Marco swoops in and kisses me on the cheek. He's doing that a lot tonight. It's pretty obvious he's ecstatic with the reception the show has received.

"Marco, I'm trying to get Miss Taylor to give me the scoop on her relationship with her costar. She's being cagey. Care to elaborate?"

"Dear lady," Marco says, "if I could figure out what's going on between my leads, rehearsals would have been far less fraught with tension and angst. Then again, the show would have been lifeless. Whatever's going on between them, I pray it continues. Now, let's talk about the fabulous write-up you're going to give us."

Marco puts his arm around the woman and leads her away.

I barely notice. Ethan's still staring at me. Amid all this excitement and energy, he calms me.

He excuses himself from the women around him and walks toward me, so handsome in his suit. People congratulate him as he passes, and even though he acknowledges them, he keeps his attention on me.

When he reaches me, he holds out his champagne glass.

"To us."

"To us," I say, and clink his glass. "We were amazing tonight, even if I do say so myself."

"We were," he says, "but I wasn't toasting the show."

He leans in and kisses my cheek. "You're so goddamn beautiful, you make me think very bad thoughts. Please stop."

I sip my champagne and resist fanning my face. "Funny. I was about to say the exact same thing to you."

The rest of the night is a blur. We spend time with his parents and sister. Chat with Tristan and his date. Have our photo taken for a slew of social pages. And through it all, a simmering tension crackles between us.

Every look is filled with heat and expectation. Every touch sends sparks twisting through my abdomen.

When the party wraps up, he's there with my coat. As he slips it on, he presses a soft kiss to the side of my neck.

I shiver and close my eyes.

"Sorry," he says and steps away. "I just . . . I'm finding it very difficult to keep my hands off you tonight." He shakes his head and laughs. "Well, let's be honest, I find it difficult to keep my hands off you all the time. Tonight is just extra tough."

TWENTY-TWO

BEGINNING OF THE END

Three Years Earlier
Westchester, New York
The Grove

Erika walks into the room like she's carrying the weight of the world on her shoulders. There's absolute silence. The tension is palpable.

After Saturday night's showcase, agents, directors, and producers had the weekend to submit offers. Now, it's the moment of truth when we find out who's been offered what.

"First of all," Erika says as she hugs a stack of envelopes, "let me just say how proud I am. The quality of your performances on Saturday was excellent, and I couldn't have asked for any of you to be more committed in sharing yourselves with your audience. Having said that, for those of you who don't have firm offers, don't despair. It doesn't mean you're not talented, and it certainly doesn't mean you're not employable. It just means you weren't right for the roles being filled."

She walks around the room and gives out envelopes. Ethan gets two. So do I. A handful of others get double offers. Most get one. A select few don't get any.

Aiyah sits with empty hands and bursts into tears. Erika hugs her and assures her the work will come.

I open my envelopes with shaking fingers.

The first one is from a repertory company in Los Angeles that wants me to become a permanent member. They perform contemporary pieces and work on a profit-share basis.

When I open the other envelope, I have to read it three times to fully understand what it says. It's from a producer. He wants to do an off-Broadway production of *Portrait*. Fully professional. Five weeks of rehearsal, plus a tentative six-week season. He's already secured the rights and wants Connor and me to be his stars.

I look over at Ethan. He's frowning at one of his letters. I say his name, and he looks up.

"What is it?" I ask.

He holds up the two pieces of paper. "Well, in the first one, the Lowbridge Shakespeare company wants me to join their next European tour, doing Mercutio in *Romeo and Juliet*."

"That's fantastic!"

"Yeah."

"Then why do you look shell-shocked?"

He shakes his head. "The other one is . . . it's the New York Shakespeare Theater. They want me to do *Hamlet*."

"Which role?"

He looks dazed. "The lead. I guess they liked my monologue."

"Oh my God, Ethan, that's incredible!"

"Yeah. I can't believe it."

"Believe it. You're amazing, and your offers prove that. Why aren't you happy?"

"I am, it's just . . . I have no idea which one to choose. The European tour is a longer contract, but the other one . . . I mean, it's *Hamlet*. For years, I've been saying I'd give my left ball to play that role."

"Then do it. It's one of the most coveted male roles out there. And you would absolutely hit it out of the park."

He shrugs. "I hope I would. But, hey, what about you?"

"Well, I've been offered a spot in The Roundhouse in L.A."

"Seriously? Those guys are impressive. Their productions are cutting edge. And the other one?"

"Well, the other one is off-Broadway."

"Are you kidding? Jesus, Cassie, that's great!"

"Yeah, I know . . ."

"I'm sensing a 'but.'"

I take a breath. "It's for *Portrait*."

He blinks. "As in, *Portrait* with . . ."

"Connor. Yeah. They want both of us."

He's really trying to keep his expression happy. "For how long?"

"Eleven weeks to start. Then, if it does well . . . who knows? A few months. A year if we're really lucky."

He nods. "Wow. A year. That's . . . wow. Amazing opportunity."

"Yeah. I guess."

A knot forms in my stomach. It feeds off the furrow in his brow and the dark energy that swirls around him.

He almost manages to shake it off when he takes my hand in both of his. "Seriously, Cassie, it's unbelievable. I'm really happy for you."

"Really?"

He smiles. "Really."

He's very convincing. Then again, he's an excellent actor.

Present Day
New York City, New York
The Apartment of Cassandra Taylor

"I can't look."

"Me, neither."

"Where the hell is Cody when you need him?"

"I'm hoping he's asleep. It's six a.m."

Ethan and I are sitting cross-legged in the middle of my living room with a stack of newspapers and printouts from various blogs sitting between us.

Reviews.

The verdict on our show.

"Okay, you read the *Times*," I say. "I really can't handle that."

"Fine. Then you have to read the *Post*," says Ethan. "That guy shook my hand for way too long last night. And he stroked it a little."

"Fine."

We both pick up a paper and flick to the arts section. I read the *Post* review. As I do, my face becomes hotter and hotter. When I reach the end, I glance over at Ethan. He's frowning at the *Times* and shaking his head.

He puts the paper down and exhales. "Well . . . that was . . . unexpected."

"He liked it?"

"No. He loved it. Loved everything about it, except for the script, but said all the other elements worked so well, it didn't matter."

"But he liked us?"

He nods. "Absolutely. And I quote: '*The two lead actors have the kind of mesmerizing chemistry that will have audiences returning to this show over and over again. Most of the people I spoke to on opening night have already planned their return visit. It's that kind of magic that will ensure this show has a long and prosperous future. A must-see night of theater.*'"

"Wow."

"Exactly."

The rest of the reviews are all pretty similar. They all love the show, particularly the chemistry between Ethan and me. By the time we're finished reading, I'm so embarrassed by all the praise, I feel like I need to splash cold water on my face.

I also feel strangely emotional.

"Hey." Ethan touches my face. "You okay?"

"Yeah. Just . . . happy, you know?"

"You look like you're going to cry."

"Shut up. Talking about it will make it happen." I blink and will the tears to go away.

"I'm sorry."

"Don't apologize! That's worse than talking about it. Dammit." I blink faster, but it's too late. The tears fall in fat streams down my cheeks. Ethan cups my face and wipes them away. It only makes it worse.

He pulls me into his arms, and I cry. It's been a long time since I cried happy tears. He presses his lips against my forehead and strokes my hair.

It feels so good . . . so absolutely and emphatically right, it makes me cry harder.

Three Years Earlier
Westchester, New York
The Grove

He hasn't touched me for nearly a week. Well, he's touched me, but not the right way. Not how I need him to.

He's shutting down and pulling back, and it makes me sick to think I'm just as powerless to stop it now as I was last time.

Still, I have one thing to try. One desperate play in what I'm suspecting is an unwinnable game.

"I'm going to tell Erika I'm passing on *Portrait*."

He looks up from his book and frowns at me. "What?"

"I'm passing. I'll take L.A. instead."

"Cassie—"

"I mean, it's still an amazing gig. Plus, it's not like Broadway's going anywhere. I'll get there some other way."

He lowers his book and sighs. "Don't be stupid. You can't turn it down. Especially if you think you're doing it for me."

"I think I'm doing it for us. I know how crazy it must make you to think about me doing that show with Connor eight times a week."

"So what? Making me part of this decision is ridiculous. It's your *career*. You need to do it."

"Not if it means losing you."

He rubs his eyes. "If you don't take it, you'll lose me anyway, because I'll never forgive myself for fucking up something so important. Please, Cassie. Take it."

"But—"

"No, this is not up for discussion. You've been given an amazing opportunity, and I'm not going to let you sabotage it because of me. No fucking way. You tell Erika you're taking it, or I will."

He slams his book closed and shoves it in his bag.

"Where are you going?"

"Home."

"But what about our Arts in Society final?"

"I'll study by myself."

"Why are you so angry with me?"

He slings his bag over his shoulder and turns to me. "I'm not angry with you. I'm angry with me. Angry that you think you need to sacrifice your career for me."

"Ethan—"

"No, Cassie, this is fucking crazy. This isn't love. It's fear. You're afraid of my reaction, and you're letting it rule your judgment. What the hell am I doing to you?"

"You're not doing anything! Sometimes to make things work, you have to make compromises."

"This isn't a compromise! This is you giving up your dream for me, and it pisses me off that you think you have to. That I've made you think that."

"You haven't, I just—"

"Please stop. I've tried really fucking hard to just breathe through this thing with Connor, but I can't, and you know it. But this? It isn't the solution."

"Then what is? Is there one? Because you're really starting to worry me here."

His expression softens, but he doesn't reassure me. I don't know if he can at this point.

"I have to go."

"Wait."

He stops, one hand on the door. I go to him and make him look at me. He does it grudgingly.

"I love you." I stand on my toes to kiss him. He inhales and wraps an arm around me, and even though he kisses me back, it doesn't last long. When he pulls away, his hand is still on the doorknob.

"I love you, too," he says as he cups my cheek. "That's the problem."

He pulls open the door and heads down to his car. I watch him until he's out of sight.

Present Day
New York City, New York
Graumann Theater

When I arrive at the theater, I dump my bag in my dressing room and go to find Ethan. He's been helping me with some meditation techniques, and even though I'm not very good at them, he's a patient teacher.

Of course, Tristan lost his shit when he found out about it. Well, to be honest, he rarely loses his shit, but he did go quiet for a long time and stare at me in a hostile manner.

He's been trying to get me to meditate since the night we met, and I've always dismissed it as a waste of time. Needless to say, Ethan and I aren't the most popular people in his book right now.

I go to Ethan's dressing room, but he's not there. His voice is echoing somewhere in the theater, so I follow the sound.

When I get backstage, I see him talking on his phone and pacing.

"I don't know about this. I mean, the show's only been open a month. We're barely getting on our feet. Yes, I know it's a fantastic opportunity but . . ." He scrubs his face and sighs. "I am listening to you. I get that. And no, this has nothing to do with Cassie. I just . . . I don't know if the time is right for this."

On hearing my name, I slink back into the shadows.

He finishes the conversation by saying, "I'll think about it," and I quietly slip back into his dressing room as he hangs up.

When he appears a minute later, he seems surprised to see me.

"Oh, hey."

"Hi. You okay?"

"Yeah. Good." He puts his phone on the counter and sits on the floor. "Ready?"

"Sure."

He hardly looks at me. We go through the routine of our meditation, but it's obvious his mind is somewhere else.

My meditation is crap. My breathing is choppy, and all I can do is wonder what the hell that conversation was about and why he's hiding it from me.

We finish our cycle and when I open my eyes, I get the impression he's been staring at me the whole time.

"You want to snuggle?" he asks quietly.

I stand and shake my head. "No, I don't think so."

"Everything alright?"

"Yep." I can feel all the parts of me that have recently started opening up begin to wilt under the weight of whatever's going on with him. I've been getting better at trusting this new him, but now . . . the doubt is back.

"Cassie . . ."

"I'm fine. I just have some stuff to do."

He grabs my hand. "Wait. What's going on?"

I shake my head. I'm incapable of confronting him, because I'm terrified of what he'll say. "Nothing. I just don't feel like snuggling tonight."

I pull my hand free and walk out. I need to get away from him.

I can't even comprehend what I'd do if things went wrong again.

TWENTY-THREE

SINK OR SWIM

Three Years Earlier
Westchester, New York
The Grove

I feel like a submarine.

It's a weird analogy, but I remember seeing a movie when I was a kid in which a sub had been hit by a torpedo. There were all these compartments that started filling up with water, and people were racing through corridors and sealing airtight doors behind them so they wouldn't drown.

The way Ethan's been acting recently is making me close off all the areas I had opened up to him when we got back together, and the torpedo hasn't even hit yet.

Ethan notices. He sees me pulling away just as he has. We talk about how we're going to spend some time together in New York after graduation, but it's never with any conviction. I don't think I could fake conviction now if I tried. Everything is desensitized and nothing hurts.

Conversely, nothing feels truly good, either.

We still have sex, but it's like the intimacy is just fading away. In the past, I might have fought against it, but not anymore.

I'm not the caretaker of this relationship. I took on that responsibility once and was nearly ruined by it. If he thinks I'm going through it again, he'll be sorely disappointed.

I think we're both waiting for the other to magically fix us, all the while knowing it's not possible.

Present Day
New York City, New York
Graumann Theater

We start on opposite sides of the stage, and through the next scene, we're slowly drawn to each other. It's a metaphor in movement, and I take a deep breath and open myself up, letting emotions attach to each word.

"Someone once said, 'If you love something, set it free. If it comes back, it's yours. If it doesn't, it never was.'"

The lighting is dim, but as we move toward each other, it brightens slowly.

"You don't believe that?" Ethan asks.

"I do, but the thing is, sometimes people want to leave because they're scared, or misinformed, or insecure, or confused. And it's at those times . . . those hard, definitive moments when two people stand on the brink of falling or flying, that you have to ask yourself: Do I let this person go? Or do I make sure, before they take one more step toward the door, they know all the reasons they should stay?"

He drops his head. "I didn't need a reason. I needed an excuse."

"Why?"

"Because when I found out about your family and your money, I didn't think I was good enough for you. Or good for you."

"Well, that's just stupid. Thinking you're not good enough because of money?"

"To be fair, it was money *and* power."

"I have zero power."

His gaze intensifies, searing my skin. "Over me, you do."

Now, we're toe to toe, and I put my hand on his face. "I didn't tell you about my family because it wasn't important. Just like ribbons and fancy paper have no relevance to the present that's inside. I wanted to be valued for more than just the expensive label. And you gave me that. You made the plain, unwrapped me feel like the most precious thing in the world."

He kisses me, and the rest of the lights fade as the spotlight tightens to contain just us. A whole world encapsulated in a single shaft of light.

"So yeah," I say, "I don't believe in loving something enough to set it free. I believe in loving it enough to fight for it. To yell and scream and beat my fists until they know . . . they understand . . . that they're mine, before they make the choice to walk out the door."

He touches my face, gentle fingers trailing down my cheek. "I'm glad you didn't let me walk away."

"Me, too. Otherwise, I would have had to follow you."

He kisses me as the spotlight fades to black, and there are a few seconds of silence before the audience explodes into applause. It takes me a few moments to let go of Sam and Sarah and return to Cassie and Ethan, but when I do, the lights come back up, and we take our bows.

I get the familiar rush of adrenaline from having a good show, but underneath it is an undercurrent of anxiety. It's been there since I overheard Ethan's phone call earlier in the week.

We head offstage and back to our dressing rooms, and I stew for the entire time I'm taking off my makeup and getting changed.

By the time Ethan knocks on my door, I'm close to fuming.

I yell, "Come in!", and he's barely closed the door before I'm leveling my finger at him.

"I really wanted you to tell me without me having to ask, but it's driving me insane. What are you hiding from me?"

"What?"

"You know what I'm talking about. You've been cagey all week."

"Cassie . . ."

"You promised I could trust you! Told me you were an open book. Was that all just bullshit?"

"No."

"Then tell me. I heard you on the phone the other day. I know something's going on. You said it had nothing to do with me, but I'm pretty damn sure it does."

He sighs. "There was a casting director in the audience last week. She wants me to go to L.A. to guest star in the new hit HBO drama. It's a pretty big role, and my agent is pushing me to take it."

"Then why don't you?"

"Because . . . we've only been open four weeks, and we're making real progress offstage, and . . . I don't want to go."

"Ethan . . ."

"There'll be other opportunities. It's not like I'll be blacklisted for turning it down."

"No, but you'd be a complete dumbass if you did."

"See? This is why I didn't tell you."

"Because I'd tell you to take it?"

"Yes."

"That's dumb."

"No, it's not." He stands and comes over to me. "I want to stay here and do this fucking amazing play with you every night and not fly to the other side of the country for a week. Why is that so wrong?"

"Because it's only a week, and we'll be fine without you. This is a really fantastic opportunity. Has your agent cleared it with the producers?"

"Yes. They're concerned about disappointing audiences, but at the same time, they think the publicity would be great."

"It would be."

"So you wouldn't give a shit if I went away for a week?"

"Of course I would, but I'd survive. We may need some extra rehearsals to make sure your understudy is ready to go, but Nathan's quick. He'll be fine."

I don't miss the way he almost flinches then shoves his hands in his pockets.

"Oh, God, please tell me the reason you don't want to go isn't because you're freaking out about me performing love scenes with your understudy."

He shakes his head. "That's not it."

He doesn't look at me. Alarm bells go off in my head. "I feel stupid for even saying it."

"Just do it. You're freaking me out."

He takes a breath. "I don't want to leave you. I've been there and done that more often than I should and now that. I've worked so fucking hard to get back here and be with you . . . I don't think I can do it."

"Ethan—"

"No, you don't understand. Here, I get to touch you and kiss you every day, even if it's only in the play. How the hell can I leave that?"

"It's only for a week."

"A week without you feels like a year. Trust me. I know this."

I go over and put my arms around him. He squeezes me so tight, it's almost uncomfortable.

"You can do this. You need to."

"Why?"

I pull back and level him with my serious face. "Remember what you said to me years ago, right before you left? You said, 'There's only so much you can watch someone sacrifice before you realize they're changing who they are for you, and not in a good way.' Well, that's what's happening here. I love how far you've come and all the strength and courage you have now, but not doing this because of me? That's just wrong. Call your agent and tell him you're taking the job."

"Cassie . . ."

"Seriously, Ethan. Do it. I'll be waiting here when you get back."

He hugs me again, and I run my fingers through his hair. "You know, Dr. Kate said something interesting today. She said people are too obsessed with conquering their fear when they should just learn to accept it and do stuff that scares them anyway."

He exhales against my neck. "I'm scared to leave you again."

I pull back and look him in the eye. "Do it anyway."

"I love you," he says as he cups my face. "You know that, right?"

"You tell me every day. How could I forget?"

One of these days, I'll accept my fear of saying it back and do it anyway.

Three Years Earlier
Westchester, New York
The Grove

Finals week is hell. I wander between classes in a daze. I'm exhausted from spending time with Ethan and avoiding all the things we should be talking about, and preoccupied with detaching my emotions so I can concentrate.

My final acting assessment is pretty much a disaster. I'm so shut down, I can't even conjure up the most basic emotion, so I fake my way through it and hope Erika doesn't notice.

Of course she notices.

Even before I'm finished, I can see the disappointment on her face. When I look at Ethan, I see disappointment, too, but on him it goes much deeper.

That night, we talk about what's going to happen after graduation. He tells me his mom and dad have offered to let me stay with them in Manhattan until I get an apartment of my own, but he doesn't sound happy about it.

I ask him when he starts rehearsals for *Hamlet*, but he avoids the question. In fact, he avoids most of my questions. In the end, I give up.

Just before he leaves, he kisses me for a long time, but it does nothing to dampen my paranoia.

The next day is Saturday. Ruby's boyfriend is out of town for the weekend, and she drags me out of the apartment to try to get me out of my funk.

We go shopping and have lunch. I pretend I'm having fun, but she's not buying it.

By the time we get home, she's had enough.

"Okay, that's it. What the hell is going on with you and Holt?"

I sigh. "I don't know."

"God, this is frustrating." She flops onto the couch. "You guys have been weird for ages. Is he still freaking out over Connor?"

"I don't know. I think that's part of it."

"But he told you to take the gig, right? I mean, why would he do that if he knew he couldn't handle it?"

"He wants me to be successful."

"But then he'll be miserable?"

"Yes."

"Wow. He's trying to do the honorable thing. It almost makes me like him. Of course, knowing he's miserable might be part of the reason."

I glare at her.

She rolls her eyes. "Have you tried talking to him?"

"A little. He's being evasive."

My phone rings. I check caller ID before answering.

"Hey, Elissa."

"Cassie, you need to get over here." She sounds panicked, and a bit like she's been crying.

"Are you okay?"

"No. I don't care that I'm not supposed to say anything to you. Just get over here."

She hangs up, and my paranoia flares into full-blown anxiety.

"Ruby, can I borrow your car?"

"Of course. What's going on?"

"I have no idea, but I have a feeling it's bad."

Twenty minutes later, I pull up in front of Ethan's apartment and run up the stairs. My mind swirls with a thousand different scenarios as I bang on his door. Even though I'm trying to control my panic, I can already feel my heart crumbling, waiting for the inevitable Ethan-shaped fracture it's about to endure.

Within seconds, Elissa opens the door. Her eyes are bloodshot and furious.

"Maybe you can talk sense into him. I can't. If he asks, I didn't call you."

With that, she leaves and slams the door behind her.

I walk into the apartment to find boxes everywhere. Most are half full and messy, and when I walk into Ethan's bedroom, I see more of the same.

He walks out of the bathroom with an armful of toiletries and freezes.

We stare at each other for a few seconds before he says, "What are you doing here?"

"I could ask you the same thing." I glance around at the boxes. "You're packing early. I thought you were staying here until the lease runs out in two weeks."

He doesn't say anything. Instead, he looks at the ground. My heart is beating so fast, I can feel it in every inhale.

"Ethan?"

"I was going to tell you . . . I just . . . I didn't know how."

A chill runs down my spine. "Tell me what?"

He takes a deep breath and lets it out. Then he does it again. I try to ignore the warning bells going off in my head.

"I turned down *Hamlet*. I'm taking the job in Europe. I'm leaving in three days."

I stare at him, and I'm so full of adrenaline and nervous energy, I let out a sharp laugh. "No, you're not."

He unfreezes and dumps the toiletries into a black duffle bag. "Yes. I am."

I knew this was coming, yet as much as I'd tried to prepare for it, I'm still stunned into silence. The pain in my chest takes my breath away, and all the places I'd tried to protect with numbness flare and burn.

I can't say anything, so I just nod.

He shoves his hands into his pockets. "I've tried so hard to find an excuse to stay with you, but I can't. I've tried to conquer my issues so I didn't infect you with them, and I've failed. Every day I see you shut down a little more, and I know it's my fault. If I stay, I won't just kill your spirit, I'll kill your career. I can already see it affecting your acting, and that fucking slays me. I can't do it, Cassie. I can't drag you down with me. As much as it kills me to go, it would ruin me more to stay."

I swallow with effort, while desperately trying to deaden the pain. I breathe in and out a few times. Hold myself upright and tall, and pretend this isn't happening.

He's leaving me.

Again.

He told me he could be in a relationship with me, but it was a lie. A beautiful lie I really wanted to believe.

I'm so incredibly stupid.

"Cassie," he says as he takes a step toward me. "Please say something."

"What do you expect me to say?" My voice is flat and disconnected. I beg my emotions to be the same way.

"I don't know. Tell me you understand."

I look at him, still dazed. "I don't."

"Tell me you don't hate me."

That makes me laugh. It seems strange that I can make such a happy noise when I'm filling up with misery. "When did you make this decision?"

"Right after we were given our offers."

I stare at him. "But . . . you took *Hamlet*."

"No, I didn't."

"So you *lied* to me?"

"No, I never told you I took it. You just assumed I would."

I'm so close to screaming my head off, it's scaring me. "When exactly were you going to tell me? On your way to the airport?"

He looks down at his hands. "I've tried to find the courage to tell you dozens of times. Then I think about actually leaving, and this . . . hole . . . opens up inside me, and it hurts too much for me to even think about it."

It hurts him too much to tell me he's *leaving me*?!

My throat constricts as pain spills into my chest like molten heartache. I try to slow down my breathing. To push down my anger. I can't.

"Fuck you, Ethan! I offered to pass on *Portrait* to save us, and you wouldn't let me!"

"*Portrait* isn't the problem!" he says and steps toward me. "Even Connor isn't the problem. The problem is me, and how you are when you're with me. It's not healthy, Cassie. I want to give you so much, but all I do is take, and I'm going to end up like a lead weight around your ankles. You can't tell me you don't already feel it happening."

"So you're leaving? Running away like that's a solution?"

"I don't know what else to do."

"You could stay! Fight for us. For me."

"I have been fighting! And losing! Don't you fucking get it? You're better off without me. You always have been. I was just too in love with you to admit it. Now I'm doing the only thing I can think of, and you should be fucking grateful you'll finally be free of me."

He's panting and wet-eyed. I'm trembling with emotion.

There's so much I want to say to him, but it jumbles and trips over itself until I'm left with nothing. No clever barbs. No entreaties. No begging him to change his mind.

Nothing.

Nothing.

No. Thing.

My heart beats like a living wound inside me. I close my eyes against the pain.

After a few breaths, bitterness floods my system, and I finally go numb.

It's strange. Like a natural anesthetic.

When I open my eyes and look at him, I feel impassive and cold. Shut down. Part of me registers that I've gone into shock, but I don't care.

I shrug. "I guess that's it, then."

"Cassie . . ."

"You're going to miss graduation."

"If there was any other way—"

"Have a good trip. I'm sure you'll be a fantastic Mercutio."

I turn to leave. When I'm almost at the front door, he yells, "Wait!"

I stop but don't turn around. I feel him behind me, close but not touching.

"Cassie, I . . ." He exhales and it ruffles my hair. "I hate this. I hate myself. Please . . ."

He touches my hand, but I pull back like his fingers burn. Then I do what I should have done months ago. I walk away from him and don't look back.

Present Day
New York City, New York
Graumann Theater

We walk out of the theater, exhausted. Besides doing the show every night, we've been coming in during the day to make sure Ethan's understudy is fully prepared to go on tomorrow night.

Working with Nathan has been interesting. He's an excellent actor, and even though our chemistry is very different, I think the audience will still respond to it.

Ethan has been surprisingly cool about our love scenes and even gave Nathan some advice about where to grab my butt to make lifting me easier. When I saw he was totally fine, it gave me the confidence to relax and just do my job. At that point, I could swear I heard Marco breathe a sigh of relief.

Ethan and I walk home in silence, hands occasionally touching. The familiar ache of wanting him stirs and intensifies. It gets steadily worse as the hours count down to his departure. My panic adds to the mix and demands I do something about it. Touch him. Kiss him. Remind him of all the ways I can make him happy, so he doesn't even consider not coming back.

When we reach my apartment, we both shuffle nervously. This is going to be good-bye, and that thought makes my veins run with ice.

"So . . ." he says, and gives me a smile. "I guess I'll see you in a week."

"You're going to be amazing. Enjoy yourself, okay?"

"I'll try."

We stare at each other for a few seconds before he steps forward and hugs me.

His breath is warm on my neck as he whispers, "I'm going to miss you so fucking much. Promise we'll talk every day."

"We will."

"You and Nathan are going to be great together."

"I'm still going to fantasize that he's you."

"Good." He pulls back. "I love you." He kisses my forehead, and I lean into his chest.

When he steps away, I almost lose it. The disconnect is immediate and painful.

"Stay," I say as I step toward him. "Come in and have some wine, or whatever. Stay for a while."

He puts his arms around me. "If I come in, I won't want to leave."

I stroke his jaw. "Then stay all night. Your flight doesn't leave 'til tomorrow."

He tightens his arms and sighs. "Cassie . . . we can't."

"Why not? I want you. You want me."

"Your therapy—"

"Is going really well. Dr. Kate is happy."

"She wouldn't be if she knew we'd slept together."

I trace his lips. "She doesn't have to know."

He takes my hand away from his face and kisses it. "Yes, she does. And you dialing your sexiness up to eleven is an unfair weapon to use against me."

I look up at him and try not to seem as desperate as I feel. "Just five minutes?"

"If I stay here for even one more minute, I'm going to forget all the reasons I shouldn't make love to you. If I do that, I'll have no chance of getting on that plane tomorrow, and my agent would murder me, and possibly you. So I'm going." He doesn't move.

"Okay."

"Tell me you'll miss me."

"I'll miss you like crazy."

He lets out a long breath and grazes his fingers down my face. "See you next week."

"Okay."

I watch as he goes to the elevator and pushes the button. Then I watch him step inside and wave as the doors close.

I stare at those elevator doors for a long time.

They don't reopen.

TWENTY-FOUR

ENCORE

Three Years Earlier
Westchester, New York
The Grove

The shower water runs cold, and I realize I've been pressing my forehead to the tiles for a really long time. I get out, wrap myself in my robe, and crawl into bed.

I've barely left it for the past three days. Barely eaten.

Ruby is spending the week in Hawaii with her rich Australian boyfriend, so I don't even have her to kick my ass. I haven't told her about Ethan. I can't.

She warned me this would happen. I should have listened.

My phone rings, and I check caller ID before ignoring it.

It's him.

Again.

He's called dozens of times, but I never answer. I don't know what he thinks I possibly have to say. It's not like I could change his mind. I don't even think I want to anymore.

Fuck him.

Fuck him and all the ways I still love him.

When it stops ringing, I call the local pizza place and order a large pie with everything. I figure if I'm going to spend the evening wallowing, I need the appropriate supplies.

Half an hour later, there's a knock on the door, and my stomach rumbles. God bless thirty minutes or less.

I stop dead when I open the door to find Ethan standing there with my pizza. Every hair on my body stands on end at the sight of him. I want to be hard and unaffected that he's here, but I'm not. My heart races as my numbness begins to fade.

He holds out the box. "I . . . paid the guy for you."

I snatch it from him with trembling hands.

"Oh, you paid for my pizza? Well, that makes up for you being the world's biggest bastard. Thanks."

I shove the door, but he stops it with his hand. "Cassie, please—"

"Let go." He has to leave. Now. Before I fall apart.

He steps forward so his body is blocking the door. "I'm leaving to-morrow. I came to say good-bye."

Just the word is enough to bring me to the edge of tears.

Good-bye.

Not "See you later," or "See you tomorrow," or even "I'll call you."

Good-bye.

I turn away and fight for air as I take the pizza to the table. I don't invite him in, but he comes anyway. When the door clicks shut behind him, I clench my jaw so hard, my teeth grind.

I don't turn around. If he has something to say, he can say it to my back. My face will give everything away.

"I know you don't want to see me, and I know I've hurt you, it's just that . . . fuck, Cassie, I never wanted it to end like this. Ever. But there's only so much you can watch someone sacrifice before you realize they're changing who they are for you, and not in a good way. You were perfect how you were. I'm hoping that when I'm gone, you can go back to that."

I can't respond. He doesn't get it. Doesn't understand that by trying to make me better, he's only making me worse.

I drag in a breath and hate that it contains a sob.

"Cassie . . ."

Then, he's wrapping his arms around me. I don't mean to turn in to his chest, but I do, and then I'm not numb at all. I'm a heaving mess of pain and regret, and although I can't really comprehend that this is the end for us, my heart is telling me it is.

"Cassie . . . God, please don't cry. Please . . ."

He cups my face and dries my tears. His lips are on my forehead, and my cheek, and it makes me furious that despite everything, he still feels so good.

"Cassie . . ." He kisses me softly on the lips. Once. Twice. I grip his shirt. Press against the skin beneath. He kisses me a third time, and I don't let him retreat. I kiss him violently. Give him some of my bitterness. He tightens his arms around me and doesn't even pretend he doesn't know what's going on.

He does.

We both do.

As we get rougher and more desperate, we both know this is the only good-bye we'll have. Words are no good to us. They never were. They're useful at communicating everything that's wrong with us, but this is the only way to express why we're so right.

It's not going to make him stay, and it's not going to make it hurt less. It's just going to give us both one last glimpse of what might have been if our story was a romance instead of a tragedy.

We tug and pull at each other as we stumble down the hallway and into my bedroom. Half his clothes are already off. The rest don't last long. My robe hits the floor. He's not gentle when he lays me down and buries his head between my thighs. There's a desperation in him that I haven't seen since the night before he broke up with me the first time, and I know it's because he already has one foot out the door.

I close my eyes and grip the bed, trying to keep my emotions from ruining me. I'm successful for a while. He makes me come, and I'm fine. He kisses up my body, and I'm okay. He settles between my legs, and I'm wavering. He looks into my eyes as he enters me, and a giant fault line cracks down the middle of my resolve. He slows everything down so much, it seems like he doesn't want it to end, and I'm cleaved in two. One part is vibrant and pulsing with pleasure. The other is withering and dying. The trusting part. The loving part.

He thinks I can go back to being the person I was after this? It's impossible. The damage is done. He's poisoned the woman I used to be. Long after he's gone, I'll still be toxic.

I don't orgasm again. My body is too busy mourning his loss even while he's still inside me.

When he comes, his face is buried in my neck, and even though I've banned myself from crying, it happens anyway. My tears are silent, but I know he can tell. Just like I can tell why he stays so still afterward. Why his arms are so tight around me, his breathing so uneven.

Why he wipes his face on my pillow before he climbs off.

He rolls onto his back. Throws his arm over his eyes. I don't move. I can't.

If I do, I'll shatter like glass.

"Cassie—"

"Nothing you say is going to make you leaving me okay. Nothing. Ever."

He takes in a shaky breath. "If there was another way—"

I turn my back on him and face the wall. It's too hard having him here now. It just makes me want to beg him to stay, and that's something my pride won't allow.

"You need to leave."

He doesn't move.

"Now, Ethan." I try to sound strong, but my voice cracks. It's no wonder. Right now, all I am is a giant collection of broken pieces being held together by the sheer determination to not let him see me crumble.

The bed moves as he stands, and I just stare at the wall while he collects his clothes and gets dressed. I don't know how I thought we'd end, but it certainly wasn't like this.

I think in my most stupid, optimistic daydreams, we didn't ever end.

What a joke.

I can feel him hovering in the doorway. Watching me. Hoping I'm all right.

I'm not. Right now, I can't even comprehend a time when I will be.

"Cassie—"

"Get out."

"Maybe one day . . . we can—"

"Get the fuck out!"

My throat tightens when I hear his sigh of resignation. It closes up completely when he whispers, "I'm going to miss you," before he leaves.

When I hear the front door close, a sob rips out of me. It's followed by another, and another, until I'm drowning and gasping for air.

Eventually I calm down enough to breathe, and head into the shower. I wash away every remnant of him. As I do, I vow that I'll never let another man affect me this way.

Never again.

I also vow that for the rest of my life, I will never hate anyone as much as I hate Ethan Holt.

Present Day
New York City, New York
The Apartment of Cassandra Taylor

Ethan is due to leave tomorrow, and "restless" doesn't even cover how I'm feeling tonight. "Climbing the walls" is closer, but still not frantic enough. I feel unhinged.

All I've done since Ethan walked me home is check my watch and count down to the time until his flight leaves. It's now ten hours and forty-two minutes. I look at my bed and consider trying to sleep, but even though it's two o'clock in the morning, I know it won't be possible.

Tristan's resonant snoring echoes down the hallway, and it's enough to make me want to scream. I have to get out.

I pull off my robe and get dressed. When I head down to the lobby, I tell myself I'm going for a walk. Just a walk. When I reach the street and hail the first cab that passes, I tell myself I'm just going for a ride. And when I pull up in front of Ethan's apartment building, I tell myself I'm a filthy, dirty liar for not admitting where I was going and what I was planning on doing.

More specifically, who I was planning on doing.

I punch in his security code and open the door. His building is quiet. When the elevator opens on his floor, I almost lose my nerve and leave. He's probably sleeping. He's definitely trying to avoid what I'm going to ask him to do. This is such a bad idea on so many levels, and yet, right now, it seems like the most imperative action I've ever taken.

I stride down the hallway and knock on his door. I expect to have to wait minutes before he opens it, bleary eyed and half asleep. Instead, it opens within seconds, and he looks even more wired than I feel.

"Fuck, no," he says, and for a second I think he's going to shut the door in my face. "What the hell, Cassie?"

"What?"

"You're here."

"I know."

He rakes his fingers through his hair. "You're supposed to be at your place. Far away from me and sleeping. Preferably in an ugly flannel nightie."

"Ethan—"

"Do you understand how hard I've fought to stay away from you tonight? I've been pacing around my living room for hours, trying to resist temptation. And now you show up here, looking like that?"

"Like what?"

He waves his hand at me. "Edible. Horny as hell. Fucking beautiful. Choose one."

I take a step forward, but he holds his hand out to stop me. "No way. If you step into this apartment, all that talk tonight about us waiting, and your therapy, and blah, blah, blah, 'We shouldn't have sex' will be out the window. You need to leave."

I stop just as my toes touch the threshold. When I'd fantasized about telling him I was ready to be intimate, I'd anticipated him being a little more enthusiastic. I mean, I know he's trying to do what's best for me, but that was always the problem. He sucks at knowing what is best for me.

I take a tiny step. "Ethan, listen—"

He backs up. "Don't do it. I really won't be held accountable for my actions. It's been three years, Cassie. Three fucking years. The things I would do to you . . ." He shakes his head. "You don't even understand."

"What if I do understand? What if I have things I want to do to you as well?"

He closes his eyes and drops his head back against the wall. "Jesus, seriously, with that comment?"

I step through the door and close it behind me.

He opens his eyes. "Cassie, we'll undo everything."

"I don't care." I put my hands on his chest. "I need this. And as you keep saying, so do you."

"I don't want to screw this up."

I stroke his face. "What's the worst that could happen?"

"You find the intimacy too confronting and panic. Shut me out. Shut our relationship down."

I roll my eyes. "Who would do something like that?"

"I'm serious."

"It's not going to happen."

"Do you forget that I've been exactly where you are right now? It might."

"Ethan, I love you, but you really need to stop thinking so much."

He freezes. Eyes wide. "What did you just say?"

I take a step back. "Uh . . . what I meant was—"

"You said you loved me." His panic seems to have vanished.

"Yeah, I did, but—"

"You didn't mean it?" He moves closer so he can stroke my cheek. "If you didn't, it's okay. Or if you did, and you're not ready to admit it, that's okay, too. Just . . . tell me."

A strange sense of calm comes over me, and I remember something he said a couple of months ago: Whether or not he loved me wasn't dependent on a word. It was just fact, pure and simple. Even if I don't say it, it's true, so why bother denying it anymore?

"I meant it," I say quietly. I expect to be hit by an anxiety attack, but instead all I feel is relief. Intense, long-overdue relief.

His smile is blinding. "Yeah?"

I take a deep breath and smile back. "Definitely."

He stares at me with so much joy, I want to kiss him all over. Instead I pull his head down and settle for his lips.

The initial shock freezes us both in our tracks. This isn't a stage kiss. No choreographed emotions filtered through our characters. This is us. The way we should be. The way I never thought we could be again.

We draw back, just a little, and stare at each other. We're actually going to do this. After all this time.

I feel like I should be more nervous, but then I realize all of our moments have been leading us here. Even the painful ones.

I look for hesitation in him. Self-protection or second-guessing. Instead, I see concern for me and overwhelming love.

It's more than enough.

It's everything.

He cups my face. Kisses me harder. There's a thrill of familiarity about what we're doing but with a completely new edge.

The lust is still there, as knee-buckling as ever, but there's something deeper. It winds through my body and anchors me to him. In the past, this soul-deep connection came and went in fleeting, infrequent moments, but now, it's where Ethan lives.

I'm still terrified, but I want to live there with him.

Make him the first and last man I'll ever have.

We keep kissing as we stumble down the hallway into the living room. I tug at his shirt, but he pulls back and tries to catch his breath. "We don't have to go so fast."

"You haven't had sex in three years, and you want to slow down?"

"The last time I had sex, it was with you. I've waited a long time for this. I want to savor it."

"You're getting on a plane in"—I look at my watch—"nine hours and thirty-eight minutes. Are we really wasting time discussing this when we could be getting naked?"

"You make a compelling case."

He pulls off his shirt and kisses me again. God, I've missed kissing him, which is crazy because we kiss every day onstage.

But not like this.

Never like this.

If he kissed me like this during the show, the sex scene wouldn't be simulated.

It proves just how much he's been holding back to avoid scaring me.

He presses me against the wall and reacquaints himself with my breasts. I grip his shoulders to keep myself upright. Shimmering heat whispers under my skin. It curls and releases in my stomach, making my heart hammer and my blood sing. Everywhere Ethan touches me burns a little brighter than the rest.

Every other man who's ever touched me fades from my memory. It's always been him. Even when I wanted to forget, my body remembered.

He pulls off my T-shirt, and when his mouth connects with my chest, I anchor my hands in his hair and pull him forward. Urge him to take more.

All of me. Everything I am is for him.

He lifts me, and I wrap my legs around his waist. Then he's moving. Pressing and grinding, and unashamed of how hard he is.

We get more frantic. Desperate and impatient, we communicate with low sounds and needy hands.

He pulls me away from the wall and carries me down the hallway. When we reach his bed, he's barely laid me down before he's tugging at the rest of my clothes.

I kick off my shoes, and he attacks my jeans. His concentrated frown as he works them down my legs is all kinds of sexy. When I'm only in my underwear, he pauses and stares.

"Goddamn." He shakes his head. "No matter how much I fantasize, the real you still takes my breath away. It always did."

I sit up and remove my bra. He swallows hard.

"Shall I remove these?" I ask as I hook my thumbs into the waistband of my panties. "Or do you want to?"

His expression turns predatory. "Oh, I want to. I very much want to."

He grabs my ankles and drags me to the edge of the bed. Then he pulls my legs up onto his torso.

"This fantasy was one of my favorites," he says, as he slides off my panties and kneels in front of me. "You have no idea how much I've been looking forward to this."

He starts at my ankle. Soft kisses and slow torture as he works his way up. Every piece of skin he isn't touching is jealous and desolate. Everything else sparks and fires through my veins. Powering a deep, spinning ache.

He takes his time, and all I can do is close my eyes and grip the sheets. He knows what he's doing. Self-assured. When he closes his mouth over me, I arch so hard I'm barely touching the bed.

I talk to God. A lot. I tell him Ethan's name. A lot. Everything spins and flutters, and I alternate their names in tight whispers.

"God . . . Ethan . . ."

I struggle for coherence. I don't remember him ever being this good. I mean, he was always amazing, but this? It's beyond words. For a man who hasn't done it in a long time, his skill level is . . . oh, God . . .

I can't even think anymore.

His hands never stop moving, and every touch winds me tighter. I'm floating so high, I feel like I'm four feet above the mattress. He keeps me there, hovering on the edge of sensation and satisfaction. Then, with a flick of his tongue and a curl of his fingers, I'm crashing back down, dizzy and breathless.

I can't move. My brain has checked out. Breathing is an alien concept.

He kisses back up my body. I summon enough strength to wind my fingers through his hair, and he hums against my skin. His voice does things to me even his hands can't.

"I've missed seeing that," he says. "You look incredible when you come."

While keeping my eyes closed, I stroke his arms as he continues trailing kisses all over. The feel of his muscles helps pull me out of my daze. Makes me hungry for more.

It's my turn, so I push him onto his back. I can deliver just as much sweet torture as he can. I start on his neck. He responds with noises that border on animalistic.

I kiss him everywhere. Touch him like it's the first time, all over again.

In a way, it is. Every incarnation of him has owned me, but this one actually deserves to.

When I get to the waistband of his jeans, I lick and nibble his hips. He sounds like he's in pain. Judging by the tightness in his crotch, I'm sure he is.

I unbutton his jeans. He's mumbling things I can't understand as I pull them off and start on his legs. He swears under his breath and buries his hands in his hair. I revel in my power over him.

He's barely holding himself together. I don't blame him. If I hadn't had sex for years, it would only take a single touch to completely unravel me. His control is remarkable.

The dark fabric of his boxer-briefs clings to every inch of him. I run a single finger down the swollen length. He squeezes his eyes shut and pushes out a long breath. I do it again, and he slaps the bed before gripping the covers.

I move down to stroke his thigh. "Do you want me to stop?"

He keeps his eyes closed but grabs my hand so he can pull me up to his face. "Just let me do this for a while." He kisses me and turns us so we're both on our sides. Then he pulls my leg up to his hip and presses his erection against me, trying to acclimate himself to being with me again.

We kiss and grind, and it all feels so good. His hands move over me like we've never been apart. The rhythm of him is intoxicating.

"Is it okay if I touch you now?" I ask.

He nods. "I was about to start begging."

"Did you fantasize about me touching you while we were apart?"

"Every single day. Sometimes, multiple times a day. Fantasy You was a total nympho."

I move my hand between us and palm him. He moans, and I smile. "So, kinda close to Reality Me, then?"

He flops onto his back. "Yep. Pretty much. Dear *God*."

I kiss down his neck. Graze my teeth across his stubble and taste his skin. Kiss his Adam's apple as he makes a long, low noise. The buzz on my lips tickles. All the while I stroke him through taut fabric. Run my hands over trembling muscles.

He pants and alternates between watching my slow trek down his torso and pushing his head back into the bed and cursing.

When I reach his belly button, he stops breathing.

"You okay?"

"Yep," he says, his voice tight. "More than okay. Just . . . trying not to embarrass myself."

"Not possible."

I pull down his underwear, and he lifts his hips to help me get them off.

And then, there he is.

He watches me stare. He's so familiar, but it's like I remember him from a dream. I trace the shape of him. Wrap my fingers around the perfect thickness.

He always was perfect. In the past, I thought my inexperience had informed my opinion, but now I've had other men, and none of them compare.

I was naive to think they would.

I lean down and brush my lips over the silky skin. He groans, and I know he won't be able to endure much of this. Already, his abdominals are trembling.

I use my tongue, and he's practically vibrating with restraint. When I take him in my mouth, I hardly have time to savor the sensation before he's grunting and pulling me off.

"God . . . no. No, no, no, *no*." He clenches his jaw and moans as he comes all over his stomach and chest. I watch in fascination. Was there always this much? Or is this what extreme sexual frustration looks like?

Good God.

When he finishes, he draws in sharp, shallow breaths and covers his face. "Fuck, Cassie. I'm so sorry."

I pull his hands away and kiss him. "Don't be. That was . . . impressive. Like a special effect. Can we do it again?"

He chuckles as I grab tissues from his nightstand. "You're asking permission to make me come like that again? Hmmm, let me think."

Even as I wipe him down, he reacts and swells proudly before my eyes. "Well, I was just being polite. Lord knows you get annoyed when I orgasm you against your will."

"One time. And only then because I was embarrassed. The orgasm itself was still mind-blowing."

"As mind-blowing as the one you just had?"

"No. I don't think anything's going to top that. Ever."

I crawl up his body and kiss him. "I take that as a challenge."

Now I see a little fear. "God, help me."

We kiss and touch each other with more confidence, and even though we've already taken the edge off our lust, it flares again. It speeds our hands and roughens our touches. Our mouths are gentle, but everything else is heavy with need. Urging us to take the last step in cementing our reconnection.

This is the part that makes me nervous. I want him more than I've ever wanted anyone, but if I'm going to freak-out, it will be when he's inside me.

The pain of him making love to me before he leaves is singed into the parts of my memory that still ache to recall it.

Of course, he's going to leave this time as well, but he intends to come back. Promises me he will. Caresses me in such a way that I believe if he doesn't, he'll suffocate. That I'm his oxygen.

I will away my anxiety and concentrate on him. It's easy enough. He's extremely talented at distracting me.

When he rolls on top of me and works magic with his fingers, my patience is at an all-time low. There's a sharp ache that won't be satisfied with fingers or empty climaxes. It demands him. All of him. I tell him as much, and he fumbles in his nightstand drawer for a condom.

When he presses back onto his knees so he can roll it on, I kiss his chest. Stroke his shoulders. I can't seem to stop touching him.

He groans his approval and pushes me onto my back, and when he lays his full weight down and kisses me, I reach between us and urge him inside.

He freezes when he realizes he's there, and pleasure, wonder, and what looks a lot like gratitude light up his face.

He frames my face with his hands. "Are you sure about this? It's not too late to stop."

"Yes, it is," I say as I stroke his back. "I need you."

"Are you just saying that because I'm leaving?"

"No. I'm saying it because I'm tired of denying it."

He kisses me gently and pushes in a little more. We both inhale.

"Cassie . . ."

"Oh, God . . ."

He drops his head to my shoulder, and we just breathe.

"I'd forgotten," he whispers. "How could I forget this? Jesus."

He rocks back and forth; tiny movements that bring him farther and farther inside. I close my eyes and grip his shoulders. He's not the only one who's forgotten. How did I used to fit all these emotions inside me? I feel like I'm about to explode.

His hips continue to withdraw and retreat, and each movement fills me a little more. I watch, fascinated, as his face morphs from disbelief, to awe, to determination, and finally to love. More than there's ever been. How did I live for so long without him looking at me like that?

When his hips finally rest against mine, I wrap my legs around him and just hold him still. I can feel my panic simmering and growing, but I don't want this to end, because then he'll leave. He'll leave, and I'll be empty, and I can't live like that anymore.

"Hey," he says as he strokes my face. "It's okay."

"I know."

"I love you. I don't even have the words to tell you how much."

I pull him down to kiss me. It helps ease my tension. When he moves his hips, that eases it even more.

He kisses me to distraction as he thrusts, long and slow. He's in no rush for this to end, either. For the first time in years, I feel what it's like to make love. Everything feels too intense, but he guides me through it. Soothes me with his hands and mouth. Inflames me with his steady, determined rhythm. All the while he whispers to me about regrets, apologies, love, future. Tells me how beautiful am. How long he's waited for this. How he can't wait to get back to me so he can do this, over and over again.

I don't know how long we make love, but he has me on the edge so many times, I lose count. When I eventually climax, it's like a full-body seizure that seems to go on forever. He talks to me through the whole thing. When he eventually comes with a long groan, he's never looked more beautiful.

We stay wrapped around each other for a long time. Just breathing. More satisfied than either of us has been in years.

I guess I fall asleep, because when I open my eyes, the sun is blazing through the windows.

He's leaning on his elbow, staring at me. It takes me a moment to understand where I am and why I'm with him. When I do, I can't stop my smile.

"Hey."

He kisses me. "Good morning."

"What time is it?"

"Late. I have to go soon."

"I'll come to the airport with you."

"No. Stay here."

"But—"

"Cassie." He strokes my face. "Please. I want the last image I have to be you naked in my bed, not tearing up in an airport. Stay here while I'm gone. Eat my food. Use my shower. Rub yourself all over my sheets. That would make me incredibly happy."

I push him onto his back and snuggle against his chest. I just want to hold him. Have him for as long as I can.

We lie there and doze. Later, when he eases out from under me to go shower, I hug his pillow and breathe in his scent.

I keep my eyes closed when I hear him moving about. As if not being able to see him preparing to go means it's not going to happen.

Except, it has to.

And it will.

Lips brush against my cheek, and I open my eyes.

He's holding out a small velvet bag with a note. I frown.

"Open this after I'm gone," he says, before placing it next to me on the bed.

"What is it?"

"A gift. I bought it when I was in Italy years ago, but I never had the guts to give it to you. I guess now I do."

When he leans down to kiss me, I stop myself from dragging him back to bed and begging him to stay.

"I'll see you next week," he says as he strokes my face. "I love you."

I take a deep breath. "I love you, too."

He smiles. "I love that you love me. You have no idea."

"I think I do. Remember when you sent me that e-mail with those thousand 'I love yous'? Pretty sure I felt then how you're feeling now."

He sits on the edge of the bed and runs his fingers through my hair. "I love that, too."

"You're just full of love today, aren't you?"

He leans down and grazes his lips across mine before whispering, "Understatement of the century."

The door buzzer sounds, and he grunts before standing and adjusting himself.

"That's my car. I have to go." He kisses me again, long and lingering, before grabbing his bag. "I'll call you when I get in."

"Okay."

He heads toward the door, but before he gets there, he stops and turns back to me. "Can you just pull that sheet down for a second?"

I smile and pull back the covers.

He groans and bites his lip. "Fuck me. Best brain-Polaroid ever."

I laugh, and he heads toward the door. "Gotta go before I forget why I can't bang you again."

"Bang?" I say, mock-horrified. "What happened to 'make love'? You're so crass, Ethan Holt!"

"You love me crass!" he calls down the hallway. "And you love it when I bang you like a Japanese drum!"

And with that, the front door closes behind him.

I flop back against the pillow and sigh.

I miss him already.

I'm reflecting on how incredible he was last night, when my phone buzzes on the nightstand. I pick it up and read the message.

<Miss me already, don't u? The feeling is mutual & I'm still in the elevator. Don't forget to open your present. I love you.>

I smile and open the velvet pouch. When I upend it, a heavy gold heart on a chain falls into my hand. It looks old. Antique. And, if I'm being honest, a little banged up.

I open the note.

Dear Cassie,

I've been wanting to give this to you for ages, and after the incredible gift you gave me last night, I figured the time felt right. I found it in a little antique shop in Milano while I was touring Europe. I don't know why it caught my eye, but I had to buy it for you.

The thing is, it's not perfect. It's had a lot of owners, some of whom haven't been kind to it, and it bears the damage to prove it. In a way, it represents me. Sadly, I guess it also represents you.

The thing that occurred to me is that despite all the damage, it's still beautiful. In fact, I think it's even more beautiful because it's not perfect. It's taken me a long time to understand that just because something isn't pristine, it still has worth. You taught me that, even though I resisted believing it.

When I think about us, I often wonder what would have happened if I'd never met you. Would I have had the motivation to change? To address the crap from my past?

The truth is, it wasn't just meeting you that made me realize I had to change. It was meeting you, then losing you. Twice. Being away from you made me face the ugly truth about myself, and after the accident, getting back to you was all the motivation I needed to tackle the issues that had handicapped me for years. You made me want to be better, and as much as I did it for myself, I also did it to be worthy of you.

So, I guess this is me, giving my heart to you. Cheesy, huh? Also, kind of redundant since you've owned it from the day we met.

It seems like we've taken such a roundabout way to get to where we were last night, and I know that's my fault. But despite all the things I would have changed about our journey, I'd never want a different destination. It's always been you. Beautiful, amazing, talented, loving you.

Thank you for giving me this final chance. I promise, you won't regret it.

As I look at you now, I really have no idea how I ever walked away. Thank you for saving me. And for forgiving me.

On a related note: You're outrageously beautiful when you sleep. Do you know that? I can't stop looking at you.

Speaking of that, I took some photos of you with my phone. Sweet

*or creepy? I'm hoping you come down on the side of sweet. I just
needed something to take with me. I already miss you.*

*Okay, I'd better wrap this up, because you're going to wake up soon,
and I want to be next to you when you do. In fact, I want to be there
every morning when you wake up, but I guess that's a longer discussion for another time.*

*I love you, Cassie. Always have. Always will. Keep my bed warm
for me while I'm gone. I promise to help you make good use of it when
I get back.*

Ethan

I stare at his words. After I've reread them a dozen times, I slip the
necklace over my head. The heart nestles right between my breasts.
Nothing I've ever owned has looked so perfect.

I swore I wouldn't cry when he left me this time, but he's making
that very difficult. At least now they're happy tears.

I grab my phone and send him a message.

*<Love the necklace. Wearing it now. Loved your letter more. Your
words were beautiful. But most of all, I love you. Call me when you
land.>*

I pull the covers over me and inhale what's left of his smell. If you'd
told me three years ago that one day I'd end up in Ethan Holt's bed,
texting him love notes, I probably would have punched you in the
face.

Now, I can't imagine being anywhere else.

I remember the card Ethan gave me on opening night. It read, "*People
are like stained-glass windows. They sparkle and shine when the sun is
out, but when the darkness sets in, their true beauty is revealed only if
there's a light from within.*"

He meant it to be about me, but I wonder if he knows how accurately it describes him.

This him.

I fall asleep to images of the two of us, smiling and surrounded by light.

TWENTY-FIVE

FINAL BOW

Present Day
New York City, New York

Dr. Kate studies me, and I hide my smile behind my hand.

"You look different today. Happy?"

"Yes."

"Very happy."

I can't deny it. I don't want to. "Yes."

"Well, judging by the way you're glowing, I'm assuming you and Ethan . . . ?"

She doesn't have to finish the sentence. Just like I don't have to answer it. My expression must tell her everything.

I nod, and she writes in her book. I don't miss her slight smile.

"You're not angry?" I ask.

"Why would I be angry?"

"Because I thought, maybe you thought . . . that I wasn't ready."

"Do you feel ready?"

"Yes."

"Then that's all that matters. I can't put a timeline on your happiness,

Cassie. Only you can do that. As long as you feel good, we're achieving something."

"I do feel good, but also . . ."

"What?"

How can I tell her what I'm feeling, when my swirling emotions don't fit into any one category? Happy/cautious. Ecstatic/terrified. Elated/anxious.

"He left yesterday." Just saying the words makes my chest hurt.

Dr. Kate studies me for a few seconds before asking, "How are you coping?"

"I don't like it. I miss him."

"Missing him is good."

I look out the window and watch the clouds change shape. "It feels strange to admit that. To acknowledge I need him. For so long, I thought needing him showed how weak I was."

"And now?"

I spot a cloud that looks like a love heart and smile. "Now, I see that letting myself need him is the strongest thing I've ever done. The bravest."

"They say fortune favors the brave."

I think about arriving on his doorstep. Convincing him to make love to me. Finally letting him in again.

A shudder of pleasure runs up my spine. "I guess it does."

I lean against the wall of my dressing room. I've been struggling with my focus exercise and just can't seem to get into the zone. Last night was the same. I'm betting tomorrow night will be, too.

It's not that I find it uncomfortable performing with Nathan, but getting into character without Ethan is much more difficult than I thought it would be.

I shake out my tension and roll my neck. I have ten minutes. I need to get my crap together.

I walk down the hall to Ethan's dressing room and open the door. A waft of his scent hits me as I turn on the lights, and I inhale deeply.

Within seconds, I feel better.

I sit in his spot in front of the mirrors and touch all his stuff. Not that he has a lot. Pancake makeup, powder, hair goop. Eyeliner he never uses because his lashes are stupidly long and dark.

I open a drawer and find a book called *Awakening the Sacred Body*.

Oh, Ethan. Reading a little pornography, are we? Naughty man.

I flip through it, expecting to see diagrams of sexual positions. I'm sorely disappointed. There are very few pictures, and those I find show a middle-aged Chinese man demonstrating various meditation poses.

Party pooper.

As I flick through to the back of the book, a photo falls out. It's of Ethan and me. We have our arms around each other and look genuinely happy. I remember the moment well. It was taken at the opening night party of *Romeo and Juliet* in our first year of drama school. Jack Avery took it just after he'd read our first glowing review. I'd felt like I could float off the ground that night.

I run my finger over Ethan's face. His smile is so beautiful, it makes me sad to think I didn't see it that much in the time we spent at college.

"He took that picture all over the world, you know." I turn to see Elissa leaning against the door frame. "Well, all over Europe, at least. Looked at it every night before he went onstage. I'm surprised you can still make out your face."

"I have the same picture at home," I say. "It's the only picture of us I kept. All the others were torched in a drunken purging ceremony."

"Valentine's Day?" Elissa asks.

"Yep."

"Had a few of those myself over the years."

I put the picture in the book and replace it in the drawer. When I turn back to Elissa, she's smiling.

"What?"

"I spoke to Ethan earlier."

I'm immediately nervous. Did he tell her we slept together?

I try to play it cool. "Oh? How is he?"

"Even over the phone I can tell he's on cloud nine. Am I right in assuming something happened between you guys?"

Her face is so hopeful, I can't lie. "I guess."

I can see her almost vibrating with happiness. "Well . . . okay. That's . . . wow. Great."

"Elissa, it's still really early."

"I know. But, it's going to work out this time. I have no doubt." She comes over and hugs me. "He's been crazy in love with you for years. He's not going to screw this up. I'm certain that right now, my brother is the happiest man on the planet."

"Well, I guess we're both due a little happiness, right?"

"Absolutely." She hugs me again, then pulls back. "Now, get your ass in gear. It's five minutes 'til places."

"Okay. Be right there."

When she leaves, I go over to the closet and find Ethan's warm-up clothes. I pick them up and hug them. When I close my eyes, I can almost imagine it's him.

Two minutes later, I try my focusing exercise again.

I nail it.

His face appears on the screen, and I want to reach out and touch him.

"Hi," I say and exhale with relief.

He sighs and licks his lips. "Wow. Hi. Fuck, you look so good. I feel like I haven't seen you in weeks."

"We spoke last night."

He scoffs. "That was a lifetime ago."

He glances over his shoulder, and I can make out the dimly lit interior of his trailer. "I don't have long to talk. We're between scenes. I'm waiting for them to reset lights."

"You're shooting all night again?"

"We finish when the sun comes up."

"That's your costume?"

He looks down at himself and smiles. "Yeah. Sexy, huh?"

He's wearing a ripped white T-shirt stained with blood. The left side of his face is swollen and bruised, and his bottom lip is split.

"Hmmm. Yes, very rugged. Your bruise makeup is impressive."

He chuckles. "Uh . . . yeah. Not all of that is makeup."

"What?"

"We filmed the big fight scene last night. I weaved when I should have ducked and . . . well . . ."

"No!"

"Yep. Pow. Right in the kisser."

"Oh, Ethan."

"It's okay. I've had worse."

"When?"

He rubs the back of his neck. "Whenever my anger used to get the better of me, I'd go to this bar in the city. It was pretty rough."

For a moment, I think about what this means. "You went to deliberately get into fights?"

"Well, I went to beat the crap out of someone, but occasionally, they got the better of me."

"Oh, God. Is that why your knuckles were always a mess?"

"Pretty much."

"Ethan . . ."

"I know. Stupid, right?"

"Not stupid. Sad."

"I haven't done that in years."

"Do you still get the urge to?"

He pauses. "Sometimes. When I'm tense."

"When was the last time?"

"Three months ago. The night before we started rehearsals. I was nervous about seeing you and was praying like hell I had the strength to not fall in a heap if you told me to go fuck myself."

"I did tell you to go fuck yourself."

"Yeah, but you didn't mean it."

"Yeah, I did."

He frowns. "Really? Wow. I totally misread that moment. Just as well. I probably would have fallen in a heap. Just like I did last night when the stunt man clocked me."

"Did it hurt?"

"Not compared to being away from you."

I sigh. "I want to kiss you so badly right now."

"Yeah?" He leans forward.

"Kissing you is the first on a very long list of things I want to do to you right now. I'd start with your mouth, and finish with . . . well, if I had my way, I wouldn't finish. I'd have all of you, all the time."

He stares at me and sets all my insides ablaze.

That look has always brought me undone. A lot of men have desired me over the years, but not a single one has ever looked at me like that. Like he belonged to me just as much as I belonged to him.

Someone knocks on his door, and he looks over his shoulder. "Damn, they're ready for me."

"Hey, I'm ready for you, too."

He turns back to the screen and leans forward. "I'm going to need you to hold that thought for two more days. Can you do that?"

"Fine. Go. Be all tough and whatever."

"Talk to you tomorrow?"

"Okay. Love you." It just comes out. I cover my mouth. When the hell did I become so comfortable saying that to him? We've been back together for a matter of *days*.

"Cassie?" he says as he fights the world's smuggest smile.

"Don't blame yourself. I'm irresistible. I love you, too."

* * *

I don't sleep well while he's away. My thoughts are too loud. My body too cold. All the ways I've forgotten how to miss him come rushing back at an alarming speed.

The day he's due to come home, I'm so nervous, I feel sick. I shave my legs. Wash and blow dry my hair. Take extra care with my makeup. Smear myself in body lotion that makes me smell good enough to eat.

And I do it all with trembling hands.

Anticipation? Yep. I have it. In spades.

In the cab on the way to the airport, I close my eyes and breathe deeply. I can't believe how uptight I am. It's like I'm about to go on-stage and haven't rehearsed.

But I have. He has. We've prepared for this scene before but never got to perform it. The happy ending. We've tried tragedy. It didn't work for either of us. What we're doing now is new.

I make my way to the arrivals area. There's a buzz in the air. People of all ages are milling around, thrumming with excitement like I am as they wait for their loved ones.

Wow.

Ethan is my loved one.

It feels weird to admit that.

People trickle out of the doors, and I lock my knees to stop judder-ing my legs. Two little kids beside me are bouncing. I'm jealous. Bounc-ing would feel pretty awesome right about now.

An anxious-looking man emerges from the doors, and the kids scream "Daddy!" before they run and engulf him in tiny-armed hugs. It makes me smile.

More people walk through as friends and family surge forward to greet them. I stand on my toes to see over heads and crane my neck. I understand they're all happy to be reunited, but they need to get the hell out of the way so I can see the doors.

I catch a flash of messy hair. After pushing between two large men, I see Ethan standing there, tall and gorgeous, frowning as he scans the crowd.

I yell his name. Well, more like scream it. The men beside me turn and stare. My care factor is in negative digits.

Ethan sees me, and for a moment, he freezes. His expression makes my lungs tighten.

Then he pushes through the crowd, apologizing as he all but throws people out of his way to get to me. I'm also too rough.

When he's a yard away, I launch myself at him. He catches me and buries his head in my neck. I'm dangling off the floor. Holding on for dear life.

He's here. Home. With me.

I finally breathe.

"Thank God you're here," he says, lips against my throat. "Fuck, I've missed you."

He lowers me to the floor and cups my face. His focus drops to the heart pendant nestled between my breasts. "Oh . . . wow. That . . ." He smiles and shakes his head. "I always knew it would look amazing on you, but that's just . . . perfect. You're perfect."

He kisses me deeply, and my heart rate doubles. He sucks on my lip, and that's it. I'm all over him. Hands in his hair, and gripping the back of his neck, him pulling my hips forward, and curving his hands around the top of my ass. I realize we're engaging in an obnoxious public display of affection, but I don't even care.

"Baggage claim," he says breathlessly.

"We need to pick up my bag."

"Leave it here. We'll buy you new clothes."

"Okay. Cab?"

"Yep."

He kisses me again, and all plans of leaving are temporarily waylaid. He wraps his hands in my hair and pulls, just enough to drive me crazy. More than enough to remind me why we were talking about cabs.

"We have to get out of here," he says as he pulls me in for a hug. "But first, give me a minute to try and deflate this raging boner. Tell me something horrifying. Distract me from my intense need to fuck you on this ugly carpet."

"Uh . . . okay." I struggle to concentrate. "Well, one of the regular fans who came to the shows this week said she thought Nathan and I had better chemistry than you and me."

He pulls back and frowns. "The fuck? Are you kidding me?!"

"Nope. She said she liked your performance better, but that Nathan and I made a better couple. He was gentler."

He shakes his head and laughs bitterly. "The reason Nathan's gentler is because he's not holding himself back from ripping your clothes off in front of a theater full of people. That's not chemistry. It's lack of passion."

"She also knitted you a cardigan and wanted to know if you were single."

His incredulity drops. "What did you tell her?"

"That you don't wear cardigans."

"I mean, about me being single."

I run my finger over the pattern on his T-shirt. As if my face wasn't hot enough, more blood rushes to my cheeks. "I said . . . that I thought you were spoken for."

"Thought?"

"Well . . . yeah."

He tilts my head up.

"Spoken for? I like the sound of that."

He kisses me again. Softer but still intense.

"Next time you see her, you tell her I'm most definitely spoken for. And she's fucking nuts if she thinks Nathan has better chemistry with you. I invented chemistry with you. Everything else is just pretend."

As if to demonstrate, he kisses my neck, and I swear, he's trying to kill me in a public place. Everything burns and aches, and if he keeps doing that thing with his tongue, my legs are going to give out.

"Do you think your bag will be at the carousel by now?" I say, short on breath and patience.

"If not, fuck it. There's nothing in it that can't be easily replaced. Except my journal." He ponders for a second. "Actually, we'd better go get it. If anyone finds it, they'll know how depraved I really am. And it's all about you."

He takes my hand and leads me down to baggage claim. His strides are long, and I have to trot a little to keep up.

"Hey, I'm wearing heels. Not so fast."

He stops and turns to me. "Do you think people would stare if I threw you over my shoulder? Because I really want to do that. Then I can ogle your ass and just run."

The look in his eye is a little manic. For a second, I think he's going to do it. Then he spies the heavily armed security officer a few feet away.

"Excuse me, sir?" he says, and the guard looks at him. "Would it be acceptable to carry my girlfriend like a sack of potatoes in order to get out of here quicker and make sweet love to her?"

The guard's mouth moves, but he resists smiling. "No, sir, that would not be acceptable."

"Piggyback?"

"Nope."

"Put her on a trolley?"

"No."

"You're no fun."

"So my wife keeps telling me."

Ethan takes my hand again and continues toward the baggage carousels. He walks a little slower, but not much.

As soon as we get there, he spies his bag and quickly grabs it. Then he drags me out to the taxi line and after we get in and he gives his address, he puts his arm around me and sighs.

I lean against his chest and close my eyes. Every part of me is relieved to have him home. Even the parts that are incredibly uptight about having him home.

"So, you called me your girlfriend back there."

"You caught that, huh? Are you mad?"

I think about it for a second. "No."

"Freaking out?"

"A bit."

"Okay. I can deal with 'a bit.' Tell me your concerns about being called my girlfriend."

I look down at my fingers and shrug. "I don't know. It just seems too soon."

"Cassie, I've been in love with you for more than six years. How is that too soon?"

"I mean, this time around."

He pauses and tightens his arm around me. "Listen, this isn't a *time*. This is it. The end. Last stop on the relationship train. I thought I'd been clear about that."

Simultaneous shudders of joy and panic travel through me.

"Okay," he says as he cups my cheek. "Here's what's going to happen. You're going to forget I called you my girlfriend. I'm going to take you back to my place, peel off your clothes, and make sweet love to you until you beg me to stop. At no time will I repeat the 'girlfriend' comment, nor pressure you about labeling our relationship. Which should be labeled 'fucking awesome,' by the way. I'm just happy to be where we are."

"Which is, where?"

"Together." A beat later, he coughs/says, "Forever," then gives me an innocent smile. "What? Why that look? I didn't say anything."

I laugh and kiss him. We're still kissing when we pull up outside his building.

He throws money at the cabbie, and the whole trip up to his

apartment is a blur of making out and juggling his bag. As soon as we stumble through the door, the bag is dropped, and our clothes become the enemy we must defeat at any cost.

It turns out the clothes win, mainly because we don't have the patience to get completely naked. Or even half naked. Or make it to the bedroom.

As soon as he has my panties off and I have his jeans unbuttoned, he takes me against the wall. It's not gentle. I don't want it to be. It's heavy thrusts and strangled moans and full of seven days of longing.

Neither of us lasts very long. I cry out first. He follows a few thrusts later. We cling to each other as we shudder and sigh. When we're both boneless, we stagger to the bedroom. The rest of our clothes come off on the way, and the second time is less hurried but no less passionate.

After the third time, we both fall asleep within seconds.

The fourth time is hours later in the shower. He washes me very thoroughly. Everywhere. With his tongue.

We never make it to dinner.

He makes vague noises about a fifth time, but I'm exhausted. Instead, we lie in bed and watch movies. He strokes my back while I draw patterns on his chest. I can't remember a time when I've felt so content or relaxed. Maybe not ever.

It feels so right, I want to cry.

"Ethan?"

"Hmmm?"

"If you want . . . and if you only do it when we're in private because I don't want people at work giving us crap . . . you can . . ." I take a deep breath. "You can call me your girlfriend."

He stops stroking. "Don't mess with me, Cassie. If this is a joke, it's not funny."

"I'm not joking."

He stares for a full five seconds. "You're serious?"

"I am. Is that okay?"

His face twitches. "Yeah. That's okay. Very okay. Extremely fucking okay. Excuse me. I'll be right back."

He gets out of bed and goes into the living room. Then I hear him open the doors onto the balcony and scream, "CASSIE TAYLOR IS MY GIRLFRIEND! FUCK, YEAH!"

I hear the doors close before he calmly walks back into the bedroom and crawls into bed.

He clears his throat and says, "So, yeah. Good. That's settled. You're my girlfriend. Which makes me your . . . ?"

I sigh. "You know what it makes you."

"No, I'm not sure. What's the word?"

"You're my . . ."

"Yes . . . ?" He's nearly vibrating with expectation.

"Do you really need me to say it?"

"Only if you want to make me the happiest man in the world. No pressure."

I shake my head and get up. "I can't believe I'm doing this."

I go and open the balcony doors while praying no one can see me, because being naked in front of random strangers is not my idea of fun.

"ETHAN HOLT IS MY BOYFRIEND! FUCK, YEAH!" I fist-pump to no one in particular, then scamper back inside.

When I jump back into bed, Ethan pounces on me. Within a second, he has me pinned to the mattress and is lying between my legs, conspicuously and impressively hard.

"That was, hands-down, the sexiest goddamn thing you've ever done."

"Oh yeah?"

He practically growls when he says, "Fuck, yes."

Without any more discussion, we go for round five, and it's more amazing than the other four put together.

* * *

A week later, Ethan stands behind me and fiddles with his hair in the bathroom mirror. This is the third time he's done it. Marco made him get it cut last week, so it's a little shorter than usual. He hates it. I think it's sexy.

So is his nervousness.

He finally gives up and sits on the bed while I finish my makeup.

"What do I call them?" he asks.

"I mean, 'Mr. and Mrs. Taylor' seems wrong, considering they're no longer married."

"Then call them Leo and Judy."

"Yeah, but don't you think that's a little disrespectful?"

"I call your mom and dad Maggie and Charles."

"Really?"

"Yep."

"Wow, my girlfriend's so rude."

I laugh and walk over to him. "You didn't mind so much this afternoon."

I stand between his legs, and he runs his hands up my rib cage, then palms my breasts. "Yeah, well, I've never done that particular thing on that part of your body before. It was hot. Plus, you were kind of insistent that's what you wanted. Also hot."

"Well, considering I now have a boyfriend eager to fulfill my every sexual whim, I may have come up with a list of things I want to try."

"Really? Like what?"

I lean down and graze my lips over his. "If I tell you, it won't be a surprise."

"I don't like surprises," he says as he pulls me onto his lap. "And speaking of which, if you do that thing with your finger again without warning me or using appropriate lubrication, you're going to be in trouble."

"What sort of trouble?"

"The kind where I spank the hell out of your gorgeous ass 'til you can't sit down."

"Ooh. Have you been peeking at my list?"

He groans and pulls me against his now-impressive erection. "Fuck me, woman. Do your parents know you're pure evil wrapped in sex?"

"No. And if you want to make it through this dinner alive, I'd suggest you not mention me and sex in the same sentence in front of my father. He has many guns and probably thinks I'm still a virgin."

"What would he do if he knew I took your virginity?"

"I'm not sure, but I suspect it would involve your balls and some sort of crushing device."

I kiss him and climb off to finish my makeup. He stands behind me and wraps his arms around my waist.

"What happened afterward with us was screwed up," he says quietly. "But the actual first time . . . Was it okay? When you think about it, do you just get pissed, or . . ."

I lean back into his chest. "Even though you bailed on us a few weeks later, my memories of that night are . . ." I smile as a shiver of pleasure runs up my spine. "I can't even tell you how incredible that night was. I never regretted you being my first."

He leans his chin on my shoulder and looks at me in the mirror. "It was the most amazing thing I'd ever experienced. Despite freaking out over how much I felt for you."

"You were pretty talented at the freak-outs," I say, and turn around so I can put my arms around his neck.

"Yeah. I thought I was over all that. And yet, the concept of meeting your parents brings it all back to me."

"You'll be fine."

"What if they don't like me?"

I give him a reassuring kiss. "They will."

"What if they don't like my food?"

Another kiss. "You've made vegan crap actually taste good. My mother may hit on you."

"What if I randomly say 'fuck' or 'sex'? Or 'My God, you two made a gorgeous daughter, and let me tell you, she's an animal in the sack'?"

"Don't."

"Well, okay then."

There's a knock at the door, and he practically jumps away from me. I laugh. "Ethan, chill."

He rolls his neck, and it cracks loudly. "I'm fine. I'm good. Operation Impress Your Parents is a go. Let's do this."

We head down the corridor, and he veers off into the living room. When I open the door, I hug my parents fiercely. I don't get to see them very often, so every visit is precious.

"Come in," I say and lead them down to the living room. Ethan's there, standing awkwardly, hands in pockets.

"Mom, Dad . . . this is Ethan."

He steps forward and extends his hand. "Mrs. Taylor, Mr. Taylor . . . it's a pleasure to finally meet you. Cassie's told me a lot about you."

Mom and Dad shake his hand in turn, but I don't miss how Dad narrows his eyes. It's to be expected, I guess.

For the most part, I think dinner goes well. Ethan tries way too hard, but my mom adores him. He's very charming. He even manages to get Dad to talk about football for a while, so I guess that's a good sign.

After dinner, Mom and I do the dishes as an excuse to leave the boys alone to talk. Surprisingly, Ethan has a lot to say, but I can't make it out from the kitchen. Whatever it is, it makes my Dad happy, because just before he and Mom leave, he shakes Ethan's hand with both of his. He hardly ever does that. It's like his version of a man-hug.

When I ask Ethan about it, he says it's between the menfolk.

Whatever it was, he seems relieved it's over. I am, too.

Ethan's the first man I've ever introduced to my parents. I'm hoping he'll also be the last.

There's a dull thud as Ethan pushes me up against the dressing room wall and tugs at the zipper to my costume.

"Hey," I say, "you're not allowed to do that anymore, remember? Karen has banned you from undressing me."

"Karen's a killjoy."

"She's in charge of costumes, and you've ripped three zippers this week alone."

"Then she should make them stronger."

"Or you should wait until I'm out of my costume before getting horny."

"Impossible. I'm horny all the time. It just happens to be worse after I've been kissing you all night onstage."

He tugs impatiently at the zipper, and sure enough, it rips.

"Shit."

"I told you."

"I'll buy Karen another bunch of flowers."

He pulls the top of the dress down and starts kissing my chest. I'm trying not to groan when there's a loud rap on the door.

In a second he's released me and passed me my robe. I slip it on as I yell, "Just a second!"

Ethan sits on the couch and tries to look nonchalant. I gesture to his erection, and he crosses his legs and drops his hands in his lap.

Subtle.

I open the door to find Marco.

"You two realize everyone in the building knows what goes on in here after the curtain comes down, right? And Karen has made a voodoo doll of you, Ethan, which she sticks with pins every time you damage a costume. It now looks like a porcupine."

Ethan chuckles.

Marco frowns. "It's not funny."

"It's a little bit funny."

"I think I liked it better when you two hated each other."

"Yeah, we get that a lot."

"Well, when you've quite finished molesting each other, please come to the lobby bar. I have someone who wants to say hello."

"Can you give us fifteen minutes?" Ethan asks. "I wasn't anywhere near finished molesting her."

Marco sighs. "You have five minutes. And make sure Karen is stocked up on Valium before telling her you've ruined another costume. I saw her talking to a burly Italian man the other day. I can't say for certain she wasn't taking out a hit on you."

Ethan laughs as Marco closes the door, As soon as it's shut he's on his feet and grabbing at my robe. He really does become a clumsy Neanderthal when he's horny.

"Stop," I say and slap his hands away. "This robe is silk."

"I know. I bought it for you."

"Yes, and I love it, so stop trying to shred it."

I pull off the robe and carefully remove the rest of my costume.

He watches with hungry eyes. "Now?" he asks, his voice low.

"You have sixty seconds," I say, and the words are barely out of my mouth before he's kissing me.

Despite his obvious impatience, I love how rough he is when he's desperate for me. It feeds my ego. Not to mention my lust.

He goes to work on my neck. "Oh, God. Okay, so . . . maybe ninety seconds, but that's it."

"Please shut up and put your hand in my pants."

"Hell, yes."

His zipper is a little sturdier than mine and copes with the rough treatment as I yank it down. Then we have a frantic two minutes of giving each other as much pleasure as possible without getting naked.

He's not good at keeping quiet. I'm not much better. No wonder everyone in the theater knows about us.

When things start getting too steamy, we grunt in frustration and step away from each other. It's not easy. We clean up and pull on our street clothes in frustrated silence, and just before we head out the door, he pins me to it and lays his weight against me.

"Just so you know, when we get back to my place, I'm going to fuck you until you scream my name so loudly the neighbors call the cops."

"What if I make you scream my name first?"

"Even better."

We kiss once more then head out. When we reach the bar, we see a familiar dark-haired lady.

"Erika!"

She opens her arms as we approach, and Ethan and I hug her. "Ethan. Cassie. It's good to see you two. You were both wonderful tonight."

"You saw the show?"

"Yes. I loved it. I even brought a group of first years from The Grove. I think seeing two of our alumni up there provided a great deal of motivation. They can see where all their hard work may lead one day."

"I wish we could have met them," Ethan says.

"Well, perhaps you will. I was hoping to convince you both to come to the school next term to give some master classes."

"I'm guessing you'd like me to impart my wisdom about working with masks," Ethan says with a smile.

Erika laughs. "I'm sorry, did you say 'working with masks,' or 'failing miserably with masks'?"

"Hey," Ethan says. "I failed brilliantly. In the history of The Grove, no one has failed masks more spectacularly than I did."

"Well, that's true."

Ethan takes my hand, and I don't miss how Erika sees it and smiles.

"You know," I say as I lace our fingers together, "if you tried masks now, you'd be much more successful."

Erika looks at us warmly. "I think you might be right, Miss Taylor."

Marco orders champagne, and we spend a couple of hours reminiscing about our time at drama school. Apparently, Erika is a cheap date, because after two glasses, she gets a little happy and does impressions of Ethan and me when we first met. Then she does us bickering, complete with silly voices and loaded stares. I laugh more than I have in years.

I'd forgotten all the good times I had at college. For too long, what happened with Ethan eclipsed all the fond memories. Now I'm glad I can look back and smile.

"It was clear to everyone but the two of you that you'd end up together," Erika says. "It was certainly clear to me. You two had a serious case of plove."

"What the fuck is 'plove'?" Ethan asks. "It sounds like a disease."

"It's a mixture of passion and love."

"Isn't all love passionate?"

"Not necessarily." Erika leans back in her chair. "You can love something without being passionate about it. Conversely, you can be passionate about things you don't love. It's when the two converge that real magic happens."

She looks down at the table like she's talking to herself. "It's the subtle shudder when you hear the other person's name. The times when you think about their smile and find it impossible to keep a straight face. It's those small, precious moments you wish they were with you, because nothing means anything until you share it with them. More than passion and love alone, it's that internal alchemy that makes them a part of you."

She takes a deep breath and sighs. "You two were lucky. You ended up together. It doesn't always happen that way. Sometimes you meet the person who alters you forever, and for one reason or another, they don't become a part of your life. The problem is, you never forget them."

She lifts her glass to us. "You've both fought for your happiness. Enjoy it. You deserve it."

Under the table, Ethan squeezes my hand. I squeeze back. I guess we'd never considered Erika's private life before. She'd always seemed so untouchable. Maybe that's because someone once touched her, and she never recovered.

I can totally relate.

Before we leave, we talk with Erika about possible dates for the master classes. Then we hug her and Marco and say good night.

Our taxi ride back to Ethan's place is quiet. We hold hands. I lean on his shoulder. He strokes my fingers and stares out the window.

I guess we are lucky. Our ending could have been very different. If Ethan hadn't had his epiphany in a hospital bed in France, we might have never seen each other again. It took him making the first move to put us on the path of healing and redemption. So I guess even though he had a major hand in breaking us, he was also the architect behind putting us back together.

It makes me sad to think Erika didn't get that chance. I guess a lot of people don't.

When we get back to Ethan's apartment, he silently leads me into the bedroom and just looks at me for a long time before kissing me gently. It still amazes me how he can leave me breathless by simply brushing his lips against mine. His hands are warm on my face as he tilts my head, and steals even more of my breath with the soft sweep of his tongue.

We take our time removing each other's clothes. The concept of fucking has been forgotten. This isn't about fitting body parts together. It's about the two of us needing to be joined. Sharing that incredible sense of rightness we only get with each other.

No one else has ever controlled my pleasure with such instinctual ease as Ethan, and no one ever will.

Erika called it "internal alchemy," and I guess she's right. It's not like Ethan does anything different from the other men I've had. It's just that his skin speaks to mine on a different frequency. The pulse of his blood powers the tempo of mine.

We kiss for a long time before he lays me down and presses himself against me. So warm. Hot in places. Soft lips. Flexing muscles under heated skin. He murmurs things as he moves his mouth over me. Tells me how beautiful I am. How much he loves me. How grateful he is to have me.

It's all foreplay. Every groan-tinged word. He doesn't even know how sexy he is. Not just his body but his stained-glass heart. All the pieces of his past and present welded into place. Cracked and imperfect, but beautiful nonetheless.

My heart must look the same to him.

"I need you," he says as his lips graze my breast. "Always."

I pull him closer, but it's not enough. I run my hands down his back. Feel the muscles as he shifts and grinds.

Finally, he pushes inside and oh . . . there's nothing else.

Nothing.

No one.

Just this. The perfect slide of him.

"Cassie . . . God. Oh, God . . ."

I can't talk. Words are pointless, anyway. As if this could be described. I could speak every language in the world and still not have enough words to express how I feel about this man.

I settle for kissing him. I make noises around his tongue. He does the same around mine. We both know exactly what we're saying: *This is precious. This is love. This is something I'll never take for granted, because I know how it feels to be without it.*

We're not quiet as we wind each other tighter. We sigh and grunt with the intensity of it. Quiet really isn't an option with feelings this big.

As I crest, I tell him I love him and moan his name. Repeat it, over and over again. Get louder as he increases his pace and stop breathing when I'm as high as I can go. I almost scream it when I snap and fly. He carries me through all the layers of pleasure. I float for so long, I feel dizzy. Then he's crying out my name, and his movements are erratic. Hips move back and forth to the rhythm of his orgasm. Staccato and unsteady. He's tense and still for what seems like minutes, then heavy relief hits, and he sinks down and wraps me in all of him.

We hold each other and breathe. Dazed. Ecstatic. More in love with each other than we ever thought possible.

As the fog lifts, our hearts slow. Fingers stroke subconsciously. He rolls off and pulls me to his side until my head is on his shoulder, my hand over his heart.

I trace patterns. I think they're random, but when I become lucid, I realize they're words. *Ethan. Love. Ethan. Mine. Always.*

He's tracing patterns, too. Also words. I'm dozing off, but I recognize some of them. *Cassie. Beautiful. Mine. Need. Love.*

Then he traces two words that make me stop breathing. When he traces them again, I'm wide awake.

On the third time I feel the tension in him. He's wondering if I've understood. His expression says he hopes I have, and he watches me, desperate for an answer.

I push up on my elbow and look at him. I'm blinking too fast, but I can't help it. The naked vulnerability in his expression makes me well up.

He gazes at me and brings a single finger to my chest. Then he traces the words one more time and finishes by uttering the world's softest, "Please."

My eyes spill over. My throat is so tight with emotion, I can barely get out my whispered, "Yes."

I kiss him and repeat it, just to make sure he understands. "Yes."

He sighs in relief as I kiss all over his face and neck. "Yes, yes, yes."

His eyes spill, too. So relieved. So happy. So beautiful.

We celebrate by making love again, and I know without a doubt, I've made the right decision.

I think about how I was six months ago and marvel over where I am today. It's hard to believe.

I don't think I ever fully understood before what a profound ability humans have to change, especially with the right motivation. We're capable of remarkable evolution. Not just physically, but mentally.

Emotionally.

Although some of us get lost in the labyrinth of our own insecurities, it's possible to find our way out. Ethan's proof of that. I guess, in my prouder moments, I am, too. Neither of us is perfect, that's for sure, but when we're together, our deficiencies are complemented by the other's strengths.

When I look at Ethan now, I don't just see the damaged young man who hurt me in a misguided attempt to protect me. I see the man who struggled against the doubt and darkness inside himself and fought with all his might to change. And there's something about his immense determination to be more than he was that makes him more beautiful to me than ever. There's compassion in him now, not only for others, but especially for me. He's known the loss and defeat I've felt. He's walked in my shoes. And I've walked in his.

I have no doubt we'll continue to fight and grow, and I have no illusions that the rest of our journey is going to be smooth, but I do know that whatever burdens we encounter will be halved because we're together. As a couple, we have more than enough strength to achieve whatever we desire and, fortunately for us, we've never desired anything as much as one another.

That's where our future lies.

Together.

Writing our own unconventional and dramatic love story, one page at a time.

ACKNOWLEDGMENTS

There's never enough space to thank everyone who deserves it, particularly the plethora of amazing book bloggers and reviewers whose passion and enthusiasm have driven both *Bad Romeo* and *Broken Juliet*. Ladies (and a few gents), I can never truly thank you enough for your awesomeness. You know who you are.

There are some absolutely brilliant readers groups out there that make me smile every day (One-Click Addicts and Vixens—I'm looking at you), and they are filled with some of the most generous and supportive souls you'd ever hope to meet.

To my amazing Street Team—you ladies rock my world. I'm so grateful for all that you do.

To three amazing ladies who give me advice, stroke my hair, and keep me (moderately) sane—Caryn, Heather, and Andrea. I adore you.

To my Filets—I wouldn't cope with life, let alone the craziness of the book world, if it wasn't for you.

To two of the best women I know—my agent, Christina, and my editor, Rose (as well as their fabulous teams at JRA and SMP). One day I'm going to drag you to a karaoke bar and sing the world's sappiest version of "Wind Beneath My Wings," and then you'll know exactly how much your support and expertise mean to me. (And will no doubt be really embarrassed by it.)

To the wonderful Haylee from Pan Macmillan Australia—the best mum a book baby can have.

To my incredible husband, who works tirelessly so that I can sit on my butt for hours every day and write. You're my Ethan, sweetie. I adore you endlessly.

And to my boys, Special K and Doctor X—you guys make everything worthwhile. Not just these books, but life. I love you more than words can express. (So norty, but no twubble.)

And finally, to every single person who has read these books and taken the characters to heart—whether you be friends or strangers, bloggers or just lovers of words—I'm so grateful for your taking this journey with me. I truly love you more than Ethan loves Cassie, and that's one helluva lot. I wish you all a spectacular and joyous Happy Ever After.

Leisa x

Their love was always destined to be star-crossed.
Don't miss Elissa and Liam's story.

Wicked Heart

Coming autumn 2015

extracts reading groups
books
competitions new
discounts extracts
extracts discounts
competitions extracts
books reading groups
new events
books
events extracts books
books new titles reading groups
interviews
reading groups
books events extracts extracts events new reading groups
discounts interviews books
new books events events
events new new books extracts
discounts extracts discounts
www.panmacmillan.com
extracts events reading groups
competitions books extracts new books